CHADURANG
THE CURSED WAR GAME

To request permissions, contact Shankar Subramanian at shankarsubs0@gmail.com

ISBN: 979-8-218-58233-3

Editing and Design: SARAS Works (www.sarasworks.com)

Cover Design: Shankar Subramanian and SARAS Works

First Edition: 2025

Disclaimer: This is a work of fiction. Any resemblance to actual persons, living or dead, is purely coincidental.

"Chaudrang weaves the strategy and intensity of chess with the tapestry of Indian mythology, creating an adventure that will captivate young minds and inspire a new generation of chess players. Believe in your moves, trust your journey—every game, win or lose, shapes you into a stronger player and a better thinker."

- Awonder Liang
Third-youngest American Chess Grandmaster (at the age of 14)

TO ALL SCHOLASTIC CHESS KIDS...

Scholastic chess players experience a whirlwind of emotions during tournaments. These young competitors enter the tournament hall with a mix of excitement and nervousness, knowing they've prepared hard and are about to face a series of intense mental battles. As they sit across from their opponents, the pressure mounts, and they must focus intensely on every move, calculating and strategizing while managing their nerves.

During the games, they experience a range of emotions. A well-executed move or a clever tactic can bring a surge of confidence and joy, while a mistake can lead to frustration or anxiety. The thrill of capturing a crucial piece or checkmating an opponent is exhilarating, but the sting of defeat, especially after a long, hard-fought game, can be crushing, lingering painfully on the ride home as friends, parents, and coaches relive the game—questioning moves, teaching lessons, and replaying every moment.

In the moments between rounds, as they wait for the next match, these players often reflect on their previous games, learning from their mistakes and savoring their victories. The atmosphere is charged with anticipation, as they know that each game could be a step closer to victory or a harsh lesson in resilience.

Outside the tournament hall, their friends, family, and coaches wait with bated breath, sharing in the highs and lows of each game. The emotional support from loved ones is crucial, as it helps them cope with the pressure and remain motivated, regardless of the outcomes.

By the end of the tournament, these young chess players emerge with a deep sense of accomplishment, having tested their limits, learned valuable lessons, and proven their fighting spirit. Whether they win, lose, or draw, the experience is a testament to their dedication and passion for the game.

To all the scholastic chess kids who pour their hearts into every match, this book is dedicated to YOU!

Shankar Subramanian

Chapter 1

The Knight of the Dark Forest

e was unusually careful despite being familiar with his surroundings. Even his horse sensed its rider's uncustomary caution. Its muscles stiffened, ready for flight at its master's command, to cut through the forest ahead, like an arrow piercing damp air.

It wasn't fear, since knights didn't know fear. It wasn't the right time yet, and they both knew it.

They still had to sneak through the village before they could hit the dark trail. The full moon's light cast hazy, constantly shifting shadows, reminding them of the dangers that lurked at every corner of the treacherous village that only a few entered and fewer still managed to leave, alive. Yet, even the sinister village posed no threat for Aarjen, the revered knight of the Dark Forest, who served none other than the great rishi, Vyas.

The rustic village of Karri-Yur was at the edge of the Dark Forest. A deep ravine, chiseled by a tortuous river, separated the village from the forest.

Aarjen had been through Karri-Yur a few times. It was usually his last stop before entering the perilous Dark Forest of Mount Karri. Once, he had even undertaken an overnight sojourn to track and kill a beast. However, this time, he wanted to avoid soliciting any attention from the loathsome creatures, the potbellied rakshasas that resided there. The wild, pudgy, troll-like creatures, malevolent and murderous, were known to kill their own for no real reason.

It was a full moon night, which meant the creatures were stupefied and intoxicated with fermented roots and shrooms. A thick mix of smoke and fog blanketed the air, aiding Aarjen's stealth mode; the heavier fog settled to the ground while the lighter smoke danced to the tune of the breeze, mildly shifting over the broken, thatched roofs.

Aarjen knew that it was only a matter of time before they sniffed him out from more than a mile away, and he would send them on a wild hunt for a tasty meal. Fortunately, unlike their cousins—the shapeshifting marisans, who inhabited the Dark Forest—the rakshasas possessed neither the skills nor courage to duel a knight.

The knight and his majestic black horse wore a light armor of dark, rugged hide. Fastened to the saddle, within the grasp of his left hand, was a thick, leathery sheath, from which extended a round handle made of oxidized metal, draped and bound with raw hide. Every now and then, Aarjen's cold fingers gripped the handle.

He took stock of his chakras—the metal disks that were arranged neatly in hard leather sleeves that were hung from the saddle. He touched the disks in an order that only he understood and pressed his finger against the sharply filed edge of a disk. It responded to his touch with a motorized whir. The horse's ears twitched, acknowledging the familiar sound, but it didn't flinch. Aarjen pushed the chakras to the center and tightened the straps of the armor. He didn't have to touch his sword to know that it was hanging in his baldric by his side, ready to be drawn at any moment. Other hunting knives of different sizes and shapes remained concealed under the broad leather strap.

Aarjen proceeded to check on his peregrine falcon, perched on a short metallic fixture on the padded shoulder of his leather jacket. The bird carefully clasped Aarjen's finger with its powerful beak, like a wrench snuggly fitting around the head of a bolt. A bird that size could easily snap his finger in two; here, it signaled its eagerness to fly by briefly fluttering its wings and adjusting its perch posture.

The pavement was broken and dangerously uneven. Muddy puddles reflected the moonlight as the horse steered itself, treading on the damp grass by the side of the pavement to muffle the sound of its powerful hooves. Its steamy breath disappeared into the thick fog at regular intervals. A few paces away from the edge of the dilapidated alley, Aarjen spotted the trail he must take, meandering downward into oblivion.

The eerie silence was broken by a shriek from a nearby hut. A brief, high-pitched yell, followed by a scream, rent the air. Aarjen ignored the unsettling sounds.

"A fight that resulted in a victim," he murmured but stayed focused on his course.

Timing was everything. He glanced at the large blood moon, signaled his horse to stop, and popped open a hand-held brass instrument with the flick of a finger. He peered at the moon through it, while fine-tuning its setting.

"Just a few more hours, my friend," he said to the horse, leaning over and gently patting its muscular neck.

The fog thickened, causing moisture to collect and roll down the leathery surfaces that armored the knight and his horse. From the sudden gush of a cool breeze, he could tell that a storm was approaching the village. At the trail's edge, Aarjen maneuvered his horse into a steep berm and descended to the ravine at a brisk gallop. When he neared the stone bridge spanning the chasm, he cautioned his horse to slow down. Although the river was narrow, the rudimentary stone bridge seemed never-ending, its far end disappearing into the foggy haze by the river below. Aarjen steadied his horse at the entrance of the bridge and observed the moon one last time with his instrument.

A flash of lightning was followed by a loud crack of thunder, signaling the proximity of the violent storm.

Aarjen heard a thud and a muffled grunt. Before his horse could react, a hideous underworld rakshasa—the kind with an enormous belly and uncanny resemblance to humans—jumped in front of him from a slanting tree above and landed on a steep boulder. His horse kicked its forelegs wildly, even as Aarjen tried to calm it down. The large, snarling canine carnassial of the creature glowed in the dark, despite being disfigured by ugly stains. The pudgy, potbellied rakshasa wielded a crude dagger made of bone in its stretched, disproportionate arm. It wobbled back and forth as it tried to balance itself on an uneven boulder. Its blood-red eyes, however, remained fixed on Aarjen.

"Give me the bird." Its speech was slurred; it spoke in the local rakshasa language that Aarjen was familiar with.

Evidently, the creature's intelligence, however puny, was dulled by intoxication. Although impulsive and stupid in general, no rakshasa in its right mind would attempt to challenge a knight. It was suicidal.

"It's not for sale," Aarjen said with a straight face.

He positioned his horse by the edge of the broken bridge. A narrow ledge separated him and his horse from hurtling into the gorge several feet below.

"I'll slash your throat, drink your blood, feed your body to the mudalas in that river, and then I'll take your bird, you stupid human," the rakshasa shouted, splattering saliva with every word.

"It's a shame you are too drunk to know who I am," Aarjen said sternly.

The creature cursed.

"Find another rakshasa to pick a fight with," warned Aarjen.

The furious creature lunged at Aarjen, but the knight had already given his horse the signal to begin its journey into the forest. The falcon screeched, and the horse sprang forward. Aarjen's timing was perfect. He caught a glimpse of the creature landing on the boulder below the bridge with a thud. The rakshasa tumbled to the bottom of the gorge and lay by the edge of the river, its body limp, rendered that way by broken bones and injuries that bled profusely.

Within minutes of the creature's blood tainting the murky water, several dark, shiny-scaled creatures surfaced from the river and swiftly slithered to the bank. The largest of them darted out of the water with great force. The crocodile-shaped mudala crawled only a few feet on its fours but quickly assumed an upright posture. Saliva drooled from its massive snout, as it awkwardly balanced itself with its long, leathery tail and ambled toward the rakshasa's limp body. The other mudalas followed suit.

They all glanced at the full moon, pounded their chests and began to devour the dying rakshasa.

The horse dashed through the dense fog under the hazy moonlight. It would be pitch-dark inside the forest, but Aarjen was not fazed. He could always count on his horse, which, even while galloping at full speed, kept up its rhythm and elegantly adjusted its stride to the contours of the uneven ground.

Aarjen removed the leather blindfold placed on the falcon; the bird adjusted its vison to its surroundings and positioned itself on Aarjen's stretched arm. The peregrine falcon then flapped its wings a few times and soared above the speeding horse. After a quick survey of the landscape, it flew back and perched on its master's shoulder.

Aarjen reassessed his plan to outsmart and outpace the shapeshifting marisans—the powerful and ruthless hunters of the underworld who monitored those who entered and exited. These rakshasa species—unlike their shorter, stouter, human-looking relatives—had a wildebeest-looking head with thick crescent-shaped horns that curved backward. They stood over seven feet tall with muscular, hairy, bluish rakshasa humanoid bodies.

It was Nami—the annual cosmic occurrence when all three moons appeared full. While all creatures were dull and sluggish during this time, marisans remained a lethal threat to strangers who strayed into the Dark Forest. Nami also triggered the abundant growth of a poisonous mold, which enveloped the forest floor with a sinister, hazy greenish glow.

"I can count on your speed," Aarjen said, ruffling his horse's mane that bounced in sync with the smooth motion of its hooves.

Given their gift of night vision, they were both undaunted by the total darkness that blanketed the forest. Aarjen knew an intruder alert would be signaled across the forest soon. Only a few of the marisans would join the initial attack, but once they learned the identity of the evasive knight, they'd attempt to follow Aarjen to find the secret path to Mount Meru—their only chance to find the gates into Lord Indra's world.

Twang—Fizzip—Thud—Grunt.

The first arrow zipped by Aarjen and hit something hard, maybe a tree, but Aarjen hoped it was another rakshasa that had carelessly stepped into the arrow's path. A few seconds later, many arrows rained down from behind in batches, all abruptly interrupted by trees. They pierced the trunks with the familiar vibrating twang. His falcon tightened its grip as it sensed the presence of the rapidly approaching creature from the direction in which the horse was headed.

Aarjen hoped he would reach the Ye-Root Tree—the oldest and the largest light-trapping tree of the Dark Forest—by the time the creatures surrounded them. Like all the other trees of darkness found only in the Dark Forest, the Ye-Root Tree sponged up every speck of light that infiltrated the canopy, making its surroundings pitch-dark.

Bearing a striking resemblance to a banyan tree, the Ye-Root, which had originally taken root at the heart of the forest, spread thousands of acres from its main trunk by sprouting thick strands of roots from its branches that reached the ground during Nami. It slept through the year, waking only during the full moon to sustain its growth, catalyzed by the light-producing chemicals stored in its bulky nodes. Once the roots sprouted, the nodes exploded, releasing tiny, heated spines, accompanied by bright flashes of energy.

Acutely aware of the danger of the exploding darts, the rakshasas carefully closed in on the knight from all directions.

Aarjen approached the Ye-Root tree cautiously. His horse came to a full stop when it reached the enormous base of the Ye-Root. Formed over centuries, dozens of trunks had grown close together.

The knight stuck his index finger in the center of the largest metal disk and launched it with a smooth, steady movement. He eased his horse into the gap between the thick tree trunks and took cover. The smooth disk transformed into a spinning chakra with sharp, serrated edges and sliced through a dozen low-hanging nodes containing the explosive darts. The sudden flashes of bright light from the nodes dazzled the rakshasas. Blazing darts sprayed at the dazed creatures, instantly killing or severely injuring them.

The north rim lay at the very edge of the rakshasa world. A seemingly bottomless abyss puckered with mountain peaks, mostly hidden beneath dense layers of cloud, marked the boundary. The marisans knew that under the constantly changing pattern of the clouds was a secret passage formed for the rishis and the knights to cross from one world to the other, leading to Mount Meru—the entrance to Devastella and the land of the immortal devas.

Aarjen's horse thundered along the bright rim; its edges, made of glazed rocks, reflected the radiant moonlight. With little time to waste, he had to evade the lurking marisans before taking the path to Mount Meru. With his thermal-imaging vision, Aarjen spotted two shapeshifters camouflaged as boulders, concealed among lifeless, cold rocks. As expected, within moments, they pursued the horse, transforming into two werewolf-like creatures. Two more marisans, cloaked as trees, transformed and joined the pursuit.

Aarjen's bird swooped in front of him to begin its careful task of leading the horse through a secret passage riddled with dangerous obstacles. When the horse approached a wide ledge at the rim, the bird dipped its wing, made a sharp turn and flew straight over the abyss. At a short distance from the rim, the bird dove into the cloud below and disappeared. The horse leaped over the ledge to where the bird had disappeared.

Aarjen held himself close to his horse. He was counting on its agility and ability to precisely follow his aerial guide. A slip would be unkind, even to a knight of his stature.

Aarjen's horse landed in the middle of a flat rock, invisible from above the clouds. Then, within a few strides, the horse jumped again, following the bird, which now glided up and down like a dolphin swimming on the ocean's surface. The only way to find the landing rocks was to follow the cue of the trained peregrine falcon, which had the ability to quickly spot the shifting path that took on a pattern continuing randomly in all directions, from up above.

Within the first few leaps, two of the four followers missed the landing and plunged to their death. The other two fought for landing space behind Aarjen; their energy was waning, but their determination to follow him persisted.

"Keep up the knight's move just a few more times, and we'll be home, my friend," Aarjen told his faithful horse as it jumped twice forward and once sideways, sometimes twice sideways and once forward.

As they neared their destination, the horse took a final leap forward, forcing the marisans to take a leap bigger than they had ever attempted before. Crashing on the mossy edge of the precipice, one of the creatures desperately struggled to grasp on to any protrusion. Quickly transforming its hairy legs into arm-like limbs, it managed to latch on to a protruding rock and pull its weight onto the flat surface above. Within seconds, the other pursuer, clearing the abyss, landed smack on the creature, knocking it over the edge of the rim. Without wasting much time, the former continued its pursuit of the knight.

Aarjen's horse eased its pace along a narrow path that wove through misty gray columns of clouds, packed with energetic, gusty winds. Sporadic lightning brightened their path. At a distance from the fast-gathering clouds emerged the face of Maeg, the guard of Mount Meru.

"Who goes through the gates of Mount Meru?" thundered Maeg.

"Greetings, oh great guard of Mount Meru, this is Aarjen, the knight…"

"*Stop!*" Maeg's voice roared across the valley. The clouds darkened and churned into a rumbling vortex. Aarjen tightened the laces on his overcoat and clutched the saddle swell. The horse lowered its face and shut its eyes as the bird tucked its wings and snuggled into Aarjen's overcoat. The gust of wind was followed by a hurtling lightning bolt, which safely passed Aarjen, his bird, and the horse but struck the last of the stealthy creatures that had managed to cross the abyss. An immediate calm followed.

"The knight of the Dark Forest!" Maeg, the master of the clouds, said in a booming voice. "I sensed a covert follower close to you, and I wasn't sure if it had somehow gained control over you. I apologize for the stormy welcome."

Aarjen waved his hand. "No apology needed, oh great one."

"Welcome to Mount Meru. The knights are the friends of the people of Meru."

"I have an urgent message for Indra, and I need your help to get through to him quickly," Aarjen requested. "My horse and bird are tired from the journey, and your help is greatly appreciated."

"Of course," said Maeg. "I understand you are in a hurry now, but when you return, please stay at the gate city of Mount Meru. You'll enjoy our hospitality, Aarjen."

Aarjen placed his right hand over his heart and bowed to Maeg. He felt a soft breeze lifting them. Floating on a gentle current, they drifted to Devastella, the land of the immortal devas. Finally, his companions would get some well-deserved rest. But Aarjen was restless.

He had just returned from Mayastella—the forbidden place of illusion—and he had some disturbing news for Indra. The world, created by Indra's daughter, Maya, was infested with deadly tantrics. Its keeper presumed dead. More importantly, a long-forgotten curse was about to be revived. The dangers he had just encountered while crossing the Dark Forest paled in comparison to the perils the devas had brought upon themselves.

Chapter 2

The Chicago Chess Kids

Downtown Lake Villa was small and quaint. Its single street—seldom called by its actual name, Center Street—was paved with intermittent sections of brick and asphalt and lined with closely spaced streetlamps, attached with lantern-looking fixtures and colorful fall seasonal banners that loosely fluttered in the cold wind. The street itself was just four blocks long, yet had four annoying stop signs, apparently installed with the hope that decelerating drivers would be tempted to stop and check out the street-side stores.

The new Fifth Third Bank building, with its elegant red brick and black glass facade, was located at one corner, and the popular Lovin' Oven bakery was on the other. Antique stores lined the streets on one side, and the popular Prairie Bar & Grill was on the other side. The Pass Pawn was located between the Lakes Bicycle Shop and JP's Boutique store. Those who were not familiar with downtown Lake Villa often mistook Pass Pawn for a pawnshop, but it was in fact a chess club for kids and young adults. In a curious coincidence, the club was located diagonally across the street from EZ Pawn, an actual pawnshop that sold chess sets, among other items, such as medieval gear, old musical instruments, antique game boards, clocks, coins, baseball cards, and old china.

Most of the stores lining Center Street were single-story reddish-brown brick buildings with red or blue awnings and huge display windows. For several days, the weather in the Chicago area had been depressingly gray and rainy. The temperature had steadily dropped from the high sixties to close to freezing. The cheerless weather forecast called for rain to become sleet, the first of the season. Rain glistened in slanted lines around the dull halo of the streetlights and the flashing amber light of a distant truck that had sprinkled de-icing salt, which looked like broken glass strewn on the road. Damp brown leaves swirled with the gusty wind and piled by the edge of the sidewalk.

Center Street was deserted, and most stores were closed. A few cars braved the weather out of necessity. Some quickly pulled in front of Pass Pawn and hurriedly dropped off the kids, who said half-hearted goodbyes to their chaperones then darted inside for an evening chess class. Across the street, a tall man pushed open the door of EZ Pawn, wiped his wet, salty shoes on the thick mat, and stepped in. The familiar electronic door chime alerted the store owner, who stood behind the counter and gestured to someone inside the adjacent room.

"Well, well, it is the man himself. Must be an important package then?" the lanky, shaggy-haired store owner asked the man entering the store. "A long trek, eh, Turner?" he smirked. The scar on his leathery cheek stretched from his chin to his right ear.

"You are as warm as the weather, Scrappy," replied the tall man. "I would have preferred to pick up my package directly from FedEx rather than walk across the street to see your friendly face, but I was told that you somehow convinced Monty to give you my package. I see you are still a very curious guy."

Scrappy, not listening, was busy nosing around the medium-sized rectangular box addressed to Greg Turner.

"Something heavy." He moved the box up and down. "More chess books, eh, Turner? But you need more than books! Your boy needs the heart of a champion and not them books. Winning ain't taught in your fancy schools, Turner. It's instinct. Like my Nikku. He is going to do it again to your boy in six months!"

Every time Scrappy saw Coach Turner, he trash-talked. He disliked everything about the coach, his kids and the club. He hated that Brendan, a high school junior, had been ranked among the nation's top 20 kids in chess for his age group since age five, and gleefully reminded Turner at every opportunity that Brendan had yet to win the national title. And to make things worse for Turner, at last year's competition, Scrappy's stepson, Nicolas, had pulled an upset by winning the final round against Brendan, ruining Brendan's long-anticipated shot at the title.

Of course, like all major tournaments, the win by Nicolas had been marred by a bitter controversy and feud, but in the end, the tournament officials had decided in Nicolas' favor. While the verdict was final, the conflict continued to smolder.

Ever since, Scrappy had become more confrontational and obnoxious, gloating over his stepson's superior chess talent. More so, he remained aggravated by the coach and his son's cool composure, both of whom had somehow managed to shrug off the disappointment.

"It's just a game, Scrappy. Now, if you don't mind, I would like to have my package. Looks like your first customer of this month just found your store." Mild exasperation tinged Turner's tone.

The blaring electronic chime sounded again as a young woman stepped into the store. She tugged at her wet jacket and pushed back her faux-fur trim hoodie, exposing her damp red hair. Water dripped from her coat and her beautiful, cold face. Beside her, holding her arm, was a little girl bundled up in a pink parka, staring at her mother's shoes.

The woman looked around, then bent down and whispered something to the girl. The girl nodded. The woman then took one of the antique chess pieces on display and placed it on the girl's palm.

"*Do not touch anything!*" Scrappy yelled, startling them.

"Oh…I am…I am sorry," the woman said politely. "I was just showing my daughter a chess piece." She snatched the piece from her kid and carefully replaced it on the board.

"You can show it to her without *touching* it," Scrappy said in a firm, unfriendly tone. "Can't you read that big *Do Not Touch* sign, lady?"

The young woman approached the counter without making eye contact with Turner. "My daughter cannot see, so I wanted her to feel the chess piece with her fingers," she said, her voice akin to a whisper. "She has never touched a chess piece before." She raised her voice slightly to make her case.

Turner picked up on her strong Irish accent.

"Well, if she can't see, then what's the point of showing her a chess piece? It's not like she's going to play." Scrappy scowled and wagged his finger at the lady.

"I just..."

"You break a piece, you buy the whole set, and it is not a cheap set." Scrappy stuck the price tag in her face.

"We just came to buy some juice," the woman said, her voice shaky. "All the other stores are closed. Let's go, Sidney." The woman turned around, gently nudged her daughter and guided her out of the store.

Turner shook his head, grabbed the package, and glared at Scrappy. "I don't believe this. You are a scumbag!" he yelled before stepping out of the store and slamming the door behind him.

Turner saw the woman open the rear door of her green Subaru Outback and help her daughter into the back seat. She leaned over and said something into the girl's ear. The girl nodded in response; the woman patted her head before closing the door. She slipped into the driver's seat, lowered the window slightly and glanced outside. True to the forecast, the rain was beginning to freeze, and Turner could see the shimmering ice crystals through the bright LED beams streaming from her car. When the woman caught Turner's eye, she shook her head vigorously, quickly looked away, and began reversing her car. Turner took a couple of quick but careful steps on the icy pavement. "Excuse me, ma'am!" he shouted over the noisy mix of the hum of the motor, clatter of wiper blades, the howling wind, and fast-falling sleet.

Turner could see she was avoiding eye contact with him.

"*Excuse me, ma'am!* Your daughter dropped her glove!" Turner frantically waved the tiny pink woolen glove by the driver's window, hoping to get the woman's attention. Without smiling, she lowered the window halfway and finally made eye contact. From her look, he could tell she simply wished to get away from him.

"I am sorry for what happened in there." He tried to keep his voice above the background noise as he handed her the glove. "He is a brute. I can get your daughter some juice or water; my chess club is right across the street."

"No, thank you!" she replied firmly. "Thanks for this!" She waved the glove at Turner.

Turner felt sorry for the girl but understood the mother's cautious response.

"Okay, I…I completely understand," he stuttered, clutching his coat as the cold wind brushed his face. "If…if…your daughter ever wants to come to a chess club, it's called the Pass Pawn." He pointed a finger at his building.

The woman cast a cursory glance at the illuminated window, which displayed numerous trophies. Turner could sense she was trying to come up with a quick excuse to slam her foot on the accelerator.

"Mommy, can we go to the chess club now?" her daughter pleaded from the back seat.

"Not now, honey," the woman said in kind tone.

"Please, Mom. I want to learn to play chess," the girl insisted.

Before her mother could answer, a little girl and a tall boy stepped out of the chess club.

"Dad!" the girl across the street hollered, stepping out into the sleeting rain. "The boys are playing anti-chess and bughouse again."

"I'll be there in a bit, pumpkin. It's cold. *Don't get wet.*"

"Who are you talking to, Dad? I thought you didn't like Scrappy!" his daughter teased.

Turner looked at the woman and shook his head. "That's my daughter. As you can see, she speaks her mind."

The woman finally cracked an awkward smile.

"You have a call, Mr. Turner!" Another kid yelled and darted into the icy rain, much to Turner's annoyance. "Mrs. Reynolds will be late to pick up Jack."

"Okay, I'll be there in a bit. Will you all get back inside?"

Suddenly, little heads, like curious prairie dogs, lined up across the large glass window, pressing their foreheads on the glass, cupped hands blocking the glare.

Turner shrugged, as if to say, *Sorry, I have to go.*

"Boy, it looks like those trophies have large heads," she laughed. "How old is your daughter?"

"Nine, but thinks she is nineteen."

"Can we go there, Mom? I'm thirsty," the girl pleaded again, trying out a different excuse.

"Okay, sweetie, just for a few minutes." The mother turned to look at Turner for approval.

"You can park in front of the club," Turner said, pleased with her decision.

He felt oddly guilty for what had happened to them inside the pawnshop. His heart went out to the little girl and her mother.

Turner's young son, Brendan, stepped outside, along with their adorable wheaten terrier, Newton, to welcome the visitors. As he was about to close the door, he glanced at the pawnshop.

"Dad, who's that?" Brendan asked, peering into the icy rain.

"Who's who, Brendan?" Turner hung all the coats.

"Someone looking at us from the corner of Scrappy's parking lot."

Turner peered into the dark and empty street. "Huh, probably Scrappy, getting mad that I invited his customers in." He shrugged.

"I don't think so. Someone much shorter than Scrappy," mumbled Brendan.

The first thing that caught Sidney's attention was the soft jingle of the mini wind chimes hanging from the door as Brendan closed the half-glass door behind them. Sidney had a keen sense of hearing and loved pleasing sounds. Some days, she'd imagine running through a field of wind chimes with different melodies.

The main hall of the chess club was filled with loud banter, laughter, chess pieces slamming on chessboards, and the ticking of clocks. None of the kids stopped to greet the visitors. Roshan, whom the kids called Ro—despite his protests—continued playing anti-chess with Jack, slamming his chess piece on the vinyl chess board with every move. Rachel, Sebastian, Martin, and Lauren were nosily engaged in a game of bughouse, a derivative of chess where the players were allowed to share and place captured pieces anywhere on the board as they played in pairs, swapping chess pieces between them. Little Austin and Kevin had turned their chess pieces into imaginary cars, airplanes and aliens.

Brendan had slipped into another room; his little sister, Madison, was focused on her coloring. Malik was by the vending machine, once again trying to get a soda without feeding it any money, while Max and Kirin attempted to shake the huge snack vending machine, hoping something would fall.

"Listen up, everyone," Turner called out. When no one responded, he repeated his greeting in a louder, firmer tone.

This time, the kids gathered around Coach Turner—everyone except Brendan, who was still in the office room, solving chess puzzles on the computer.

"Brendan, are you going to be here?" Turner called out to his son.

Brendan had just started solving another chess puzzle, and he knew his father would give him 30 seconds before calling his name again. His mind worked fastest in those 30 seconds. The puzzle was simple—white to move and mate in three. Brendan stared at it for 15 seconds, quickly wrote the answer, and walked to the hall before his dad could call him again.

"Everyone, say hello to Sidney and her mother, um…"

"Nora," the woman announced. "I am so glad to meet all of you."

At first, the boys stood around, grinning, but when Turner cleared his throat a few times, a couple of the kids mumbled a "hello" and a "hi". Madison quickly ran up to Sidney and asked if she wanted to play chess. Newton promptly jumped up and followed Madison, vigorously wagging his stubby tail, attempting to lick Sidney's face in excitement.

"I can't see," said Sidney, pointing to her bright blue eyes. "But I would love to learn the game from you." She hugged Newton and giggled before her mother could react. "Show her the chess pieces, Maddie," Turner said to his daughter. "Let her feel the differences between them for herself," he quickly added. "You can then explain the game to her."

Then, he turned to Malik. "Have you taken anything from the machine today?"

"No, Coach." Malik pouted and did not make eye contact with the coach.

"Good. I want you to get Sidney some orange juice."

"I've got some change," Nora offered.

"That won't be necessary," Turner said, rolling his eyes. "Malik has figured out a way to make this machine spit out the cans without feeding it money." He lowered his voice and whispered to Nora, "He knows I am okay with it."

"Thanks for having us over. I know she'll never be able to learn chess, but at least she'll know how the game is played," Nora said, her tone conveying her sincerity.

Turner silently observed Sidney. She let her fingers run over every piece from top to bottom while paying attention to Madison.

"I think she will be able to pick up the game with a bit of help." Turner removed his reading glasses; he looked thoughtful.

"You are kidding, right? She cannot see anything, Coach," Nora said to Turner.

"Do you know there are several blind grandmasters all around the world? Chess is a mind game, and one can visualize the moves without looking at the board," he said.

"Like how the girl sees the pieces upside-down on the ceiling in *The Queen's Gambit*," said Max, laughing.

"But she was…"

"Shh." Turner shook his head.

"I was going to say, she was a grandmaster, Coach," Ro said, shrugging his shoulders.

"Nora, let me demonstrate something for you. Might be a bit hard to follow, but it will be amusing," said Turner. "Brendan, call Bob Raj," the Coach said.

"Guys, guys! Brendan is going to play a game with Mr. Raj over the phone. Who's going to set up the board and play for him?"

"Me, me, me, meee, *please*, Coach? *Me!*"

An instant chorus erupted around the room with almost all the kids volunteering to participate in blindfold chess.

When Coach picked Max and Ro, there was a collective groan, but the students wasted no time in crowding around the two students whom Turner had delegated to play for Brendan and Coach Bob Raj.

Bob Raj, an international master with a rating of over 2,100, was a chess coach originally from Jamaica. As usual, he was enthusiastic about playing a game with Brendan.

"Let me bring a notation book, man," he told Brendan in his thick Caribbean accent. There was a brief pause.

The kids loved the boisterous, philosophical, sometimes-difficult-to-understand coach. Turner briefly chatted, explained the purpose of his call, and persuaded Bob Raj to focus on the game.

Brendan stood, facing away from the board.

"I have never seen this type of chess set," Nora told the nearest kid, pointing to the green-and-white-checkered vinyl chessboard and the tall off-white and black plastic chess pieces that accompanied it.

The squares on the top and bottom rows of the board were lettered A to H, and the squares on the side of the board were numbered from 1 to 8. The white pieces were arranged at the bottom from A to H, 1 to 2. Next to each board was a rectangular clock.

"Is that a digital clock?" she asked.

"Chronos GX are the best," a kid shouted.

Turner hit the clock for Brendan. "Start!" he said loudly.

"E4," said Brendan without seeing the board. After one of the boys made the move he'd just called out, Brendan wrote it down in his notation notebook.

"E5," said Bob Raj instantly.

Brendan wrote his opponent's move as well in his notation book.

The game continued as each player called out his next move within seconds of each other:

Nf3, Nc6;

Bc4, Bc5; Nc3, Nf6;

d3, d6;

Bg5, h6;

Bh4, O-O;

O-O, Bg4.

The first several moves were spontaneous and reactionary, as though they had memorized the sequence of every move. Coach could tell Nora was impressed as she watched with her hands on her cheeks, intensely observing the game.

"*No kibitzing!*" One kid accused another of prompting a move.

In about ten minutes, the pieces were all over the board as the game developed. Fewer and fewer pieces remained on the board as the players began capturing and exchanging each other's pieces. The only reference the two players had on what pieces were left on what squares on the board was the numbers and letters they had noted down in a notation book.

"All right, guys, you can stop now; it's getting late." Turner stopped the game and said goodbye to Bob Raj.

The kids groaned.

Turner explained to Nora how the rows on the green-and-white chessboard were labeled. "So, if you know the board and the positions well, like most experienced players do, it is easy to remember where your pieces are by simply looking at your notation. That's why, Nora," he stressed, folding his reading glasses, "with the help of a computer-aided chessboard, I believe your daughter can play this game."

The front door opened, drawing Sidney's attention to the soft jingle of the wind chimes. "Hey, Coach!" said the middle-aged woman with smooth, dark skin, short, straight hair, and a larger-than-life smile. "I need to pick up Martin early today; he has a lot of homework."

"Hello, Mrs. Thompson." Then, "*Martin!*"

"I see he's quickly starting another game with Jack. Could you please kick him out of there, Coach?" She raised her voice so that Martin and Jack could hear.

Her comment was immediately followed by a muffled protest from Martin.

"Hi, I'm Shirley," the woman introduced herself to Nora.

"Hello! I am Nora. Pleased to meet you."

"You must be…" Shirley turned and her gaze settled on Sidney. "That girl's mother?"

"How did…"

"It's time to go, Martin. Martin!" yelled Turner.

"This is how we know the kids and their moms. The coach starts to yell their names aloud on Mondays and Wednesdays and sometimes Saturdays!" Shirley chuckled.

Nora instantly liked Shirley. "You are so funny."

"I don't think so," mumbled Martin as he passed his mother. "Hey, Mom, check out this meme." He swiped the images on his phone.

"Oh, no. Not now, son." She winked at Nora.

Nora burst out laughing and said goodbye to Shirley.

While Turner was busy with the parents who trickled in to pick up their kids, Nora browsed around the chess club. Newton followed her, wagging his tail sporadically.

There were four large rooms. The first room was the display room with the tall glass window. Numerous trophies and chess paraphernalia filled the room. To her right was a small office room with a large wooden desk by the wall, upon which there were two laptops, a flat screen monitor that looked disproportionally large, and an old printer that was connected to the dusty desktop computer on the floor. Unruly wires crisscrossed behind the desk. The wall across from the computer desk was lined from floor to ceiling with shelves filled with chess books on opening games, middle games and end games. There were puzzle books and books on strategy. Among the smorgasbord of framed certificates and patents mounted on the wall in an unorderly fashion, the biggest one read *University of Chicago, Doctor of Philosophy*.

She stepped closer and read the name scribed elegantly in cursive: *Greg Turner*. "PhD in mathematics!"

She also read some of the newspaper clippings describing Turner's accomplishments in the field of number theory. '*Greg Turner must be a brilliant man*', she thought, reminding herself to google him later.

"Do you want me to show you around?" a voice asked politely. It was Brendan.

"Sure!"

"Dad doesn't like to display these. My sister Tara and I did it for a Father's Day. He's achieved a lot."

From his blush and the twinkle in his champagne-brown eyes, she could tell Brendan was very proud of his father.

"Tara is your older sister?"

"Yes, she's in the Air Force. A test pilot." Brendan beamed with pride.

"Wow! Who won all of those?" she asked as they walked by a room full of trophies.

"Tara and I won most of these. Those tall ones are all team trophies won by the club. They just give out a lot of trophies in chess," he said with a hint of warmth in his expression as he pushed his curly, long brown hair away from his forehead.

"Is your dad your coach?"

"Yeah, but a couple of grandmasters help me out as well."

"Was your dad a university professor?"

"He still is," Brendan politely corrected her. "He teaches at the University of Chicago in applied math, but he's been on sabbatical since Mom died of cancer."

"Oh, so sorry to hear about your mother," Nora said.

Brendan nodded and changed the topic quickly. "I think we can teach Sidney how to play chess. I have taught a lot of kids over the years. She seems pretty sharp!"

Nora and Sidney were the only people left after all the other kids departed.

Nora felt the club would be very beneficial for her only daughter. The kids were friendly and considerate of Sidney, and Nora was impressed with their passion for the game. Briefly, she wondered about the coach's wife.

"It must be getting late for you. I hope you don't have to drive too far. It's nasty outside," Turner said from the front room.

"No. We live close by, in the Eagle's Nest subdivision."

"Oh, are you new to town?" Turner asked Nora.

"Yes, we just moved here recently. From Dublin," Nora added quickly anticipating Turner's question.

"Ohio?" asked Turner

"Ireland. My husband was from here, but I met him in Sligo when we both worked for the same pharma company," she said with a blank stare. "He passed away last year," she said without getting into the details.

She looked at Sidney, who was giggling and chatting with Maddie.

"You can always bring Sidney here," Turner said quickly. "She seems to have hit it off well with Maddie."

"It will help me to get to know some parents as well." Nora gently reached for Sidney's arm and guided her to the door. "Looks like you had a lot of fun, sweetie!"

"Yes." Sidney nodded in the direction of her mother's voice.

As Nora opened the door, Sidney's face lit up when she heard the pleasant melody from the wind chime again.

While Nora buckled up her daughter in the back seat, Sidney felt her mom's cold cheek. She then moved her hands over her mother's cold nose.

"You look so beautiful, Mom," Sidney told her mother. "Pink looks good on you," Sidney added even though Nora had no pink on her.

"Not as beautiful as you are, my dear," said Nora, her eyes welling up with tears. "I wore pink just for you, hon."

As Nora waved goodbye to Turner, Sidney felt a chill go through her spine. Her head suddenly hurt, and she felt dizzy. She felt the presence of someone around her and turned to the window. At first, she thought it was something in the car that had fallen on her, but soon, she realized it was more of a feeling. Her sudden reaction made Nora look in the rearview mirror.

"Honey, is everything okay?"

"I am not sure, Mom. I just felt . . .I am just tired, Mom," she said hastily.

As the car drove away, a mysterious figure silently lurked around the corner of the street. The hunched creature with a wildebeest head was as tall as the side entrance door of the Pass Pawn Chess Club. It slowly moved through the sleety rain, its eyes glowing red as it walked toward the building.

For the first time, the creature felt as though someone had noticed it. Humans were usually impervious to the creature's existence, yet its presence had been felt very strongly by a child. The creature was confused, even infuriated. It could not account for the sensation of having been perceived.

The creature hesitated for a moment. It slid into an obscure corner of the street to blend in with the darkness and to rid itself of any followers, namely the knights of the rishis, who guarded the worlds that didn't belong to the creatures.

The brief hesitation caused the creature to deviate from its original plan of breaking into the Pass Pawn Chess Club. It reached the front of the chess club, only to stare at the bright headlights of Coach Turner's SUV. The coach was heading back home with his kids. The SUV veered by the creature and splashed icy water on it. Neither the coach nor Maddie noticed the creature hunched by the sidewalk.

But Brendan did, and Newton reacted by barking, as though he'd heard a coyote. Brendan first thought it was a deer, but it was too tall for a deer.

He caught a fleeting glimpse and yelled to his dad, "What is that?"

"What is what?" asked Turner.

"A big animal," said Brendan, turning to see if he could see anything.

"Must be a deer," said Turner.

Brendan was not convinced, but within minutes, he forgot having seen a strange creature, as he was distracted by texts from his friends.

"Oh, by the way, Dad," Brendan said, remembering something, "Monty mentioned he'd be delivering a large package. Since it's very heavy, he said he'd go ahead and put it in the storage room with the other chess supplies."

"Huh? I don't remember ordering anything recently. We'll deal with it tomorrow, Brendan," he said, waving it off with a casual flick of his hand.

Chapter 3

Indra's Distress

ndra, the immortal king of the devas, was disturbed by the wailing of the shunk. The melancholic sound from the sacred conch, discernible only by a chosen few, blasted through his head. He had not expected to hear the sound of death *now*, during a time of such prosperity, so its occurrence made little sense to the lord of weather, war, and wealth. After all, it was mostly through his efforts that harmony among all the known worlds had been established.

Indra was no stranger to threats or peril. He had a history of invoking the wrath of mortals and immortals, sages and monks, and gods and demons with his inherent and incessant habit of displaying his valor. However, his innate goodness and sense of justice had ultimately triumphed, allowing him to harvest sufficient support from the seven great sages of the worlds to thwart any serious consequence to his exhibitionistic actions.

Collectively known as the saptarishis, the seven great sages, the most powerful wizards of all time, led simple lives in the mountains and forests of the mortal worlds. Their powers and knowledge exceeded that of any of the kings. The rishis ensured all mortal beings established civilizations through different time periods since the beginning of their mortal existence.

Of the seven rishis, Vyas was the most revered and powerful. So, why had the sound of death resonated in a place where death did not exist? Were the asuras, whom he had learned to trust, betraying him *now*? Harmony was at its best between the devas, the immortal guardians of the living during the day, and the asuras, their equivalents at night.

Only a few could answer his questions: Samudra, the queen of the Oceans; Baga, the lord of the asuras; and Vyas, the great rishi.

"I think I heard the sound," Indra said to his queen.

·What sound?" his queen asked, trying to listen to the sound.

Indra thought of Maya, his beloved daughter and the architect of illusion for all the worlds he governed, and wondered if she would know anything about the origin of the sound.

"The wailing sound of the shunk," Indra said.

"From the conch Queen Samudra gave you?"

Indra closed his eyes and visualized the conch.

A simple yet sublimely beautiful object—shiny, smooth pearly-white outside with a pink hue inside. A circular golden sleeve bordered its open mouth. Indra could see the celestial symbols of the rishis carefully inscribed on the glossy curves of the shell's spiral surface. "The shunk is a catalyst of life beneath the oceans of a new world," said Indra. "When the rakshasas came close to stealing the shunk, Lord Baga and I protected the jalas with our forces and thwarted the attack," Indra added, recalling the attack on the jalas, the beings of the water world.

"Samudra was grateful for your timely help," Indra's queen remarked.

"The queen of the oceans gifted Lord Baga and me with the shunk and honored us as guardians of life for the new worlds. The conch has the ability to warn its guardians of any threats or distress to life with a wailing noise. I reckon Baga would have heard the wail as well."

"You should talk to your council," his queen advised.

"We'll need to quickly prepare for the battle."

"Battle?" the queen asked, perplexed.

"Yes, if the warning is true, all bets are off. Everyone is a suspect until proven otherwise. Baga and Samudra will arrive at the gates of Mount Meru in full force. I need to find Aarjen. He is my only connection to the dark world of the rakshasas."

Indra hurried to his court to meet with his trusted council members, whom he had summoned urgently. The mighty palace of marble towered in front of him. He raced through the garden of the devas without stopping to admire the exotic flowers or to check on his white elephant mount, Hiravat, who had served him with utmost loyalty in many gruesome battles.

At the steps of the court, Indra was greeted by Agni, the lord of fire. The ever-radiant Agni was adorned in his usual flaming-orange-red robe.

"Indra, what's the matter? You summoned us with great urgency."

"Has everyone arrived?" Indra asked sternly.

"Yes…" said Agni, surprised by the seriousness in Indra's tone.

Indra paced the turquoise-blue floor that appeared like still water, reflecting the colorful ceiling above, like an upside-down vaulted basement deep under the floor. The tall columns that supported the ceiling appeared to sink into a layer of rippled water. He entered his court, where kings of all the worlds assembled to make crucial decisions.

Indra waved at his council—Varuna, the lord of rain; Surya, the lord of sun and light; and Vayu, the lord of wind. They welcomed Indra by placing their right hand over their heart and subtly bowing their heads.

Within the flamboyant chamber, decorated thrones were mounted on short pedestals, raised several steps above the ground. While the thrones' framework was constructed with dark, gleaming mahogany wood, it was crafted with enough gold to raise the question of whether they were wooden thrones embellished with ornate gold or golden thrones with exquisite woodwork. Their square bases and circular backs were lined with velvet and padded with soft cotton from the plains of the Pulikat River.

"Indra, this council is yours," Agni said after completing the council formalities swiftly. A flash of Agni's flame rolled through the chamber.

"I can sense your concern, Indra," remarked Surya.

The members of the council quickly exchanged glances, as if to gauge each other's level of awareness of Indra's concern.

"My dear friends, at sunrise, I heard the wail of the shunk."

Everyone knew he was talking about the conch.

"Where is Maya?" Indra gestured at the empty throne by his side.

Agni shook his head, unaware of Maya's whereabouts.

Vayu was about to speak, but stopped when the empty throne next to Indra distorted and faded in irregular, flickering patterns. The almost-translucent throne altered its shape, folded in the center and slowly transformed into a ghostly human form. Within seconds, the blurry shape sharpened to reveal a radiant young woman.

Maya's glassy form floated a few inches above the pedestal, where the throne had been set. Her brown hair, with partially braided strands, flowed well past her shoulders under her thick crown braid. Her beautiful face glistened in the glow of Surya, who was seated across from her. Her long green dress kissed the surface of the pedestal. Her brilliant eyes reflected the colors of the objects she gazed at. Maya glided gracefully toward Indra, reflecting a spectacular array of the elements—the light from Surya, the heat from Agni, and the great storm of Vayu and Varuna.

"Father, I was in search of information for you," she said politely, her voice echoing through the chamber.

"I'm glad you're back in time," Indra said in a relieved tone. Maya served as the link between the council and all the distant worlds.

"There is disharmony, but I cannot explain its cause."

"Could it be the doing of the asuras?" asked the powerful king.

"The asuras are our allies, Indra," Varuna said quickly. "They want harmony now more than ever, as they cherish the brotherhood created between the two kingdoms. I know my brothers, and I have remained close to them." Varuna's voice was stern but composed.

"We must assemble at Mount Meru, where Baga and Samudra will be battle-ready, following the shunk's warning protocol…" Indra began.

"March to the battlegrounds?" Vayu asked, incredulously. "Are we preparing to fight with them or against them?" he asked with great concern.

"For the sake of all worlds, let's pray it's with them and not against them, but that will be decided at Mount Meru," Indra said grimly.

###

The battlefield of Mount Meru was at the geographic intersection of three distinct worlds. It was here that the bright, lush meadows of the land of the devas, foothills of the dark mountains of the asuras, and the deep blue oceans of the jalas melded. He who controlled the gates of Mount Meru controlled the gates to the worlds, and the gods protected this place with all their might.

Adorned in his lustrous battle gear, Indra thundered down the rolling meadows on his four-tusked white elephant, Hiravat, flanked by the fiery golden chariots of Surya and Agni. As they blazed toward the dark mountains, Vayu and Varuna stormed behind Indra, making it seem like a million warriors were charging across the plains. Maya gracefully glided by her father, weathering the elements.

At the sight of Baga's massive army, comprised of an endless sea of strong, armed women and men on black horses, elephants, and other creatures that belonged only to the asura worlds, Indra signaled to Hiravat to slow down.

The crowd roared as Indra approached their fearless leader, Baga, who stood on a silver chariot, his dark, muscular arms folded across his colossal chest. Like Indra, his council flanked his chariot.

Maya greeted Baga with respect and embraced him. She then went back to Indra and signaled to him. Her illusionary powers ensured congeniality among the great warriors, even at times of crisis or hostility.

Indra waved to Baga and let out a laugh. "Why this spectacle, great lord of the nights?" His arms swept across Baga's vast army, his tone reflecting friendly sarcasm. "Mine is just an army of five," he added.

Baga glared at the devas. Of the four councilmen, he studied Varuna the most and then finally nodded at Maya. With a flash, his army disappeared, leaving behind only five of Baga's trusted aides.

"That's more like it," said Indra. As he dismounted from Hiravat, the storm behind him calmed immediately. "I see Maya serves both of us well." Indra acknowledged Maya's incredible display of Baga's might through illusion.

"INDRA!" said Baga, his voice deep and loud. "What does the shunk's warning portend, my friend?" He unfolded his arms. Baga was colossal, dark as the night, and handsome.

His chiseled face was punctuated by feline, sparkling amber eyes. His dark, bushy, dumbbell-shaped mustache—the trademark style of the asuras—neatly spread across his upper lip like a landscaped hedge. Unlike his royal peers, the traditional apparel he wore was simple, consisting of silver-plated leather armor and a thick, dark kilt that flowed down below his knees. A heavy pewter double-headed ax with a short, heavily carved black wooden handle hung upright by his waist. His attire was less ornate, more warrior-like, even during times of peace. Baga was not wearing his crown, as he had been in the middle of playing his stringed instrument—a diligent daily routine—when he suddenly heard the discordance of music through the shunk.

The last time he'd met Indra, he had gracefully accepted defeat in a wager and given away his prized stallion, Ashvat. It had been a fair competition, but still, Baga realized, albeit a bit late, that Indra had hustled him into the competition. Annoyed with himself and his clever opponent, he'd vowed to be more cautious in future dealings with the king of the devas.

For centuries, especially during times of harmony, the devas and asuras played war games, such as Chadurang, and had friendly wagers with high stakes. The competition was intense but amicable and ended in celebratory revelry, in which both the winner and the loser participated with equal enthusiasm.

"Looks like neither of us knows what's going on, Baga." Indra quickly got to the point.

Baga nodded. "I was hoping *you* could tell me…"—he jumped out of his chariot—"…if you suspect anyone, um…at your end who would betray the brotherhood."

"No. The devas have nothing to do with this," Indra assured him. "We should work together, Baga."

Maya floated between the two kings, connected with their minds briefly, and conveyed a message from the great rishi Vyas, advising them to join forces at the time of distress.

"Mighty king Indra, the great rishi has spoken. Our cooperation, like the strings of an instrument in the hands of a skilled musician, begets cosmic harmony," Baga said with dramatic flair. "Together, we can destroy evil."

The ocean rumbled in the distance. It receded, leading to the build-up of a tidal wave. An enormous waterspout spiraled toward the kings on shore, molding itself into a ghostly water figure. As the column of water gained strength, Maya inserted herself into the column and abruptly arrested its momentum, taking the form of water.

"Welcome, great queen of the jalas," she announced the arrival of Queen Samudra.

Maya was Indra's closest confidant. Legend had it that the gods had created Maya when Indra, having lost his beloved mortal daughter, pleaded for her spirit to be returned. They granted his wish by reviving her spirit as the creator of all illusions for the new worlds. The overjoyed lord of the devas had named her Maya. Her infinite creative powers made Maya an indispensable presence at gatherings of rishis, leaders, and the councils of various worlds. Indra had come to depend on her discretion and judgment.

"Indra and Baga!" said Samudra. Her voice was like billows from the ocean depths. "If the warning of the shunk is unheeded, everything we swore to protect in the living world will cease to exist." Samudra spoke with animation. "Evil will reign, destroying the living and raising the dead. The rakshasas will take control of the mortal worlds, slowly and painfully devouring every other form of life."

"Why would the rakshasas prevail?" asked Baga, raising his voice. "The creatures are powerless. They have lacked a strong leader for ages."

"They never had one!" said Agni, shaking his head.

"Well, they did with Kumba, the rakshasa king…" Varuna chipped in.

"Listen, I don't have the details," Indra quickly said, interrupting Varuna. "All I can tell you is, in the cycle of life and death, there will only be death. We'll be long forgotten."

"The great rishi Vyas, the fourth guardian of the shunk, will have some answers for us," said Indra.

"I have a message from the great sage Vyas." Maya spoke clearly. "The Curse of Bhrigu has begun! We are at the mercy of weak mortals."

"The knight of the Dark Forest will have the answers," Indra said grimly.

Chapter 4

Chess and Football

It was an unusually sunny and warm fall day in the Chicago area. Students were sent home early to make time for parent-teacher conferences, but instead of rushing back home, Brendan and Max decided to sit outside by the school football bleachers and play some chess.

Ever since the *Chicago Tribune* had run an article on chess in Chicago and featured Brendan and a few other kids from the Illinois chess circuit, the school principal—an avid chess player himself—had encouraged Brendan to start a chess club in the school and keep a chess set in his locker. It was a soft, zippered rectangular black nylon case that resembled a flute case with two handles and a shoulder strap. The green-and-white-checkered vinyl mat was rolled up and placed inside the case beside an enclosed pouch that contained the large plastic black and white chess pieces—thirty-two of them. Inside this case, Brendan almost always placed his black Chronos clock and a notation pad.

Because of all the publicity that Brendan had been receiving from the multiple school PA announcements and the numerous articles and trophies that the school showcased, his fellow students, in general, acknowledged that his chess talents were up there at some top national level.

But chess was no real sport, like football, and Lake Villa was all about football! Unlike the Chicago city schools, where chess was embedded into the curriculum, most Lake Villa residents had football on their minds. It was peak football season, and the school's most-talked-about and publicized female kicker, Alex, was not performing so well.

Brendan rolled out the chess mat and set the pieces. Max pulled the clock out and tried to set it for 5 minutes for Brendan and 20 minutes for himself. He hoped the time advantage would help him overcome such a skilled opponent.

"Oh, c'mon. We don't need the clock," said Brendan. "Let's just play. You are going to lose anyway."

"No way. I need some time odds," insisted Max.

Brendan just smirked and shook his head.

Although Max had never won against Brendan in a serious game of chess, on rare occasions, he would catch Brendan off guard. And when that happened, Max made sure that the world heard about his crushing victory over a future grandmaster.

"Oh, have you seen our new kicker?" asked Max, pointing to the football field.

"Nope. I think she just transferred this year from another state. Pretty cool," Brendan replied.

The board was set up in seconds, and the boys zipped through the first ten moves or so. Each knew exactly what the other was going to play, as established by the pundits for their named opening moves and their countless variations. About the twelfth move or so, Max paused briefly to think. The game had already progressed beyond book predictions, and a new pattern had emerged as a result of a swift and cunning attack by the superior player. Just when he was about to move his knight…

SPLAT! Something smashed into the board.

It took a few seconds for the boys to understand what had struck the board. The impact was so hard that it sent the pieces flying over the shriveled vinyl mat. Max jumped up in shock and then realized that it was a football. "Ha-ha. That was funny, dude. Right on the money," said a boorish student in football gear.

"You got them, Joe," a heavyset student in uniform with a bulging belly concurred with his taller teammate. "Looks like you nerds need to start over again with your checkers," he said, grabbing his football and adjusting his cup.

"These are not checkers, you moron," Brendan responded with a snicker while picking up the pieces. "Of course, when your IQ is less than your shoe size, you would not know any better. Why don't you and your buddy go pound your brainless heads against each other so that we can get back to our game of CHESS?" said Brendan.

"Let's see you start a new game. Go on," said Joe, aggravated.

"We don't have to," said Brendan. "We know exactly where we were, so we can continue where we left off." He set up the board the way it had been before the football landed on it.

Joe and his stout friend Nate looked at each other, fist bumped, and walked away toward their practice.

"Morons," said Brendan, settling back on the bench. "This is why I stopped playing football."

"Let's just go inside and play. It's getting chilly anyway," said Max, his voice a bit shaky.

"No. We can't let a couple of bullies bother us. I want to play outside."

Max collected his thoughts for a few minutes and made his move, but not where he had originally intended to move before the ball dislodged the pieces.

Brendan shook his head. "See what I mean! You just hung your queen! There are going to be a lot of distractions like this. It is important to isolate yourself and focus…"

THUD.

The ball crashed onto the chessboard and sent the pieces flying again; one of the pieces hit Max on his forehead. Joe and Nate were clearly amused as they cheered each other with high-fives.

Brendan collected the scattered chess pieces, but he also quickly grabbed the rolling ball and held on to it.

"This is trouble!" Max said.

"Give us the ball, Brendan," said Joe. "You guys should have known not to mouth off to football players. Let's see you remember your game now."

"If you want the ball, you'd better apologize to Max," Brendan said, standing tall.

"You've got to be kidding me," said Nate.

"I am not talking to you, dude!" said Brendan, pointing his finger.

"You know that's not going to happen, Brendan. Mustangs don't apologize," said Joe.

"Hey, man, if you are that tough, how come you got your butts kicked last week by the Falcons?" Max muttered but with difficulty.

Nate lunged forward, but Joe grabbed him by his jersey and yanked him back to prevent Max from getting pummeled. This gave Max enough time to dart up the bleachers.

Brendan, who was 6 feet tall, was never afraid of standing up to anyone in school, even those who were older than him. Besides, he was friends with many of the senior football players and had established a good network of students. Many teachers and students liked his pleasant and unassuming personality.

He held out his strong, long arms at the boys. He knew they just picked on the weaker kids.

"Come back, Max!" shouted Brendan, still holding on to the ball. "These guys will be off the team if the coach spots them bullying others. They might get suspended, and even they are not that stupid."

"What's going on, guys? Where's the ball?" a person in uniform and a helmet hollered from a distance. "Coach wants you back at the practice." It was a girl.

Max recognized Alex, the kicker who had moved from California. She was much taller than the two football players, even without her helmet.

The two jocks quickly exchanged glances and waddled toward Alex, who jogged and met them by the bleachers. They mockingly laughed at the chess players.

"Cut it out, guys," Alex snapped at the two football players in front of Brendan and Max. "We need to focus on our game, and you don't want to get into trouble again, Nate." Alex pressed her finger against the heavier kid's padded shoulder. "You know Coach doesn't approve of this behavior. You might want to apologize to those guys for messing up their game," she added.

"They can start a new game, Alex. What's a big deal?" asked Joe.

"They don't have to, they can just continue where they left off," she said.

"Can we have our ball back?" Joe asked.

Brendan ignored them. "Your turn, Max," he said, squatting on the football. "Let's finish the game, and if you like, we'll start from just before you lost the queen."

He could hear the football coach yelling at them to join the practice.

"C'mon, man! Don't make me take the ball from you," said Nate.

"Try me," said Brendan.

"Um…sorry, guys. Sorry for bothering you. I just…" Alex started apologizing but abruptly stopped talking, studied the game, and asked Max whose turn it was to move.

Max exchanged a quick look with Alex before making his move. "Look who's distracted now," he said, capturing Brendan's knight.

"Are you sure about that, dude?" asked Brendan, shaking his head and moving his pawn without wasting any time on the clock.

They both executed a series of moves in succession and suddenly, both Max and Alex gasped as Brendan marched his rook down the file toward Max's king, ending the game.

"Touchdown and checkmate," Brendan and Alex said in chorus.

Brendan knew only one other person who associated a back-rank checkmate with a touchdown! It was a simple chess-football analogy when a rook marched down the board to checkmate the opponent's king, just like an uninterrupted running back charging down the field for an easy touchdown. It was a kid he'd grown up with in his neighborhood a long time ago. Brendan looked up, and when he recognized Alex, he jumped up, knocking over the chess set and the clock.

His heart raced as he locked eyes with Alex.

He saw an equally surprised Alex standing in front of him with her mouth open.

"Alex Sherwin?" Brendan burst out as the others watched with puzzlement.

Alex brushed her wavy brown hair with her fingers. "Brendan! It's been so long!" She reached out and squeezed his arm. "You've become tall. I didn't know you went to this school. Do you still live in the city?" she asked.

Brendan stood, grinning, his eyes still locked with hers. "Uh…We moved a couple of years ago after Tara joined the Air Force." He continued. "Oh, wait, you are the new kicker?" he asked, finally making the connection.

"Didn't I just tell you?" Max mumbled.

"Yes, for now," said Alex. "Only if I survive this season," she added. "Things are not going too well."

"You know each other?" asked Joe, surprised that a cool girl hung out with chess nerds.

"We grew up together," Alex said, patting Brendan's shoulder. "Football and chess are all we did. It was great."

The football coach yelled at them to get back to practice.

"It's really nice seeing you, Brendan. I'll catch up with you soon," Alex said. "He sacked his knight. I didn't see it either, but we'll get him next time," she said to Max with a wink. She blurted out her phone number to Brendan and sprinted back to practice.

Halfway down the field, she made a sharp turn to her left, and as she anticipated, the ball that Brendan threw spiraled in the air and landed in her outstretched hands with perfect timing! Alex pumped her fist in the air. Without looking at Brendan, she waved at him and continued running.

Following Brendan's enthusiastic narration of the afternoon's events, Turner called his old friend and former neighbor, Dwayne Sherwin—Alex's dad and a football coach—to reconnect with him. Dwayne and Turner had been neighbors for more than ten years on the south side of Chicago.

Dwayne had introduced football to both Alex and Brendan at a very young age. Dwayne was also a decent chess player, and his neighborly friendship with Turner was nourished by evenings the two men shared across a chessboard. The kids were naturally inclined to learn both games. Initially, Brendan was more attracted to football. He was good with the ball. However, Brendan was more influenced by his father's interests and preferred chess to football. He did not like being tackled by other kids. Alex, on the other hand, was more focused and played chess better than Brendan for several years. Turner saw a lot of potential in Alex and liked her drive to win. However, as Alex got older, she chose football over chess. When her family had moved to California, she'd lost contact with Brendan and the board game.

Dwayne and Turner finally met up at Fog Cutter Diner. Dwayne talked about his daughter's success in football as a female kicker but also conceded that Alex was going through a difficult phase in her life. She was missing too many field goals and had difficulty performing under pressure. Dwayne felt the move, the school, et cetera, might have affected her concentration and hence her performance.

Both Turner and Dwayne agreed that it would be good for Brendan and Alex to get together, and Dwayne promised to send Alex to the chess club.

The following night, two black Ducati Superbike 1199 Panigale S motorcycles roved around Turner's chess club and stopped in the narrow alley behind the club. Two riders in dark matching race gear and helmet surveyed the unfinished storage room of the chess club from the outside. It was Aarjen, the Knight of the Dark Forest, and Kaia, the Knight of the Earth.

"Do you think this is ground zero?" asked the tall male rider, adjusting his headset.

"Yes, it is," his companion replied, pushing her visor up. "The Kats were here. I can still smell them."

"Is the artifact here?" he asked.

"Not yet, but it will be here soon," she replied, peering inside the building.

"This human boy and his little friends…" the man said, walking closer to the building. "It could get very dangerous, and someone could die," he said coldly. "How are they going to handle it?"

"It's not their fault and they don't have a choice," she defended the children. "We have to protect them when the worlds collide and the attacks begin. We'll be back soon," she said, getting back on her bike, turning it around, and accelerating away from the chess club as her partner raced behind.

Inside a distant, abandoned barn, a vampire Kat, hanging upside-down from a rusted iron beam, stirred briefly, sensing the presence of a deadly hunter. But as the threat quickly disappeared, it settled back into its slumber.

"I will wait for the signal to attack the children," it mumbled as it shut its large red eyes.

It was a Saturday afternoon, just before Christmas. The schools had already closed in Lake County, and the holiday mood was at its peak.

Much to the annoyance of his students, Turner decided to have special coaching sessions on Saturday mornings for a select few to begin preparations for the Chess Olympiad—the prestigious Olympic chess event that the US Chess Federation in Chicago was scheduled to host during the summer.

Finally, after years of seeking the distinction, Chicago had won the privilege of hosting the Summer Olympic Games, and there was excitement all around the city in anticipation of the event. Although chess was not included as an Olympic sport, the International Olympic Committee and International Chess Federation had decided to conduct a Chess Olympiad prior to the commencement of the Summer Olympic Games to promote the game and give it an international stage.

The Olympiad was originally intended for the world's top professional talent; however, with a large government push toward enriching school and college curricula, it was decided that the Olympiad would include world scholastic and high school tournaments. Navy Pier, customized to host special events during the Olympics, had been selected as the tournament's venue.

Turner was setting up the boards with his younger kids while Brendan was setting up the computers. When the phone rang, Turner took the call in his office. Brendan noticed that his father appeared to be happy to talk to the person on the other end.

"When?" asked Turner and waited for a response, leaning back on his chair. "Why don't you send Alex over this morning, nine-ish? I have invited a few kids," the coach said loudly.

Brendan was immediately excited by the prospect of Alex joining them.

"Is Alex coming over, dad?" he asked as soon as his dad hung up.

"She might," said Turner. "Dwayne said the football season was not that great for her. He just wants some change of pace, and we think it would be best for her to spend some time with us. The kid's talented, and we could use her help."

The front door opened with the familiar jingle. It was Nora and Sidney. Sidney was wearing her favorite purple jacket and the pink woolen parka from New Zealand. She opened and closed the front door one more time just to listen to the sound of the chime. When she heard Maddie's voice from inside, she quickly released herself from her mother's gentle grip and attempted to dart toward the voice. Nora quickly reacted, held her close, and removed her heavy jacket.

"Now, you can go," she said, winking at Maddie.

"Hey, SID!" Turner greeted Sidney loudly. "You look beautiful, kiddo," he said as he watched her hug Maddie. He wanted to add, *as beautiful as your mother*, but, rightfully, the compliment remained an unspoken thought.

Sidney had long, wavy red hair, just like her mother's, whose fiery locks were her defining feature. She had a pretty, round face with a pointy nose. Her deep blue eyes were more highlighted because of her constant gaze.

It had only been a few months since she had been introduced to chess, and she had already picked up the game after some initial frustrations. The coach's colleague at the University of Chicago had provided software that helped visually impaired children learn the game and spent time at the club to get Sidney acclimated to the program.

Nora waved at Turner. She had been bringing Sidney to the club almost every other evening, and she enjoyed visiting the club as much as her daughter did. Over the months, she had become good friends with Coach Turner and had gotten to know more about the charismatic single dad who had lost his wife to cancer. She noticed with gratification that Sidney had no trouble blending in with the other kids, who had almost stopped noticing her inability to see.

Ro, Max, Austin, and Jack all arrived at about the same time, and the quiet club erupted with noisy activities.

Coach Turner herded them into the coaching room, where he asked the kids to set up several boards. A large green-and-white-checkered chess mat that represented a chessboard hung on the wall across from the tables. Flat magnetic cutouts in the shape of the chess pieces were stuck to the board at their respective positions. The coach utilized his old-fashioned hanging board to analyze games and tactics for the first 30 minutes of all his coaching sessions. He would set up the pieces on the board and challenge the kids to find the best moves to solve the chess puzzle. Even the parents who dropped their kids off at the club often stayed back just to watch the kids resolve complex chess problems.

"Guys, you need to work harder—a lot harder—to do well at the national tournament," Turner said, raising his voice.

"Olympiad!" Ro piped in with his characteristic impulsiveness.

"If we learn and practice *every day*," Turner continued, ignoring Ro, "we'll have a decent shot at a good placement at the nationals, but it is not going to be easy."

"It's internationals, Coach!" added Max. It was his turn to interrupt.

"Brendan will beat Scrappy Junior and become the international champ," added Ro.

"Someone should get Scrappy Junior a new clock," said Max in an altered voice.

Austin laughed.

"Now, stop," Turner said. "Let's not waste our energy by being silly. *All* of you have a good chance at the titles next year. You are all in different sections, but you cannot be underprepared. This is also the first year you get to play as a team. So, this is the most important tournament for all of us. We are going to work hard and play hard, but we are going to have fun as well. Are you all ready for it?" asked Coach, scanning the room and looking at each of his students.

"Yes, sir!" Sidney giggled.

"You are going to shock a lot of players," said Turner, who had already approached the tournament directors about including her in the regular tournament. He knew that it required bending some of the rules, especially the *you touch a piece, you move that piece* rule.

"Now, are you ready for this?" Turner asked the group.

A chorus of, "Yes!" echoed; of course, a few rolled their eyes.

The kids quickly got busy with the session, and Coach Turner focused on the end game.

"Many people lose their games simply because they fail to come up with a strong finish." He looked at Austin and asked, "Austin, what should you pay attention to?"

"Stalemate!" said little Austin.

All the kids, except Sidney, cheered. Despite the celebratory atmosphere, she felt a chill run down her spine as a shadow silently moved across the corridor toward the storage room.

In the midst of the eerie quiet, an uneasy feeling descended, and goosebumps emerged on her skin. A monster, moving in the shadows, was silently preparing the unfinished room for the delivery and storage of precious cargo from a distant water world. Just as the tension peaked, a sudden jingle from the door chime distracted her. Thoughts of fairies playing in a field quickly replaced the darkness that briefly seized her, and Sidney, despite the sense of lingering unease, resumed playing chess.

Chapter 5

The Curse of Bhrigu

E nough of your beauty sleep, Aarjen." A familiar voice and touch woke the knight of the Dark Forest. "You look well rested." It was Kaia, the Knight of the Earth.

"They are waiting for you!"

Aarjen pulled his pillow over his head and turned away. "I worked hard to get here. *I am tired!*" His voice was muffled.

"You have slept for an entire day! The council is waiting for you. Remember, you told Maya that you have something urgent to tell them." Kaia tugged at the pillow.

"How is my horse?" He finally looked into her hazel eyes.

"She's exhausted but holding up well. The stable keepers are pampering her," Kaia reassured him.

"She deserves it. Without her, I would be dead." Aarjen pulled himself up and leaned his shoulder on the finely crafted mahogany headboard.

"It's good to see you. I am glad you are back in one piece. There is something terrible going on out there, right? I sense it. Whatever it is,

Aarjen, I am going back with you." She sat next to him on the bed. "Yeah, let's go talk to the council."

"Welcome back to Indra's palace." Maya gleefully reached for their hands at the entrance of the palace. "Father is anxiously waiting to talk to you."

Instantly, they found themselves transported into Indra's court.

"Aarjen, what do you know about the wailing shunk?" Indra asked without wasting too much time.

"Great king Indra." Aarjen took a quick knee. "The Curse of Bhrigu has begun! The curse of your war game, Chadurang, has now become a reality."

"What game? What curse?" asked a baffled Varuna.

"Maya can help us remember the details of what happened a long time ago. Not all in my council know about the curse," said Indra.

Maya closed her eyes and let her memory unfold in the form of holographic images that the council members could see.

During turbulent times, when the worlds had been at war with each other, the devas had fought bitterly with the asuras. To prepare themselves for the war, the devas crafted a war game called Chadurang. People who excelled at this game became highly skilled warriors in real battles.

Eventually, the animosity between the asuras and devas ended, and only sporadic threats from the rakshasas existed, but together, the devas and the asuras kept the latter under control. The use of war games declined with time. Only a select few, like the warriors and knights, continued practicing Chadurang, and the war game was reduced to a sport.

Indra himself was highly skilled at the game. It was he who introduced the art of Chadurang to Maya and wished for a game where the players would be taken to a magical world of illusion.

At Indra's suggestion, Maya developed an exciting form of a war game, in which the players would embark on a journey into the magical illusionary world called Mayastella while playing Chadurang.

To retain the original essence of Chadurang, the contestants always assembled in a chamber, where a large, ornate, traditional Chadurang board made of jade was placed in the center over a stone pedestal. The board was square with a checkered design of alternating dark and light colors. The chamber itself was apportioned between night, depicting the strength of the asuras, and day, representing the power of devas.

Chadurang was designed to be played at many levels—from a simple two-player game to a complex team game, whereby the players used information about events transpiring at Mayastella and applied it to the game.

The most advanced and exciting form of Chadurang, however, involved war games where the players embarked on quests to Mayastella, where they interacted with illusionary, ghostly characters called the poiz—meaning false creatures, or creatures that were not real or alive.

Poiz, while illusionary, existed only in Mayastella. Sparse in matter, their weak composition made them cloud-like and too fragile to sustain existence long enough to morph into real living beings. Although ephemeral, the poiz played a crucial role in the game, as some became allies of the players, providing them with useful information, while others were deceitful and battled the players. The easily destructible poiz were harmless and incapable of causing any real danger to the players.

As the players engaged with the illusion of Mayastella, returning to the chamber frequently allowed them to study the positions and the patterns on the platform and isolate themselves from the treacherous illusions. The game was intended for brave warriors and was emotionally unforgiving of the fainthearted. Returning to the chamber was the only way out.

The game was quickly popularized across the worlds by Indra and Baga, who remained the uncontested masters of the game.

However, soon, Indra's interest in the existing format of the game began to wane. With an unparalleled thirst for challenge, he commissioned Maya once again to modify the game with trails that intertwined illusionary creatures that could become dangerous when they mixed with reality.

Maya sought the help of the rishis, but the rishis warned Maya of the dangers of creating an unsupervised world of artificially induced illusionary life forms that would be forced to mix with real and potentially dangerous creatures.

To Maya's surprise, Dur-shi—an apprentice sage of the rishis—offered to help her. "The rishis are too conservative and controlling," he'd reasoned. "Maya's world deserves a rich variety of life, like the other worlds."

Dur-shi then helped the queen of illusion establish the nijaz—real creatures that were an assortment of living creatures but were unique to the world of Maya. Thanking the rishi-apprentice for his generous gesture, Maya vowed to keep the creation of the nijaz a secret from the rishis and the knights.

Nijaz quickly proliferated. They evolved into different species and took various forms. Although the Nijaz were similar to other life forms, their life's essence was created and coded in such a way that they could not survive outside Mayastella.

Maya ensured that the poiz and nijaz were generally amiable to the players at the outer sphere of Mayastella and could only become progressively antagonistic as the players' journey neared the inner sphere.

With the introduction of the nijaz and the poiz, Indra's game quickly transformed from a simple war game to an adventurous and sometimes dangerous expedition, involving numerous conquests marked by milestones. This was one game of which Indra could never grow weary, for the expedition, the creatures, and the laws that governed the conquests changed with every game.

Each conquest required the completion of multiple tasks. The team that achieved the most tasks had an advantage over the other team and secured a head start toward the next conquest. The outcome of the game was always unpredictable. At any time, a losing team could emerge as the victor by fulfilling the ultimate purpose of the expedition.

Indra and Baga had immersed themselves in mastering this new source of entertainment in the absence of threat from any real enemies.

"You might recall that Chadurang was our way of life for a while, until…" Indra finally spoke.

"The curse," Surya spoke for Indra. "The Curse of Bhrigu."

"A curse of our own rishi. Why?" asked Varuna.

"The expeditions were becoming more complex, and Maya began to observe certain strange and inexplicable changes in her world that made her uncomfortable," Indra continued.

"A hint of tantrics," Maya explained.

"Dark magic?" asked a surprised Varuna, his voice booming across the court.

"Yes, the illusionary world appeared to be on edge, as though preparing for a transformation of the poiz into evil soul-hunting beings."

"I warned my father that something that I didn't understand had exerted its influence on these expeditions," said Maya. "My illusions were becoming dangerously real...*and dark.*"

"No need for tantrics to infiltrate a mere game," said Samudra, who neither liked the war games nor participated in them.

"At that point, I reached out to rishis Bhrigu and Vyas," said Indra.

"That was the right thing to do," said Samudra thoughtfully.

"They were upset with us for creating and exploiting life in the world of illusion without their approval. Then, they scolded Dur-shi for breaking the core values and rules that bound the great rishis."

"Um...And rishi Bhrigu cursed you for that, Indra?" asked a surprised Varuna.

"No...no," Indra said hesitantly, unwilling to allow the shadow of blame to fall on Maya.

"I learned my lesson," Maya interrupted him. "Then, I explained to them that these expeditions had helped us understand real threats and be prepared for any attack from the forces of evil. It was a hard argument. Bhrigu was still stubbornly opposed to the game; however, the great Vyas agreed that he would persuade Bhrigu to allow some form of the game to exist in Mayastella with proper checks and balances in place.

"We created a plasma layer in the inner sphere of Mayastella and banished the tantrics into the plasma, where they cannot escape without a soul. We monitored Mayastella for the presence of tantrics but found none outside of the plasma. Mayastella was a safe place for the quests," Maya sounded defensive. "While we were waiting for Vyas's approval, Baga and I discovered that at the center of this world—at the innermost sphere, past the plasma layer of Mayastella—rested Kumba!"

"What?" Samudra jumped, sending seawater flowing down the turquoise floor.

"Kumba, the rakshasa king? But didn't Kumba die before the war began?" asked Varuna.

"Killed by the rakshasas, his own creatures?" asked Surya.

"Isn't that why our war against the rakshasas ended so quickly?" asked Chandra, the lady of the moons.

"No one saw him alive or dead," said Baga. "He just disappeared before the peak of war."

"We had reasons to believe that he might have somehow found his way to the center of this newfound world of Maya, where he took refuge with a secret ally until he could gain enough strength to retaliate. Until then, no one would even look for him there," Indra added.

"Kumba was no coward, Indra," argued Varuna. "Why would he hide when his strength matches our strength? Besides, how could he possibly enter this world that is so well protected by Maya and cross the plasma layer?"

"I was as surprised as you all are, when I first heard about Kumba," Indra admitted. "We asked ourselves the question, what if Kumba had never died, but somehow found his way to the center of Mayastella by simply playing his own game, without Maya's knowledge?"

"We needed to find a way to ascertain the existence of the most dangerous of all the rakshasas who could be building his forces with the nijaz we had created," said Baga.

"True," agreed Surya. "The situation called for answers."

"Baga and I decided to get the answers, even before we received approval from Vyas that we could resume the game," Indra said. "But we did not involve or inform Maya."

"We believed that the path to the center would be the most treacherous one *if* Kumba was really there," said Baga. "He would have created obstacles and laid traps, knowing Indra and I often entered the expedition. And even if one reached the center of this world, where we suspected him to exist, defeating him was not likely to be a trivial task."

"Baga and I focused our energy to unlock the secret gates to the center and find Kumba before anyone could suspect our intentions," Indra continued.

"Ahh, now, this explains why you spent so much time in Mayastella, Indra," said Vayu.

"We believed we had another opportunity to defeat Kumba once and for all," said Indra.

"That is, if he were still alive," qualified Baga.

"Where does the curse fit in all of this?" asked Samudra impatiently.

"Things were going as planned until, suddenly, while we were in Mayastella, secretly finding our way into the inner sphere, Maya informed us that Bhrigu was seeking us with urgency. Since we could not readily reach the rishi, we informed Maya to let the great Bhrigu know that we'd exit Mayastella soon to meet with him, but we never heard back."

"But..." Indra paused, recollecting the painful incident. "Little did we understand the plight of the sage Bhrigu."

"The attack on the villages?" asked Varuna.

"Yes. The rakshasas seized the opportunity to attack rishi Bhrigu's ashram when the rishi was away and up in the mountains for his annual penance. Our distraction with Mayastella provided the creatures with a real opportunity to plan their raid."

"But we did warn and protect his village from the attack," said Agni.

"Someone helped orchestrate a bigger, well-timed second attack," Indra explained.

"The onslaught began after Bhrigu left his ashram," said Baga. "Bhrigu's disciples vigorously defended their homes against the attack, but soon, they were outnumbered. Finally, Dur-shi—the rishi's apprentice who was visiting the ashram—saved the day." Indra sighed.

"Wasn't Dur-shi the apprentice who was disciplined by the seven rishis for misuse of powers?" asked Varuna.

"Yes, he had returned to the ashram to apologize and ask for forgiveness from rishi Bhrigu. The timing of his visit could not have been any better," said Indra.

"When Bhrigu returned, he was shocked and enraged by the devastation. He felt let down by the kings and the lords who had sworn to protect the rishis.

In his rage and despair, Bhrigu cursed them: "*Listen, O devas and asuras, the vain leaders of the worlds. Perish you will of this game you play. As I suffer, you will, and as I did, you will beg for mercy! Powerless you shall be, as your fate one gloomy day might rest upon the weak and the frail.*

"The curse of the sage is akin to words written on stone. Bhrigu was hurt deeply, and the words poured from his heart. He wanted the devas and asuras to feel his pain," Indra spoke with remorse.

"Even though we helped Bhrigu rebuild his ashram and showered him with the respect he deserved," added Baga.

Indra paced back and forth, paused, and then continued, "It was several moons after the attack when Vyas and the other sages approached Bhrigu and asked him about our fate. 'The curse will destroy the worlds the devas and asuras are protecting. They made a mistake, so let us find a solution. We need to find a way to reverse the curse,' Vyas had reasoned with Bhrigu.

"Bhrigu agreed and set forth some criteria under which his curse would become effective, and in addition, he foretold that the shunk would send a warning if those requirements were about to be fulfilled," said Indra.

"And what were those conditions for the curse to be effective, Indra?" asked Varuna.

"The war game must be played on the original Chadurang board by me, Lord Baga, or our direct descendants against the rakshasas in an official competition initiated by a rishi or a sage."

"Indra, didn't you destroy the board and seal outside access to Mayastella?" asked Agni.

"I was about to, but Dur-shi, who had come to the rescue, requested Bhrigu to build a small ashram in Mayastella as tribute to those who had fallen in the fight against the rakshasas. Concerned with Dur-shi's unorthodox practices in the past, some of the rishis and the knights objected to Dur-shi's proposal. However, the sage-apprentice had already garnered Bhrigu's approval to become the guardian of Chadurang," said Indra.

"Unbeknownst to any of us, Chadurang disappeared and has somehow found its way to the human world," said Baga.

"Now, we have heard the warnings of the shunk," said Surya.

"Which means the rules are about to be broken. The Curse of Bhrigu is about to fall on us," added Vayu.

A noisy chatter erupted among the councilmen and women. The members were concerned, and many questions were asked.

Finally, the knight spoke: "Not only is Kumba at the center of Mayastella, but I am afraid immortals are now at the mercy of mortal children, who will be forced to play the game of Chadurang."

Chapter 6

Chadurang
Comes to Life

ustin, the youngest chess player in Coach Turner's club, was popular with the parents. Barely six years old, he was already about to finish second grade. He enjoyed playing competitive chess and had developed a reputation for beating most kids in his K-1 section. With his social demeanor, he was quick to make friends of all ages. He enjoyed mingling with the club's older kids, who readily accepted him and entertained his comments. His favorite players were Ro and Brendan, whom he followed everywhere during the tournaments. They treated him like their own sibling and took him under their wing.

When they were not around, Austin sat in a corner of the hall and played with his Hot Wheels and miniature die-cast fighter planes, which he carried in his bright yellow mini backpack. Austin played with his cars, no matter where he was. He would lie on the floor and move his toys at his eye level. In his imaginary world, bad people and aliens were always attacking the good people, and planes were flying everywhere, trying to defend the good people against laser attacks from malevolent forces. Sound effects and hurling objects punctuated Austin's improvised battles. Parents who accompanied their kids to the tournaments adored him, and coaches snooped around him, hoping to lure his parents to their coaching camp.

"Watch out for stalemate," Coach reiterated for the umpteenth time. He believed in repetition, especially for the younger kids. "Do not get greedy and surround the opponent's king with too many pieces."

"Okay," said Austin, holding on to his favorite white Aston Martin DB9 model.

"If your opponent's king cannot move without getting into a check and there is no other move, then it is a stalemate," Coach stated the obvious. "Remember, you don't win if there is a stalemate. It's a draw—you and your opponent get half a point each. This has already happened to you in two critical games, and I'd rather it didn't happen again. Let me go over some examples."

The class got intense, and the coach went over many scenarios. He addressed different weaknesses of his students individually and then finally paired them up and let them play games against each other or online.

The chess session was interrupted by loud knocks on the front door. Sidney perked up. She heard Coach Turner greet someone, and they chatted for a while. Coach called Brendan and said something to him.

A noisy exchange of greetings between Brendan and the visitors followed. From the voices, she could tell two people—a girl around Brendan's age and the other a man who was possibly Coach's age—were visiting.

Coach said goodbye and left with his friend. The door closed with the familiar sound, and Brendan and his guest joined the students inside.

"Guys, this is Alex," Brendan announced. His voice was playful. "She's the new kicker for the Mustangs…A good football player but a lousy chess player."

Sidney heard a playful push and a stifled laugh—likely Alex's.

"Just kidding," Brendan said. "She's good at chess too."

Max was the first to greet Alex.

"As a kicker, could you kick his butt?" Ro pushed Max and chuckled.

"Very mature, dude," said Max.

"Um…it feels like I am good at neither now," said Alex.

"She's joining the club," Brendan continued. "Be nice to her."

After brief conversations with the students, Brendan proceeded to show Alex around.

"Look, it's getting cloudy and really dark outside," Sidney heard Ro tell Max. They were in the office, playing chess online.

They talked about the winter storm advisory flashing on the Weather app. The radar was tracking a massive blue-and-purple patch that was supposed to roll through the area within the hour. Sleet, followed by six to ten inches of snow, were expected to add to the existing mess.

Sidney, acutely sensitive to sudden noise, let out a startled scream when a gust of wind flung the front door open and slammed it with a loud bang on a metal desk that sat very close to the doorway, knocking over a heavy trophy that served as a paperweight. She heard the paper and other stuff on the desk falling over everywhere as the wind chime clattered wildly.

She felt something—something that gave her the chills again. She had felt this way once before…as though someone or something very close was watching her.

Max and Ro jumped up, hearing the sudden burst of commotion. Max almost knocked the chair over. They both quickly ran to the front room to shut the door, gather the papers, and set things in order.

"Is your dad back?" Max asked Brendan, who had joined them.

"I don't think so," Brendan replied.

"Who opened the door then?" asked Max, looking around.

"The wind," Brendan responded nonchalantly. "Who else is here on a Saturday morning?"

"The wind shut the door too?" asked Ro.

Brendan just shrugged. He looked outside to check for any familiar cars, but didn't see any. The kids inside were unusually quiet, focused on their games.

As Brendan entered the office, through the corner of his eye, he caught a quick glimpse of someone swiftly darting across the hallway toward the storage room. "Is someone inside?" he shouted and hurried into the room, where he found all the kids playing, except Sidney.

"Where's Sidney?" he asked Maddie.

"Oh, she just went to the restroom," she said without looking up.

"Alone?" asked Brendan, irritated.

"Yeah."

"Maddie, it is so dark there. You need to turn on the lights and help her out."

"I am scared to go there, Brendan. And she told me that the light won't help her," Maddie said, somewhat shame-faced.

"Then, call one of the boys. You can't…" Brendan didn't want to waste any more time arguing with his little sister.

He hurried to the restroom. It was dark. The door was closed and it was eerily quiet. "Sidney, are you there?" he called out. "Sid, are you okay?"

There was no answer. He stepped closer to knock on the door, but the door was not locked. When he pushed, it opened gently. She was not inside.

Brendan's heart raced, and blood gushed to his face. He turned his attention to the storage room. The room was unfinished and cold. Too many loose articles were lying around. Sidney could very easily fall and get hurt.

"Hey, Sidney. Are you there?" he shouted.

"I don't think she would have gone there; the door is closed, Brendan," said Ro, who had joined him by then. "That's a difficult place to get to even if you can see well," he said.

"Maybe she strayed into the room accidentally," said Brendan.

Brendan pushed the storage room door open and peeked inside. "Sidney, are you in there?" he asked faintly at first, but then repeated it in a firm voice.

A hazy blue glow, similar to the light from a computer monitor, filled the room. The light flickered as a layer of fog covered the floor.

"Is that smoke on the floor?" asked Ro.

"I don't think so. It feels more like moisture, like mist," said Brendan, carefully lowering himself to examine the murky layer and fanning it toward his nose.

"Do you have a freezer here?" asked Ro, shivering and crossing his arms close to his body.

"No...nothing. This is just a storage room."

The haze came from the center of the room, where a bulky package lay on a makeshift table made of large plywood board and plastic crates. Across the room, Brendan could see the silhouette of Sidney standing still, her back turned toward the door.

The boys froze.

Finally, Brendan, who felt his throat tighten, tapped Sidney on her shoulder. He wanted to call her name, but his voice failed him. She was cold and stiff. He shook her gently. Ro hurried inside and stood next to Brendan, breathing heavily.

"Sid, are you all right?" Brendan's voice sounded louder than he'd intended in the cold storage room.

Sidney finally moved and held Brendan's wrist firmly. Her hand was shaking, but her grip tightened.

"Look, the light seems to be coming from that...that box...that package," said Ro, his voice barely audible. "Maybe it was packed with dry ice."

"I don't think so," said Brendan, swallowing hard.

He remembered the large package from Monty. Why would anyone send anything packaged in dry ice to the club?

"Maybe they shipped it to the wrong address. Let's open it," said Ro.

They cautiously leaned over to examine the four-foot-long square package, which was already partially opened. When Brendan flipped over the thick cardboard, the blue glow intensified and spread across the room.

"Wow, look at this!" whispered Ro, as he flipped open the second panel.

Brendan studied the rectangular object. It was breathtakingly ornate, made of a light green, stone-like material, and embedded with shiny, colorful gemstones.

It sat on a well-fitted black marble platform with gold trim, supported by four short legs that resembled the large paws of a lion on each corner.

Beautiful geometric designs and shapes of celestial objects were etched into the slab. At the center, there was a square checkered area that was encircled by strange, inscribed symbols.

"This is awesome! Where did you get this from?" asked Ro.

"Dad must have ordered this, but when I mentioned the package, he didn't remember ordering anything." Brendan examined the board without touching it. "Where's the light coming from?" He looked for the light source but couldn't locate it. He leaned over and looked at all slides. "Must have batteries inside," he said, moving his hand closer to the side of the board.

"Where is it? I want to touch it!" said Sidney, lunging toward the makeshift table as though she could see what Brendan was up to. Her tone was harsh, and unusually possessive as if she were drawn to the object by some inexplicable force.

She reached out to the board. The glow seeped through the room as though someone had turned a blue LED strip light on. With her slender, cold fingers, she carefully felt the board, first sliding them over the sides and then the indents, the designs, the embedded gemstones, and the inscriptions. She felt the planets and the geometric shapes, and when she touched the checkered squares, the entire board lit up. Several beams of blue and green light shot out of the sides of the circular slabs, horizontally spanning the room. Sharp laser beams cut vertically through the mist from the checkered squares around the center and, one by one, multiple lines of lights formed a grid over the checkered square.

Brendan and Ro watched with amazement as holographic images of celestial bodies—planets, stars, and galaxies—projected through the glow.

"Dude, the graphics are really cool," said Brendan excitedly.

Max heard muffled voices coming from the storage room, but he didn't want to venture inside. Suspecting that his friends might be in the room he hated so much, yet driven by curiosity, he mustered enough courage to move halfway closer to the room. When he saw a hazy blue light seep through the partially opened door of the otherwise dark interior, he badly wanted to look inside.

"Hey, Maddie, who's in that room?" he shouted.

"No one, Max," Maddie responded uninterestedly.

"Is there a monitor or TV inside?"

"No, Max. It's just a storage room."

"Then, what's that light? I bet the guys are in there. Can you check?" he asked.

"Why don't you do it yourself?" Maddie asked in a high-pitched voice. "Are you scared?" she giggled mockingly.

"Oh, come on. You know the place much better than I do, and Coach will get mad at me if I go there."

She shook her head. "That obviously has not stopped you before," she mumbled. "Come with me!"

Austin, with a tiny Hot Wheel car in hand, quietly followed them into the room.

Brendan was fascinated with what he saw. A strange-looking game board was coming to life. It made a series of clicks, causing the shiny stones to sparkle.

"Oh, cool." Austin was the first to speak as they crowded around the board. "Can I play with it?" he asked innocently.

"You guys are not supposed to mess with Dad's stuff," warned Maddie sternly. "I bet he ordered a special board for Sidney from the university for her to play in the tournament," she said.

The heavy door behind them slammed shut, startling everyone, except Sidney. The kids shivered as frost formed on the floor and the walls. Peculiar crackling and static noises were heard from within the board as beams of light from it spanned the room.

Then, everything went silent.

"How the heck does it project the light up there? Did you press any buttons?" Ro asked Sidney.

"Sidney! What's the matter?" asked Brendan when Sidney shuddered.

"I am getting a bad feeling when I touch this." Sidney's voice trembled.

"Then don't touch it," he said, pulling her arm away from the board.

"Someone is watching us!" said Sidney, her tone deepening.

"We are inside a storage room with no light. There is no one here, and the door is shut, Sidney," Max said. "You guys are just trying to mess with us," he said, forcing fake laughter.

"Let's just get out of here. It's really cold," said Ro.

"*Shras Ni Chadurang…Ni Chadurang…Noos!*" A loud voice exploded through the board.

Austin screamed and grabbed Brendan's pants, pinching him in the process. Brendan winced and moved but held Austin close to him.

An image appeared—a frail, hairy-faced old person, with sandy hair knotted up over his head like a bun. His beard was shaggy and long, and his eyebrows were as thick as his droopy mustache. He had a frown but appeared serene. He looked like a wizard. The holographic image slowly rotated 360 degrees. He seemed to be studying the audience, who was watching him in awe.

"*Shras Ni Chadurang…Ni Chadurang…Noos!*" The face repeated the strange words, only louder this time.

"What is he saying?" asked Max.

"Don't know," said Brendan. "Who is this dude?"

"Some foreign language," said Ro.

"I think it's made in China," said Max.

"It doesn't sound anything like Mandarin!" said Ro.

"How do you know? You are Indian!" Max shot back, his tone sharp.

"Exactly. That's why I know it sounds more Indian than Mandarin," Ro countered confidently.

"So, what's he saying?" asked Max.

"I don't know, dude," said Ro.

"Smart-ass!" mumbled Max.

"Shuddup, guys," Brendan called out.

Swoosh. The hand of the sage came out from the bottom of the grid and swept across the board, as though he were directing his audience to do something. He held a Y-shaped wooden object that resembled a large catapult without the sling. His frown intensified as the frequency of his hand gesture increased. The wizard spoke other strange words but always finished with, "*Ni Chadurang Noos!*"

"He wants us to do something," said Max.

Both Max and Ro giggled and imitated the image while Austin looked at them, confused but with a grin. Ro examined the table and the package while Brendan searched under the board. Even when he lifted the heavy object, the projection of the image remained perfectly clear and unchanged without distortion.

No one noticed they were being closely watched by a creature lurking in the shadows. A creature whose patience was quickly waning.

"How do we turn this off?" Maddie asked.

"Show...*Ras Nee Chadurang Ra...Nee...Ass.*" Max made up some similar-sounding words.

"Don't do that," snapped Sidney. "They are watching us."

The face continued repeating its phrase.

"This is stuck," Brendan said, desperately looking for a switch to turn it off.

"What do we do now?" asked Ro.

Sidney raised her hand and inserted her palm across the green laser grid lines over the checkered board. The face's orientation in the grid changed, and it looked directly at Sidney. A chorus of "*Ni Chadurang Noos,*" erupted from inside the board.

The frown on the creepy wizard's face was replaced by a crooked grin, and he seemed content with Sidney's maneuver. Two open hands appeared, making a gesture of welcome. The satisfied wizard stroked his beard with one hand, waved the Y-shaped wooden piece at Sidney, and uttered strange words.

"Oh my God, the creepy old man is talking to you, Sidney. He is asking you to do something," said Ro.

"It's probably some kind of an image sensor." Max examined the board.

Although Sidney couldn't see the images, the board was clearly responding to her, and Brendan could tell she could feel it.

"*Namas!*" She repeated. "*Chadurang Ni Noos.*"

"How does she know the words?" whispered Brendan. "Are you making up words, Sidney?"

Sidney didn't respond. She remained focused on her activity.

The light changed from green to red, like fiber optic lights. It moved down to the level of the grid lines above the checkered squares, creating green grid lines across the red glow. The sage pulled a small maroon cloth pouch, tied with a thin silver string, and motioned it toward Sidney and spoke again.

"*Let the games begin,*" a hoarse voice said from somewhere inside the room. It was the creature that had been painfully observing them.

"That's English!" said Brendan, spinning toward the voice, almost losing his balance and tripping over Ro. "Is there another speaker somewhere?"

"The sound came from over there." Max surveyed the dark corner of the room. "Good surround system, eh?"

There was a loud thump on the door. The noise was deafening inside the cold room. For a minute, no one moved. They waited in silence, hoping that the noise would go away, but the knob on the door turned, and the thumping resumed.

"Hey, guys, are you in there?" asked Alex, much to the relief of those inside.

Max, who was closest to the door, reached the doorknob and pulled it. But the door wouldn't budge. "It's stuck," he shouted.

"What do you mean, *stuck*?" Brendan asked, puzzled.

They tried to force the door open as Alex threw her weight behind the force.

Finally, the door flung open, almost bringing Alex to the floor.

"What are you guys doing here?" Alex strained to see. "There is no light here."

Her eyes hadn't adjusted to the darkness, and she couldn't see the others standing around a table. The board had completely shut down.

"Boy, this room is cold!" Alex clutched her shoulder with one hand.

"You have a call. Someone wants to talk to you—right now!" Alex thrust a phone at Brendan. "She says it's urgent. She even used the word *emergency*."

"Who?" asked Brendan.

The door banged shut behind them again. There was darkness, except for the light from the phone and a pair of glowing red dots in a corner across the room.

"What's up with this door?" yelled out Max.

"Can someone turn the light on?" Alex asked loudly.

"I think the bulb's out," Brendan flipped the switch a few times.

Sidney shouted some strange words, and the board lit up again.

Alex jumped away from Sidney, startled. She stumbled, but Brendan caught her.

"Hello? Hellllooo? Can you hear me? *Brendan?*" said a faint voice through the phone. "*Brendan*, you need to hear me out if you are there. This is important; it's about the board...Brendan?"

Brendan held the phone close to his ear. "Hello?" His voice was feeble.

Several images orbited inside the glow. They were small but complete images of a queen, a knight, a sage, a chariot, and a soldier. Slowly, the queen's image became more prominent. She was dressed in a simple white silk gown, embellished with red roses and golden embroidery. A small silver diamond tiara highlighted her dark, flowing hair. She wielded a thin silver sword. The image moved up as the other smaller images circled around her at the base of the light. She faced Sidney directly and said some words.

"Brendan, you have to stop the girl from interacting with the image," pleaded the voice on the phone.

"Who are you?" asked Brendan as he watched the image of the queen interact with Sidney. As he moved closer to Sidney, the signal on the phone got choppy.

Sidney stretched out her hand.

"Are you the one who sent this board?" Brendan adjusted the phone to get a better signal.

"Bad things could happen if…I can explain…but you need to pull Sidney away from the board." The connection was spotty.

"Hello? I can't hear you properly. The signal inside is not good. Who… *hello?*" Brendan spoke loudly.

It was too late for Brendan to comprehend and act on the caller's warning. Sidney had already touched the image of the queen. A bright light flashed and snaked through Sidney's hand. A circular portion of the board rotated, and an arrow aimed at Sidney.

Once again, the sage appeared and spoke in a strange language.

A slot opened from the side, and a beautifully carved stone game piece, which resembled a modern chess piece queen with roughly the same dimensions, rolled out.

"Tell me what's happening," the women's voice on the phone asked sternly.

"A chess piece just rolled out," Brendan said into the phone.

"Like a queen?" asked the voice.

"Uh-huh," said Brendan.

"Okay, I am going to access your phone's camera," she said.

"Now, take the piece and give it to Sidney. Ask her to hold on to it," said the woman.

Brendan complied with the request. The piece was made of stone, heavy and cold to the touch. Suddenly, he was obeying a stranger on the phone, but she seemed to know something about the electronic game board.

"I want you to listen to me carefully. The next few steps you take are crucial. Sidney will need a team of players, and I suggest you be the leader and pick your players," the stranger suggested.

"Chess players for a chess team?" asked Brendan, scratching his head.

"Um, yeah, but do exactly as I say," the voice said as the signal strengthened. "I want you to be strong, especially in dealing with what you are about to see now, okay?"

"There is more to this?" asked Brendan.

"You haven't seen anything yet," she said as Brendan put her on speaker. "I'll guide you and your friends through it. You are the captain."

"Captain of what?" asked Brendan.

"Of your Chadurang team! Are the other kids still there with you?"

"Yes," replied Brendan. "Cha—what team?" he added.

"What do you see now?" the woman asked.

"A wizard, the old guy again. Wait, it is changing. I see…I see…"

"An elephant," Max, Ro, and Brendan all shouted in chorus.

"A big white elephant, and it's running around in circles," said Brendan.

An elephant with large tusks raised its trunk and charged, destroying everything in its path. Then, it came to a complete halt. The realistic image created a certain excitement in the room.

"Brendan, let Austin place his hand on the board and touch the elephant," said the voice.

How does she know Austin? And why would anyone pick a six-year-old kid? thought Brendan, but he turned to his little friend.

"Austin, could you put your hand on the board, at the center, just like Sidney did? It is your turn."

"No. I want to go home," said a teary Austin, moving away from the board.

"I'll do it," said Max, looking at Brendan for approval.

Ro volunteered as well.

"You have to convince Austin," said the voice. "For the sake of the keeper's notebook."

"Who?" asked Brendan.

"Never mind. Just talk to your little friend," she requested.

"Okay, I'll try." He lowered himself to Austin's eye level. "Hey, Austin, see, everybody wants the elephant but I think you should have it. Don't you have a cool stuffed one in your backpack?" he asked.

"Mr. Trunks?" A single tear rolled down Austin's cheek. "Mr. Trunks rides a motorcycle." A thin smile emerged on his troubled expression.

"Yeah, that's right. This one is like Mr. Trunks. It is all yours; if you put your hand there, it will give your Mr. Trunks cool powers too," said Brendan.

Austin shook his head and pulled away.

"C'mon, Austin. I'll give you some of my Hot Wheels," Brendan offered.

"Okay, I'll touch the board if you stay close to me," said Austin, liking the trade offered by Brendan.

Austin had barely placed his hand at the center of the board when the elephant raised its front two legs and trumpeted. The thin, aperture-looking door, to the slot opened again, and Austin picked up a curved piece, which looked more like a tusk of the elephant than the elephant itself.

"There are no elephants in chess," said Max.

"I think it is the rook," said Ro. "If you keep the rook upside-down, it looks like an elephant's leg. So, Austin is the rook?"

"But this doesn't look anything like an elephant's leg," Max argued.

As the boys contemplated elephant anatomy and Austin's role in the game, the image changed again. The elephant changed to a knight on a black horse, galloping across the board. The knight turned and waved as the horse stopped and kicked its front legs in the air.

"The knight is yours," said the woman on the phone.

Brendan walked up to the knight and placed his hand on the board. The image moved up Brendan's hand, giving the illusion of the horse galloping up his arm. The knight then reached out with his sword and seemed to lay it on Brendan's shoulder. The slot opened, and Brendan took the object, which looked very similar to the knight piece of a chess set. An unmanned chariot, drawn by two horses, followed the knight.

"Max will take that," prompted the voice.

Brendan invited Max to take the chariot, but Max didn't want anything to do with the strangely interactive artifact. He hesitated, but Brendan nudged him. "The lady is testing it out, Max. This is just a game board. It's not going to hurt you. What are you worried about?" he gently teased him.

Max gathered his courage and gently touched the board. Immediately, a person jumped into the chariot and drove off with great speed. This time, a small chariot-looking piece was pushed out.

"The wizard is back," Brendan said into the phone.

"You need to pick two more players," said the voice on the phone. "But not now. I'll let you know when the time is right. Now, ask everyone to move back to the door."

"Hey, what about me?" asked Ro as Brendan signaled the kids to move back.

The face of the wizard began to deform slowly, turning into something ugly.

Brendan directed everyone closer to the door.

"Yuck…look at that thing," Ro cried out.

"This one is probably for you, Ro; it looks just like you," said Max.

"What is *this*?" asked Ro, trying to look away. A chill went down his spine.

A slimy, long, greenish-brown creature with resemblance to a Moray eel, eerily squirmed above the board. Unlike the other holographic images, it was much bigger, towering over them like a floating snake. The kids gasped.

Even Brendan took a step back when he saw the creature.

It had a large, hairless face with the skin texture and color of worms. Two luminescent bulging eyes that dilated and contracted at steady intervals spanned the face. Its aquiline nose, resembling a mosquito stinger, dangerously protruded above two sharp fangs. Two locks of thick, S-shaped hair hung loosely from either side of its otherwise bald head, which seemed to have sprouted out of a tubular body that loosely tapered into an extended tail that lashed like a whip. It had two tiny limbs for hands with pointy, slender, fingers and overgrown black nails. The creature appeared to be searching for someone.

Unlike the sage, the creature spoke no words. It opened its mouth wide and hissed, displaying its fangs and spiky teeth. It appeared agitated and angry.

Sidney's attraction to the light began to wane. She seemed content to hold on to the ornate queen piece that had rolled out of the strange board.

"That thing is called the theel. It is a dangerous creature, and it is looking for the rakshasas to play against your team."

Brendan didn't quite understand the next steps of the game, but before he could get an answer, he noticed something big slowly moving toward them from the dark corner of the room. He could see the silhouette of a hunched figure, almost the size of the door. The outline of two bat ears, along with scaly wings and its shadow spreading almost half the length of the wall, appeared to grow in the faint neon-green light from the board. Its red eyes glowed. The light musky odor that lingered in the room intensified.

The thing let out a shrill, exposing its fangs, pushing out two puffs of breath that condensed instantly, like bursts of steam rolling from a locomotive. The kids froze. This was not a hologram. It was real.

Austin was the first to scream.

Brendan and his friends stepped back from the creature that blocked the entryway to the room. Ro, Max, and Austin backed themselves to the wall, slid down to the floor, and huddled, holding each other. Alex stood next to them in the nearly dark corner of the room. Everyone, except Sidney, was screaming.

"Listen, that thing is not there to hurt you or your friends," the voice on the phone assured. "There are two of them in the room," she said. "Brendan …Brendan, point your phone at the creature that looks like a—"

"A-a-a vampire?" said Brendan, voice shaking.

Swallowing hard and barely able to talk, he aimed his phone at the bright red eyes.

"A vampire? I was looking for a wildebeest," said the slightly surprised voice, which appeared to briefly consult with another person before continuing.

"Well, looks like they have sent a kateri—a vampire that drifts in and out of our worlds."

"*Our worlds?*" said Brendan.

This part of the game was too realistic and spooky.

"The other is a shapeshifter, and you cannot see it until it reveals itself."

Shapeshifters and vampires? What is she talking about? Some kind of Dungeons & Dragons live game?

"They'll make noise, but only to intimidate you."

The beast ambled close to the board. Even in the darkness, they could tell its face was scaly and pale. Someone tried to open the door, but it wouldn't budge. There was commotion in the room.

The creature let out a gust of breath toward the screaming children. The fumigating effect of its breath was immediate. The kids calmed down, as though drugged. The creature adjusted its wings by briefly expanding and closing them, like an umbrella. The eel hissed with excitement on seeing the beast.

From the flicker of the glow, Brendan could tell something else was moving.

The light brightened to reveal the rough, hairy hand of another creature, almost human, with pointy, dark nails. It had a stout, pudgy face, a broad forehead, and cat-like eyes under bushy eyebrows. It sported a thick mustache that spanned beyond its face like a machete. The hair that flowed back from the top of its forehead was oily, wavy, dark, and dropped down to its shoulders. It had a wide mouth with thick red lips that partially covered the dull white teeth and a pair of curved cuspids on either side. It stuck out its thick red tongue. It was short, like a troll, with a bluish skin color, had a big belly and disproportionately lengthy arms. It wore a dark wraparound outfit with frills, but its upper body was bare, exposing its thick bristly chest hair, over which hung a necklace that appeared to be made out of tiny pieces of bones loosely strung on a leather strap. The creature wore loose golden metal anklets and bracelets.

The two creatures stood close to one another. Neither paid attention to the horror-stricken human children.

"Keep your phone steady," said the calm voice on the phone.

"Okay, I get it. This is a show by your company for the board—a real demo Dad must have organized," Brendan said, finally rationalizing the situation.

"I wish," said the woman. "You are looking at two of the worst kind of underworld creatures—these are collectively called rakshasas."

Brendan was speechless. If this was a show or a demo, it was too realistic.

The floating eel's image morphed into a queen when the vampire touched the center of the board.

"It's the same queen," Brendan said.

He looked for his friends, but they were all crouched in the corner, transfixed by the board, as if hypnotized. The queen transformed into a bony zombie. Her eyes were sunken, and her skull protruded into the tiara. Her lips had turned black. Her shiny dark hair had become thin, gray and disheveled. Her teeth had decayed. She had become the cadaverous version of the beautiful queen he had just seen. The horrifying specter of the queen created an unpleasant wailing noise when she floated within the neon glow. She glided across the outstretched hand of the vampire creature and swept a jagged sword across its hand. A flash erupted, and the creature winced in pain. When a red scar appeared on the creature's hand, it looked at the ceiling and let out a wild, deafening cry.

A chess piece rolled out, which the creature grabbed before quickly disappearing back into the darkness.

The kids snapped out of their spell, and Brendan could tell that the vampire creature was approaching them. Austin ran to the locked door, screaming. He tugged at the door handle, and when it did not yield, he became hysterical. Ro and Alex rushed to help him out.

"Open! Open the door! Mommy, Mommy, Mommy," he yelled.

Alex tried to help him while Max stood frozen, staring at the vampire.

There was another grunt and a gush of air from the vampire, but this time, its foggy breath was not directed at the kids.

"Okay, this is enough. We want this to stop," Brendan demanded to the person on the phone but there was silence on the other end.

"Can you hear me?" he hollered.

But there was no response.

"Hello! Helllooo! Hello!" Brendan swore under his breath and redialed, hoping to regain the lost signal but the line was dead.

"Let's just break the damn door and get out of here," said Alex. "I've had enough of this nonsense."

The lights of the board abruptly went dead as it lay on the table, lifeless, just as it should have always been. The creatures stood, sniffing the air and pounding on their chests, as though they had accomplished their mission, whatever it was. The storage room door flung open, letting a stream of light and a gush of fresh air inside. Austin and Max scrambled out, ignoring the two strangers who had opened the door.

Real people at last! thought Brendan.

He had never been this happy to see strangers walk this far, unannounced, into his father's chess club. While the bright background light from the hall and the darkness to which his eyes had adjusted prevented him from seeing their faces clearly, he could tell that the couple—a woman and a man—were tall and had hair down to their shoulders. He could smell their damp leather outfits. He noticed they hadn't bothered to wipe the snow and slush off at the entrance, which would have normally bothered him, but considering the situation they were in, he readily welcomed the strangers.

"Uh...are you the one...?" asked Brendan searching for words.

Without responding, the woman squeezed past the kids crowding the entrance. Her companion went to the other side of the room. The woman spotted the game board first and briskly walked toward it, pointing a shiny object. The man approached the board with a similar object but from the other side. They spoke in a foreign language.

"Why is everyone talking in a foreign language?" asked Alex. "And who are these guys?"

"These are good people from far away," Sidney said, in a surprisingly calm tone. She held on to Ro's hand, who helped her get to the door.

"How do you know that, Sidney?" asked Ro.

"I can feel it," she replied.

Brendan paid attention to what the woman was saying. Even though he didn't understand a word of their conversation, he recognized her voice and her speaking style.

"Hey, you were the one on the phone!" he cried out to her.

She nodded carelessly, focusing on her intrusion into the dark room.

"I am calling my dad," he said. "What are all those..."

Before he could finish his sentence, he heard an unpleasant grunt and a gut-wrenching shrill.

The sound had come from the ceiling.

The vampire spread its wings, spanning more than half of the ceiling. Its two hairless, muscular legs with dark, sharp, long talons tightly clutched the wooden beam. Twisting its neck, it hung its head low and sneered at the strangers.

The man reacted. He stepped on the sides of the corner where the two walls met and ascended effortlessly, defying gravity, to the ceiling, where the creature dangled upside-down. He violently swung a shiny, long dagger at the beast, but it whipped its tail and pounced away from him, forcing him to strike the metal surface protruding from the unfinished portion of the ceiling. A streak of sparks erupted with a loud clang. The man followed the beast almost in the same stride, and the noisy pursuit continued as hunter and hunted crisscrossed the walls. The man's blows landed on it at least once.

The woman paid no attention to the skirmish her companion was embroiled in. She examined the board, using the same shiny, cylindrical instrument she had used to scan the room. A thin stream of green parallel laser beams engulfed the board. She adjusted the beam to widen its span across the entire room from the floor to the ceiling while maintaining its razor-thin sharpness and then slowly swept the room with it. She stopped the light at the far corner, where the parallel beams converged, and assumed the shape of the fat-bellied creature standing against the wall. The creature scrambled to the door, and in its haste, it pushed Alex and Ro to the floor and darted into the hallway, knocking over a table and sending the chess sets and the clocks flying across the hallway. Austin, Max, and Maddie stood, speechless, in the hallway, not knowing what had gone past them.

"That thing ran out into the street," said Ro.

The man cornered the vampire-looking thing and pressed the tip of the long dagger against its throat. The beast crouched in the corner, its muscles tense, its mouth wide open and drooling, and its fangs exposed. It appeared much smaller in size, and its fiery red eyes were fixated on the stranger. Brendan couldn't tell if the creature was about to fight the man or flee the building, like its partner, but he suspected there would be some bloodshed.

Whatever the man mumbled, it seemed to have irritated the creature.

It let out another cry, and much to Brendan's surprise, in a deep voice, it uttered in English, "*You have already lost!*"

The man said something, spat at the vampire, and positioned his blade as if he was ready to pierce its heart.

The creature laughed as it continued to speak in English. "You are a bit late, knight. I don't have what you want; you can kill me in front of them, but that will only make things worse. You must worry about the girl now. The game is over!"

The woman intervened and hurriedly spoke to the man in their shared language, as if pleading with him. She then steered the boys away from the door.

The man shook his head and angrily sank two-thirds of the blade into the drywall right behind the beast. The beast scrambled to the door on its fours, barely fitting through the doorway.

At the front entrance, it stood on its hind legs, stretched its wings, and warned the man, "When I see you again, knight, you'll be *dead!*"

It disappeared, just like the other one.

The kids stood in silence.

"Okay, we need to talk," said the woman in a friendly but firm voice. She led them away from the room into the hall where the vinyl boards were set up. The woman knelt in front of Sidney at her eye level as the others gathered around her. "Sidney, my name is Kaia." She introduced herself. "I am here with my partner, Aarjen, and we are here to help you."

Kaia was a tall and elegant woman. She seemed middle-aged, with sharp features and a friendly countenance. Brendan noticed some resemblance to the holographic queen that they had just seen on the board, but the color of her eyes, her skin tone, and the dark, highlighted hair were different. She appeared more athletic than the graceful queen, perhaps because of the strange biker attire she wore.

Sidney's eyes gazed into Kaia's as though she could see Kaia. She extended her hand to touch Kaia. When Kaia moved closer, she put her hand on Kaia's cheek, like she'd always done to her mother. She appeared to take an instant liking to Kaia.

"These are bad things, aren't they?" she asked innocently. "I am glad I could not see them, but I sure could feel them."

"Yes," agreed Kaia, "but we are stronger and smarter."

"Why…why are they here?" asked Max.

"That thing said something about the game and the board. What does it mean?" asked Brendan.

"We'll explain all of this, but first, we need to keep this a secret," said Kaia.

"A secret?" asked Alex. "We need to tell Mr. Turner about this."

"I know you should, but this situation has to be an exception for two important reasons," Kaia replied calmly. "First, no one will believe you. Second, the creatures will harm anyone who knows about this secret, so for the safety of others, we need to keep this to ourselves. Brendan, I will make sure we tell your father soon, when the time is right, I promise, okay?"

"But what about us? Aren't we in danger?" asked Ro.

"We are here to protect you," Kaia said. Aarjen stepped closer to the kids and nodded.

"I am not sure I understand any of this," said Brendan. His confused look was not any different from that of the others. "Who are you, and where are you coming from? How do you know our names?"

"We'll tell you everything, but before we do, Sidney needs to finish what she started. We drove the creatures away before they could get the best of the situation," she said, making eye contact with each of the kids. "But we want to make sure that we benefit from this advantage."

"What should I do?" asked Sidney eagerly.

"You two…" Kaia picked Alex first and then Ro, "…let's get back to the board."

"No way!" said Ro.

"Why me?" asked Alex. "I play football and not chess," she sounded defensive.

"We are not concerned about your ability to play chess. Not yet, anyway," said Aarjen. "There is more to this than the game. Let's wrap this up before the coach comes back." Kaia escorted Sidney back into the storage room and made Ro and Alex follow them.

Aarjen broke into a smile for the first time.

"Does anybody want to play chess with me?" Aarjen directed their attention to the vinal boards set up in the main hall. "I am sure you all will beat me easily."

His smile and friendly comment seemed to ease the tension a bit.

"My mommy has asked me not to play chess with strangers," said Austin, "but I am sure I can beat you. I came in fifth in the national championship." He stuck out five little fingers at Aarjen as they walked to the chess room.

"Would you like to see some magic?" Aarjen asked as he sat on the chair next to the table with the chessboard.

"Haven't we seen a lot for one day?" asked Max.

Aarjen responded by raising his eyebrows and tilting his head at Max. He reached into the pocket of his leather outfit and pulled out an antique figurine.

"This is also a chess piece. Can you guess which one?"

Austin examined the heavy stone piece, as big as the chess pieces used in the tournaments.

Aarjen adjusted the angle of the piece so that Austin could see the knight better.

"It is a…knight?"

The carving on the jade stone piece was beautiful with exquisite details. The horse appeared wild and free. The knight stood by his stallion in total harmony, clenching his sword tightly in one hand, as though he were ready to ward off an imminent attack, while gripping the reins with his other hand. Aarjen showed the piece to the kids and then dropped it on the green-and-white-checkered board. The piece landed on its base, wobbled briefly, and positioned itself upright.

The vinyl board appeared to dissolve at the base of the knight, and the now-familiar blue glow rippled across the board in concentric circles around the knight. After the second or third ripple, the stone figure slowly transformed. The knight jumped onto the horse and extended his sword while the horse began to gallop, faster and faster, but remained at the same spot on the chessboard. The board had almost disappeared, and in its place, a constantly changing scenery appeared as the horse galloped across the valleys and hills, streams and forests.

The kids huddled around the table with excitement, looking closely at the galloping horse.

"It looks so real," whispered Austin. He looked under the table to see if there were any concealed controls.

"It's magic," said Aarjen.

"Can I touch it?" asked Maddie.

"Sure, you can."

Maddie carefully placed her finger at the edge of the board—the portion that remained as the vinyl mat—and slowly moved it toward the hazy outline of the image. Her finger began to sink in the glow, as though she were immersing it in water. Her finger faded away as she moved it toward the center, where the knight was placed. Maddie pulled her hand back quickly when the image suddenly disappeared, and the board reverted to its vinyl form.

"What happened?" she asked.

"You must have touched the knight," said Aarjen, smiling.

They continued to play with the magic piece until Kaia returned with Alex, Ro, and Sidney.

"Are we ready then?" asked Aarjen.

"We are," said Kaia and glanced at Brendan.

He nodded. A lot would depend on him. Kaia had designated him as the leader after explaining to Brendan they had been chosen to activate a magic chessboard, which would make them play against creatures called rakshasas. The game was played like chess, but it would take them to another world on quests. There was no turning back since a long-forgotten curse had been activated, and Kaia and Aarjen—the knights of the rishis—were there to protect them.

It was all a bit murky for Brendan. He was not sure what was real and what was an illusion. His immediate task was to keep all that had happened a secret, even from his own father. The strange occurrences of the afternoon would no doubt test anyone's credulity. He'd call it computer games and Halloween costumes if Maddie or Austin revealed to Coach the events that had just unfolded. Brendan didn't want any part of this, but Kaia had warned that the creatures would harm him, his friends, and his family if the chess kids did not play the game.

"Okay, listen up, everyone," said Kaia. "You have seen a lot today, but we can assure you that the creatures will not bother you anymore. My friend and I will keep the chess pieces that came from the magic board, but the board will stay here. It will not work until the tournament begins. Brendan knows what to tell his dad, and he now has my number, so he can contact me anytime."

The kids had numerous questions, and Kaia patiently answered as many as she could, but Aarjen didn't say much. When she saw Coach Turner's car pull up, Kaia hurriedly concluded the discussions. As they exited the club, the coach approached them with a curious expression.

"Can I help you?" Turner asked them, looking up and down at the oddly attired people in his chess club.

"We were just looking at the chess sets you had displayed in the window. We talked to your son inside; he informed me that this is a chess club. Fine young man you have there!" said Kaia. "You must be Coach Turner."

"Yes, this is more of a chess club than a chess store, but I do have a few different kinds of chess sets, nothing fancy. If you like, I can show you more. Do you play the game, or do you have kids who are interested in chess?" Turner asked.

"Thanks. We might come back later, Coach. There is a board inside that caught our attention. An antique stone set that looks quite unique. We collect old chess sets and are certainly interested in it. I have left my number with your son. Please do give me a call if you get other buyers; we might bid for it as well."

Turner frowned. "Oh, there is another store across the street that sells antique items," he added with some hesitation. "You...you might find a better variety there, maybe even the real collectible kind." Although Turner did not want to give a plug for Scrappy's store, he was always ready to provide helpful information to anyone.

"Thank you, Coach," said Kaia. She extended her hand for a firm handshake. "My name is Kaia, and this is my partner, Aarjen. I am sure we'll see you again soon. You have some great kids here—awesome chess players."

She waved at Brendan, who was watching from inside, and without offering much information to the coach, they left.

Brendan heard the bikes pull away from the club as his father shut the door behind him.

His friends left the club that day after making a pact with each other not to talk about what had happened in the chess club.

The curse was unleashed. The game was about to be played.

###

While the rakshasas didn't exist in the human world anymore, a small group of dangerous human-like descendants of the rakshasas known to the knights as the 'earth dwellers' had colonized Earth and existed among the humans. They secretly served the rakshasas and helped them infiltrate Earth, whenever and wherever possible. Kaia detested the earth dwellers.

Turner was by himself at the chess club on a Sunday morning. He did not pay attention to the visitor entering EZ Pawn.

The earth dweller introduced himself to the suspicious Scrappy as a TD, a tournament director, from the Illinois Chess Association. He pulled out a folded brochure of the interactive chessboard from its pocket, showed it to Scrappy, and gave a lengthy explanation on how the board connected to computers and other devices and allowed easy access to all the games played on the board in real time.

"Viewers will watch the game anywhere, even if a network connection is not readily available." The earth dweller tapped the section in the brochure that highlighted the board's capabilities.

He explained to Scrappy that the board had been erroneously sent to Turner's chess club, Pass Pawn, across the street by the manufacturer and that Turner was planning to sell the board to some strangers. He tried to convince Scrappy to get the board from Turner. He promised that Scrappy had a stake in appropriating the board, especially if his son had to play in the upcoming tournament.

Convinced, Scrappy rushed across the street and talked to Turner, who insisted that he was not aware of any such board. However, when Scrappy showed a package receipt, Turner checked his storage room. Sure enough, they found the antique-looking board under the opened cardboard package.

He was reminded of the odd visitors who had expressed interest in antique chess sets in his store.

"How did I not know about this board? When was it delivered and where did it come from?" Turner asked himself.

Both Turner and Scrappy were intrigued by the workmanship of the board. Neither could figure out how this board could project a game or connect to other devices, as the man had described—there were no obvious USB ports, connectors, wires, batteries, or anything that remotely resembled an electronic component.

Turner didn't cherish the idea of turning the board over to Scrappy—he was suspicious of the pawnshop owner's intentions. He tried reaching Brendan on his phone, but the call went to his son's voicemail. The coach then had a long conversation with Scrappy. Finally, he took pictures of the board and said he'd only allow the chess association to borrow the board until he found out where the board had come from.

Chapter 7

The
Counterplan

large delegation of Indra's allies had gathered for dinner at the private quarters of the devas' king. Baga, Samudra, and their councils attended. There was no big feast or festivities, owing to the seriousness of the situation. However, it was by no means a simple meal.

"Five young human children have been selected to play this game against the rakshasas," said Aarjen. "The game they'll begin playing, called chess, is a primitive form of Chadurang, to which it bears a close resemblance."

"So, everything depends on how these children play the game?" asked Lord Baga.

"Yes, so we really need to understand how the curse plays out," said Aarjen.

"And, hence, why we are gathered here," added Vayu.

"To understand what can be done to save the worlds and to act immediately," Queen Samudra said emphatically.

"The rakshasas are trying to get free access to Mayastella by playing Chadurang. The children will open the portal to Mayastella, which will give the rakshasas the freedom to infiltrate the world of illusion," said Aarjen.

"Sidney, the child who cannot see, will be the first to open the entryway. The rakshasas know the human children will be lost in a strange world, confused and terrified. The quest will force them to lead the rakshasas closer and closer to Kumba with every game they play. The expedition will end when they find Kumba, and the war of the worlds will begin," said Kaia.

"So, how do we help the children win the war game?" asked Baga.

"We are trying to fully comprehend how their talent in a game of chess would manifest in Mayastella since the two are interconnected, just as in Chadurang," said Aarjen.

"And what the kids do in Mayastella will have a bearing on how they move their pieces in the chess game they play on Earth," said Kaia.

"I am afraid their weak minds will be vulnerable to being manipulated by their deadly opponents," said Baga.

"Then, as the curse portends, we are truly at the mercy of the *weak*!" said Surya.

"Vyas believes that this weakness might also be their strength," said Indra. "If the humans succeed in this game—as Vyas predicts they will—and begin to get closer to Kumba, then the rakshasas will interfere with the competition and try to take control."

"So, how do we help the children win the war game?" Baga repeated his question.

"Who are the allies for the rakshasas in Mayastella if Kumba is sleeping?" asked Samudra.

Aarjen opened the bag Kaia had tossed over to him and pulled out a large book with a thick leather-bound cover and aging pages.

He thumbed through it carefully and finally landed on a page that was brightly colored. "This is an old book of Yan, the revered keeper of the Mayastella, whose tragic disappearance has left us searching for answers."

Aarjen then raised the book up, and Maya used her illusionary powers to project the page over the long dining area.

An ugly creature with an eel-like body and an odd head emerged.

"This is the theel," said Aarjen.

"This creature existed only within the confines of the inner sphere of the Mayastella. It was an illusionary creature, not of flesh and bone, with no real threat to the outside worlds," Kaia explained.

"Now, the theel has changed into a tantric." Aarjen revealed to the viewers how the once-unreal creature now revealed genetic markings of the soulless tantric of the plasma. "It has evolved to adapt to its surroundings by developing tubular eyes that can see well in total darkness—a characteristic quite common in the rakshasa underworld. The rishis believe that the theel is now trying to hunt souls of the living. In the absence of the keeper, this creature has found a way to join forces with the other soulless tantrics to exploit Mayastella. Its mission now is to infest Mayastella with rakshasas," said Aarjen.

"Even the rakshasas don't trust the theel, but somehow, they have found ways to use each other," said Kaia.

"How did an illusionary poiz become a soulless tantric, cross the plasma, and wander freely in Mayastella? Does this have anything to do with the keeper's disappearance?" asked Samudra.

"There's a greater force behind the theel, Lord Samudra," warned Aarjen. "We don't know who this is and would like to find out before evil takes over."

"What do you propose we do then?" asked Samudra. Like the other members of the council, she was unsure what was being suggested.

"It is time for us to join the expedition and prevent unwelcome changes," Aarjen said. "Halting the curse by taking Chadurang back or preventing the tournament from happening is a short-term measure that will fail to address the real threat behind the uprising and, ultimately, to prevent the inevitable. For the sake of protecting the worlds, we need to be on the offensive and fight evil instead of allowing it to take control of this situation."

"Are you recommending we go with the kids to Mayastella?" asked Varuna.

"Yes. Kaia and Aarjen will accompany the human children," Indra advised.

"You have my full support," said Baga, first to endorse Indra's plan.

"Let's get ready for the battle," ordered Indra.

Chapter 8

Strength of the
Weakness

Turner was unusually irritated on this Sunday morning. He had just answered an early phone call and found out that for the first time in the history of U.S. chess, a qualifier tournament was going to be held to establish the eligibility of players to play in the Chess Olympiad. The qualifier was also intended to determine the rating of the contestants and how they would be paired up at the main event.

"This is not good for the kids. We should be encouraging them to play in all the tournaments regardless of their rating and not discourage them. We cannot put unnecessary pressure on them," Turner argued with the tournament director, Randy.

"I understand," said Randy. "But the sheer volume of players is too much to handle; there will be more than 2,000 participants, mostly kids running around. We don't have the manpower or the facility to host an event that big. The pairing for each round will take a long time, and the tournament could go on forever. People will get frustrated. This is an international tournament, Turner—the Olympics, you know—and Chicago cannot look bad."

"Listen," said Turner. "That is your problem. The kids cannot be penalized for your inability to handle volume. What kind of message are you sending to young chess players?"

"It's everybody's problem, Turner. I just called to inform you of the decision that has been made. I am not asking for your opinion. Every country will hold a preliminary round to select their players, and we should follow the same rules."

"Sorry you feel that way." Turner hung up on the TD.

Turner had to get his students ready for the qualifier. He not only wanted all of his students to qualify but also wanted his core team players placed at the top. He resented the fact that Scrappy would be working the system to get his stepson a better rating and position by pulling strings. Turner believed in doing the right thing, qualifiers or no qualifiers. He was an honest man; winning was important to him, but he would never value victory over integrity. His attitude had gained him respect not only from top chess players and coaches, but also, more importantly, from the parents of his students.

The previous year had been a particularly challenging year for him and his students. Although many of his students had performed well, they had let opportunities slip at crucial moments and hadn't won any individual or team championships. With the sudden news about the qualifiers, he was pressed for time. He decided to address their weaknesses briefly but spend more time developing their strengths.

The students arrived at Pass Pawn after a two-week holiday break. The boards and the clocks were all neatly set up. This was the first time the students were seeing each other after the mysterious storage room incident, and only Brendan and Alex had had a chance to discuss the incident during the holidays. Brendan had called Alex to inform her about Scrappy's visit to the club and his dad's decision to allow the board to be used at the Chess Olympiad.

The kids instantly noticed that their coach was in a terrible mood. Coach Turner seldom acted irritable toward his students, even when they didn't live up to his performance expectations, but on occasion, certain people—like Scrappy, the pawnshop owner, and Randy, the tournament director—were known to trigger an unpleasant mood change. This was one of those days.

"Roshan, you play too *fast*. You are not in kindergarten," Turner said sharply within a few minutes of opening his coaching session, catching everyone by surprise. Harsh public criticism was never his style. "Your rating is seventeen-something, and you are the No. 2 kid in Illinois in your age group. You cannot play all your games like you play blitz." Turner was referring to the speedy version of the game that many kids loved to play.

In a typical national tournament, each player played seven round-robin games. The pairing of each player was based on their ratings and the number of games they won or lost. Each player got 85 minutes on the clock, and at the end of each victorious game, they had to play the next round against an opponent who had a similar standing in the tournament.

The rounds got tougher and tougher as the tournament progressed. Winning a round gave a player one point while a draw resulted in half a point. It was rare that more than one player ever won all their games in the national tournament, getting a perfect score of seven points. When two players won the same number of games or had the same points, then the winner was decided by a tiebreaker scoring system, which involved computer calculations that factored several variables, including the strengths of the opponents and the players each player had defeated.

Max elbowed Ro, but neither of them chuckled, as they usually did.

"How much time did you use up on the clock in the last game?" Turner asked Ro sternly.

"Um…I think it was more than 45 minutes, Coach," Ro responded.

"Can you look it up in your notation book?" Turner asked.

"I didn't bring it, Coach." Ro's voice was barely audible, and his face turned flush.

"Didn't I ask you to?" Turner looked at Ro's parents standing by the wall in the back of the room and shook his head. "He needs to pay more attention to my instructions."

They nodded with a perplexed look.

"Next time, I will not let anyone attend my session without their notation book or the answers to the puzzles. *Am I clear?*" the Coach boomed.

"I brought the puzzles," Ro's voice matured to a serious tone.

The coach ignored him.

"Assuming you used up 45 minutes for your game, Ro—although it felt like you were out in less than 10—you used up about half your allotted time! And how much time did your opponent—what's his name, the kid from Texas?" Turner snapped his fingers. "Gomes, right?"

"Gomez!" prompted Ro, knowing the coach was not very good with names. "70 minutes, Coach."

"You see, Gomez used up his clock wisely and thought through every move," Turner noted.

"But he *lost* that game, Coach," said Ro. "I crushed him in time."

"But that's beside the point. When you play with really good players, don't play like you are playing blitz," said Turner. "You need to balance your time so that you can pause to think through your moves and so you don't run out of time and lose the game. Let's focus on your clock work. Take time to think several moves ahead. Do not wander around the hall when it is not your turn."

Turner's list of to-dos prompted Roshan's friends to defend him.

"Ro is very good in blitz," said Austin.

"But, Dad, Ro does keep the time pressure on his opponents," said Brendan, feeling guilty about his father's mood. "He thinks on their time. That's his strength. You have always liked to focus on the strengths and not the weaknesses, Dad," said Brendan.

"I agree, Brendan. But in a national tournament, he needs to slow down and use the clock."

"And use your head, Ro." Max whispered in Ro's ear.

"Max, let's see where you can improve." The coach scanned through Max's MonRoi—the electronic notation device.

"Max, I like the way you think. You are very focused," he began on a favorable note. "But with you, it's always analysis paralysis," Turner continued.

"Pa-ral-y-sis?" Max shrugged.

"That's correct. There are times when you get stuck—really stuck. Like when you played against Chang." Turner slipped on his glasses and pulled up Max's game against Chang at the national tournament.

He quickly went over several moves on the wallboard, moving and removing magnetic chess pieces on the specially designed board used to illustrate game strategies to a group of learners. Coach then paused.

"You see, you were doing well up to here. Your position is very strong but look at what she pulls on you." Coach moved a piece. "She surprised you with an offensive move, sacrificing her rook, and you completely froze here."

The coach then explained how Max could have countered.

"Sometimes, you need to take risks, Max. Learn to make sacrifices to finish the game. The objective is not to save your queen or keep all your pieces, but to checkmate your opponent's king. Don't be afraid of taking risks—strategic, calculated risks, of course."

Ro gripped his own neck with both hands, as though choking, and stuck out his tongue at Max. Max bit his lips and refrained from engaging with Ro.

"We are going to study the games of Mikhail Tal," Turner told Max. "Tal is the master of sacrifices and surprise attacks. He took calculated risks that paid off in big games. He cornered his opponents into going on the defensive. Such clever maneuvers make up the beauty of this game."

Like Ro, Max was spontaneously sociable, sharp-witted, and well liked; however, unlike Ro, Max hated taking risks. He disliked speed chess and was uncomfortable making hasty decisions—a trait he'd developed in childhood after an incident in a swimming pool when he almost drowned. Since then, Max had adopted a tendency to play it safe in everything he did—from riding a bicycle to spending money on toys or even when playing cards. Max was particularly cautious while playing chess. Most of the time, he benefited from his unimpulsive approach; however, when he faced unpredictable and aggressive players who didn't follow the rules, he struggled.

Like Max's parents, Turner cringed when watching Max lose a game, especially the ones fought to the very end when each player had only a few pieces left on the board.

"Okay, Coach," said Max. "I don't like sacrificing my queen."

"Let's take small steps, Max. It's not just about sacrifices; it's about taking some chances to achieve your goals. I'll work with you. We'll have to learn this together."

"Speaking of achieving goals ..." He turned his attention to his own son and asked, "What are our goals this year, Brendan?"

"To win the championship," said Brendan without hesitating.

Brendan had had this conversation with his father many times since the last national tournament, and he did his best to avoid this topic.

"Last year, you were in a position to…"

"You know they cheated, Dad," Brendan interrupted his father. "I don't know how, but they did it. There's no way that I would have run out of time. I just didn't want to fight it," he said, shrugging.

"But…" Turner tried to continue.

"It was just a game, Dad. You have said many times yourself that we are NOT like them."

Brendan disliked talking about the suspicious incident of the previous championship game and was upset with his father for suddenly raising this issue in front of his friends.

"I agree we are not like them, but we need to fight when we need to. We cannot give up even when someone cheats. You could have become the champion last year, but that game put you behind. You and I both, we should have fought it with the TDs, but we didn't, and Scrappy thinks we are weak. I don't want you to be perceived as someone who gives up."

"I don't give up!" Brendan said, his voice shaky. He snapped his pencil into two under the table. "You know I don't give up, Dad. We cannot worry about what other people think. You have always told me that."

"Let's go get 'em this year. It's your year; you have worked hard to get here, and you deserve it." Turner spoke firmly.

"It's your year, Brendan," said Max.

"Yeah, Brendan," added Ro, and soon, the entire class applauded Brendan.

Brendan shrugged and shook his head. He strongly felt that he hadn't given up and had done everything right.

Somehow, Scrappy Junior's clock had been tampered with, and it suddenly reduced Brendan's remaining time in the game by 24 minutes. Brendan couldn't comprehend how it could have happened; he was confused. By the time he realized he had been cheated, it was too late. Although Turner alerted the TDs, no one paid attention to the clock, and he couldn't contest the decision.

Several coaches speculated that Brendan had lost due to his careless attitude. They specifically pointed to Brendan's tendency to walk around and become distracted during his games. This implied that he was not giving his best to win crucial matches. A few recent losses, including the one at nationals to Nicolas, had quickly tarnished his reputation and branded him as lacking the fortitude to be a champion. Brendan was ready to change this unfair perception for the sake of his father, who had devoted his coaching life to nurturing Brendan's talent for the game.

"Max, pair up with Ro. Austin, you play with Sidney," Turner instructed. "Jack and Alex will pair up, and Brendan will play with me. After you play the first game, switch colors. If you played white, play black."

"What should Austin and I do better, Coach?" Sidney sensed Turner walk by them.

Turner patted Sidney's head gently. "Be yourself, Sidney, and play hard. This is your first big tournament, and we'll focus on you getting qualified. If you and Austin solve all the puzzles I gave you, you will be fine."

Turner leaned over Austin's chair. "Young man, you are going to start notating, right?"

"It is too hard," pleaded Austin, pouting. "I also don't like puzzles. They are boring."

Austin did not like to notate. He found it very distracting to write down his moves during the game. He did not like solving chess puzzles either since his methodology and approach to solving puzzles were so different from those of the others. He was very visually oriented and saw patterns that were not obvious to other players.

"Well, you have to start soon, Austin. That's the only way to go over your games—good and bad ones—and learn from them. Remember, only if you get through the qualifiers—"

"What are qwalifiers?" he asked, prompting Turner and some of the students to burst out laughing.

###

Most parents were upset that the once-every-two-years super-nationals tournament in Tennessee during spring break was tagged as the qualifier tournament. Some of the parents who hadn't planned to attend the super-nationals suddenly had to scramble to make travel arrangements and were not thrilled about the US Chess Federation's last-minute decision to introduce a new barrier.

The Gaylord Opryland Resort of Nashville was ready for the challenge. Adept at handling an influx of visitors, the resort put on a friendly face and braced itself for the arrival of more than 4,000 guests.

Turner's team had arrived a day early. From the twelve representing his club, many had arrived independently while some, including him, had driven from Chicago in a convoy.

The tournament was to be held in the grand ballroom. Two rounds on Friday afternoon, three rounds on Saturday, and the final two rounds on Sunday. There were also tournaments on two variations of chess: blitz, which was the speed chess tournament, and bughouse, a novel form of the chess game, in which a player played with a partner against two other players. While both kinds of games were fast and entertaining with only five minutes of playing time, in bughouse, the partners helped each other by capturing and exchanging enemy pieces that could later be placed anywhere on the board to defend or attack the opponent.

Brendan had convinced Alex to join them; Alex had initially resisted the idea of spending three days of her spring break in country music land, playing chess, but the idea of hanging out with Brendan appealed to her.

"Let me get this straight," she'd chuckled. "You want me to spend ten hours with you in an SUV to get to Nashville and then play chess for three days?"

"Yes! Just forget the chess. We can chill in Nashville, check out Vanderbilt University, do stuff," Brendan had reasoned.

After some initial resistance, she agreed to take the trip with Brendan and the rest of the kids.

The first round was to start in less than an hour, and Austin was still asleep. His mother was scrambling. She had been awake since 6 a.m. She had already made two trips to the coffee shop, brought breakfast to the room, and nervously packed snacks, juice boxes, Austin's toys, and his chess bag. Austin's brother, Jack, had been up for about an hour and, much to his mother's dismay, was watching TV.

"You'd better warm up, Jack. Look at some puzzles, some openings, or whatever. Turn off the TV," she scolded, but Jack protested.

"Why don't you wake your brother up?" she snapped, and Jack quickly responded by turning the TV off.

Austin woke up with the usual plea. "I don't want to play today. My tummy hurts," he moaned.

Austin felt uneasy before tournaments, especially the big ones that involved traveling. His condition improved once the games started, but getting there was not eventless. To make the situation worse, the brothers picked on each other, requiring parental intervention.

"Why don't you bring Mr. Trunks, dear? You'll be fine, I promise. You are going to do so well today," she added, sitting next to Austin and running her fingers through his soft brown hair.

"But, Mom, I don't want to play today," Austin pleaded tearfully.

"How about you go talk to Brendan and Ro? They're waiting for you." Her voice was intentionally animated to quickly change her strategy.

There was a soft knock on the door.

"You guys ready?" asked Nora, gently guiding Sidney into the room.

"Sure, we are!" Austin's mom replied with a bit of sarcasm.

"Austin has decided not to play today," Jack continued to provoke his brother.

"*Mommy!*" cried out Austin.

"Hi, sleepyhead. Get up! It's time to go. Do you want to walk with us to the hall?" Sidney said to Austin.

The sight of Sidney cheered up Austin. "Let me get my cars," he said, jumping out of the bed. "My tummy hurts, but I'll go with you," Austin added as an afterthought as he grabbed his Hot Wheels tote bag.

While walking down the spectacularly built atriums of the Opryland Resort, the kids were struck by the splendor of the place. Sidney was quiet and held her mother's hand tightly. She was uneasy. She was engulfed with the same feeling that she had experienced several months ago—as though someone or something was watching her.

She stopped. She could smell the creature, the same musky smell that had emanated in the storage room. The encounter was real.

"What is it, hon?" asked Nora.

"Nothing, Mom, just my shoes," she said.

The registration site was swarming with kids and parents. People bumped into each other and huddled in front of large Styrofoam boards with the list of players.

"This is only the primary section!" someone yelled. "Where's elementary?"

"Why don't they put up more boards and lists?" someone else yelled.

"They are always understaffed," added another frustrated parent.

"That's because not many parents volunteer these days," scoffed a TD, who tried to squeeze his way through the crowd.

"Why can't you post this online or have an app?" suggested a young woman.

"*We are working on it!*" the irritated TD shouted.

Away from the chaos, Brendan and Alex were hanging out by a large fountain.

"I can't believe they combined high school and scholastic tournaments at the same place. There are just too many people," said Brendan.

"You need to watch your back," a stranger cautioned them from behind.

It was a woman, wearing dark glasses, seated on a bench by the walkway, where the morning sun's brisk rays beamed through the atrium glass.

"Excuse me?" Brendan wasn't sure if she was talking to him.

"You heard me. Things are about to change. We have waited longer than expected. They are here. They are watching you," she said.

"Who?" asked Brendan, trying to get a closer look at the woman.

The voice was familiar, but the face was not until Brendan walked closer to the bench.

"Kaia? What are you doing here?" he asked, surprised to see her.

"Sit down." She offered them space on the bench. They hesitantly sat down. "I recommend you wear it," Kaia said as she gave Brendan a slender leather bracelet with a small crystal hanging from it.

"I am not going to wear this thing around my wrist. It looks like something a…"

"A girl would wear? I didn't think you were the kind who cared," Kaia interrupted.

Alex tapped Brendan on his shoulder. "You might start a trend here."

"What's it for?" he asked, seriously.

"This will help you find me. Do you remember all the game pieces that came from the board?" she asked.

"How could I forget? Your friend took it. Is he here as well?"

"You'll see Aarjen soon. The pieces are in this bag." A leather pouch hung on a thin strap around her shoulder.

"What's going on?" Alex asked.

"You never came back for the board. It is gone now," Brendan didn't answer her, and spoke to Kaia instead.

"I know where the board is, Brendan. We'll take care of it. Just focus on your tournament. I am here to warn you the creatures are watching you and your friends. So, put that bracelet on," she said.

"They are here?" Brendan asked, looking around.

"Very much so, but in the form of earth dwellers—they look like humans but behave like the creatures. They blend well with the humans but can transform into creatures quickly," Kaia said. "But don't worry; they'll not interfere as long as we stay close. Put that thing on, and I'll see you again soon." She glanced at her watch.

"It is getting late. The first round is starting in fifteen minutes." Alex got up and slipped away from them.

Brendan glanced at his phone to check the time. "We'll see you again?" He confirmed with Kaia, then hurried to catch up with Alex.

###

After more than an hour's delay, the pairings were up. There was a computer glitch, and all pairings were messed up. The officials scrambled to get things sorted. The TDs were cursing. The crowd was becoming unmanageable.

Austin sat on his knees in the corner and played with his tiny red Matchbox car. His mom let him have his playtime—anything to get him back to a good mood to play in the tournament. Skipping a round would be deemed a 'bye' and would yield Austin only half a point out of two, considerably decreasing his chance of doing well in the tournament.

But Austin was persistent with his excuse.

'What's wrong with him today?' she asked herself, frustrated.

"Austin, you have to play, buddy," Max encouraged.

"My tummy hurts," Austin whined.

A row of tiny toy cars was lined up by the wall. Austin knew every car by name and model—Tesla Model 3, Ferrari Enzo, Aston Martin DB12, Lamborghini Diablo, Maserati Ghibli, and many more high-end cars that most kids his age had never heard of. Tiny F-22 Raptors flew over the traffic jam. Missiles launched from the jets while the bad guys were being neutralized. Even some aliens had managed to infiltrate the setting.

"How do we get him to play today?" Austin's mother asked her husband over the phone.

The pairings were already up, and it was a very easy round for Austin, but he didn't want to play.

As Austin motioned his fighter jet over the cars, it slipped from his hands, slid across the hallway, and landed near a man standing by the little stream that wound through the resort.

The man was short with dense facial hair and a big belly. His arms were extraordinarily long. One look at him, and Austin scrambled to his mom, who was on the other side of the room, still talking on the phone.

"I have a plane that actually flies," said the man. His voice was hoarse.

Austin didn't look at the man. He knew not to talk to strangers; besides, he didn't really care about the man's offer. He continued walking away from him even though he wanted his toy back.

"Just watch." The man gestured to Austin.

A sudden roar of an engine and a jet, which looked like Austin's own, accelerated and blasted toward the line of toy cars. Austin couldn't believe what he saw. His toys were coming alive. The jet soared past Austin's white Aston Martin DB9, turned around, and fired. The car dodged the strike but was struck by an incoming missile. It rolled over with a fiery crash. A police car raced down the line.

The action got louder and bigger for Austin. He stood there, motionless, for a few minutes until the jet just dropped down, reverting to its toy form.

"I told you," said the man. "I have cool toys."

Austin dashed to his mom.

His mother, having noticed the man talking to Austin, immediately diverted her attention to him.

"Hi!" the man said. "Is he in the tournament?"

"Don't ask," said his mom. "He's not feeling well. The one tournament we wanted him to play."

"Don't worry. I have a great toy for him. My kid is playing in the tournament, too, and he also brings his toys," the man said.

He then extended his long arm and offered the toy airplane to Austin. "I'll give this to you if you play in the tournament today."

"See, Austin, this nice man wants to give you a toy if you play," his mother encouraged.

Austin tugged at his mother's handbag and tried to avoid eye contact with the stranger. Everything he had imagined seemed to come alive a minute ago, but nobody else appeared to have noticed it. He then abruptly reached for the new toy and agreed to play in the tournament.

"I'll make sure we return the toy," his mother said, after thanking the man.

The first round was a disaster for Sidney. Her opponent was much stronger and experienced. However, it was confusing for the other player to play with a player who couldn't see.

"Why are the rules different?" said the rude father of Sidney's opponent. "*She* can touch the pieces while my son cannot?"

"Yes," said the TD. "I am sure you can understand why that is the case, can't you?"

"But how will my son understand?" he still protested.

"I am fine, Dad. I understand the rules," said the kid quickly, embarrassed by his father. "It is clear and fair."

"Thank you. Raise your hand if you have any questions," said the TD. "I am glad the kid gets it," he mumbled as he walked away.

The boy shook hands with Sidney and started the game, but Sidney was nervous and disoriented. The boy ended up winning, and Sidney was crushed.

"Good game," the boy said politely.

"Don't worry. This is your first tournament game ever, Sidney," consoled Turner, who just couldn't bear to see the child cry. "You'll do well in the next round, I promise."

The first round was a breeze for Brendan. It was eventless, and he finished the game in less than 30 minutes. He waited for Alex to come out from her game, which she surprisingly won.

"This is tough," said Alex with a wide grin. "I am not sure why I am doing this."

"It will make you a better football player," Brendan said reassuringly.

"I see it has already made you a good comedian," she laughed.

"I know it sounds odd, but I see patterns everywhere, all the time. I remember things when I use these patterns. Things like locations, directions, even how people move around." Brendan paused, realizing that Alex might not feel the way he did. "Maybe you'll see it one of these days too!" He flicked her forehead gently with his finger.

"Let us just get out and throw a football," he added quickly, changing the topic.

Alex decided to throw the football instead of kicking it. She had a good arm, and Brendan knew it. After two caught passes, the ball was overthrown on purpose. Brendan leaped in the air but was only able to tip the ball, which found its way into a swampy ditch with a splash.

"Couldn't read me after all, could you, grandmaster?" Alex shouted, wagging her finger in the air.

"I read you all right, but just couldn't catch a ball that was so overthrown. You need to work on your throwing skills, spiral queen." Brendan headed to the ditches. "Now, come and help me find the darn ball."

The shallow, marshy ditch was tens of feet wide. At an angle, Brendan could see light hit the marshy bottom. Tall grass and plants with wildflowers surrounded the ditch and made it look like a scene popped out of an oil painting by Bob Ross. The dried brown grass brush with fallen branches and twigs served as a perfect camouflage for the football.

"It has got to be here. I heard a splash, but couldn't see where it fell," said Brendan.

"I am sure we are in the right pl—*Snake!* S-s-sn…"

"Yeah, we should watch out for them. This far down south, there might be some poisonous ones too."

Not realizing what his friend had encountered, Brendan continued to mutter until he turned around to see what Alex was up to. He froze, like Alex.

In front of them, a purplish eel-like creature squirmed as it protruded out of the swamp water, its tapered bottom immersed in the water, its ugly head positioned at Alex's eye level. It had bulging eyes and a sharp aquiline nose. Its mouth barely covered its sharp, jagged teeth and the two extended fangs. It was the same creature whose image they had seen before in a dark storage room.

But this time, it was real; the creature was flesh and bones, just a few feet away from Alex, staring directly at her silently.

"Oh my God! It is that thing," muttered Brendan after finding his voice. "She called it the theel."

Instead of running away, Brendan took a couple of steps closer to the creature. Only the creature's head turned, tracking Brendan's movement as its hunched body stayed fixed. It looked like a large serpent, ready to strike its victim.

Brendan slowly reached for Alex's hand. "It has my football," he whispered.

Hiss. It sounded like it was quickly releasing steam upon hearing Brendan's voice as it stretched out its slender lizard-like limb with dark, long, sharp nails clutching the football, as though giving it to Brendan.

"Let's get out of here, before this thing kills us," said Alex, swallowing hard.

Brendan continued to stare at the creature. It made a guttural noise and whipped its tail in the water. The theel then glided up in the air like a kite. It looked vicious when it looked down on them with its feline eyes becoming blood-red.

Brendan wanted to flee but his legs failed him.

"The wristband!" Brendan thought of the safety bracelet that Kaia had given him.

He reached into his pocket and tried to feel the thin leather band, but just when he touched the bracelet, Alex tugged his arm, causing the bracelet to slingshot out of his pocket. The theel tossed the ball and caught the bracelet.

Its eyes reflected the crystal's light, and it let out a shrill upon close examination. It looked back and forth between Brendan and the wristband. Its red eyes reverted to its original form, and a translucent layer flickered back and forth, as though the creature was blinking rapidly.

Brendan was spellbound. His throat went dry, and his heart raced. Before he could say something, the creature dove into the swamp and disappeared.

Brendan stood next to Alex in silence for what felt like hours. He expected the theel to reappear, but there was no trace of it.

"Where did it go?" he asked, finally able to speak.

"No idea. Let's get the hell out of here," Alex hollered.

"Why did it suddenly disappear?" Brendan asked, puzzled.

"Because of me," said a voice from behind. It was Aarjen. "Never lose the crystal. It has powers. In the wrong hands, it would become extremely dangerous. You were supposed to wear it at all times," said Aarjen sternly, approaching them.

"It fell out of my pocket when I was about to wear it," Brendan said, looking at Alex for support.

"It was my fault." Alex defended her friend.

"I believe you!" Aarjen nodded his approval. "Don't worry. I took these back from the theel." Aarjen tossed the shiny piece to Brendan but kept the football. "Works better on your wrist than in your pocket. Don't ever try to communicate if it shows up again," he warned.

"How did you...I-I didn't see you." Brendan tried to form a sentence while making random gestures with his hands.

"Never mind how I got this from that thing."

"What is that creature, and why is it here?" Alex couldn't remember the man's name.

"It is a lost soul, trying to find its identity. It has a mission now—an evil one. You are about to get very familiar with it. It is not going to hurt you now, but it can if things don't go its way," said Aarjen. "You are going to encounter more of these strange creatures, and most of them are wicked and heartless. The journey you are about to go on requires courage."

"Journey?" Brendan frowned.

"I'll give you more details tomorrow night after you're done with the tournament. Kaia and I will meet you both in the main atrium by the waterfalls," said Aarjen.

Aarjen nodded, as though he saw someone at a distance, and abruptly walked away.

As Brendan and Alex watched him, Aarjen reached the large tree that was fifty or so yards away, turned around, and threw the football with a perfect spiral. He waved at them and disappeared behind the trees.

Alex held on to Brendan's hand as they hurried into the lobby.

Turner was quite happy with the way things were turning out in Tennessee. His kids were winning. At the awards ceremony, Sidney was in the limelight. The chief guest highlighted her perseverance and skills. People applauded her extraordinary ability to not only survive but also succeed in the regular tournament. The TDs and the US Chess Federation were praised for allowing kids with disabilities to play in regular tournaments.

"This is a new era in chess," said the mayor of Nashville, who spoke in front of a large audience at the convention center, "a game that allows mind over matter."

The event kicked off the spring country music festival. Nora was interviewed by a local reporter. Teary-eyed, she unselfishly gave the credit for her daughter's performance to Coach Turner and the Chicago chess kids. An article in the online version of the local newspaper highlighted Turner and his coaching style. It even mentioned Alex, a high school football kicker who had reentered the world of chess.

Scrappy was annoyed by all the attention Turner was receiving. His stepson, Nicolas, had excelled in the tournament as well, but was not mentioned anywhere. His hatred for Turner deepened.

That night, in an abandoned slaughterhouse several miles away from Opryland, four creatures convened to celebrate the achievement of a small milestone in their master's grand plan.

A potbellied rakshasa sat nervously between two marisans. Although they all belonged to the rakshasa family, they detested proximity to one another. However, it was not the shapeshifters that the potbellied rakshasa was nervous about; it was the treacherous crocodile-like mudala that ambled out of the water. To the mudala, the potbellied rakshasa was an easy meal and a delicious one, too, but the formidable wildebeest-headed marisans were a threat and did not offer easy access to its prey. Besides, this meeting was called by a higher order. There were bigger issues to be discussed than eating one of its distant cousins. It grunted and perched itself on a rock, salivating.

The faint glimmer radiated by the shiny skin of the theel disturbed the darkness the creatures preferred.

"Do you know why we are gathered in this mortal world?" the theel hissed in a primitive rakshasa language. The marisan grunted with disgust. It had heard that the soulless theel was working for an unknown, evil, power-seeking master who had initiated a scheme to awaken the demon King Kumba and unleash the rakshasas to destroy the worlds, but it did not trust the theel.

"Our plan is beginning to work," the theel said. "Today, we made sure that the human children will play in a real Chadurang tournament that will allow us to get to the sleeping king. Your entry into Mayastella will open doors for a great future for our species. But I remind you that this is just the beginning, and our master commands you not to engage in any foolish acts in the mortal worlds, however tempting it might be."

The potbellied rakshasa kicked at some dirt and spat on the floor. "What is the purpose of bringing us here and keeping our hands tied from harming the humans? There is wealth to be made. We will not wait for some stupid g—"

The rakshasa winced as the theel zapped it with a flash of electric charge, hitting it square on his chest and tossing it a few feet in the air. It landed with a thud. Blood dripped from its mouth; its fingers and toes twitched. It was still alive.

"The potbellied rakshasas are fools," the theel hissed. Its tail was still glowing and its eyes were bulging. It slithered through the air like a dragon and abruptly stopped a few inches from a marisan's face. "You have no idea what is about to happen, do you? The worlds could be ours for the first time. Our master will allow us free rein over this world, and the mortals will be yours for you to slowly destroy. Yet, you fools can't take simple orders. I will not hesitate to kill any of you if you fail to obey the master's orders."

The provoked marisan grabbed the theel by its throat, but the electric jolt from the theel's tail was too overpowering, even for the beast twice the size of the theel. It abruptly let the theel go and gasped.

"The knight awaits your death. Save your might for when it's needed," said the theel, snarling at the zapped marisan.

The fallen potbellied rakshasa regained consciousness and tried to get up but fell on its back again. The marisan kicked the helpless creature as the other rakshasas laughed.

"Drink this, you fool," said the marisan, finally offering the rakshasa some fermented dirty water. "The theel has a point. We'll put up with this for just a short while. Soon, we will become immortals."

The creatures were excited at the prospect of ruling the worlds. They raised their heads as though smelling success, pounded their chests, and then feasted on freshly killed cattle.

"The knight will try to help the kids, but he has no idea of what's in Mayastella. They are still looking for the board," the theel laughed.

"The creatures think that we are looking for the board," Aarjen raised his voice just over the live country music band.

Alex, Brendan and Sidney sat across from Aarjen at a round table. Kaia sat next to Aarjen. They both looked out of place with their long, rugged leather coats, laced-up boots, and tanned skin tone.

"We want them to believe that we are a step behind in our plans," he said.

"What plan?" asked Brendan.

"Let me give you some background first," said Kaia. "The worlds are governed by laws." Kaia explained to the kids about immortals and mortals, their powers and responsibilities.

She described the role of devas, asuras, and jalas and their rulers, Indra, Baga and Samudra. "These laws are upheld by the rulers of these worlds to ensure that each world is held to its lawful boundaries and the forces of good and evil are kept in balance. However, forces are forever working to upset this balance, and we need to intervene quickly when evil works to create lawless worlds, where order will cease to exist. But sometimes, trouble finds a way to overcome the powerful, partially because of their own doing," added Kaia. "The curse…"

"The curse," said the theel to its soldiers. "The powerful Indra was cursed by his own rishi." It scoffed. "He thought he could hide by simply not entering Mayastella, but our master has found a way to get back at them."

"What is our role?" asked a shapeshifter.

"To make sure Earth dwellers do their job of playing the game well. When the portal opens, we will follow them and take control," responded the theel.

###

"So, do we continue to play chess in this other world called Mayastella?" asked Brendan. He couldn't comprehend how a world of illusion could exist and how playing chess could influence what happened in this world.

"No, your journey into this world will be different, almost like entering into a video game while playing it, but your actions are interrelated. The creatures will have one goal in mind—to get to Kumba."

"Who?" Brendan chomped into a crispy nacho chip, loaded with melted cheddar cheese, refried beans, and jalapeños. Carelessly, he allowed a thin stream of sticky cheese to roll down the side of his mouth. Alex, irked by the clumsy display, quickly shoved some napkins at him.

"Kumba," Kaia repeated.

"Kumba?" Brendan shouted, but suddenly realized that the band had stopped playing and he was yelling.

"Nice!" said Alex. "You just hollered with your mouth full."

"Kuuummmmbaaaayaaa!" Brendan drew the attention of some high school girls at the next table, who chuckled as Alex rolled her eyes. Wound up a little, he snapped his fingers and moved his body to the beat of the next song kicked off by the band.

Aarjen's face tightened. He wanted no attention from anyone, particularly the Earth dwellers. Brendan's behavior angered him.

What he didn't understand was that even the mature, soft-spoken Brendan behaved his age, especially after a long day of chess and when surrounded by teenagers and nachos. After all, he'd just turned sixteen.

"Look at me, Brendan; this is very serious. One small mistake can kill innocent people. We had a reason for picking you, so do not disappoint us," Aarjen said sharply.

"Harsh words," said Alex, reacting quickly. "I don't think Brendan or any of us wanted to be part of this. You guys claim to come from some faraway place. Weird things start happening, and suddenly, you blame him for having some fun? That's not fair." She almost slammed her tall plastic cup on the table. A piece of ice flew into the basket of nachos.

"Why us? Why don't you go find someone else to do your job?" asked Brendan. His face turned red with anger and embarrassment.

"It has already started," said Aarjen, trying to keep his voice calm. "Whether you like it or not, you have exposed yourself and your friends to the creatures, and they are going to make you play. If you walk away now, the creatures will hurt you, your friends, and your family." He paused and continued, "I tried to tell Kaia I had my doubts about your abilities, but she convinced me that you are right for this task. Your attitude has proven Kaia wrong."

Brendan stood up abruptly, almost knocking his chair back. Alex did the same, shaking her head in disapproval.

"Aarjen, we need each other," Kaia said with a calm yet firm voice, trying her best to soothe the rising tensions. She held Aarjen's arm, as though to prevent him from walking away to find another solution to this problem. "I am afraid if we let the kids go, the creature will find a way to harm them," she said.

"Thanks for the food," Brendan said politely to Kaia.

"Please listen, Brendan. Aarjen is not making this up," Kaia said. "The creatures will hunt you down. They'll hurt you and your friends really badly if you leave us now. They are killers."

Brendan had already started off, but he stopped and hurriedly walked back to take Sidney with him. He lowered himself to the height of the table and spoke to her.

"C'mon, Sid. Let's get back to the room. Sorry you had to listen to all of this." He then removed the bracelet with the crystal and gently tossed it onto a thick layer of napkins on the tray.

Kaia held on to Sidney's hand for a moment, then let her go. "Don't be hasty, Brendan," she cautioned.

Aarjen had already shifted his attention to two short, stout shadowy figures in dark hoodies, observing them from the walkway atop the cascading, tropical-themed waterfalls that stood more than two stories tall.

Kaia quickly slipped into her long leather jacket. "Let's split ways," she told Aarjen, and began following the kids.

"Are you mad, Brendan?" Sidney asked, trying to keep up with his hurried pace.

Alex, who was walking alongside Sidney, prompted Brendan to slow down.

"I'll be fine," said Brendan.

"Excuse me," a hoarse voice from behind called out to them. "Excuse me, is this yours?" asked a short, pudgy man in a dark hoodie, holding out a rectangular black nylon bag by its two short handles.

Brendan immediately recognized it as a chess kit.

"I don't think so," Brendan said, shaking his head. He hesitated, then took a closer look at the chess bag. "That's not mine," he confirmed.

"I think it is," the man insisted and tossed the bag at the kids with his unusually long arm.

"I am sorry—" Brendan's objection was cut short by the chess bag hurtling at him. He caught it awkwardly. As he was about to drop it, a plume of pungent dust erupted from the bag, making him dizzy and nauseous. Brendan dropped the bag and grabbed the railing. He felt light-headed. His legs unable to support his weight, he fell to the ground. Suddenly, things went dark.

When Brendan regained consciousness, there was noisy chatter around him. Alex was helping him sit up.

"Brendan? Brendan, are you okay?" Her voice was muffled and seemed far away despite her blurry image being just inches from him.

Brendan wobbled as he pulled himself up and leaned against the railing with difficulty. He blinked a few times, then wiped the bitter saliva and dirt off his mouth and chin. He looked around, breathing heavily.

"Sidney! Where's Sidney?" he asked, his voice barely audible.

Alex, suddenly aware that Sidney was not next to her, frantically looked around.

"Sidney," Brendan tried to shout, but his voice continued to fail him. With a trembling hand, he attempted to direct attention to the waterfalls at the end of the walkway on the other side of the atrium.

Alex screamed when she spotted Sidney. "*Sidney, stop!*" Her voice was drowned by the noise of falling water.

Somehow, Sidney had found her way up to the artificial indoor waterfalls. She was standing precariously at the edge of a slippery rock, tens of feet above the turbulent stream.

"What the heck! How did she get up there?" Alex sprinted across the walkway leading to the top of the falls.

"Hey, kid, you can't go there! Step back," someone from the crowd below shouted.

Two guards sprinted behind Alex.

"Oh my God! Look at that kid!" a woman screamed.

From where he sat, Brendan saw Sidney with her arms stretched out, searching for someone or something to grasp on to. She was obviously confused about her whereabouts and the commotion around her. Behind her, at a reaching distance, Brendan saw the man in a dark hoodie who had tossed the chess bag at him. Instead of whisking Sidney away from the edge of the rock, he merely pointed toward the base of the wall, as if warning that the child was about to fall.

Brendan gasped helplessly. The unfolding events made him dizzy.

He saw Alex at the junction of the walkway and the waterfall facade, made of concrete in the shape of large rocks, but she would still have to run up to the top of the wall and climb down the rocks to get to Sidney.

"Sidney, don't move," Brendan cried out, gathering his strength.

Suddenly, a tall woman in a long coat effortlessly jumped over the 4-foot railing and onto the rock and pushed the stranger in the hoodie away from Sidney. Unable to hold on to anything, the fellow rolled down several feet below into the tropical thickets. It was Kaia. She swung her arm around Sidney, pulled the child close to her, and landed back on the walkway.

Before the security guards arrived at the scene, Kaia disappeared with Sidney.

Brendan felt sick. He was upset with himself for losing Sidney.

"It's not your fault," Brendan heard Aarjen's voice just above him.

"Grab my hand, kid," Aarjen said. "You have been poisoned with shroom dust."

Brendan wiped his tears and looked up. He was glad to see Aarjen.

"Poisoned?" Brendan tilted his head up, perplexed. He continued wiping the bitter, splattered saliva under his lips with his T-shirt.

The high schooler tried to get up, but his legs buckled. He felt a sharp, burning sensation on his scraped-up left hand as thin streams of blood drained and collected at the bottom of his elbow. Brendan winced as he wiped the blood on his jeans. He then reached out and grabbed Aarjen's hand and pulled himself up with great difficulty.

"Shroom dust is a neurotoxin. It weakens your muscles. Take a few whiffs of this, and you'll feel better," said Aarjen, handing Brendan an amber-colored vial that looked like a miniature pawn chess piece with clear, oily liquid inside.

"Sidney…Is she with Kaia? I thought she was going to…" Brendan felt a tight knot in his stomach, thinking of Sidney at the edge of the rock.

He shifted most of the weight from his lean, 6-foot-tall frame onto Aarjen, who seemed to support him effortlessly, like a pillar. Without questioning, Brendan lowered his face and inhaled from the vial. He didn't smell anything. Pain shot through his neck and shoulder. When he inhaled a couple of more times, he picked up on the faint flowery odor and he liked it. The sweet fragrance intensified when Brendan took a deep breath from the vial. He felt his body relax. Aarjen capped the vial and put it away.

"Sidney is safe. If we are not careful, someone could die," Aarjen said in a calm voice. "Call your friends and make sure they are okay."

Just as Brendan felt his pocket for his phone, it buzzed.

"Hey," Brendan said.

"It's Alex. Are you okay?"

"Where are you?" asked Brendan, exchanging glances with Aarjen and slowly starting to walk. "Have you seen Kaia and Sidney?"

"I'm with them, Brendan. Sidney is fine. Ro and Max are also here."

"I was poisoned," Brendan stuttered.

"Yeah, Kaia told me what happened. Someone also tried to hurt Max, but Kaia saved him as well."

"What?" Brendan tried to raise his voice, but his throat hurt.

"Brendan…Max almost got killed," Ro took the phone from Alex. "The giant guitar prop over by the arcade came crashing down, and luckily, Kaia pulled him away before it crashed. I was right behind him and could have been hit too."

"He was far behind…He was not in any danger!" Brendan heard Max shouting into the phone.

"There are two of those guys in hoodies, trying to hurt us. Kaia wants us all to meet up at the pizza place near the arcade, so we can talk. Can you check with Aarjen?" asked Ro.

Aarjen nodded in agreement. "The antidote will make you very hungry soon." He patted Brendan's shoulder.

"Welcome to Paisano's Pizzeria," the greeter said cheerfully at the entrance of the restaurant. "You can sit anywhere you like."

Soft music complemented the dim lighting and quiet ambience. Other than two families seated in booths by the window, the restaurant was empty.

"Are you closing soon?" Kaia asked politely.

"No, we are open for a while," replied the greeter. "Looks like most of the chess families left today after the tournament. Please take your time and enjoy."

"Thanks," Kaia said, smiling.

She quickly led the kids to a large circular booth at the back of the restaurant. Max and Ro were the first to slump down onto the oversize, cushioned beige seats. They slid around to the middle of the circular table, and others followed from both sides.

Evana, the pleasant greeter, also took their order. "How did you guys do in the tournament?" she asked, reading Ro's chess-themed T-shirt.

"You are looking at champs," Kaia said.

"Awesome, y'all!" Evana said. She air-high-fived the kids and left with their order.

"Those short guys in the hoodies are Earth dwellers who work for the creatures," Kaia said.

"So sorry for what happened, Sidney." Alex gently squeezed Sidney's hand. "I saw Brendan faint, and I got scared…And distracted."

"I want each of you to keep this with you at all times!" Aarjen placed four thin leather straps—each with a small, almond-shaped crystal attached—on the table. The crystals shimmered with colorful sparkles under the soft light from the large pendent fixture hanging above the table.

Kaia took one and tied it around Sidney's neck. She tucked the pendant underneath her shirt.

"I hope you understand the seriousness of the situation now," Aarjen said. "You cannot walk away from the Curse of Bhrigu. You are all in this whether you want it or not. You could get killed if you are not careful," he said, looking at Brendan.

"What do you suggest we do?" asked Brendan.

"A serious task requires dedication and execution—no half-hearted approach," Aarjen said, gently hitting the table with his fist.

"I don't do anything half-heartedly," said Brendan, turning away from Aarjen.

He was tempted to storm out of the restaurant, but he contained himself. He had been accused of not doing his best and giving up once before, and he did not want to hear it from a stranger. He spoke to Kaia. His voice was tinged with resentment. "If you think we can help, then we will. If I was chosen for a task, I'll finish it for you even though this is all a bit bizarre. I am not a quitter."

"Good," said Aarjen without much expression. "I am not here to judge whether you are a quitter or not—that's up to you to prove for yourself— but I need someone who is courageous and has the maturity to deal with complicated situations."

"Can you just tell us what we should be doing?" asked Brendan, again speaking to Kaia instead of Aarjen.

Kaia exchanged glances with Aarjen, then nodded. The pizza arrived just in time for the kids to eat while hearing the story of Kumba.

"Legend has it that Kumba was the only underworld rakshasa emperor who was able to successfully unify and rule all species of rakshasas." Kaia continued the story where she left off. "He was a warrior whose strength was unmatched in any world. He soon became the most powerful underworld emperor of all time."

"Even though Kumba was a rakshasa, he was different," Aarjen said.

"Kumba..." Kaia paused for a brief second, as though collecting her thoughts. "He is a rakshasa with asura blood. He realized that he could bring some order to his species and unify them even if it meant using excessive force. For his effort, he won the respect of even the devas, asuras, and the jalas."

"Then, what happened?" Alex raised her eyebrows.

"With power comes greed and enemies. Kumba had good intentions of aligning with the kings of the other worlds, even if they were his natural enemies, so there could be peace. But some of the rakshasas saw this as a sign of weakness, and they rebelled. Eventually, Kumba started building a large army of deadly fighters."

"When Indra, the immortal king of devas, realized that Kumba could not be persuaded to stop his build-up of a formidable rakshasa army, he reluctantly joined forces with the asuras and jalas to wage war against the rakshasa king," said Aarjen.

"Without any warnings? Just like that?" asked Brendan.

"There were plenty of warnings and negotiations, but the conflict escalated over the years. Small skirmishes between the worlds spread like wildfire, and war was inevitable," said Kaia.

"Now, the rakshasas are trying to get to him before us," said Aarjen.

"What is he doing in Mayastella?" asked Ro.

"Hiding?" asked Max.

"*Hidden* would be a more appropriate term," said Kaia.

"Um...Not sure I follow," said Brendan.

"Well, the story takes a turn here. An event occurred, unknown even to the mighty Indra," continued Kaia.

"A secret event?" asked Alex.

"Kumba's queen, Suhela, born a rakshasi—a female rakshasa—possessed a rare duality. Although her lineage marked her as a creature of formidable power, she defied the stereotypes associated with her kind. Raised by Atri, the healer and kindest rishi of all time, who discovered her abandoned in a forest, Suhela exhibited an uncommon kindness toward others. Her devotion to her foster father and the great rishis earned her not only the rishis' favor but also bestowed upon her great wisdom and unparalleled beauty."

"When Kumba saw Suhela in the forest one day, he was instantly captivated, and much to his delight, his feelings were reciprocated, and soon, they married," said Kaia.

Sidney giggled, and the boys rolled their eyes.

"Queen Suhela was instrumental in the unification of the kingdom," said Aarjen.

"So, all this happened before the war?" Brendan asked, trying to comprehend the timeline.

"Yes," Kaia continued. "Suhela made Kumba strong. She secretly brought political power to Kumba with the help of the rishis but also ensured that her husband didn't endanger the devas, jalas, or asuras. However, in spite of her political influence on both sides, Kumba's power roused the suspicion and animosity of the devas and asuras toward his ever-growing army. War was inevitable.

"Suhela begged her husband to stop, but he saw no honor in backing down. Finally, Suhela sought the help and guidance of the rishis. She wanted her king, her love, alive. The rishis believed the worlds would need Kumba someday, so they wanted to save him from his enemies and, more importantly, from himself. The only way to do this, they told Suhela, was to keep him asleep in a secret place until the time was right to awaken him.

"The rishis advised Suhela to cast the spell of prolonged sleep on Kumba. They asked her to find a widow-maker, who would pose as the queen and use the venom of a sergon on Kumba." Kaia paused when she observed the boys' quizzical expressions.

"A who?" Brendan squinted.

"Widow-makers are a rare kind of rakshasis who are agents of war. In the darkness of the second new moon night, a widow-maker is selected to be bitten by a sergon—a half dragon, half-serpent creature that lives in the Dark Forest near the kingdom of Kumba. As the luminescent snake venom from the sergon's bite seeps through the widow-maker's skin, it creates an enchanting aura around the rakshasi that can mesmerize not only male rakshasas, but many living creatures. Even strong-willed deva and asura warriors have succumbed to this aura. A kiss by a widow-maker rakshasi on the dark night has seriously incapacitated even immortals whose lips are tainted with her poison."

"Is that what we saw today? A sergon?" Alex asked, suddenly remembering the eerie encounter.

"You saw a dragon today?" Max almost spat out his soda. He started coughing.

"No, a sergon is several times bigger than the theel. She has a head of a dragon and the body of a serpent. But instead of spitting fire, she bears poisonous fangs, like those of a serpent. Her scaly wings span across her body, allowing the sergon to fly, swim, or crawl."

"Wouldn't her poison kill Kumba?" asked Sidney.

"Not quite. The rishis knew that the sergon's poison, while not lethal, would have a lasting effect on Kumba. The effect of the poison would prevent Kumba from entering into a deadly war."

"So, how *did* Suhela save her husband?" asked Alex.

"Frustrated and desperate to save her husband, the queen decided to make the ultimate sacrifice by becoming the widow-maker herself without telling the rishis."

"But when the Suhela presented herself to be struck by Azi, a loyal sergon, the beast would not comply. She begged, pleaded, and ordered Azi to strike her. Finally, succumbing to the queen's desperate plea, Azi reluctantly struck her."

"Did she die?" asked Sidney.

"Not right away, I am sure," said Max.

"She can't die before kissing her husband, right?" Ro rolled his eyes.

"When the queen reached the castle," Kaia continued, "her loyal maid noticed her crying, her body cold and trembling. Suhela stumbled in front of the king, and when he held her, she kissed him on his lips. She held on to him until they both fell to the floor."

"Did they both die?" asked Sidney.

"Sidney, the whole idea is to *not* die—this is like reverse Sleeping Beauty," said Max.

"That's okay, dear. They are both still alive," reassured Kaia.

"Where is she?" Sidney asked.

Kaia placed her arm on Sidney's shoulders and gazed into her sightless eyes. "After placing Kumba in Mayastella, the rishis realized that Suhela had poisoned herself to save her husband. Sage Atri quickly sought a cure, but somehow, with someone's help, the theel found a way to abduct and imprison the queen."

"You don't know where she is?" asked Sidney.

"She is somewhere in Mayastella, and you are going to help us find her, right?" asked Kaia.

Sidney nodded eagerly.

"How?" asked Brendan.

"Playing Chadurang will take us there. But we'll be racing against the theel and its creatures, who are also trying to find Suhela. The theel has one goal in mind—to find Queen Suhela and kill her. If the theel gets to Kumba first, it will blame the devas and asuras for her death, and the king will immediately join forces with the theel. The curse will never be broken."

"Why can't the theel just get to the queen on its own? Wasn't it the one who put her there in the first place? Why play a game?" asked Brendan.

"The rishis banned Mayastella when they heard about Indra's dangerous quests. Now, the only way to get in is by playing Chadurang and finding the secrets of Mayastella," said Aarjen.

"And the secrets of Mayastella are in the keeper's notebook," said Kaia, exchanging glances with Aarjen.

"Yan was the keeper of Mayastella. The guardian of the world of illusion. No one entered or exited this world without his knowledge," Aarjen said to his attentive young human audience. "Yan was as strong as an elephant and as wise as a wizard, and he was my friend. We need to find the notebook first."

###

"Our job is to find the keeper's notebook," the theel said to the half-drunken rakshasas. "The notebook will lead us to Kumba."

"Have you lost your mind?" a shapeshifting rakshasa shouted. "The keeper is the son of Maya, who created Mayastella. He has great powers. He's a master of disguise, and he guards the secrets of Mayastella with his life."

"Yan's dead. Our master has killed him."

There was a brief silence. The creatures stopped what they were doing and looked at each other and sniffed the air and erupted with joy. They thumped their chests and pushed one another.

"When Kumba awakens and learns his beloved wife is dead, he'll unleash his powers against the devas, asuras, and rishis," the theel said with a grin, exposing a row of spike-like teeth.

The creatures relished the prospect of a war with the worlds—especially the mortal world.

Chapter 9

The Replicas

Thank you for coming here on such short notice. The rakshasas, I hear, are very active now," Indra said as he guided Kaia and Aarjen through the breathtaking garden of roses.

Kaia loved to be surrounded by the flowers of the devas. Their special aroma, the range of spectacular colors, and the velvety texture instantly calmed her senses. She walked beside Aarjen and wished he were not so preoccupied with his own thoughts, unmindful of the beautiful landscape of Indra's exquisite palace in Devastella.

"The rakshasas think we are after the board to stop the kids from playing Chadurang. But we have other plans," Aarjen said.

"I worry the theel will be unpredictable once the war game begins. The human minds are weak and will succumb to the theel's will before they even realize they are lost," Indra said thoughtfully.

"Yes, but not as unpredictable as the young human minds," said Kaia. "This is where Vyas and Bhrigu think our real advantage lies."

"So, what should we do next?" Indra asked.

"We need to make several replicas of the board," said Aarjen.

"Replicas! Replicas are easy to make, Aarjen, but they will serve no purpose in the tournament. Only Maya's Chadurang will activate the curse," Indra responded.

"Exactly, my king. I want the boards to be there as just replicas, a source of bewilderment for the rakshasas. They will have no clue when the portal opens. We will take advantage of their confusion to control the entry into Mayastella, and we will decide which child takes an active role at every entry," explained Aarjen.

"Whatever you do, we have to be one step ahead of the theel." Indra placed his hand on Aarjen's shoulder. "I am here to help, Aarjen. This is our war, and I know I am responsible for this. I truly regret this," Indra said in an uncharacteristically soft voice. "We have to protect the human children in every way possible—they are easy prey for the tantrics, who hunt for souls."

Indra led the knights toward his stable. In front of Aarjen stood the mighty Hiravat, the majestic white elephant of Indra. Aarjen greeted Hiravat by looking directly into his eyes and gently touching his trunk. Not many would dare to get close to Hiravat, let alone touch him.

"He likes you," said Indra, impressed with Aarjen's ability to gain Hiravat's respect. "I am going to show you something that will take your breath away," added Indra with excitement in his voice, drawing attention to his enormous stable that held over a hundred horses.

Aarjen had been to the famed equestrian center many times. It was the place where all the knights' horses were bred and trained and was home to some of the fastest horses of Devastella. Everything about the facility was large—the resting chambers for the horses, the circular riding pavilions, training facilities, pools, and the number of caretakers.

Aarjen faced the open, lush meadow, where many of the horses roamed freely. He whistled aloud in a pattern and waited. At a distance, a tall black mustang stopped grazing, raised its head excitedly, and thundered toward the visitors. "Here she comes," shouted Aarjen, clapping his hands with joy to see his loyal ride again. "She might be old, but she still has the strength and vigor of a young mare. Without her, I would be long dead in the Dark Forest." Aarjen's horse stopped just a few inches from him and nudged him with its large face. Within minutes, a peregrine falcon swooped from the sky and landed on Aarjen's shoulder.

"They always go in pairs," he said.

"I am not here to ride you, my friend." Aarjen gently rubbed the loyal mount's forehead. "You are free now…No more Dark Forest, no more risking your life for me. You are in a peaceful place now with your friends and family."

He patted the mustang on its back, where it bore many scars incurred on perilous past adventures, and bid it a lingering farewell. The horse hesitated for a minute, then took off toward its pack with the falcon flying overhead. At a distance, it saluted Aarjen by kicking its front legs in the air and letting out a loud neigh.

"Now, to my prized possession," said Indra, leading them to riding hall that was separated from the main stable.

They took a few steps toward the hall and stood in front of the open gate. There, in the middle of the riding facility that opened up to the rolling fields, stood the most majestic horse that Aarjen and Kaia had ever seen.

"Wow, look at him," said Kaia. "Is this the famous—"

"Ashvat? Yes, the fastest horse in this universe. Lord Baga's loyal war horse."

"His kind and precious gift to you, Lord Indra," added Maya.

Aarjen was speechless. The majestic beast and the knight stood, staring at each other.

"How does it feel to ride him?" asked Kaia.

"I wouldn't know," said Indra. "Ashvat would not let anyone other than Baga ride him. I tried my best, but he hasn't accepted me yet—probably never will. An asura horse will never allow a deva to be his rider."

"I believe in the bond and trust between a horse and its rider," said Aarjen.

"Perhaps he will allow a great knight to ride him," Indra conveyed his vote of confidence with a hearty clap on Aarjen's shoulders.

Aarjen continued looking straight into Ashvat's eyes as he replied, "Thank you, my lord."

He slowly and steadily walked toward Ashvat, who seemed to get taller with every step. Aarjen could hear him breathe as he touched the noble steed gently on his face, stroked his mane, and finally held on to his massive back. Ashvat didn't flinch. Pressing against Ashvat's side, Aarjen quickly lifted himself and threw his leg over the stallion. The instant the knight landed on Ashvat's massive back, he bolted at lightning speed. Within seconds, Ashvat leaped in the air, kicked his hind legs, and made a sharp turn. Aarjen tried to hold on, but the beast was too quick in countering his maneuvers to stay atop. He managed to fall gracefully on the soft, damp, muddy ground. Kaia and Indra gasped, but they both burst out laughing. Maya gracefully glided over to Aarjen and helped him onto his feet.

"Are you all right?" she asked while Aarjen dusted the dirt off his clothes. "I am surprised he didn't let you ride him." She tried hard to sound sincere, and not laugh spontaneously.

Aarjen shook his head. "He's too quick and clever."

"Ha-ha-ha." Kaia covered her mouth with her hands, unable to curtail her laughter.

"You can only be amused if you can do better than that." Aarjen wagged his finger at her.

"I don't want to ride him," she said. "He's too free-spirited for anyone to ride. You don't ride a free-spirited horse until he wants you to ride him. I thought you knew that."

"That's just a poor excuse, my lady," said Aarjen, prodding Kaia. "My gut tells me he won't even allow you to get close to him."

"He belonged to Lord Baga." Kaia closed her eyes for a moment and took a deep breath before approaching Ashvat.

Ashvat lowered his face and stood there still, as though awaiting his next victim.

Without hesitating, she stood close to Ashvat, gently patting him on his long neck and speaking to him softly. Suddenly, Ashvat trotted away from her, kicked his heels, and galloped at full speed. He arched along the tracks and charged toward Kaia. Kaia waited for the right moment. She timed her sprint to match the speed of Ashvat and perfectly aligned herself with him. As Ashvat passed her, she grabbed his mane and threw herself onto his back. Together, they thundered past the stable door and out into the meadows while Aarjen, Indra, and Maya watched them in delight.

"He has finally found his rider," said Indra.

Aarjen waved, then clasped his hands and bowed to Kaia. She waved back to him from the distance.

Brendan met with Aarjen at the chess club two weeks after returning from the qualifier tournament.

"Wait, you want to break into Scrappy's pawnshop and steal the board?" Brendan asked, scratching his head and pacing back and forth. "Why not just ask him to give us the board?"

"I didn't ask you to take the board from the store. I want you to get to it first," Aarjen said patiently.

"I can get shot, you know. Besides…"

"Brendan, I want you to do this," Aarjen said sternly. "I am sure you can figure out a way."

"And what do I do when I find the board?" Brendan asked.

"The board has a hidden mechanical replicon embedded inside. If you bring the part, we can make several replicas of the board and confuse the creatures during the tournament. We can control the game and protect you better."

"Can't you pose as customers and take it yourself?" asked Alex.

"No, we have to take care of something while you access the board," said Kaia, quickly exchanging glances with Aarjen.

"Can we count on you, Brendan?" asked Aarjen.

"Okay. We'll do it tonight after Scrappy leaves." Brendan shook his head.

Alex, Brendan, and Ro waited until Turner left. Brendan had convinced the coach to leave early, promising to lock up the club. Alex watched the pawnshop from the large window. Ro peered through a pair of old binoculars.

"I don't see any movement." Ro strained his eyes. "Are you sure they are still there?"

"Don't you see the big *Open* sign on, Ro? Is it too far for your binoculars?" Alex gently tugged at his binoculars to annoy Ro.

"Maybe they forgot to turn it off," Ro argued.

"What about the half-open door? Did they forget to lock it as well?" she asked.

"Maybe they left it open to make it easy for you and Brendan," he said.

"There he goes," Brendan, said watching from the office room. "Scrappy has left the building."

"How come Nicolas didn't leave with him?" Alex asked.

"Scrappy goes to some warehouse on Fridays with his shady cronies," Brendan replied.

Scrappy and his cohorts got into his beat-up pickup truck, and it roared past the chess club, ejecting a plume of thick, dark smoke.

"Junior has to clean and close the store up," Brendan said.

"Ro, keep watching and text us if you see someone pull up to the shop. And lose the stupid binoculars, dude," Brendan said in a tense voice.

"Don't take too long. I don't want to be here alone."

"Wooooo, the CREATURES are coming," Alex teased Ro before darting off.

The curtain behind the pawnshop door moved, and Scrappy Junior peeked behind the oval glass pane as the two friends crossed the street and approached the shop. He could not conceal the surprised look on his face. He cracked open the door.

"My stepdad is not here and I am closing shop," he said nonchalantly, looking past Brendan at the empty street.

"Hey," Brendan said with a neutral expression. "This is Alex. You might have seen her in school—our kicker. She…she wants to look at some stuff…a gift for her dad," he said, peeking inside the store.

"This place is full of stuff, so what kind of stuff?" Scrappy Junior asked without looking at Alex, who noticed that he didn't look anything like his stepfather, Scrappy. He was of medium height and build with long, dark hair and thick, matching brows. He had pleasing brown eyes and a defined chin.

"Some old ch—" Brendan was going to say *chess sets*, but Alex quickly chipped in, "Baseball cards. Yes, I am looking for baseball cards—some old ones. Do you have any? I'm sorry. Are you closed already?" She grinned and nodded toward the glowing *Open* neon sign.

"Um…just about, but you can come in." Scrappy Junior opened the door just enough to let them in one at a time as the annoying buzzer blared.

"Thanks, man," said Brendan, looking at some random items inside the old glass, wood-framed countertop.

There were all kinds of antique objects. One section of the room housed colorful porcelain ware and stacks of oil paintings, leaning against the wall. Another section was crowded with an assortment of vintage furniture. Wooden cabinets with glass doors with crystals and other trinkets lined the walls. There were knives and old guns in one cabinet and chess sets and checkers in another. Alex saw some pattern in the clutter. An old cash register was in the middle of the hall on a counter that also contained a built-in glass display case with watches and jewels. To their left, tucked away in a corner, was another room that looked like an office area, and to the right was a doorway to a cage-like storage room, enclosed by two wide metal screen doors. Behind the locked screen doors on the second shelf, Brendan spotted a large package, from which a corner of the chessboard jutted out.

"Are you looking for any particular type of baseball cards? Players? Era?" Scrappy Junior asked Alex politely.

"Uh? Oh no, no, I am just looking for regular stuff for my dad," she replied. "Not the expensive ones, you know."

She searched for words but couldn't come up with any baseball personalities. Scrappy Junior walked to the cabinet behind him, whistling softly. He opened the locked door and pulled out a small box. He took out some cards and neatly laid them on the countertop.

Alex peered into the deck but her interest was just pretense. There were some cards of Hank Aaron, Willie Mays, Babe Ruth, Jackie Robinson, Yogi Berra, and many others of that era. Some were even signed.

"How much are these?" She picked up and examined a few.

"Three dollars apiece," he said, looking at the side of the box. "You can get them on eBay, but we price them good. These are just knockoffs or copies, you know," he added, chuckling.

Brendan was surprised to hear so much talk from Scrappy Junior. They rarely talked during the tournaments. His stepfather was always around, yelling at him for some reason or the other.

On a small desk by a wall, behind the counter, Brendan noticed that a chessboard was set up, and it looked like Junior was going over some puzzles.

"I'll take these three," Alex said. "Do you have more inside?"

"I don't think so," Scrappy Junior answered firmly.

"Can I look around to see what else you have?"

"Um…Okay…But I am about to leave…You can come back tomorrow and spend more time." Despite his hesitation, he seemed accommodating.

"You have some cool antique clocks here," Alex noted.

"Yeah, some of them change time without warning," Brendan said with a snicker.

"Wh-what?" asked Alex, raising her eyebrows.

"Uh…Listen, I had nothing to do with any of it, man," Scrappy Junior blurted out, not looking at Brendan.

An awkward silence ensued.

"Let me check in the back room to see if we have more cards." Scrappy Junior darted into the back room connected by a narrow corridor, as if to avoid further conversation.

Alex looked at Brendan and raised her eyebrows and cocked her head in the direction of the cage room. Brendan nodded, quickly glanced inside to made sure Scrappy Junior was not looking at them, and quietly darted into the darkness of the storage room. Within moments, Scrappy Junior returned. "I have nothing in the back," he said, clearing his throat and rubbing his stubble.

Brendan had positioned himself behind the partially closed door and could see and hear Scrappy Junior through the gap between the door and jamb.

"Oh, it's okay," said Alex, "Thanks for looking. I'll take these three. Um, I am sorry. I didn't catch your name." She didn't want to call him Scrappy Junior, like the others.

"Nicolas," he replied eagerly.

"Nicolas. I like this store." Alex pulled out a ten-dollar bill. "I might come back for that clock." She took a closer look at an old mantel clock on the corner shelf with a cherry wood casing. "My dad loves old clocks."

"Thanks," Nicolas said cheerfully. "You should come back. You know, most people don't call me Nicolas…I like that name," he said sincerely. His eyes then shifted across the room.

"Where's Brendan?" he asked.

"Brendan just left. Someone's at the club," Alex replied briefly looking across the street.

"But…I didn't hear the buzzer," he asked in a suspicious tone.

Brendan could hear his heart race in the heavy darkness of the room.

"Buzzer? Yeah, yeah, he just ran out," she said, awkwardly raising her voice.

"Hope it was not something I said?" he said with a sigh. "You know, things just happened last year at the national tournament. It was a pretty close game, but Brendan ran out of time suddenly."

Brendan was surprised that Scrappy Junior was discussing the game he wanted to forget so badly.

"We were playing with my clock," he said, turning toward the chess clock by the chessboard on the desk. "He had 28 minutes left, and I had 26. The next time I looked, he only had two minutes. I am not sure how. Brendan felt that something had happened when he stepped out to the restroom. I had gone to get some water myself."

"Uhhh…Maybe you both didn't pay attention to the time?" Alex said, trying to buy time.

Alex's suggestion irritated Brendan, and he almost bumped his head against the door.

"No, we both knew we had time. That was not the issue."

"Something was wrong with the clock then?" Alex prolonged the conversation. Brendan vigorously nodded and whispered to himself, "*Cheaters!*"

"We'd checked the clock many times, and this had never happened before," he said aloud.

"Who was winning?" she asked.

"Equal material, but many thought Brendan had a better position."

Brendan was surprised by Nicolas' candidness.

"But I saw some good moves myself. It was a tight game, and I felt that I had a chance—at least for a draw," Nicolas continued.

"Didn't you, too, feel that something was odd with the time? And no one else noticed?" Alex asked.

"*Thank you,*" Brendan mouthed.

"Of course. I was very confused. But it was a very intense game. You know…There were four people watching the game, and somehow, no one paid attention to the time."

"Have you gone over the game?" Alex asked.

"No! I hope, someday, Brendan and I can just pick up where we left off and finish the game."

"Thanks for the cards," Alex suddenly, abruptly, ended the conversation. "I'll try to come back tomorrow for the clock. It was nice to meet you, Nicolas." She hurriedly picked up the cards and opened the front door.

The entry buzzer startled Brendan. He watched her wave at Scrappy Junior and leave. The place was suddenly filled with silent darkness.

Brendan watched Scrappy Junior switch off the neon sign, clean up the counter area, and go in and out of the store a few times with empty boxes. He finally stood in front of the security alarm keypad and attempted to activate the alarm several times, but the system repeated the same error message. Thankfully, he never came to the storage room to close the windows that Brendan had cleverly cracked open to prevent the alarm from activating.

Brendan heard him curse loudly, as someone outside impatiently flashed the vehicle headlights and blared the horn a couple of times. Nicolas yelled out some foreign words and stormed out of the store, slamming the front door shut. Moments later, the vehicle screeched away into the night. Brendan could hear his heart pound again as sweat broke out on his forehead. He waited for 10 solid minutes, which seemed like an eternity, and then called Alex.

"It's all clear," Alex said in a muffled voice.

"This place is creepy," said Brendan. "Get here fast. I have the storage room window open," he said, breathing heavily into his phone.

Within minutes, Alex was by the window. Brendan leaned over and pulled her up and was surprised by how effortlessly she climbed through the window. When she moved her hoodie back, her thick auburn hair briefly brushed Brendan's face. Brendan was holding her close to him, and their eyes locked in the glow of Brendan's dim flashlight.

"Did you see the board inside?" Alex stepped away and tied her hair back into a knot.

"Yes." Brendan directed the dull beam of light at the shelf behind the cage-like screen doors.

The metal door was bolted and locked with a large iron padlock with a disproportionally large keyhole.

"Great, this stuff is locked," she whispered straining her eyes. "Why don't you use the phone light? It's brighter."

"Too bright." Brendan closed the window blinds. "I found this flashlight on the shelf."

"Where do you even look for a key in this place?" Alex asked, exasperated.

"I don't know. You look there, and I'll look there."

"It is spooky in here with all this weird, old stuff. From the look of the lock, I would imagine it would be one of those old hollow keys with a large head. My grandpa had locks like these in his tool shed." She tugged at the lock.

Brendan looked inside the drawers. He didn't see anything. As he turned around, he caught a glimpse of a shadow move across the wall under the faint light. He stood still for a minute, trying to adjust his eyes to see beyond the boundaries of the shadows. It was in a direction away from where Alex had gone.

"Is that you, Alex?"

There was no answer.

"Alex?" Brendan raised his voice.

"What?" came a faint reply from the other room.

"We have been looking for the stupid key for a while now." He yanked the lock a few times and pushed the screen door.

The sudden blue glow on the desk and the buzzing noise that followed startled them. They looked at each other and listened.

"There!" He reached for the pile of papers on a small coffee table, from which the sound originated. "It is just my phone." He quickly grabbed it.

Ro's name appeared as the caller on the screen. "Hey?" Brendan's voice was barely above a whisper.

"What's taking you so long? Is everything okay?" Ro's shaky voice filled the room.

"We are trying to find the key to the screen door," he said impatiently. "You just watch and text instead of calling if someone pulls up to the store. How does it look?"

"It's totally dead. Don't take too long. My dad will be here to pick me up in less than an hour."

"Okay!" Brendan hung up.

"Let's think. Either Scrappy takes the key with him or he hides it in the store. Neither of them is too practical since the stuff on the shelf is inventory that Scrappy probably needs access to frequently." Brendan tried to infuse logic into the situation. "The key cannot be too far from here."

"This is frustrating. I can't believe that we have been asked to do this. Where're Aarjen and Kaia when we need some help?" said Alex.

"Ouch!" Brendan suddenly winced as a sharp hook protruding from the wall entangled with the thin leather strap of his crystal charm and snatched it off his wrist. He cursed.

"Your wristband is now glowing! Everything glows these days," said Alex.

The soft blue light spread as the crystal shone like a mini keychain light from where it hung, exposing a large key hanging on the side of a short wooden shelf. "It's the key. It's the key." Brendan struggled to keep his voice low.

"Finally!" He pulled off the key and unlocked the heavy lock. He then took the leather bracelet and crystal and slipped it back on his wrist.

Carefully, Brendan, the taller of the two, entered the cage and reached for a large box that stuck out. "Boy!" Brendan said, grunting as he tried to lift the box, arms shaking, muscles tensing, and elbows bending as he carefully lowered it.

"Just don't drop it," Alex said, helping him set the board on the large desk nearby.

Several blocks behind the shop, out in the open field, inside a dilapidated barn, six human-sized vampire kateris were perched upside-down on the large metal beam. One of them opened its blood-red eyes and spread its scaly, large wings. It let out a shrill to awaken the others.

"Someone is touching the board," said one of the kateris.

One by one, they dove from the beam and swooped out of the barn.

Brendan slowly opened the cardboard carton.

"We need to flip the board to get to the part," said Alex. "Count to three?" she said.

They jointly and carefully flipped the board upside-down on three.

Brendan pulled out a piece of folded paper from his pocket, containing instructions from Aarjen. He felt a sudden gush of air on his face as he started reading the instruction. A lamp on the shelf above swayed. Creepy shadows rolled across the walls.

"What was that?" asked Alex, looking around nervously.

"Let's get the part and get out of here," said Brendan in a hushed voice.

A network of thin silver rods about the size of 20 gauge wire neatly spread from the center to the edges of the board, like a printed circuit board.

Brendan inserted a small cylindrical object, which Aarjen had given him, with hundreds of tiny protrusions—like the rolling drum of an old musical box—into a matching slot and waited.

"I didn't hear any clicks," Alex said.

"You have to wait for a few seconds."

It felt like hours before they heard a faint click. Two long wooden strips at either side of the board slid downward, exposing the ends of the silver rods embedded in the board. The terminus of each rod was marked with an illuminated symbol.

"I'll read, and you press the symbols," said Brendan.

"Go slow," said Alex.

"Okay. First, the lightning symbol, it is the fourth from the top," he read out slowly.

Alex counted and pressed the symbol, and its glow disappeared.

Fire, water, air, mountain, queen, elephant, and knight—all the lights from the symbols were switched off in that order. Brendan tried to turn the cylinder counterclockwise, as per the instruction, but it wouldn't budge.

"Oh, I forgot. I am supposed to use this tool to move the pin." He pulled out a shiny object that looked like a picklock from his pocket.

A thin diaphragm shutter opened, exposing a small compartment. Blue charges randomly sparked around a floating marble-like object. Brendan carefully reached inside the space with the tool, pushed a lever, and allowed the sphere to gently float into a black leather pouch.

A terrifying loud shrill made them both dive behind the large desk. The bookshelves shook violently, and heavy thuds moved rapidly across the walls, floor, and roof.

"We got the part. Let's get the hell out of here," shouted Alex, squeezing Brendan's arm.

"We have to put this board back up, Alex. We don't want Scrappy to call the police."

They hurriedly set the board back in order and closed the box. Brendan wiped his sweat off the package with this sleeve and pushed it back on the shelf.

"What's that smell?" asked Alex, pinching her nose.

"It's not me," said Brendan. "I thought it was you."

"Me?" Alex shook her head. "This smells like dead animals, dude!"

They nervously looked around.

Shadows were creeping up on them from all directions.

"The kateris are in," said Aarjen. "It's time for us to surprise them."

"I prefer to take them down before they expose themselves to the kids."

Aarjen and Kaia drew their long knives and slipped through the window, like silent shadows. Aarjen spotted the largest kateri swooping down the attic as though the roof didn't exist. Two other kateris followed.

By the time they sensed the presence of the knights, it was too late. Aarjen grabbed the large one by its neck, and as it tumbled to the floor, he pressed his long knife against the critter's throat. The shelves shook vigorously on impact, and Kaia prevented a ceramic lamp from crashing to the floor.

The other vampire kateris swooped in to attack Aarjen, but Kaia unleashed her disks, injuring at least two of them. She stabbed the third. With their leader still under the forceful grip of Aarjen, they were disoriented by the ambush.

Kaia stepped closer to the cowering vampire kateris, her long, bloodied knife poised at them. "I'll kill you all if you ever come close to the kids," she warned.

Aarjen kicked the large kateri, and it rolled on the floor and slammed against a nearby wall. After finally managing to scramble away from Aarjen, it hesitantly spread its wings and flew into the darkness.

The remaining two vampires followed their defeated leader. Later, the creatures would kill their leader for the unsuccessful mission.

Ro was relieved to see Brendan and Alex finally emerge from the shadows. His father had arrived and was waiting for him in the car. Brendan signaled a thumbs-up and waved to Ro as he got into the car.

"Hey, thanks for your help." Brendan put his hand on Alex's shoulder.

"We did it." She reciprocated Brendan's gesture by wrapping her arm around his waist. "We got what we wanted."

"And then some," said Brendan.

Alex raised her eyebrows.

"Look at this." Brendan pulled out a small leather bundle. "I found this wrapped in the corner of the box. I don't know what it is, but I think it has something to do with that board."

He set the bundle on the table and slowly opened it. Inside were four chess pieces, two of them were black and the other two were white and they all looked like pawns.

"These might come in handy when we play in the tournament." He hurriedly put them back when he heard a knock on the door.

Aarjen and Kaia stood outside.

"We have something for you." Brendan welcomed the guests.

"I know," said Aarjen. "You both did good. Really good!"

"How do you know?" asked Brendan.

"Let's just say that we were watching you from a distance and helping you unlock locks and preventing lamps from falling on your head." Kaia winked at Alex.

"Thanks for watching out," said Brendan.

Aarjen gave an amicable shrug.

Brendan handed the black pouch to Aarjen. Without looking at its contents, he put it inside a small bag he carried.

"When do we meet again?" asked Brendan.

"We'll be in touch with you," said Kaia. Then, Kaia and Aarjen thanked them and left.

That night, in his room, Brendan briefly thought of the conversation between Nicolas and Alex inside the pawnshop when he had been hiding in the small storage area. Scrappy Junior had sounded sincere. Could it possibly be that he'd had nothing to do with the clock? Brendan had not been aware that Scrappy Junior, too, had left the board when he went to the restroom. *Was Scrappy Junior simply trying to escape blame, or was it all his stepfather's doing?* "I am not going to worry about the past," he told himself. "Time to focus on the future." His thoughts shifted to Alex, which made him happy. It felt good to be with her.

Chapter 10

The Boards Arrive

The young computer technician had begun his day early to get a head start with the network setup at the tournament hall. He had much to do, yet he kept staring at the strange chessboard. He wanted to examine underneath the board, but since it was too heavy, he pushed it to the edge of the table and lowered his head below. He stood up and scratched his stubbly brown beard.

"You have been staring and poking at it for almost 30 minutes now, Steve. What are you looking for?" asked his colleague and friend, Katie.

"I am trying to figure out how this thing works. The squares light up when you place the pieces, but I can't find the power source or the power switch," he said, bewildered.

"Probably has some kind of sensor." Katie was not too curious about the inner workings of electronic gadgets. "It's big enough to have a rechargeable battery pack."

"Maybe," he said. He muttered something and moved a piece on the board, and the corresponding square lit up. The color of the light changed from white to red when a piece was captured.

"How is it going, Steve?" asked the US Chess Federation chairman. The chairman was accompanied by the TD from Illinois. He placed his hand on Steve's shoulder. "Does this thing do what that man said it would? Have you figured it out?" he asked loudly, as though addressing a crowd.

"Um, it does things on its own, Gary," Steve told the chairman. "I can't control it, but it does do a lot of different things."

"It's no good if we can't control it. I don't want any problems during the tournament." The chairman sounded annoyed and anxious.

"It automatically lights up, Gary," Katie shouted and laughed, irritating the chairman.

"This could be too distracting to the players," said the TD, adding fuel to the fire.

"How do you turn it off?" the chairman asked.

Steve shrugged his shoulders and then moved a pawn to d4.

"*Ni Chadurang…Noos!*" a voice from the board announced.

"What was that?" the chairman asked, frowning.

Katie giggled.

"Something in a foreign language," said Steve.

"Can you make it speak in English? Or better yet, make it *not say anything at all?*" the chairman asked.

"Gary, I have been searching for switches or controls for a while, but I can't find any," Steve admitted.

Two other officials huddled around Steve. They carefully lifted the heavy board and looked underneath, but found nothing.

"Oh, also," Steve continued, "holographic images randomly pop up. This was probably designed as an interactive game. Modern technology in an antique style."

"Call that guy and ask him to take this junk back," the chairman said angrily. "You know him well, right?" He asked the TD from Illinois.

"Scrappy? Yeah. I bet somebody dumped this in his pawnshop for a quick buck, and he's trying to make something out of it. I'll call him," the TD replied.

"Wait!" said Steve.

His laptop screen flickered a couple of times and displayed an image of a typical electronic analysis board with the standard chess icons, representing various pieces, on the blue and white squares.

"D4," the electronic voice said in English.

"Gary, this is connecting on its own—without internet connection, external receivers, or devices," said Steve.

"I guess it's modern technology, folks." The chairman moved another piece.

"E4," said the computer, then, "Knight F6," shortly after another move.

"Try moving a piece randomly," said one of the other technicians, amused by the board.

Steve moved the rook over the pawn and put it in the middle of the board.

The lights on the board dimmed.

"Illegal move! Illegal move! The game will be shut down in 20 seconds—19, 18…" The computer started a countdown.

Steve quickly retracted his move.

"Resume game," announced the computer.

"Ha! Look! Look at this, everyone," said Steve with a short burst of laughter and a few clicks of the touchpad. "So cool. I can select from a menu of images for the chessboard and the pieces." He displayed a variety of representations of the board and the pieces in splendid color and graphics.

"I got an idea," Gary said, rubbing his chin. "We can use this as Board One and project the games played on this board. Everyone can watch the game on Board One."

"We can have the grandmasters analyze the game that is being projected," said the TD.

"Hey, that thing is on my computer too," a man from the corner of the room shouted. "How do we turn it off?"

Katie walked up to the desktop setup in a corner of the room. She turned it on and waited for a few seconds. "Well, this one has it too. So, this is streaming on all computers without internet connection or Wi-Fi. That's the kind of technology I like. No fuss, no mess." She clicked her fingers in the air.

"Let's play a game," said Steve to the other technician and rapidly moved the pieces.

One after the other, the computer screen picked up the moves. When a piece was captured, the images transformed into a video game mode with impressive graphics. They watched a knight emerge and eliminate a soldier.

"Is this just a prototype?" asked the chairman. "Can we get more of these?"

"I thought you didn't like the board," said the TD.

"Well, now, I do."

"Frankly, I don't think Scrappy knows anything about this board's capabilities," said the TD. "But I'll call him."

"Excuse me," said a deep voice from the entrance of the room, followed by a loud knock on the open door. It was a tall man in a dark suit. "Can I see the chairman of the USCF?"

"Can we help you?" asked the TD, speaking for the chairman.

"Are you the chairman?" asked the man.

"I am the chairman, but we are a bit busy now." Gary was curt.

"I hear you are planning to use one of our special boards for the major event," said the man.

He scanned the room to see if he could spot the board.

"Which board might that be?" asked the chairman, awkwardly positioning himself to block the board from being seen.

"Look, my time is as valuable as yours, so let's get to the point. Our technology is unique and the best in the world. We have more of those for you to use. It will make you look good."

The chairman exchanged glances with his cohorts and raised his eyebrows. His lips moved, but no words came out. He finally cleared his throat and spoke. "Do you work for the company that makes them?" he asked, stepping away from the board.

"Something like that," replied the man. "It's a secret, highly specialized project, and it has somehow found its way to you from a different source, but we are willing to work with you."

The man approached the chairman and handed him a card. Gary hesitantly took the card.

D.E.V. Holographic Games Ltd., the card read. When Gary tilted the card slightly, a holographic image of the chessboard appeared and disappeared quickly. It only had a phone number at the bottom.

The chairman didn't like the man's attitude, but he didn't want to lose the board. It could build hype during the tournament. The games could be easily streamed live without Wi-Fi issues. This board had the twin advantages of being easy to work with and entirely gratis.

"Let's go to my office." Gary suddenly wanted some privacy. "My tech tells me that we can't control the board," he added as they walked into his office.

"It is highly advanced gaming technology, and we don't want it to get into the wrong hands. We will provide tech support during the game. It will be flawless," the man promised. "Controlling the board will not be difficult for our skilled technicians."

"How many boards can you provide?" the chairman asked, offering a chair to the stranger. "I am Gary, by the way."

"One for every section. Every top game in the section can be viewed anywhere in the halls or streamed into any device—computers, tablets, or other mobile devices. No messy wires, and no need for internet connection. All at no cost to you. Of course, we are not experts in chess; you would have to have your GMs go over the games." The man stood, his gaze fixed on Gary with a stern, unyielding expression. His face remained impassive, and he withheld his name.

"Why are you being generous?" asked the chairman suspiciously.

"Great minds come to this event, and we would like to be there as well, Gary. This is a good venue to get exposure for both of us, although we didn't plan for this event," the man said, sitting back on his chair and crossing his long legs. His penetrating eyes looked directly into the chairman's shifty gaze as he continued in a casual tone, "We have more games, all based on new technology coming up. We have demo units with advanced gaming systems unlike anything you have ever seen; kids and adults will really enjoy them." He leaned over the desk and lowered his voice: "If you and some of your staff would like to test them out, we'll be happy to just give away a few of these as a 'thank you' for using our boards at the tournament."

The chairman thought for a moment. Obviously, his staff and helpers would be happy to get something in return for working so hard. He could give out some door prizes as well to raise funds for the organization. "Okay, my staff and I could test some of the demos," he said, deliberately avoiding direct eye contact with the man and hastily wiping off an uncontrolled grin. He made a conscious effort to compose himself, forcing a serious look. "You can deliver them to my office. Additionally, would it be permissible to utilize some of these as part of our fundraisers?"

"Of course, Gary." The man pushed his chair back and stood up, his six-plus-foot stature towering over the seated chairman. The chairman got up slowly.

"We are looking forward to partnering in your social responsibility opportunities," said the man. "You'll receive five new game boards along with various test units shortly," he promised.

"I want all the boards set up and our team trained by the end of the day tomorrow." The chairman quickly shifted the conversation from the freebies.

"You got it." The man nodded. His work was done.

The chairman stood in his office for a minute, studying the business card. He had never seen one like this before. He flipped the card, looking for the stranger's name, but it was not there. He rushed outside to see if he could catch the man before he left the building, but he was nowhere to be found.

Within hours, two men delivered six big boxes.

Steve spent the rest of the afternoon experimenting with the new board. When he returned to the tournament hall with the TD and the chairman, he was shocked to see all the boards neatly set up at the head tables, where the top-rated players for each section would be playing. A young woman with a sleek tablet-like device appeared to be examining the boards. She hadn't noticed them enter the hall.

"Um, excuse me. Are you with this company?" Steve asked.

"Hello," replied the elegant woman, quickly setting down the device. She was tall and attractive. Her beautiful hazel eyes immediately caught his attention.

"I am Tasha," she said. "Yes, I am the technical engineer. You must be Steve," she beamed radiantly.

Steve nodded with a big grin, pleased that an attractive woman knew his name.

"Oh, by the way…" he turned to the chairman. "This…"

"Must be the famous chairman of the USCF," completed Tasha. "I have left several packages for you in your office, Gary. Thanks to you and the USCF." Her dimples deepened as her smile widened.

Steve could tell that Gary liked her much more than the man who had shown up that morning, unannounced.

"Very nice to meet you, Tasha," the chairman said, blushing.

"I am here to make sure that everything runs smoothly. Would you like a demo? Do you play, Gary?" asked Tasha.

"Ha-ha. Not very well. You know, my game is a bit rusty. I am more into the management of the tournaments these days."

"I think you are being humble," the lady said.

"I can play," another TD immediately said in his Russian accent, wanting to be part of the conversation.

"Ah, Igor," she said, recognizing the TD. "I know you are a good player." She continued to impress everyone with her knowledge of all their names.

"Watch the projection on the wall, Gary. Igor, you're white, and I'm black—don't worry, just on the board," she added with a smile that disarmed even the flustered chairman.

Igor was the third to display a wide grin in a few minutes. Katie, who had joined them, appeared to be amused by all the men and their innate ability to lose their cool in front of an attractive woman. She rolled her eyes at Steve and shook her head.

Igor and Tasha moved their pieces.

A thin beam of light spread across the wall, projecting a clear image of a green-and-white chessboard with each chess piece represented by its icon—just like any standard computer chess game.

"How does your device project the image on the wall?" the Chairman asked.

"New built-in laser technology," Tasha said.

The graphics were incredible, and the image was stable.

"These icons can also be viewed as 3-D holographic images, like a video game. Kids will love the graphics, and if you use this versatile analyst tool," she said, highlighting some impressive features, "you can make the games educational."

The chairman started clapping his hands, and soon, everyone joined him in the applause.

The normally festive Navy Pier had transformed into a carnival for the tournament. Chess had brought a Renaissance atmosphere. The decor reflected the event with checkered banners, fictitious coats of arms, and flags from medieval times.

Actors in Renaissance clothing—kings, queens, knights, and soldiers—walked around and greeted visitors. Fake medieval battle and pirate ships lined the pier. There were plays and skits. Jugglers and jesters performed at the central stage across from the food court. The children's museum store was stocked with chess sets, chess software, chess puzzle books, and a potpourri of chess-related items. Apparel and other paraphernalia were imprinted with the Chess Olympiad Chicago logo and a variety of creative chess slogans, such as *Full Contact Chess* or *I Am a Chess Mom* or *Pawn Power*.

To manage the throngs of visitors and separate the regular tourists from the tournament crowd, access was restricted to certain areas. Tournament passes were issued to the players and their families with designated parking permits and assigned locations. The entire exhibit area on the second floor was extended and converted into the tournament hall with neatly labeled sections. The flags of all the countries participating in the upcoming Olympics hung from the ceiling, signaling the arrival of the Summer Olympic Games to Chicago within a month.

New skittles rooms—the designated rooms for teams to play unrated games of chess—and waiting facilities for families were added to the upper section of Navy Pier.

"I want to thank all of you for doing such a great job with the planning." The enthused chairman spoke jubilantly over the microphone to his staff and volunteers of more than 200 people. "This tournament serves as the kickoff for the Olympics in the greatest city of our nation. People from all over the world will be here to enjoy our hospitality, so let's make it memorable, let us make it flawless," he said with passion. "We have some great new tools that we'll be unveiling to monitor the games."

Steve stood next to Tasha. His heart skipped a beat when she looked at him warmly.

At a distance, from behind a glass door, a creature, a servant of the theel, stood still, closely watching the special board on the center table. It had an uneasy feeling about Tasha, who stood next to the board. She was not all human and had some knight blood in her. What was she doing next to the board? Should it alert the theel? Unsure, it weighed its options. The tournament was only a day away, and it didn't want any problems with the board. Contrary to the theel's warnings, the humans appeared to want to use the board for the competition. The creature was so focused on the center board, it failed to notice five other identical game boards, neatly covered by sheets, at the top of each section.

At a faraway, secret location in the world of the rakshasas, the theel carefully spoke to its evil master. "Things are in place, great master," it said.

His master sat with his legs crisscrossed over a large block of ice. His red hair was fused into thick locks and was tied up. His frail, pale, severely wrinkled skin hung loosely over his bones. His deep meditation state made his body levitate eerily over the smooth ice.

"Oh, master." It spoke again after a long pause. "The door to your empire will be opened, and soon, my master will rule!"

"I sense the return of the Seventh Knight," said the master, his eyes still closed, words echoing from within.

"There is no Seventh Knight, oh great one. You have made sure that the Seventh Knight is dead. The knight of the Dark Forest has no blood of rakshasa in him, and he cannot become the Seventh Knight. I have scrutinized all worlds for any signs of the Seventh Knight, and none exists," the theel insisted.

"Don't be a fool, theel. I see the signs are there, and I can foretell the future. The rishis are deceitful and secretive. They are desperate to find the Seventh Knight." As the master raised his voice in anger, the ice rapidly melted.

"Master, the war game is about to be played, and the journey is about to begin. I shall bring you the secrets of Mayastella and the path to Kumba." It rubbed its skinny hands with ugly, long talons.

"The game is of no interest to me, theel; that's your job. Find the keeper's notebook before they get to Kumba first. Do not communicate with me from Mayastella under any circumstances. Now, leave."

"As you wish, my lord." The theel left the master's secret chamber.

Chapter 11

The Land of the White Gajaz

 t Navy Pier, a room was designated for Coach Turner and his students. Turner had gone over the basics with his students several times.

"No back-rank checkmates. Make sure to look at all your options before you touch a piece. Notate the whole game. Manage your clock. Do not walk around and watch other games. Raise your hand if you have an issue…" He went on and on.

Parents, coaches, and students of all shapes, sizes, and cultures were sprawled across the rooms, halls, and hallways. Thousands of players had qualified to play in the tournament from all over the world, and Navy Pier had undergone an amazing transformation. The games were staggered over three days to accommodate all the sessions.

In preparation for the Olympics, the Chicago Olympics committee had expanded Navy Pier's exhibition hall to twice its size. The mayor of Chicago saw a terrific opportunity to utilize the new facility to host the Chess Olympiad event—a newsworthy event as a precursor to the Summer Olympics. Seating areas, rooms, and offices were added to the upper level while maintaining the commercial essence and the festivities of Navy Pier.

Teams from all around the world had arrived. Teams from New York, Texas, California, and Illinois dominated the U.S. delegation. Players in different team apparel congregated with their coaches, who were yelling at the top of their voices in different languages. Parents were pulling their kids aside and giving last-minute coaching and special advice—some stern, some concerned, and some worried. Participants carried a nylon chess bag, a digital clock, a notation book, and a serious look.

The place was bustling like a colony of ants, and when someone yelled, "The pairings are up!", a swarm of kids, coaches, and parents gathered around the bulletin boards with their notepads.

Regardless of how big or important a chess tournament was, its commencement was always punctuated with chaos, especially when the player pairings were posted, stemming from confusion around who was playing who, erroneous team names, misstated player ratings, and wrong section entries. Despite the touted high technology, the Chess Olympiad was no exception.

"Do NOT put your hand on the pairing lists, please. The others can't see the listings," some parent shouted at a kid.

People bumped into each other and yelled in many languages.

"ALL pairings are posted online, and the list is being projected on screens at multiple locations, I repeat!" An irritated TD tried in vain to disperse the crowd.

But the crowd around the postings persisted for several minutes until, slowly, most people dispersed, except for a few parents, who kept studying the list, as if to memorize its contents from top to bottom.

In a dark corner of a small room, a group of Earth dwellers huddled around their potbellied leader. They had been instructed to accomplish a specific task—open the portal for their master to enter the world of illusion.

"You have been selected by our great master to play the game against the humans. Here is a new opportunity for you forgotten Earth dwellers to prove your worthiness and earn ranks among the rakshasas," said the potbelly, its mouth drooling with excitement. "Once the portal is open, the theel will lead us on our quest to find the secrets of Mayastella and the path to Kumba."

###

Aarjen and Kaia were nowhere to be seen, and Brendan paced back and forth nervously.

"You are playing someone who hasn't played much in tournaments," Coach Turner said.

"Should be an easy round," said Brendan, shrugging and concealing his anxiety.

After the short commencement speech by the governor and notable guests, the TD went over the rules like at any other tournament. The same rules the players had heard repeatedly: *You touch a piece, you move it! Raise your hand if you have any conflicts.*

The TD finished going over the rules and then introduced the chairman.

The heavyset chairman adjusted his tie and cleared his throat. "In halls A, B, and C," he said, sweeping his arm to indicate the rooms, "games played on Board Number One will be projected on the wall and analyzed by the world champions in real time. We will also be streaming all the top games simultaneously. Parents, please step outside so that Round One can begin."

Sidney's fingers trembled, not because she was already playing someone on Board One, but because her senses warned her of the presence of one of the creatures. It started when she shook hands with her opponent. She knew she was getting ready to play a different game, the one Kaia and Aarjen were preparing for. She hoped her team would be there to help her out.

"Can't wait for you to make the first move, kid," whispered a voice into her ear, sending shivers down her spine. "Your world is about to change!"

Sidney felt a gush of frigid air blow on her face, as though she'd stepped outside on a cold, wintry Chicago day. She adjusted her chair to get closer to the board.

"White to move," a voice from the board repeated.

Sidney felt the pieces and positioned her finger on the pawn in front of the king.

"E2, white pawn," announced the voice from the board.

When Sidney touched the pawn, she felt the board shake. Tightly gripping the pawn, she managed to push it to the e4 position.

"E4!"

Sidney—a descendant of Indra—had activated the curse, and wars of the worlds had officially begun. Darkness settled within and around her. Her acute sense of hearing could no longer detect the sporadic coughs of the children near her, or the clatter of the chess pieces being moved or captured by a hall full of players, or the chess clocks being constantly slapped to stop time at either side of the table. The floor beneath her feet rapidly drifted as she was about to be transported to Mayastella, the world of illusion. As Kaia had explained, she would be in two places at the same time—playing chess at Navy Pier and moving through a world of illusion.

Nora sat next to Turner and the other parents to watch Sidney's game being projected on a screen. Her section was the first to start, and they were all curious to see how the streaming and the projection system would work. Tasha and Steve had completed the setup, and a brilliant image of the animated chessboard appeared on the screen. The analyst eagerly stepped up to the screen to comment on the game.

"E4, standard open..." Before the analyst could finish his sentence, a wave rippled through the transmitted image.

The pawn on e4 transformed into a young boy who was running across a grassy meadow away from a distant storm. The skinny lad with shaggy, long red hair and freckled cheeks was dressed in a raggedy leather outfit with matching sandals and had a small knife hanging from his belt.

People burst out laughing.

Sidney continued hurtling through the vortex of the dark clouds. When she reached the bottom, the storm had cleared, and she felt herself lying on soft grass.

She felt the ground around her and carefully helped herself back onto her feet. She could feel the warmth of the sun but had no idea where she was or if anyone was with her.

"Kaia, are you here? Brendan?"

Sidney heard some muffled noise around her. With her arms stretched out, she turned around and called out for help again. She felt someone standing close to her, but she could tell it was not the mean Earth dweller opponent.

"Is it you, Brendan?" she asked nervously.

After a brief silence, she heard a rustling in the nearby bushes. Someone gently touched her forehead and placed a large flower on her palm. It was as soft as velvet, and its pleasant fragrance calmed her nerves.

As the smell of the flower intensified, Sidney began to see light around her. She squinted her eyes through the glare of light and saw a faint outline of someone in front of her. Everything was so bright, but Sidney could *see*! Tears welled up in her eyes, and the stranger gently wiped a rolling tear with his slender, long fingers.

Sidney's vision sharpened. A tall, skinny, red-haired lad in crude leather clothing knelt in front of her with a big smile across his freckled, friendly face. His intense green eyes peered into hers.

"Who are you?" she asked.

The young lad gently hugged Sidney, and without saying anything, he stood up and disappeared into the tall, thick bushes.

"There you are!" said a familiar voice. "I am sorry I am late, my dear." It was Kaia, who had followed Sidney through the portal.

Kaia hugged Sidney tightly. "I know the first journey into Mayastella would have been so scary for you." She surveyed the place for any strange movements.

Kaia lowered her voice. "The rakshasas have followed you to Mayastella."

Sidney rubbed her eyes as her vision reverted to being blurry and dull. "I have a headache."

"I have made arrangements to get us back to the tournament hall through the portal, dear," said Kaia, rubbing Sidney's temples gently. "We are going to switch your board with another section and trick the creatures. They still think they are following you into Mayastella."

When Tasha received the signal from Kaia, she punched some keys into her tablet-like device and slipped into the tournament hall. The lights on Sidney's board dimmed, and it uttered random words, distracting many players around Board Number One.

"Is everything all right here?" asked Tasha, who arrived at Board Number One before any of the TDs.

Both Sidney and her Earth dweller opponent remained fixated on their game.

"What's going on with the board?" asked Steve, worried about the chairman's reaction to its sudden malfunction this early in the tournament.

"It's just a glitch in the voice system," replied Tasha calmly. "I need to reboot the system. It will just take a moment."

"Reboot now? Won't it take time?" Steve was confused and panicking.

"I got it, Steve; don't worry. We'll swap this one out with a K-1 section board. Their game has not started, and they don't need the voice feature." Tasha remained calm.

Scrappy, who was tasked with guarding the board, protested to a TD, who had joined the commotion.

"The boards are programmable. The positions of the pieces of Sidney's game will be transferred to the other board from this tablet." Tasha handed the device to the TD, who gave a cursory read.

"Of course, you can take a picture with your phone or use the notation notebook to confirm the positions," she assured them.

By the time the TD fully comprehended the situation, Tasha's team had already completed the swap, and Sidney's game resumed with the board fully functioning with voice and all.

"Where did you guys get the other board from?" asked a baffled Scrappy, but the TD shrugged him off.

"I am going to get you all fired," shouted Scrappy as a couple of officials escorted him out.

In the K-1 scholastic section, Austin was not ready to play on Board Number One. He had never won on the top board, and his brother had told him that Board Number One brought him bad luck. But Austin was surprised to see the magic board.

"Hey, this is a cool chessboard," said his young opponent enthusiastically, examining the ornate board and engaging in cheerful conversation with Austin about video games.

Anticipating the opening of the portal through Austin's game, Aarjen timed his entry into Mayastella before Austin arrived. When Austin shook hands with his opponent, his journey into Mayastella began.

Austin's entry into the portal to Mayastella was exhilarating. He felt as though he was gliding over a luscious meadow under clear blue skies. When he landed softly and gathered himself, Aarjen was standing by his side, smiling at him.

"Did you have fun flying like a kite?" asked Aarjen.

"That was cool," said Austin. "Am I in a dream?"

"Yes, it is your dream," replied Aarjen.

Austin nodded and looked around.

"We are in the land of the white elephants, Austin." Aarjen knew Austin would be excited by the prospect of exploring such a land.

"Elephants? I love elephants. I saw elephants in the Brookfield Zoo." He skipped around Aarjen.

"Austin, we need to look for my friend Yan's magic notebook. Will you help me?" asked Aarjen, lowering himself to Austin's eye level.

"Oh, sure. I like magic. What does it look like?" said Austin, with unbridled enthusiasm.

"It has a lot of colorful pictures and maps. It also has secrets. But we need to find it before the bad creatures do."

Austin stopped and held on to Aarjen's hand. "Where is your friend?"

"I don't know." Aarjen shrugged. "Some say he's gone far away. Some say he'll only appear to those he can trust."

"Will he trust us?" asked Austin innocently, squinting his eyes from the glare of the sun.

"I think he'll trust you, Austin, but probably not me. I have had a falling-out with him." Aarjen looked around as they neared the top of the tiny hill.

"*Look!* Look over there, Aarjen!" Austin shouted with excitement, jumping up and down. "Tiny little elephants."

Austin finally had his *Jurassic Park* moment. The lush, rolling green meadow across the hill from where they stood was littered with white elephants, each not taller than a calf. They were boisterous, playfully pushing each other while grazing on the field. Many were shaking their heads and trunks back and forth and their tails sideways. The scene was comical for Austin, who laughed uncontrollably.

"These are the gajaz, the white elephants," said Aarjen, who was a bit surprised by the extent to which living things had proliferated across the outer sphere of Mayastella.

"Can I pet them?" asked Austin eagerly.

"Not yet," said Aarjen, observing the elephants cautiously. "We first need to find Yan's home."

Aarjen studied the area. Knights seldom visited Mayastella, a place of illusions and tricks. He scanned the vast terrain that varied significantly in each direction. To his right, it was bright and sunny, the land was green, lush with tall grass and rolling meadows. At a distance in front of him, the mighty blue mountains abruptly rose, clouds hugging its peaks. Behind him, the rolling meadows merged into a thick forest, covered with tall green trees, and to his left darkness engulfed the forest.

Austin held Aarjen's hand tightly as he hurriedly walked by his side.

As they got close to a herd of miniature elephants, one of them stopped shaking its head, stood still briefly, and watched them walk by. The little one had large brown eyes, a broad forehead, and its trunk was only as big as the baby elephant's trunk he had seen at the Brookfield Zoo. It was white with a pinkish belly. None of the elephants had any tusks, and they all looked like they were smiling.

"Can I touch you?" Austin stuck his hand out and stepped away from Aarjen.

The elephant paused and then marched toward Austin. Aarjen reacted by grabbing Austin and moving away from the elephant. Startled by Aarjen's sudden move, the little one hurried back to its herd.

"It's not time to pet the elephant," Aarjen warned.

"Why?" Austin pouted. "He's not going to hurt me; he's just a baby."

"He might be a little one, but look over there."

A mammoth, larger than any elephant Austin had ever imagined, emerged from behind the rocks and the trees in the distance. Its sharp and symmetrical tusks protruded several feet in front, neatly curving inward. Its eyes remained focused on the visitors. Its enormous trunk was raised in the air to smell and warn the intruders. It moved slowly toward Aarjen.

Realizing the contrast in size would be quite astonishing for his young companion, Aarjen hoisted Austin onto his shoulders and hurried away from the elephants to a secure spot up the hill.

"Look, Aarjen, more giants. Are they parents?"

Aarjen set Austin down and pulled a small circular device from his leather bag. He knelt on one knee and positioned the compass-like device away from him. Needles spun and finally settled, all converging in one direction.

"What is this?"

"This will help us locate Yan's house; it picks up a beacon—a signal from the keeper's home—and will point in the direction of his cabin. That way!" Aarjen faced the dark edges of the forest.

"It is so dark on that side. Why is he there?" Austin asked, straining his eyes to find a house in the distant darkness.

"The keeper lived at the edge of this land." Aarjen lifted Austin onto his shoulders again. "We have a bit of a distance to cover."

Aarjen spotted the dull stone cottage nestled among trees as tall as the California sequoia. A faint light flickered at one corner of the house, and a trickle of smoke danced above the chimney. Aarjen wasn't sure if the keeper was alive or where to find his notebook. That would be the task for the human kid he carried with him.

Through the light from the torch that Aarjen had created, they could see the hall inside the cottage was totally empty. Austin tightened his grip around Aarjen's neck when he saw the creeping shadow of the oversize wooden rocking chair in the corner.

A long metal key on a ring, loosely hanging on the wall, swayed a few times, making a scratchy noise as the gentle draft of the wind whistled through the broken windowpane. As the torchlight did a ballet with the breeze, so did the shadows.

"Austin, can you do me a favor?"

"I want to go home." Austin pressed his face against Aarjen's shoulder.

"Don't worry; this place is safe. Can you call out for Yan and see if he's here?"

"Yan?" Austin whispered.

"Louder," whispered back Aarjen. "If he's inside, he won't hear you. Maybe he's sleeping."

"Mr. Yan, are you there? We are here to see you." Austin's voice echoed through the hallway, but there was no response.

"Tell him you are a good friend."

"He doesn't know me," protested Austin.

"If we find him or his notebook, I am sure we can learn how to pet an elephant." Aarjen tried to convince Austin.

"Mr. Yan, are you here? We are your friends," Austin called out at the top of his voice, but there was still no response.

Aarjen lowered Austin as he moved from one room to another. The floor creaked under his thick boots. With his torch, he lit all the lamps and lanterns in the rooms and adjusted them to glow brightly.

There was a simple bed in one of the rooms with a pillow as wide as the bed and a neatly folded colorful quilt. In the corner of the room was a closet with neatly hanging robes. Across the room in a nook sat a heavy wooden desk against the wall with two drawers on either side. There were several old books on the desk.

Aarjen opened another door and led Austin through a wide corridor and into the kitchen, where a lamp was already lit. Several rows of shelves with jars, cans, and bags lined the wall. An old metal stove occupied one side of the room while a dark wooden table with large chairs occupied the other.

A stone elephant figurine, holding a lantern with its trunk, was on the center of the table, and Austin was instantly attracted to two shiny glass prisms floating inside the lantern. "Don't touch anything, Austin," cautioned Aarjen. "I am sure we can find something to eat," he added, taking stock of the variety of groceries on the shelves.

Aarjen pulled out some pots and pans and got busy while Austin explored the room. Inquisitive, he inched toward the stone elephant. Although Aarjen had his back turned to Austin, he was able to observe him through a mirror on the wall by the stove.

Austin carefully opened the door of the lantern and gently touched a prism. The prism wobbled and spun freely, its color changing from bright orange to a dazzling array of colors. Austin watched the colors swirl into a holographic image in awe.

"Mr. Trunks." Austin instantly recognized the image of his stuffed elephant riding a toy motorcycle, exactly the way he played with his toys.

The stuffed elephant transformed into a strange elephant-like person, wearing a thick leather jacket; large, rounded boots; cutoff gloves; and a brown leather helmet with dark vintage aviator goggles. His short trunk was curled into the front of his jacket. The rider raced down a dusty road across a meadow with lush green grass and waved at Austin.

"Hello, Mr. Trunks!" Austin waved back.

Yan's memory prisms have triggered the child's imagination, thought Aarjen.

"Here, let me show you something, Austin," Aarjen said, serving some spaghetti-like food and moving the elephant figurine in front of him. "Think of your parents." He gently flicked a floating prism, and made it spin rapidly like a top.

Austin's face lit up when he saw his parents with Coach Turner and the other parents outside the tournament hall. He was astonished to see himself playing chess on Board Number One. The game had just begun, and they were still very much on the opening game.

"It's just like a dream. When you wake up, you'll be with your mother. Now, watch your game. How do you think you are playing?" Aarjen asked.

"My bishop is stuck. I need to bring him out soon," He rubbed his eyes and yawned.

Aarjen hoped Brendan's arrival through the portal would be helpful for Austin. It was their game, their journey; he was merely their guide and guardian.

Chapter 12

Search for the Keeper

 hen Austin woke up, he found himself staring at Brendan sitting on a chair right next to him.

"I am still in the dream?" Austin sounded disappointed.

"Yeah," said Brendan, reaching over and ruffling Austin's hair.

"How did you get here?" Austin jumped out of his bed and looked outside the window.

"The portal...I used the pawn we found with the magic board, and it put me through the portal, just as Aarjen had suspected it would."

Austin caught a glimpse of a small white elephant tugging at a low branch of the tree outside the perimeter of the cottage.

"Look, Brendan, a little one."

But Brendan was already in the kitchen, talking to Aarjen.

Austin tried to open the window, but it wouldn't budge. He tiptoed to the heavy, large wooden front door, pulled the handle with all his weight, and managed to squeeze himself out.

When the elephant saw Austin, it walked away.

"Wait! I just want to pet you. Wait!" Austin shouted, chasing it.

The friendly little beast seemed to tease him by scuttling through the bushes, but paused for Austin to catch up. He got close enough to touch its tail, but only for the elephant to run away from him again and disappear into the thicket.

Austin found himself in front of a small hut, covered in vines with large leaves and bright purple flowers. Since the door to the hut was wide open, he guessed the playful critter might have gone inside the hut.

Austin cautiously entered the hut and peeked behind a bamboo divider. The sight of an old man sitting on the floor over several layers of animal skin stunned him at first. The frail man's robe flowed loosely from his head to feet. His hair was tied in a bun on top of his head. Most of his face was covered with a thick mustache and wild gray beard. His eyes were closed.

"Are you looking for the elephant?" the old man asked in a hoarse, shaky voice.

Austin stood, speechless.

"I can let you pet him."

"Are you...Yan?" Austin asked, somehow finding courage to speak to the man.

"Yes, I am. Now, come inside, my little friend," he said, opening his cat-like eyes. The old man's intimidating look belied his kind words.

"Here's your chance, kid; you can play with that elephant all you want. Listen to me!" The creepy old man's stern offer was cut short by chatter and noise from outside.

Austin was relieved to hear Brendan and Aarjen calling out his name.

The old man's face tightened. "Listen to me," he snapped. "I don't trust the knight. *Step inside now!*" His voice changed. His body began to rise, and his legs unfolded underneath him as he floated in the air.

"I found him!" Brendan hurriedly moved Austin away from the sinister figure.

"You need to leave the hut now with Austin," Aarjen instructed. Using his night vision, Aarjen saw the true form of the creature.

The creature prepared to fight. The body of the old man began to transform. His face shrank, his eyes enlarged, and his nose protruded like a stinger. Fangs appeared at either side of his lips, and his hair receded and disappeared. His body elongated, and his hands converted into long, skinny wings.

Aarjen shut the door behind him and spat at the creature.

Agitated, the creature lunged at Aarjen, but the knight front-flipped over the attacker and plunged his dagger into its neck. As the creature shrieked in pain, Aarjen directed a beam of light from the window through the spherical crystal on the dagger's hilt. Intense light flooded the bleeding creature, boiling the blood inside its body. Aarjen put the dagger back into his bag, adjusted his eyes to normal vision, and walked out of the hut.

"What was that?" asked Brendan.

"A tantric. They are soulless creatures from the plasma layer of the inner sphere. They hunt for souls. Some have escaped by stealing a soul from another life form—an innocent nijaz or even rakshasa that might have tried to cross the plasma."

"What is it doing here?" asked Brendan.

"It must have encountered Austin while searching for Yan's notebook. You guys are easy targets," said Aarjen. "Good you still have the crystal on you." He gave Brendan a pat on his shoulder. "We need to head to the Blackstone Cave, where there might be some clues on Yan's notebook."

###

Back in the tournament hall, Austin thought for a moment on how to free up his bishop. He then fianchettoed the bishop by moving it in front of his king. His other bishop was free as well. He had finally started developing his pieces.

###

The faint roaring noise Aarjen and the boys heard at a distance grew in intensity.

"Sounds like an airplane," said Brendan.

"It's Mr. Trunks." Austin eagerly looked down the hill.

"Mr. Trunks?" asked Brendan.

"Yes, look."

A peculiar and rugged motorcycle, custom-designed to resemble an elephant, roared down the dusty, narrow path to the bottom of the hill. Its copper-colored headlight was shaped to look like an elephant's head; its trunk curved over the front wheel, and two large elephant ears spanned across the handle bar. The bike was built with a streamlined gas tank, a saddle seat, a wide rear wheel, and was fitted with a large, bullet-shaped, one-wheeled sidecar.

The rider looked exactly the way Austin had seen him in the prism with a leather helmet and vintage aviator goggles.

Aarjen quickly established that the stranger was not a tantric.

The rider pulled up in front of them, and dismounted the elephant bike.

"Hi there, young man," the rider hollered, waving at Austin. He ignored Aarjen, who stood between him and the boys, and walked straight to Austin.

Aarjen clutched his dagger and tried to stop the rider from getting to the boys, but the rider effortlessly flipped over Aarjen and landed in front of Austin.

Austin giggled at the rider's acrobatics. He squinted, looking up through the glare of the sky at the towering rider, who awkwardly removed his helmet and goggles and revealed his face. He had a domed head, and his elephant ears, tucked tightly under his helmet, sprang out with a comical flap. He had a short, ribbed trunk for a nose, which he stretched like a spring from his chin to his chest.

"Hello, young man," bellowed the rider with a strong Indian-sounding accent. Once again, he evaded Aarjen by effortlessly flipping over him.

"Austin, my friend, I finally get to meet you. Welcome to my land of the elephants. I hear you are very good at solving puzzles. I really can use your help in finding my way. I have lost my friend, but since you saw me in my good friend's prisms yesterday, I reckon you can help me find him," said the rider, sticking out his stubby hand.

Austin shook the rider's massive hand, much to the frustration of Aarjen, who was unable to get anywhere close to the stranger.

"I am not good with puzzles, and I don't like them."

"But you'll help me, right? True friends are hard to come by, Austin. The good ones you can really count on in times of trouble. Is he your friend?" Mr. Trunks asked, briefly locking eyes with Brendan.

"That's Brendan, my really good friend," Austin responded proudly.

"Do you trust him?" The rider leaned toward Austin, lowered his voice and partially covered his mouth with his massive hand.

Austin nodded.

"Nice to meet you, young fella." The rider waved and saluted Brendan, who watched Aarjen struggle to stop the rider from approaching Austin.

Brendan was intrigued by Mr. Trunks.

"Hello!" Brendan waved back at Mr. Trunks.

Mr. Trunks pulled out a flat box the size of a deck of playing cards from his pocket. When he tapped the box, it quickly unfolded into a large sheet of parchment. The rider swept his cylindrical fingers across the paper and made multiple pop-up images of miniature landscapes with mountains, valleys, and rivers appear on the sheet.

"Who are you?" Aarjen demanded answers from the evasive intruder but the rider continued to ignore Aarjen.

Arjen reached into his bag and activated his disk with his finger. No one was fast enough to evade his target-seeking disk, and he was prepared to use it against the awkward and imaginary rider.

"Take a look at my… my…friend's notebook and tell me what you see," said the rider to Austin.

"Is this the notebook that you are looking for?" Brendan asked Aarjen, who was standing a few feet away, surprised by the sudden revelation of a notebook by the stranger. Aarjen moved closer to the rider.

"This notebook has lots of secrets, young man. I found this inside the Blackstone Cave, but don't tell anyone, okay?" said the rider without lowering his voice. The rider's trunk curved upward, as if smelling the air.

"Okay," said Austin, almost whispering. "What secrets?"

"Where did you say you found the notebook?" asked Aarjen, raising his voice.

He was shocked the rider could enter the protective Blackstone Cave and survive. No rakshasa or tantric could enter the cave that bore the seals of the seven rishis.

"Secrets only my friend could read. Or his close friends," the rider added, finally making eye contact with Aarjen but quickly turning away after shaking his head.

Austin and Brendan were fascinated by the magic notebook and the images it revealed.

"Hey…We are looking at our location in the notebook. It's like a giant GPS." Brendan crouched down and looked at the colorful cartoonish rendering of their surroundings on the map.

"Here, see this river?" Austin traced the image with his finger. "This is where we saw the elephants." He tilted his head to inspect the map from different angles. "And this," he continued, pointing to the mountain behind the rider, "is that mountain."

"I see. I see," said the rider. "I am in the right place then. Now, can you tell me where my friend's cottage is?" he asked.

"I can show you where Yan's cottage is." Austin thought for a minute. He then turned the map around. "There, behind this waterfall. This boulder looks like the top of a bishop."

"Bishop?" The rider raised his eyebrows.

"Yeah, the chess piece, Mr. Trunks." With a stick, Austin drew the shape of it on a patch of dirt on the ground.

"Um, you are right. We need to go to the cottage. I can take both of you," said the rider, folding the map back into the notebook with one touch. "Come on!"

"What about Aarjen?" asked Austin.

"Who?" The rider walked to his bike without turning back. He clapped his hands, and the bike extended to expose one more seat.

Aarjen pulled out his weapon. "That's enough," he said sternly. "With what I have in my hand, I can destroy the boy's imagination in seconds, and you'll be back to being a stuffed animal in no time. These boys are here to find my good friend Yan's notebook—the one you seem to have stolen."

The rider stopped by his motorcycle and scratched his head.

"Who did you call a friend? Yan?" The rider finally acknowledged Aarjen. "Aarjen! I have heard that name before," the rider continued. "You are here to take Yan's notebook," he said, pulling the notebook from his pocket and waving it at Aarjen. "Yan is dead! He died long ago. He was betrayed by his friends who were supposed to protect him. This notebook is mine now. You can try to kill me if you want."

The rider's response caught Aarjen by surprise. He needed to understand the connection between Yan and this rider. He wanted to get to the prisms in Yan's cottage quickly.

"If you want the boys to go with you, then I go with them," said Aarjen.

"Suit yourself. You'll have to squeeze into the sidecar."

The rider didn't wait for Aarjen to settle down. As soon as the boys were seated comfortably, he took off in full throttle, almost throwing the knight off the bike. When they reached the cottage, Aarjen hurried inside while the rider was busy demonstrating the features of his vehicle to the boys.

The rider scratched his head once again, pulled his trunk back and forth, and studied the surroundings. Inside, he went straight into the kitchen and opened several cabinets. He then rubbed his forehead and spoke to the boys. "I am getting flashbacks of the cottage, some attacks, painful memories, but I can't seem to put them all back together or remember any of the details," the rider said.

"Are you looking for something?" asked Brendan.

"What do you see?" he asked the boys, unfolding the notebook.

"I see a queen," said Brendan, peering at the evolving image of the beautiful woman dressed in a royal outfit.

"I am glad you are able to see what's in the notebook, young lad!" The rider patted Brendan on his shoulder with his heavy, non-human-looking hand.

Austin was on the other side of the parchment. "That's not a queen. It's a zombie."

"What are you looking at? All I see is a queen," said Brendan. When Austin moved the notebook, Brendan saw the image change to a zombie. "Ahhh…I see the illusion," said the rider. "Someone in two forms. See what else you can find on this page. I'll be back soon."

The rider set out to explore the perimeter of the cottage.

"I can explain," said Aarjen from behind, startling the rider.

"Ahh, it's the protector! I know who you are." The rider sounded upset. "Knights of the rishis are supposed to be loyal."

The rider suddenly charged at Aarjen with his hatchet drawn. Aarjen reacted swiftly by grasping on to a low branch and swinging behind the big frame of the rider. Aarjen thrust his knee into the back of the rider, just above the waist, simultaneously throwing one hand over the rider's massive chest and pulling him back. He let gravity do the rest. The rider fell backward instantly, but before he hit the ground, Aarjen kicked the large wooden chair under him and let the rider just sink into it. Unable to recover his balance, the rider was completely under Aarjen's control. Hearing the noise ensuing from the tussle, the boys dashed out of the cottage, but the sight of confrontation rendered them speechless.

"You are a coward." The rider's voice trembled and his breathing was heavy. "You abandoned Yan and saved your own life," he accused.

"You are a bit confused and angry, and you have every right to be so," Aarjen said without relaxing his grip on the rider. "I am going to show you what happened to Yan. The whole truth."

"I know the truth!" the rider protested.

"What you see in that notebook only makes you recall some of your lost memories." Aarjen relaxed his arm and allowed the rider to calm down. "Yan's memory prisms and the information from his notebook will help." Aarjen held the prisms close to the rider.

The rider was upset but seemed to calm down.

"I don't have all the answers, but we can join forces to solve this mystery," Aarjen suggested sincerely. "Your help will save the world. Do you *want* to learn the truth?" He allowed the rider to settle back into the chair.

The rider's restless eyes were constantly shifting. He eyed his hatchet, which Aarjen had embedded into a nearby tree trunk, out of his reach. After a momentary awkward silence, without waiting for the rider's consent, Aarjen let the prisms float in front of the rider.

"Yan carried these with him everywhere. It captured everything he saw," Aarjen said, giving the prisms a light flick.

The rider reacted to the spinning prisms by moving his head back.

"The kid activated them yesterday," Aarjen continued. "This will give us a full account of what happened to Yan." Aarjen made the reluctant rider watch the images from the prisms as he narrated the events.

"When Maya created Mayastella for Indra, she wanted a trusted keeper for the world of illusion who would honor the rules and integrity of the journey and the quest inside Mayastella so a fair game was played. A keeper with the power to protect Mayastella from outside elements but also be true to its internal secrets. To limit access to this world, two gateways were created—one to enter and one to exit. Only the keeper would have keys that allowed anyone to enter or exit Mayastella."

"Oh, please, I know the keeper's story better than you do," protested the rider but Aarjen paid no heed.

"Maya searched the worlds for someone skilled at illusion, like herself, to serve as the keeper of Indra's new world. She sought the help of the kings, but they could never come to an agreement. Finally, with the help of Vyas, Maya created a shapeshifter with the strength of Indra's elephant, Hiravat, and the wizardry of a sage."

"Yan was a master of disguise and illusion," the rider said. "He was the guardian and the holder of the keys to a new world full of tricks, but what's the point? I lost my friend because no one saved his life," he said, his eyes welling up with tears.

"After the attack on Bhrigu's ashram by the rakshasas, and to prevent Bhrigu's curse from taking effect, Chadurang was banned, but we heard that the theel was trying to infiltrate Mayastella with someone's help—someone with the powers of a rishi but deceitful and evil," Aarjen said. "I rushed to Mayastella to warn Yan, but he was severely injured and was hiding in the protected Blackstone Cave."

The rider watched images from inside the dimly lit Blackstone Cave, where Yan was resting on a makeshift bed of dried ferns and vines. Aarjen emerged from the shadows and tended to Yan's injuries, comforting the keeper.

"I was ambushed by the theel," said the keeper.

"You did good by coming to this cave, Yan," Aarjen said. "The Blackstone Cave bears the seal of the seven rishis, and it was created as a safe house for you and other players. As long as you stay here, you are under the protection of the seal. In the meantime, I'll get help from the rishis."

Flashes of bright light suddenly erupted inside the cave.

"Come out of hiding, you coward," the theel shouted from the perimeter of the cave.

Yan clutched his hatchet. "Let's take that hideous thing down, Aarjen. Together, we can get rid of these creatures once and for all," Yan said, finding the strength to pull himself up.

"Listen," said Aarjen. "The theel is working with an evil force—something stronger than us. This is a trap to draw you out," Aarjen warned his friend and pleaded with him not to leave the cave.

"No, no, no." Yan shook his head. "The theel is not very smart, and I'll teach it a lesson by severing its stinger," Yan said, sharpening his hatchet on a shiny black stone.

"Someone is trying to learn the secrets of Mayastella. They are luring you to step out of your protection so they can seize your notebook and, more importantly, your memories. Do not leave this cave!"

"My job is to protect Mayastella from enemies and invaders. I'll guard my notebook with my life," said Yan, clenching his teeth and wielding his hatchet. "My notebook is of no use without my memory. I'll keep the notebook."

Before Aarjen could interrupt, Yan removed two tiny crystal prisms from a black pouch and pressed it against either side of his temples. He closed his eyes and chanted the names of the rishis. A luminous steam of energy connected the prisms to the seal of the rishis at the center of the room. The light steadily dimmed and extinguished.

When the images from the floating prisms disappeared, the rider turned his inquisitive gaze at Aarjen.

Aarjen let out a sigh. "Yan tossed the pouch with the prisms by the seal of the rishis, and before I could retrieve it, he rushed out of the Blackstone Cave."

"What happened to Yan?" asked the rider with a fierce frown.

"It was a bloody scene outside, dead creatures everywhere, but no sign of Yan or the theel or its severed tail," said Aarjen. "I retrieved Yan's hatchet, lodged between rocks several feet below at the edge of the cliff, and left it inside the cave. I returned the prisms to Maya, and now, you show up with his hatchet and his notebook. How's that possible?"

"Because I am Yan's true friend."

"No. Only Yan can use his notebook or wield his hatchet," Aarjen said.

The rider's eyes blinked rapidly. "Are you telling me I am Yan?" he asked.

"*You are Yan,*" Aarjen said. "The kid has kindled the memory prisms. You stem from his imagination."

"Am I just an illusion…not real?"

"You are very real." Aarjen put the prisms away.

"How do I know you are who you say you are, or I am what you say I am?" he asked Aarjen.

Aarjen opted to incorporate an element of drama. He felt producing proof of his identity warranted a bit of theatrics. He pulled his silver dagger from its sheath, and swept it across at rider's chest.

The rider, who had already established his footing, exerted all his weight on the chair and broke it. As he fell to the ground, he pulled Aarjen down with him with his elongated trunk and effortlessly flung him into the nearby bushes. The bulky but agile rider then sprang upright and charged at the fallen knight. With a swift, continuous motion, he yanked the hatchet from the tree and brought it down to strike Aarjen. The boys, shocked by the outbreak, screamed out loud. The edge of the blade abruptly stopped, barely touching Aarjen's neck. Yan stood still, staring at the seals of the rishis engraved in the blade of Aarjen's dagger. Aarjen let go of the dagger he tightly clutched close to his chest. His dangerous test was successful in revealing that the rider was indeed Yan, a trusted friend of Aarjen's, one who would never strike the bearer of the seals of the rishis.

"So, I am Yan!" the rider said, lending his hand to the knight.

"Great keeper of Mayastella." Aarjen tossed the prisms to the rider.

"So, what's next?"

"We have to win this war against evil. But first, we need to win the battle against the rise of Kumba," said Aarjen after they gathered inside the cottage.

"Kumba…Kumba? I remember the great Kumba," the rider said, tugging his trunk. "My instincts tell me that Kumba is not evil." Yan wagged his stubby finger rapidly.

"The kids…Look, they are happy now," said Aarjen.

"I am alive because of you, little guy." Yan gently patted Austin's head. "Mr. Trunks will always be there when you need him."

He opened his cupboard, his eyes shifting across the neatly organized shelves from bottom to top. He then reached for a square wooden box in the corner of the middle shelf.

"Did you get to play with one of my tiny elephant friends?" Yan asked Austin.

"They run away from me," Austin said, stamping his feet on the ground.

"Hmm…Now, tell me, do you know which chess piece represents an elephant?" Yan enthusiastically raised his short trunk in the air.

Austin giggled. "There are no ele—" Austin stopped mid-sentence; his eyes moved left to right, as though examining the chess pieces in his mind. "The rook," he said with an affirmative nod and a snap of his fingers. "It looks like an elephant's leg when you put it upside-down." He inverted an imaginary rook in the air with his tiny hand.

"Think again," said Yan, lightly placing his stubby index finger on Austin's temple.

"Is it the bishop?" Austin, jumped.

"You got it, son. If you notice…" Yan pulled a shiny white chess piece from the wooden box and placed it on the side of his mouth under his trunk.

Austin laughed.

"Shaped like the tusk," said Brendan.

"You look silly with a tiny tusk." Austin chuckled.

"Here." Yan tied a thin leather string around the piece and put it around Austin's neck. "This is a special gift, made of stone from the Blackstone Cave. This will not only protect you from danger, it will also allow you to contact me anytime."

Austin lifted the piece to his eye level and rotated it slowly. He rubbed the piece a few times and squinted at the strange engravings. He then looked at Brendan and shrugged his shoulders, as though uncertain on what to make out of the gift.

"Thanks," he muttered and let it drop around his neck.

"But here's the fun part, kiddo." Yan cleared his throat. "You can now play with the elephants. My friends are your friends."

Austin's eyes lit up. "Even the big ones?" He gestured with his hands stretched up above his head.

"Even the big ones."

"I have never touched an elephant before," Brendan yelled excitedly, running his hand over the rough surface of the small elephant he was riding.

As the little one picked up pace, he tightly gripped the thick folding on its pink ears as his legs dangled on either side of the elephant's bulging belly.

"Whoa…Whoa!" His nervous screams turned into boisterous laughter.

Austin and Brendan raced each other on their elephants, and when they were not riding them, the little mischievous creatures played with them like puppies.

Austin's eyes shifted across the chessboard from the center to the corners as he studied the position of all the pieces carefully. He had traded off one of his knights for his opponent's knight. His black square bishop still sat in front of his king, flanked between two pawns. His white square bishop was dangerously lined across his opponent's king, pinning the knight to the king. He was up by a pawn, and his coach liked what he saw.

"Austin's playing well," Turner said to Austin's mother cheerfully.

"Do you remember what happened to Queen Suhela?" Aarjen asked Yan.

"Kumba's queen? Um…" Yan closed his eyes and drummed his fingers sequentially on the table, trying to connect a series of forgotten events. "She was poisoned…Er, she poisoned herself, trying to save her husband." Yan thought for a moment, pushed his chair back, stood up abruptly, and paced back and forth. "The boys reminded me of something when they saw two different versions of the queen in my notebook. At the request of Maya, I opened the gate for the sick queen." Yan raised his eyebrows, and glanced up to his left, as if recalling an image in his mind. "She was so beautiful, but the poison was getting to her. Maya wanted her to be with Kumba, so that the guardians of Kumba could help her recover. I arranged for a chariot with her warrior escorts to take Suhela to the inner sphere."

"Someone abducted her," said Aarjen.

"Impossible! No one can enter Mayastella and open the gateway without my knowledge or my secrets." Yan banged his fists on the table, rattling all its contents.

"Unless it is someone as powerful as a rishi," said Aarjen. "Someone who can conjure up the theel and the tantrics. That's why they were able to attack you at the Blackstone Cave, Yan. Their goal is to kidnap or kill the queen and infiltrate Mayastella."

"But who could that be? Our rishis raised Suhela. They would never put her in harm's way." Yan shook his head vigorously as his trunk wobbled like a spring.

"Is she dead?" asked Brendan.

"No. Maya can feel her presence," said Aarjen.

"We need to find the keys to open the gateways," Yan said, hurriedly opening and closing several wooden boxes and rummaging through his cupboard. "Two gateways will open simultaneously; only one will take you to where you want to go, and the other one is a trap, so you have to choose the right one," he warned.

"Where are the keys?" asked Brendan.

Yan tapped his notebook, closed his eyes, and chanted some words. Strange letters appeared on the unfolded sheet of paper.

"Words only one Chadurang player can read…A player I can trust," said Yan.

"I can read it," said Austin gleefully, tilting his head and attempting to read the words that formed on the page.

"The…The sec-secret lies in the belly," read Austin with difficulty.

Yan set the notebook on the table, giving room for Austin.

Austin read falteringly.

The secret lies in the belly

Of the great white Ely.

It is a bit tricky,

And you have to be lucky

If you are trying to find who.

The key to your success is

Not one, but two.

Yan repeated the words with his eyes closed.

"Elyanna, sister of Hiravat?" asked Aarjen.

"Yes, Ely is my favorite, also the biggest. Hmm, what's under her belly?" He raised his elongated trunk above his head and let out a series of muffled trumpets. Within minutes, the ground trembled. A grayish-white elephant as big as a truck, its sail-like ears fanning back and forth, generating a vortex of pulsating air, slowly walked toward them. The boys stood in silence.

"That's my girl," said Yan, as Ely stood inches from his raised hand, gently making contact with the tip of her trunk.

"Meet my friends, Ely." He encouraged the awestruck boys to interact with her. Ely slowly crouched down to let them climb onto her back.

As Yan, Aarjen, and Brendan focused on understanding the clue, a tiny playful elephant tugged at Austin's shirt from the back. Austin reacted by reaching out to its trunk, but the critter teasingly turned away and gently brushed Austin with its tail. Austin latched on to its tail and skidded behind the scurrying creature.

"Stop, stop. I want to ride you."

The elephant stopped abruptly. Austin dashed to grab its ear, but in his haste, he got tangled in a thick shrub.

"Ugh...Let me go, you stupid branch!" Austin tried to wiggle away from the spring-like branches, but in the process, the leather string with the bishop talisman snapped and hurtled into the bushes.

"Oh no," he wailed, running in the direction of where Yan's gift had presumably dislodged.

"Ow!" Austin pulled his hand back from the deceptively benign-looking bushes, decked with brightly colored flowers and thorns.

The elephant had abandoned him and disappeared. The place was eerily quiet with no sight of Brendan, Yan, or Aarjen. He felt a lump in his throat, and his eyes welled up with tears.

"Brendan...Brendan...Can you help me?" he cried out at the top of his voice, but all he heard was the echo of him shouting.

Austin started to run but tripped and tumbled down the slope. Someone stopped him and prevented him from rolling farther down the steep incline.

Austin was shaken by the ordeal. He began to sob again.

A red-haired boy with a freckled face and large expressionless, deep green eyes smiled at Austin but his friendliness did not mitigate Austin's anxiety. Tears streamed down his cheeks.

"Brendan," Austin stuttered fearfully, even though he wanted to shout.

"You?" the stranger spoke to Austin. "You? Um, yours?" he corrected, offering Austin his bishop talisman with the broken string. He wiped Austin's tears.

Austin nodded hesitantly and took the bishop in a hurry.

He looked behind him and realized the stranger had just prevented him from plunging into the deep ravine. Austin took a deep breath. "Thank you." His voice trembled with fear.

"A-A-Austin?" the stranger asked, gently poking Austin's chest.

Austin nodded. "What's your name?" he asked, mustering enough courage.

"Run-Nier," the stranger replied, patting himself on his chest.

"*Runner?*" Austin asked.

"*Runner?* Run-Nier." His already-big eyes widened. "Frrieeend! I help A-A-Austin." He gestured with enthusiasm, extending his hand once more.

"Can you take me to Brendan?" Austin pleaded. "We need to find a key in the belly of Ely; otherwise, we'll be in trouble with the creatures."

"Key…Ely…Belly. Runner show Austin Eeelly," the boy said with a drawn-out accent.

He took Austin by his hand and led him to a pond close by.

"Look," he said, pointing to the water. "Ely."

"Ely is in the water?" asked Austin, perplexed.

"No." Run-Nier shook his head. "Look inside water. Big white elephant," he said.

Austin looked at the water, confused, but when he was about to look away, he saw it in the reflection.

"I see it now!" He jumped.

"The mountain look like Ely," said Runner, his eyes shining with excitement.

The pond reflected the mountain range at a distance in front of them. A mountain in the shape of a great white elephant with its knees bent, ears spanning wide, and the big trunk stretching in front for miles. It reminded Austin of Ely, Yan's great white elephant, when she crouched down to let them climb upon her back.

Austin looked up to see the mountain, but didn't see the shape he saw in its reflection. He went back and forth, looking at the reflection and then at the mountain. "I see the legs, the belly, the trunk, and the ears but all upside-down."

Run-Nier directed Austin's attention to the center of the reflection of the mountain that looked like Yan's majestic elephant. "A big cave inside the belly of Ely." Austin's heart raced when he heard Brendan calling out to him. "Brendan, I am here," Austin said, wildly waving his arms and jumping. "I found Ely! I found the belly!" Austin shouted at the top of his voice.

"Hey, you were not supposed to wander off. What are you doing here?" Brendan pulled Austin by his shoulders.

"Look, Runner…um…Run-Nier showed me Ely. He helped me solve the puzzle. I know what the clue means. Look inside the water," Austin continued, pulling away from Brendan, dropping to his knees, and frantically gesturing at the water.

"Who is Run-Nier?" Aarjen quickly surveyed the surroundings.

Austin looked for Run-Nier, but the boy was nowhere to be found.

Yan, who had joined them, quietly dropped down to the ground next to Austin and studied the reflection. He immediately understood what the clue meant.

"I know where the key is," Yan said, smiling. He patted Austin's shoulder gently.

"How come I can't see the shape of the elephant without looking at the reflection?" asked Brendan.

"The pond's water has special algae. It filters the blue and green colors and only reflects the unique white haze of Mount Ely," explained Yan. "The caves of Mount Ely—it is a beautiful place with splendid crystalline formations. We'll find the key inside the cave. Clever clue!" Yan was pleased with himself. "We'll ride to the mouth of the cave on my bike, but it's different inside."

Yan lit a torch and led his young companions inside the cave with abundant caution. The boys strained their eyes to see beyond a few feet around them, their steps faltering on uneven ground. The odor and the warm, damp air reminded Brendan of his trips to his grandfather's farm in Springfield, Missouri, during the summer. "Be careful!" Yan grabbed Brendan's arm as Brendan slipped. Water splattered under his feet.

"How far do we have to go?" Brendan took a deep breath. "I feel a bit claustrophobic."

"We have to get to the core, deep inside the mountain. I promise, the journey will get better." Yan halted in front of them and fanned his elephant ears out. "There. I can hear it. Listen!"

The boys didn't hear anything, except the crackle of the fire from the torch and their heavy breathing.

"The acoustics are better as we get closer." Yan continued to press on, bending and ducking his large domed head from the low ceiling.

It felt like the walls were closing in for Brendan, but Yan's towering presence and strength made him feel much more secure inside the cave.

"I can hear water flowing," said Brendan, paying attention. "Sounds like a stream." And before Yan responded, Brendan saw light at the end of their pathway. "Oh, are we getting out of the cave?" Brendan was surprised.

"No, we are deep inside the cave," said Yan.

The kids had to first shield their eyes with their hands from exposure to sudden brightness, but when they let their eyes adjust to the bright light, the view was simply breathtaking.

Although Brendan had been to a few caves across America, this was different—almost artificial, as though they were in a large studio setting. Twinkly, bright green and blue colorful LED-like lights were sprinkled all around them as they journeyed deeper into the cave.

The ceiling tapered upward, but the dome seemed to blend into the endless haze. Translucent mineral columns of merged stalactites and stalagmites spanned the ceiling and floor. A winding stream with clear water flowed calmly through the endless cave.

"This place is beautiful!" Brendan paused to appreciate the beauty of the cave.

"That stone looks like an elephant." Austin was looking at a large mineral deposit in front of them.

He studied all the formations closely—every mineral deposit created by the dripping water and the running stream, which had an inherent swirl and gave it distinct shape and color that invariably resembled some form of an elephant.

"Ahh, the beautiful cave of crystals, where you can let your imagination run wild," said Yan. "Our journey to the heart of the cave begins here."

"Do you mean the belly, Mr. Trunks?" Austin chuckled.

"Clever!"

"So, how do we get there? Follow the stream? Dibs on the front seat of the canoe ride," Brendan joked.

"Hmm, if that's how you want to go, close your eyes and imagine a way to get there, and we will…"

A large canoe gently floated down the stream.

"That was quick," said Yan. "You like canoes?"

"I like canoes," said Austin.

"Let's do it," said Yan, "but just be careful what you wish for in this cave. It could get a bit rough if you let your imagination go wild." Yan let out a burst of laughter.

Food was the second thing the boys imagined, and they were well served. The boys even got a chance to swim in the warm, shallow water that glimmered under the light of the crystals. Finally, they settled down into the comfy seats of the canoe and silently drifted into the deeper confines of the cave. Darkness crept up as fewer light-emitting crystals sporadically illuminated the cave, giving the sense of floating on a tranquil stream under the starry sky of a silent night.

A gut-wrenching shriek rudely jolted Brendan and Austin just as they were succumbing to drowsiness. A loud thud and a flash of fire ensued. Brendan rolled out of his seat, feeling the heat from the fire. Austin began to cry.

"You soulless, good-for-nothing creature!" shouted Yan, jumping out of the canoe.

He rushed toward the fire-spitting tantric, curled at the base of a charred mineral column. Fire spewed from the creature, which looked like a small dragon, about half the size of Yan.

Undaunted by the shooting flame, Yan brandished his hatchet and attacked the creature.

Realizing that it had provoked a formidable foe, the dragon-like creature morphed into a frail, scaly vampire kateri, like the one the kids had encountered in the chess club storage room. Its large eyes remained fixated on Yan. When the keeper raised his hatchet to strike, it shouted strange words. Yan yelled back, kicked the creature away from him, and watched it scramble up the charred column. When it reached a certain safe height, it assumed its original dragon-like form and flew into the darkness.

Yan returned to the canoe, mumbling and cursing, but when he saw the agitated boys, he faked a smile and hugged them. "It is a nuisance. I had to put the fear in it."

"Were you going to kill it?" asked Brendan.

"According to the rules of Mayastella, you never kill anything in the cave of Mount Ely," responded Yan.

"Why?" asked Brendan.

"This cave brings goodness in all. If you spare the life of your enemy, in return, they could help you later."

"But that was a tantric. Aren't they dangerous?" asked Brendan.

"Yes...It didn't think I'd see through its true form. These are mean, soulless creatures, and I doubt if this one will ever repay our kindness and help us, but there are no rules for kindness. It just needs to come from your heart without seeking anything in return. These noble values make us better than the soulless ones."

"It was scared of you," Austin said.

"I made sure that it won't bother us anymore." After that, Yan remained silent for a while, holding Austin, who sat by his side. The cave was dark, except for the tiny guiding light of the canoe.

"There it is," said Yan, suddenly standing, and his weight rocked the canoe.

"My key," he said, peering at the distant star-like gleam.

"I see the light, but I don't see any key," said Brendan, straining his eyes and holding on to the rocking canoe.

"The light *is* the key, Brendan! The intensity of the light in the mineral crystal indicates how much energy it has, and as long as the crystal has energy, it will open the gateways. When the light fades away, the gates will close," Yan explained.

"Where does this crystal get its energy from?" asked Brendan.

"From the keeper, uh...From me," Yan said. "The keeper is a source of energy! If the key is stolen, the light will fade quickly, and it will not open the gateway."

The crystal—a seven-sided object about the size of a golf ball—floated in the narrow space between the sharp vertices of a stalactite and a stalagmite, just inches away from touching each other. Yan allowed the stone to float over his palm. "This key will transport us back home quickly when I touch it," he said, but even as he spoke, its light began to fade.

"Quick, back into the canoe," Yan said hastily, carefully holding on to the crystal and awkwardly leading the way.

He squeezed the crystal between his two chubby palms, making the dim light burst into an instant flash, followed by utter darkness.

When Brendan peered through the obscurity, he saw a faint, blurry light, far away from them.

"Are we still moving?" he asked.

The light got brighter as all the lanterns in the cottage were lit. Yan and Aarjen were talking to each other. Aarjen's presence comforted Brendan. Yan had used the key to take them to the cottage.

"Without their help, I would not have found the key, Aarjen," Yan said. "They are smart and courageous. I used the energy from the crystal to get us back to the cottage."

"We need to find out how to recharge and open the gates. Perhaps the kids can help us solve the second part of the puzzle."

Aarjen read the verses from the notebook.

It is a bit tricky,

And you have to be lucky

If you are trying to find who.

The key to your success is

Not one, but two.

"I think we were lucky in many ways," said Aarjen. "First, Austin found the pond, which led us to Mount Ely. Second, we found the key with just enough energy to get us back."

"Who or what am I talking about—the key to the success is not one, but two?" Yan asked, tugging at his trunk.

"The notebook showed us two queens, and in chess, we can have two queens when we promote a pawn," reasoned Brendan. "Maybe there are two queens here too," Brendan said.

"It could be *two* gateways. You said it before—both the gateways have to be open. Only one is the right one, and the other is a trap," said Aarjen.

"The forest might have some answers for me," said Yan.

"I'll go with you. The boys will be safe here in the cottage," Aarjen told him.

"Uh-uh." Brendan shook his head. "Take us with you."

"Austin has the talisman, and I'll leave you with my prisms. We will be able to reach you in a blink of an eye," Aarjen assured him.

"Aarjen is right. You'll be safe here. Just look outside. Ely and her friends are guarding the perimeter. Not a thing can enter this place," Yan added.

Brendan sat by the window and watched Ely with awe while Austin lay on the bed, hugging a pillow bigger than him. Within minutes, Austin fell asleep. Austin didn't want to wake up, but someone was persistently shaking him, much to his annoyance. "Go away, Jack," he moaned, but when he partially opened his eyes, a friendly face with large green eyes was smiling at him.

"It's me!" said Run-Nier. "You look for two?"

Austin covered his face and turned away but rolled back immediately, shocked to see the lad who had helped him before.

"Runner? What are you—"

Run-Nier placed his long, slender finger on Austin's lips. "Shh!"

"What…What are you doing here?" Austin asked, lowering his voice.

"Two people…Use key…Run-Nier show you."

Austin understood Run-Nier was referring to the clue. "Do you know who?"

Run-Nier nodded. He unknotted the strings of a tiny black pouch hanging on his belt and emptied its contents onto his palm. A spectrum of colors dazzled across their faces from two tiny prisms that had rolled out.

"Hey, this is Yan's memory thingy," Austin said, reaching out.

"Two people…When moon high today, Yan open gateways with key from Ely, but need these prisms."

"Which two people?" he asked.

Run-Nier tugged Austin by his hand and gestured to him to follow.

Yan and Aarjen had returned. They were in the kitchen, examining the lifeless key.

Run-Nier lowered his hand to Austin's eye level and angled the prisms, bringing Yan into view.

"Yan is two people in one."

Austin tilted his head forward and peered through the prism, unsure of what he was looking at. When Runner tilted his hand slightly, he saw the distorted image of Yan diverge into someone else he hadn't seen before.

"This is Yan, the keeper," said Run-Nier. "When moon high in night, the gateway open when Yan, the keeper, and Yan, the rider, become one."

Not one, but two.

As Austin observed the images of Yan in the prisms, it occurred to him that Yan was indeed two people who held the key to the gateways. "I think we found it," he shouted, clapping his hands and jumping on the bed.

Yan reacted to the noise and rushed from the kitchen to his bedroom. "Austin, you are awake!"

"We figured it out," said Austin. "Runner just told me we need two people—Yan, the keeper, and Yan, the rider."

"Who's this Runner? Another one of your imaginary friends?" asked Brendan. But Runner had already disappeared.

"Arrrrgh," Austin said, frustrated. He searched for the prisms, but somehow, they had magically found their way to the kitchen.

"Look at Mr. Trunks through those. You'll see two Yans—the keeper and the rider!" Austin shook his head and searched for words to better explain. Where was Runner when he needed him?

"How did these get here?" Aarjen asked, exchanging a quick glance with Yan. He looked through the prisms at Yan, the rider. "Ahh, the kid's correct," he said, looking through both the prisms. "Only when the powers of the keeper and the rider are combined will the crystal work. You need to merge the two forms."

"We can make it happen with the light from the full moon of Mayastella," Yan said, flipping through his notebook. "When the prisms are combined under the light of the moon, I can energize the crystal and open both the gateways."

"And with help from all of you we can save the queen," said Aarjen with resolve.

"Young lad, you not only helped us find the pathway, but you also helped me find myself. Thank you for that," Yan said to Austin. "Also, remember this secret in chess—long-range bishops are very strong. People often don't see the attack of the sneaky bishop, so use your bishops wisely."

"When can I see you again, Mr. Trunks?" Austin asked, suddenly overwhelmed by emotion.

"I'll always be there when you want to see me, Austin; just touch that chess piece around your neck and think of me."

###

Austin found himself on Board Number One with abundant time on the clock, surrounded by other kids studying his game. It felt like he had woken up from a wild dream. It was his opponent's turn to move, and after considerable deliberation, the kid moved his queen to exactly where Austin had hoped he would. He had failed to notice the bishop that was among the pawns on the other side of the board, in front of Austin's king.

With one swift move, Austin's bishop moved across the board and captured his opponent's queen. Holding back his tears, the kid resigned.

"Good game," said Austin, shaking his opponent's hand.

Austin ran to his family, who stood, waiting among the sea of parents, and gave his mom a big hug.

"You won't believe this, Mommy. Mr. Trunks really helped me with my bishop game. That boy didn't see my bishop and hung his queen."

"I know, dear," said his mother. "That move with your bishop was simply awesome." She patted his head gently.

Chapter 13

The Gateways

Darkness surrounded the gateways to the inner sphere. Brendan felt alone without Austin, but was glad that Austin was back where he belonged. The gateway was nothing like what he had imagined. It was just a dark pathway with a square tollbooth-like building.

"Is that the gateway?" Brendan sounded disappointed. He strained his eyes to get a glimpse of the blurry silhouette of the structure engulfed in darkness.

"The gateway is simply a pathway for one to choose," clarified Yan.

"I thought we were supposed to have two of them, an entrance and an exit…But there is only…"

"Is that all you see…Only one? Are you sure?" Yan was emphatic.

Brendan peered through the darkness again. Something shimmered several feet away from the stone building. "Aha, I see another one. It looks exactly the same."

"Keep looking," said Yan. "Um…About now, three, two, one," he counted.

And there it was. Anywhere he looked, the same pathway appeared.

"Oh my God, this is making me dizzy. I...I..." His voice trailed off. "How will you know which one to take?" Brendan was bewildered.

"All gateways come in pairs, the day and night, the good and evil, the yin and yang, a pair of mirror images, or the strands of DNA. They are complementary to each other, and the only one who has the power to find the correct one is the keeper."

"When the moon is high, I'll use the key to find the correct pair of gateways," said Yan.

A shadowy figure stealthily approached them, sending a chill down Brendan's spine.

"Look over there," he whispered to Aarjen.

"What do you think it is?" Aarjen whispered back, reaching for his sword.

Brendan shrugged his shoulders, sensing Aarjen's deliberate attempt to frighten him.

"More friends, maybe?" Yan nudged Brendan.

From the shadows emerged Kaia with Sidney, Ro, and Max.

Brendan let out a sigh of relief and ran to greet Kaia and his friends.

Kaia was ecstatic to see Yan. Teary-eyed, she greeted the keeper with a bear hug and kissed him gently on his cheek. "I just cannot get over the resemblance you bear to Austin's toy, Mr. Trunks," she said, wiping her tears, laughing and holding Yan's arm. Brendan cheerfully recounted his adventures in Mayastella—how they had met Yan, the rider; played with elephants; fought tantrics; explored a cave where imagination turned into reality; and how Austin helped unlock secrets from Yan's notebook.

"Aarjen and I have to take care of a few things before the creatures arrive," said Yan. "We'll see you soon on the other side," he said and slipped into the silent night with Aarjen.

"The pawns you found hidden inside the board have been very helpful in transporting more than one person at a time. Good thinking," said Kaia, complimenting Brendan for finding the hidden pawns from the Chadurang board.

###

The wait inside the tiny, dark, cold stone building dragged on.

"What are we waiting for?" Brendan asked Kaia impatiently.

"Shh…They are here," she whispered, gripping her sword. Like Aarjen, she could smell them a mile away. "These creatures feel cheated and are angry. They will try to beat us to the gateway to get to the queen first."

A shockingly loud blast from a war horn pierced through the darkness.

Sidney was the most affected by the sudden noise. She screamed and buried her face into Kaia's arm, plugging her ears with her fingers to mute the unpleasant noise.

Brendan, instinctively curious, jumped up and tried to peek through a hole in the wall.

"I don't see anyone. Will they know we are here, Kaia?" he asked.

"They probably think we have already entered the gateway," said Kaia.

She spotted the theel herding a bunch of rakshasas, including a few short potbellies and an equal number of burly marisans. Using her night vision, at a distance, she located a few silent shapeshifters lurking as sniper attackers of unsuspecting enemies.

"They are coming this way," said Brendan.

His heart raced as he pressed his face on the wall, straining his eyes to see through a tiny opening. Ro joined Brendan, taking turns in peeking through the hole.

Max sat next to Sidney, holding her hand. He did not even attempt to look at the approaching danger.

"How are we going to find the right gate and go through it without being seen?" Brendan asked.

"I have a plan," Kaia said.

Their conversation was interrupted by another blare, but this time, it was the short, high-pitched burst of a trumpet.

"I know this sound," said Brendan, looking through the opening. "I think…"

The ground rumbled. From the side of the building, a huge white elephant rushed toward the rakshasas.

"What the—Max, check this out!" cried Ro. He had never seen a creature this massive.

"That's Yan on big Ely," said Brendan.

The theel was the first to react. It shot up, slithered through the air, and positioned itself between the creatures it led and the charging elephant.

Ely slid to a halt just a few paces in front of the floating theel. Yan cursed the theel at the top of his voice. The theel bared its fangs and shrieked back, flashes of electrical charge radiating from its tail.

"You are not the keeper!" the theel hissed. "You're his foolish friend, who's about to meet the same fate as the keeper if you don't give me the key to the gateway."

Yan leaned forward, wielding his hatchet in one hand, and took aim at the theel.

The theel countered quickly by whipping its tail and zapping Yan with a powerful arc of electricity, ejecting Yan over Ely's head.

Ely reacted by attempting to wrap her trunk around Yan's spinning body, but only managed to soften the impact of the fall. The awkward fall knocked the already-dazed keeper out cold.

Infuriated, Ely charged at the nearest rakshasa, the one blowing the horn. The potbellied rakshasa dropped the instrument and reached for its crude bone dagger, as if it would stop a charging elephant, but Ely's blow sent the rakshasa crashing into a nearby bush. The theel retaliated by unleashing its tail like a taser on the pachyderm, rendering her immobile. Yan helplessly watched his faithful friend wince in pain.

"Stop hurting her!" Yan ordered the theel.

"Now, watch your ride die, rider," shouted the theel, its aquiline nose twitching in anger.

"Do something, Kaia," pleaded Brendan.

"This is not the right time, Brendan," Kaia whispered.

"But they are hurting her!" Brendan protested.

"I know it's hurtful to see them attack our friend. But trust me, Yan is a powerful warrior, and he can handle this," Kaia said reassuringly.

Brendan, unable to witness the assault, slumped to the floor and buried his face between his knees.

"Let her go. Just take me," Yan conceded to the theel.

"You show us the gateway, and I'll spare her life." The theel reduced the intensity of its electric charge on Ely.

Yan hesitated.

"You let us through the gateway, I'll spare *your* life." The theel revised its offer.

Yan appeared to weigh his options before speaking to the theel. "How do I trust you?" he asked.

"You can't," hissed the theel, sliding closer to Yan, "but as you can see, it would suit you better if you worked for me. My master has great powers and is looking for people like you. You are more courageous and loyal than the rakshasas."

Without saying a word, Yan stood up. "Let her go. I'll show you the way, as I did for the knight," he said, raising his voice.

"The knight?" the marisan cursed. "They were already here?" It grunted in disgust, sniffing the air, trying to get a scent.

"It was the knight who betrayed my friend. He told me not to let you in," shouted Yan. "I'll show you the pathway, and you can chase the knight down…Hopefully, you'll kill each other. Remember this, you ugly worm, I am not loyal to you, your master, or that self-serving knight."

The theel flashed a sly grin and released Ely from its force. "My master will like your appetite for vengeance, rider! The knights of the rishis are no match for my master's powers. We are about to take over the worlds, and you're better off being at our side."

Yan led the theel closer to the stone building but away from where the humans were hiding.

Yan raised his mineral stone key over his head. It was not high moon yet, and the timing was perfect. The stone caught the light of the moon and illuminated the winding pathway in front of Yan.

"Um…" Yan deliberated, inspecting the trail.

"You are wasting time on purpose," the theel accused.

"I am just trying to make sure that you take the same path the knight did to the inner sphere. Aha…This is the one." Yan dramatized his selection of the path, suddenly letting out a cry and startling the potbellied rakshasa that stood just inches away from him.

"Is this the one?" The theel's tail glowed as its impatience heightened.

"I am telling you, this is the one," Yan snapped. "Look, the light on the stone is bright, and it is your last chance to take the pathway. If you are so fickle-minded, you don't have to take this one. You can wait for the next high moon, but that's your call and not mine."

"Come on, worm. The light is beginning to dim," a marisan shouted anxiously. "If this is not the one, can't we come back and kill the rider?"

The theel examined the gateway. The light from the crystal *was* dimming, as the rider had warned.

"I think the rider has a lot more to gain from letting us follow and eliminate the knight, theel," said a potbelly, snickering.

"I can smell the knight," said the marisan. "He must have gone through this gateway," it said, reassuring the theel.

"If this is a mistake, I'll have your elephant's head cut off!" the theel said and ordered his cronies to go through the gateway.

Yan watched the creatures disappear through the slowly dimming pathway to nowhere. He waited until the paths closed and then signaled to Kaia. The kids ran to Yan and Ely.

Brendan hugged Ely's trunk. "Are you all right?" he asked Yan.

"Don't worry about me, son," said Yan while tending to Ely's wounds carefully. "She'll be fine, too," he said, stealing a look at the moon. "You should get going."

"Are you ready?" Kaia flashed the prisms at Yan.

Yan bid a warm farewell to the kids. "It is a dangerous place out there, but you are in good hands. Remember, the keeper will always be there to protect you."

Yan then exposed his crystal key to the full moon's light. As the light dispersed through the two memory prisms, he adjusted the prism until the beams converged and burst with a flash, temporarily blinding everyone. For a brief moment, there was total darkness.

When a faint light reemerged from the key, Yan was gone, and in his place stood a stranger, holding the illuminated crystal. The person wore a long, hooded robe, and in the dim light, the boys could see his facial features covered with locks of golden hair. He looked nothing like the rider. His trunk was much shorter; a pair of sharp cuspids protruded from underneath the trunk. The serene brown eyes under thick eyebrows looked more human than elephant-like. The person was shorter than Yan, and Brendan could tell from the shape of the robe hugging his body that he was muscular and not bulky, like Yan.

"I look very different, but I am the same inside," the stranger said earnestly, causing a curious chatter among the perplexed children.

"What's happening?" Sidney tugged Ro's shirt.

"The rider has become Yan the keeper—they both are the same," said Ro.

The light from the crystal flowed like a stream, snaking around the nearby trees, briefly disappearing behind the bushes and reappearing. Yan led his team back to the stone house, where the stream of light ended.

"Two gateways will open—one illuminated and the other dark. Take the dark one."

"I can see the light!" Sidney said, jumping with excitement and facing its bright source.

"You can *see*?" the boys asked in chorus.

"The dark one, the one the girl can see, is your gateway to the queen," said Yan thoughtfully. "Be careful. Your path could be treacherous."

The keeper knelt next to Sidney and pushed his folded notebook into her pocket. It automatically conformed to the size and shape of her tiny pocket. "When the time is right, my notebook will reveal more clues about the whereabouts of the queen. But I want you all to remember, Sidney should open the notebook only when you are about to enter the Palace of the Ruins, not before."

"How will we know when we have reached the Palace of the Ruins?" asked Max.

"You'll see it for yourself. It's not a very welcoming place, and it lives up to its name."

Kaia let out a short, mellow whistle, and her majestic white horse arrived, pulling a covered metallic buggy with four large wheels. "My horse will take us through this journey," she said.

Kaia and the kids bid goodbye to Yan, and they watched him fade away at the edge of their dim trail.

Twilight surrounded them as the bumpy but relatively quiet buggy sped over the trail. Brendan sat comfortably on the soft, cushioned tan seat between Max and Ro while Sidney sat across, close to Kaia. Kaia was initially focused on planning and preparing for the unpredictable journey into the middle sphere; however, she soon shared her adventurous stories with her young companions.

"Are you from our world?" asked Max hesitantly.

"I come from a different world, but Earth is home to me now." Kaia gently rubbed Sidney's cold hand to transfer some warmth.

"How many knights are there like you and Aarjen?" asked Brendan.

"Seven in total. Aarjen is the fiercest of all. He is the only one who can survive the Dark Forest, the most dangerous place in the underworlds."

"What do knights do?" asked Ro.

"We serve the rishis. We seek information to help restore the balance between good and bad."

Kaia reached over to the back of the seat and pulled out a large duffel bag and handed them some items from it. "I want you all to wear these. Make sure you pull the hood on," she said, her voice stern.

Ro elbowed Max while slipping into the long, knee-length, hooded parka, and in return, Max pulled Ro's hoodie over his face. Brendan pushed them both as they flopped back in their seats, laughing.

"Eww," said Max, sniffing the parka. He hated the smell of fragrant oils.

Ro removed himself from the horseplay to help Sidney slip into her parka. Her sweet smile accentuated her dimples as he pushed her thick, wavy hair under her hoodie. "I like the smell," said Sidney, rubbing her sleeve on her nose. "Eucalyptus!"

Kaia opened the lid of a small wooden compartment under the seat and pulled out a couple of pairs of boots. "Wear these," she instructed. "You don't want to be seen as humans."

"What are those?" shouted Ro, looking at the soft, dark, crumpled boots, made of the same soft material as the parka, with thick leather soles.

"No way!" said Max, vigorously shaking his head. "They look like UGGs."

"These will not fit me," complained Brendan, looking at the smallest pair of the lot.

"Those are Sidney's. But that pair will fit you." Kaia pointed to the largest pair of boots at the corner of the compartment.

Kaia pulled two straps on either side of the boots. "These are well-designed boots; they'll adjust to your feet. Roll it up as high as possible so that your parka is over it," she instructed.

"Why do we need to wear these?" Max held one boot at his eye level.

"This gear will protect you from the creatures. It's made of material that will mask the scent and the thermal signatures of humans," Kaia said.

The buggy swayed and slowed down.

Max wiped the moisture off the frosted glass and gazed outside, trying to adjust his vision to the twilight-like surroundings. "I see some lights," Max said, trying to identify the source of dull, flickering tiki-torch-like lights at a distance. He counted a dozen or so, spread out randomly, some bright while the others intermittently faded away. "Where are we?"

"Whoa!" Max jerked back, startled by the proximity of two rakshasas riding strange bull-like creatures. One of the riders steered his dark ride at the buggy, and before anyone could react, the fat rakshasa on his massive ride reached over and pulled the reins, forcing Kaia's horse to slow down.

"Someone is attacking us!" Max shouted.

The riders shouted in the rakshasa language as the horse wildly resisted the intruders before coming to a full stop. Leaning over the window of the buggy, Kaia shouted something back at them.

"Stay inside," she told her young companions and jumped out.

The large four-horned bulls were fierce and ready to charge at Kaia, who fearlessly jumped in front of them. The fat rakshasa rider, who sat high on the dark saddle, pulled the rugged rein, and she could tell from the bulging rakshasa muscles in his heavy arms that he held his animal back with all his might. His face was plump, but his pudgy cheeks and thick lips were partially hidden by a long, bushy, and curvy mustache. Kaia eyed his curved cuspids that fanged outward underneath his mustache and gleamed under the light of the two moons. He wore a portion of a large animal skull on his head with sharp horns spiraling forward. He was clad in a tight leather vest, which only partially covered his upper body and allowed his bluish-purple belly to flow over the hump of the bull, and he had a matching tan wraparound that hung loosely from his hips to below his knees. His boots were made of hide with sharp, pointy scales. Kaia guessed they were two local rakshasa patrol warriors.

"I come here in peace," shouted Kaia in English. "We need your help." She spoke with confidence, but secretly, she gripped the dagger that was concealed under her coat.

"Strangers are not welcome to this village. We suggest you leave now," the rakshasa warrior replied in perfect English.

The angry bull snorted, lifted its front leg, and dug its massive hoof into the grassy ground below, creating a divot more than a foot wide. Chunks of grass and dirt hurled at the visitors. The rakshasa pulled the leather harness back and kicked the bull, sinking the sharp scales of his boots into the side of its belly. The enraged bull moved backward and shook its head sideways in an unsuccessful attempt to strike the boot with its horn.

"My arm is getting tired of holding my ule back. I suggest you get lost before I let go of my grip. You are about to become someone's sliced meat," the rakshasa threatened.

The ule seemed to understand and appreciate the warrior's comments. It nudged its head in the air, letting loose a wild, bellowing sound. This excited the other ule, but its mount—a much less fierce-looking rakshasa—applied a shiny whip to its back.

"You are as clever as your ule," Kaia deliberately said in their language, which infuriated the man on the ule in front of her.

He released his grip, and the bull lowered its head to charge at Kaia.

However, instead of moving forward, it fell to the ground with a thud and rolled on its side. Along with the ule, the rakshasa crashed but managed to roll away from the heavy creature, saving himself from being crushed under its weight. Dazed, he lay flat on the ground.

Kaia turned her attention to the other rakshasa, who had helplessly watched her bring the massive ule and his partner down.

"Do you want me to bring your ule down too?" she asked, revealing her dagger, and this time, he seemed to pay attention.

He dismounted the ule and controlled it by pulling the harness to the side of its face. They both grunted.

"Who are you, and what do you want?" he asked as the other rakshasa slowly tried to get back on his feet.

He was wobbly from the impact of the fall while his heavy ule continued to struggle to lift itself on its legs. Kaia didn't reply to the warrior. She had succeeded in intimidating them. She approached the struggling ule with the exposed dagger. The ule warrior's eyes widened with anxiety and fear, and the ule, recognizing the weapon, scrambled to find its footing.

Before the warrior could protest or plead, Kaia bent down, and with one swift motion, swiped her dagger across the face of the ule. The tight harness knotted through the nose of the ule snapped, freeing the ule from its master's control. Energized by a gush of unconstrained blood flow, the ule instantly jumped on its feet, but harmlessly stood next to Kaia like a timid dog.

"I am Kaia, the knight of the rishis from the mortal world. I don't consider you as my enemy. I am here with my friends, and we need your help in finding Queen Suhela."

From the reaction of the ule warriors, Kaia realized that she must have uttered a dreaded word. She sensed the ule warriors' anguish and fear.

The muscular warrior reacted first and yelled something to the fat one who had fallen from his ule.

"No. No. No queen," stuttered the fat one, shaking his head. "We'll help you with your stay, but you must leave before twilight."

"But I—"

Kaia was interrupted by a loud exchange of outcry between the two warriors.

Finally, the thin one spoke. "Kaia, the knight, listen…And do not protest." He cleared his throat with a grunting noise. "We don't know anything about the queen, and we can only help you with your stay. Just follow me."

He turned his protesting ule around, and within minutes, the fat one managed to jump back up onto his ule and ride away into the night without saying anything.

When Kaia hopped back into the buggy, she had already put her weapon away. "Cowards!" she said.

"Who were those people, Kaia?" asked Sidney. "I didn't get the bad feeling I get when the creatures are around."

"You are correct, Sidney. These are not evil beings, like the real rakshasas," said Kaia calmly. "Here in the middle sphere, the illusionary creatures we call poiz have become real creatures that we call nijaz. They might not be our enemies now, but they could be friends of the theel, so we should still watch our back."

"Wow, what is that animal? I thought it was going to kill you," said Max, his voice shaky.

"You were really good," added Brendan.

"It is called an ule, a fierce creature when provoked. These animals are trained to kill," said Kaia.

"How did you put that thing down so easily?" Max asked.

"I have been trained to control the minds of the nijaz. Their minds, unlike those of the real rakshasa, are still vulnerable to hypnosis. They also learn from each other. Did you notice how the other ule became docile after she saw me control her kind?"

"That was cool," said Ro. "Do you trust them?"

"Yes, for now."

###

"Don't you know who I am?" the ule warrior raised his voice in frustration to the guard, who only revealed two large eyes and a nose through the viewing portal of the fortified gate.

"Only warriors are allowed. You know the rules. I'll let you in, but not the others."

After much debate, the ule warrior finally decided to shift his focus from trying to convince the guard of his importance to revealing Kaia's identity. "I am traveling with a knight. I just witnessed what she could do to an ule. If you don't open the gate and let her in, you and your friends inside won't live another day to follow your rules."

The guard mumbled and cursed, keenly aware of a knight's capabilities.

"Damn ule warriors. They are as dumb as the ules they ride on. It is going to cost you," the creature said, grunting.

"Consider your spared life as your payment!" the ule warrior said with a smirk.

An old, hunched ogre cranked a clunky metal wheel and slowly opened the heavy wooden gate. The potbellied rakshasa guard stood by the troll, glaring at visitors.

The ule warrior spat at the guard as he passed by while the troll nervously recoiled from seeing an Earth horse for the first time in its life.

Inside the stone inn, the ule warrior received a warm welcome from the tall rakshasi behind the counter.

"Marra, you are back already?" she said without taking her eyes off a large, torn ledger. "I thought you were gone for a couple of moons. Is Karro not with you?" she asked, sniffing for his scent.

"No, but I have brought some visitors. Take good care of them, but make sure they leave by twilight." He leaned over the wax-covered counter and lowered his voice. "I don't want them to talk to anyone here. You don't want any trouble."

The rakshasi looked puzzled. "What visitors?" she asked, finally looking up and sniffing the air. She froze when she saw Kaia standing behind the guard. Kaia watched the rakshasi's eyes turn bloodshot in an instant. Her curving fangs protruded from underneath her lips. Her already-large forehead doubled in size, and her hair on her head and neck grew uncontrollably. Kaia stood still as the creature crouched and jumped up on the counter. Her large, scaly wings unfolded from her hunched back. She scratched the counter, peeling the wax with her talons. She finally let out a high-pitched shrill.

"Calm down," yelled the warrior. "She's a knight of a rishi."

Kaia sprang into action. Intercepting the rakshasi-turned-vampire mid-air, she gripped the creature's throat with one hand and twisted its flapping wing with the other. The kateri swirled in the air like an entangled parachute and dropped to the floor with a thud. Kaia swung around a wooden beam and aimed her landing on top of the vampire. She thrust her knee into the creature's chest as it gasped for air and pressed her dagger on its throat. Exhausted and unable to move, the kateri reverted to its original rakshasi form.

"I told you. You never listen," yelled Marra, shaking his head and laughing at the rakshasi. He turned to Kaia and said, "She's all bark and no bite. Let her go."

"I meant no harm," said the rakshasi.

"We'll blame it on our instincts." Kaia put away her dagger.

"I'll put you and your companions in special rooms, but please promise you will leave at twilight." The rakshasi returned to her spot behind the damaged counter.

"I am not promising anything. We are looking for the queen. I'll leave when you help," Kaia bargained.

"We possess no knowledge of the queen," the ule warrior said with a scoff. "When I return, I'll have many more warriors with me to escort you out of this village." He walked out without looking back.

The rakshasi hurriedly led Kaia and the children upstairs to their room, which had two large wooden cots with beds stuffed with some kind of straw. Nothing was comfortable.

"It smells like fish," said Ro, gagging.

"It is the wax that is burning," Kaia said.

She scanned the surroundings for poiz or tantrics. No traps.

"Anyone hungry? I am sure they have room service," Kaia snickered.

"Fish and chips?" joked Max.

"Blood pudding," said Kaia.

"Ule burgers!" added Ro. "Glad I am a vegetarian."

Amid the banter related to the menu options, Kaia found a way to slip out and talk to the obliging rakshasi behind the counter, who she had previously "bumped into," and within moments, someone delivered delicious, strange-looking dishes.

"Listen up, all. We'll have to move fast before the twilight—it is called trilight here." Kaia carefully moved the broken wooden shutter and looked outside the window. "It is the light from the three full moons that makes this place brightly lit. It is also when all the creatures start acting up. I am going down to the courtyard to find some answers," said Kaia, grabbing a small net sack of pungent ingee roots. "Stay inside and keep your gear on," she instructed before slipping out swiftly like a ninja.

At the end of the roofless corridor of the unfinished courtyard, four rakshasa warriors, huddled in a corner of the raised stone patio, were having a heated argument. "You guys keep it under control; otherwise, I'll throw you out," shouted the front-desk rakshasi. "We have—" She stopped speaking when Kaia approached the group.

"I'll pay money if you take me to the Ruins," offered Kaia.

"Arrrrgh—kuss marrr," one of them cursed in a rakshasa language, ready to attack the intruder who'd had the audacity to disturb them, but when he saw the sack of precious ingee roots that Kaia flaunted, his demeanor changed.

"How much for the ingee?" he asked, sticking his nose in the air to determine the quality of the roots from its smell.

"I am willing to trade these for some information on the Ruins," Kaia said.

"You've got some guts to come here and ask about the Ruins. How about we just take the roots from you instead?" shouted another with a weapon in hand.

"Idiots, you have no idea who she is," said someone who stood in the shadows of a tall column.

He took a step closer to Kaia and spoke to her in a deep voice. "You are wasting your time with these dumb and drunk gamblers; they have no information, but I have a proposal for you."

It was Karro, the fat ule warrior who had fallen off the ule.

"It's you again. Be careful what you ask for," she said.

"I know a person who can help you, but she needs you to return her favor," he said.

"I am listening," said Kaia. She knew that she could never trust a rakshasa even if it was only a nijaz.

"First, give the ingee to my friends here," he suggested.

"What do I get in return?" Kaia asked.

"My word and their silence," he responded.

"A rakshasa's word means nothing to me," said Kaia, getting close to Karro. She preferred any negotiations to be one-on-one.

"You have a nice shelter and food despite the fact that you brought humans, don't you?" said the ule warrior, much to Kaia's surprise.

"You seem to know more than what you should know," Kaia flashed her dagger.

"Show us you are really worthy of your quest."

"You are challenging me? Interesting." She laughed.

"There's a makeshift Chadurang competition tonight. How about you join our team?" asked Karro.

"What are we playing for?" asked Kaia.

"To put it in human terms, it is for power, money, and everything that comes with it," replied Karro.

"So, you are a rakshasa after all." Kaia poked his massive chest, deliberately provoking him.

"Hold your judgment for a later time. Humans are no different," Karro said, carefully pushing her hand away from him.

"I see you have some Earth dweller connections. A knight never gambles," Kaia said sternly.

"Don't flatter yourself. You are no match for our champion at this game, but the girl, the one who can't see? She's the one."

"Looks like the smell of the roots is already getting to you. I would never expose a child to ruthless creatures."

"You already have by bringing her to this world," the ule warrior provoked the knight.

"She has a purpose, and that does not include participating in your lame game," Kaia replied calmly.

"The girl who cannot see can help. Besides, as long as she's under the parka, no one will know she's human."

"You seem to know a lot. How about the older boy instead?"

"No. I have been told that it has to be this girl. She's got deva blood. Only she can do this."

"Who told you that?"

"Not any of your business."

"You just made it my business." She thrust her dagger at Karro.

"Okay, calm down, Kaia. You'll know soon. But not before the game."

Kaia tossed the roots at one of the drunken warriors, who scrambled for their share. "Deal. I'll help you with Sidney, and you'll accompany me to the Ruins."

"No, no, no. I'll only show you the way to the Ruins," the warrior said, disagreeing violently.

Sidney was nervous, but Kaia's presence comforted her jitters. "You want me to play chess?" she asked with a frown.

"Something like that, honey. The rules are exactly the same."

"But, Kaia, I can't see the pieces."

"I am not sure I have the answers, dear, but we'll find out soon," she said, holding Sidney close to her.

The event, some form of ritualistic competition, was a noisy mess. Kaia worried that the gathering of an assortment of intoxicated rakshasas would be too much for Sidney to bear, but the child was strangely calm, holding Kaia's hand.

Karro introduced himself to Sidney and showered her with kind words of encouragement. "They won't be able to see who you are, little one, or what you look like under your robe, so be brave. Besides, when I am by your side, no one will bother you," he said.

The unruly crowd roared at winning rakshasas. Many yelled and cursed at the losers. An ugly brawl erupted in a corner when two losers of the game attacked the winning players. A nearby guard did nothing to stop the fight but ultimately dragged the dead out of the premise. Vendors sold raw foot-long saltwater fish to sloppy customers with little sense of hygiene.

There was some kind of loud announcement, which unexpectedly silenced the crowd. The crowd then began to chant while thumping the floor with their feet and sticks at a steady interval.

Thump…Thump…Thump.

The dull sound of a ram-horn bugle with a slow, monotonous rhythm of a drumbeat cast the chanting spectators into a trance.

The crowd rearranged itself around the stone parapet wall, a couple feet tall, of a large but shallow well. Water overflowed from the well, but the surrounding stone gutters navigated the overflow back to its source. From the metallic appearance and the sheen from the effervescent water, Kaia guessed correctly that a water shapeshifter was about to appear, but she couldn't see its relevance with this crowd. She spotted Marra on the other side of the well with his muscular hands folded over his rakshasa-sized belly and observing the crowd.

Kaia held Sidney close to her. She tightened the hoodie around the child's ears and ensured most of the clatter and the noise generated by the rakshasas were filtered out.

As sinister chanting reached its rhythmic peak, a blob of water rose from the center of the well and assumed a humanoid shape.

"What's happening?" asked Sidney.

"A jala is about to emerge," Kaia said. "Jalas are people of the water world."

"What do they look like?"

"There are many forms—mermaids, dolphins, seahorses, and many even look like humans." Kaia paused to watch the column of water change into a cocoon, from which a shiny, silvery mermaid appeared.

"There she is," said Kaia, letting out a deep breath.

She recognized the infamous runaway jala sorceress, Neeria, who had been banished from Jalastella by Samudra for betraying the jalas. She had somehow managed to infiltrate the middle sphere with the help of an evil force, forging an alliance with the rakshasas.

"Neeria, Neeria, Neeria," the Rakshasas chanted until the blindfolded jala raised her hand from within the watery cocoon.

The crowd went silent.

"The mighty Neeria is here! Let the game begin," announced an ule warrior.

The crowd erupted.

"Bring the first challenger," the announcer shouted.

A large rakshasa and his posse pushed through the crowd and took the seats in front of the well.

"The game will begin now," said the ule warrior, striking a large gong that shook Sidney.

Neeria removed her blindfold and revealed a third eye in the middle of her forehead. Kaia knew that Neeria would use the third eye to probe the weak minds of the nijaz.

A replica Chadurang board was placed between Neeria and her rakshasa opponent.

From inside the watery cocoon, Neeria made the first move of the game with her mind as her opponent watched the piece on the board move on its own.

"What's going on?" asked Sidney.

"Neeria is playing a mind game with her opponent, dear," Kaia said.

The game continued as the players moved the pieces crisscross on the board.

"Air battle, air battle," chanted the hysterical crowd.

When Neeria's third eye opened, the crowd dropped down to the floor and bowed to Neeria.

Kaia was amused to see the control Neeria had over the weak nijaz of Mayastella.

Neeria raised her hand and made her move. The piece began to float.

"The air battle has begun," shouted the crowd as the pieces levitated one after the other.

She rained attacks on her opponent, one piece destroying the other. With every piece she captured, she drained the energy and the life of her opponent, who collapsed to the floor when the king was captured. A supporter leaned over and checked the fallen rakshasa before pronouncing him dead.

"Next opponent," shouted the announcer.

One by one, Neeria's opponents succumbed, and the dead losers were tossed into the well.

The wild crowd seemed to savor the slaughter.

"Are there no more challengers?" asked the announcer.

"The short one will play." Karro announced Sidney's participation in the game, without wasting time.

Someone must have known about Sidney's strength against Neeria, and instructed Karro to bring her to the competition. Kaia wondered who. While she was confident Sidney would prevail, she was not going to take any chances. She was ready to defend.

"It's finally our turn to play, hon," said Kaia, touching Sidney's hand gently. "I am sure you can do better than these rakshasas."

Two guards guided Sidney and Kaia to the well amid the crowd's chant in rakshasa tongue: "Power to the Neeria. Kill the short one. Power to Neeria. Kill the short one."

They pushed to get close to Kaia and Sidney as the guards controlled the crowd with force.

"I'll be the speaker for the short one," Karro shouted to Neeria's guards.

"Why?" Neeria's guard shouted back and approached Karro.

"The short one can't see or speak well. The crowd will easily get upset and rowdy if they don't understand what she's saying," Karro reasoned.

The guard exchanged glances with his partner, who hesitantly gave the approval to Karro.

"Ask her to call out the game as she would in her world. We'll take care of the rest," Karro said to Kaia.

"You'd better be right, Karro. If that thing ever succeeds in getting into this child's mind, I will cut its gooey, mutated head off and feed it to the fish, and you'll go with it for putting us through this nonsense." She reached into her bag and activated her disk briefly.

Karro and the other guards winced with the discomforting high-frequency sound.

"A warning," Kaia said, "to let you know that I am prepared for the worst."

"You will not regret helping us," Karro assured her, stepping away from the bag.

"Just call out the moves as you would in your game. Karro will translate the moves for you," said Kaia.

"The short one will move first." The announcer signaled to Karro.

"E4," Sidney said hesitantly.

The game was extremely confusing for Sidney at the beginning. She struggled to remember where the pieces were and how the game had developed.

"I can't keep track of the pieces," Sidney told Kaia when her first piece was captured. "I don't want to play anymore," she said, shaking her head and sitting closer to Kaia.

Kaia reached into her bag and pulled out her phone and ear-buds.

"This will help you relax." She helped Sidney with the tiny ear-buds.

Soothing sounds of water flowing, wind chimes, and birds chirping helped Sidney focus. Karro then helped Sidney to feel the pieces on the board and stepped back when Neeria's guard began to object. Kaia's move to calm Sidney's nerves worked. Sidney began to challenge Neeria with her clever countermoves.

Agitated by the short one's ability to counter her moves, Neeria opened her third eye and began her attack, but Sidney fought back with strong defensive placement of her pieces.

Neeria's knight moved across the board and sacrificed itself to Sidney's knight.

"I don't think my opponent knows what she's doing," Sidney told Kaia and giggled, but Neeria had already cracked open the door to Sidney's mind.

Sidney felt a soft light slowly diffuse through her mind. It was truly bizarre to see chess pieces floating all around her. Initially, it felt good to be able to see things again in her mind, but soon, her head began to hurt. At the far end of the light, Sidney saw someone smiling at her, but when she drifted closer, the face began to laugh louder and louder.

"How interesting. It is a *human child*!" the jala creature cried out. "Precious and innocent—what a treat." Neeria's laughter was hysterical. "The nijaz truly live up to their promise." She laughed.

Neeria attacked and captured Sidney's queen unexpectedly.

The light intensified, and Sidney shuddered in pain. She remained paralyzed and speechless, unable to ask Kaia for help. As she struggled to set herself free from the powerful grip of Neeria, Sidney noticed one of the chess pieces turn into a young foot soldier, who ran toward her from an obscure space of her mind, where she stood trapped under the spell of Neeria's third eye. The lad slowly reached for her.

It was the same touch that Sidney had experienced when she landed on the grassy knoll—a touch of a friend, someone she had recently met.

"Sidney," the foot soldier called out to her. His voice was soft with a distinct accent. "I am Run-Nier. Remember, I gave you the flower?"

"Yes, I remember," Sidney cried out in her mind, thankful to see Run-Nier again. "Please help me," she pleaded.

"Neeria cannot see me, but you can," said Run-Nier.

Sidney could see his face up close—bright green eyes, shiny red hair, and finally a smile that wiped her pain away.

"When I tell you to play, you play, okay?"

"I don't want to play this game anymore. My head hurts." Sidney cried.

"Don't worry. I'll show you, Sidney," said Run-Nier. "You see these footers?" Run-Nier cast a soft beam of light on a floating chess piece resembling a foot soldier. "He is your pawn; you move there," he spoke slowly.

He drew an imaginary line from where the foot soldier stood to a space somewhere in the air. When Sidney followed Run-Nier's instructions, the foot soldier stood up and ran to where Sidney had indicated, and upon reaching his destination, he turned into a pawn again.

Neeria countered.

Run-Nier instructed Sidney to move the knight up above her, and the horseman took his new position.

Sidney's move surprised Neeria.

"Now, back to your footer." He guided her attention back to the pawn she had directed to move. "You are about to find the real queen," he said in fragmented English.

The moment Sidney touched the foot soldier, he got up, ran across the light, and disappeared.

From deep within the light emerged a queen, pale and slender, as beautiful as Sidney imagined her mother to be.

"Trust your heart. It will lead you to me, and I'll be waiting for you." Her voice was reassuring.

The queen clutched her sword and faded into the light. All the pieces around Sidney began to crumble, and the shocked Neeria let out a shrill.

"Run-Nier, we did it!" Sidney shouted with joy.

"Are you all right?" Kaia asked, gently squeezed her arm.

"Oh, yes!" said Sidney. "I think I just won this game."

"You won? How—"

Kaia watched the cocoon in front of her collapse, spilling Neeria into the water below. Without the protection of her cocoon, her body disintegrated into the swirling water. The liberated crowd wildly cheered the short one. Heavily armed soldiers, who had remained hidden, took their positions, as planned by Marra and Karro. With the help from ule warriors, Marra apprehended Neeria's warriors before they could react.

"The short one has helped us defeat the dreaded Neeria and has freed our world," Karro proclaimed.

The crowd erupted with joy once again.

"This is no ordinary human child," announced Marra. "The vasana oracle prophesied the perishing of Neeria, the jala sorceress, at the hands of a sightless child. Finally, her prediction has come true!" he said.

"We will show you the secret path to the vasana oracle. She is the only one who can help you with your quest," Karro said and summoned his aide. "My trusted ule warrior will be your guide. He bears this kingdom's seal, so you'll be well protected."

An ule warrior much smaller and younger than Karro arrived with Kaia's horse and the carriage. Kaia accepted the guide. "We are grateful for what you did, but I must warn you that you are embarking on a very dangerous journey into a forbidden place," said Karro.

The path to the oracle's place was bumpy, long, and winding, but no one interfered with the visitors, as the Karro had promised.

There was a brief lull inside the buggy.

"Kaia?" Sidney's soft voice drowned in the incessant rattles and squeaks generated by the swaying buggy. "Who is an oracle?" Sidney asked, facing in the direction of where Kaia sat.

"And where is he taking us now?" asked Brendan.

Kaia looked at Sidney's innocent, smiling face. Sidney's eyes were bright yet had a blank stare. She reached over and gently touched Sidney's soft but cold cheek. "A vasana oracle is a rakshasi who lives in the Dark Forest among ape-like creatures. These oracles possess the power of prophesy and predict danger, especially to those they protect. Only a handful of them exist, and they are extremely hard to find."

"Why?" Ro asked.

"They have many enemies in the outside world. They are often hunted for their predictive powers. They live deep inside the Dark Forest, protected by vasanas—or apes," said Kaia.

"Do you know this oracle?" asked Brendan.

"I am not sure." Kaia nodded hesitantly.

The serious and watchful guard who accompanied them spoke only once during the entire journey. "Over there," he said, dismounting his ule. "My ule will lead you to the forest across the water. You'll find the vasana oracle somewhere inside the forest by the biggest tree you'll ever see. I am sure she's expecting you," he said, bowing to Kaia.

"Um, which tree?" asked Brendan, facing a forest across a wide body of flowing water.

"The oracle will find you, but this is where I take leave," he said abruptly. Before Kaia could thank him or ask him any questions, he slipped into the shadows of the trilight.

Without stopping, the ule proceeded to cross a shallow river. Its riverbed stretched wide on either bank.

"I guess we follow the ule." Kaia, shrugged her shoulders.

"Is it safe to cross this river?" asked Brendan.

"I think this is more of a creek than a river, but the current seems swift. Let's wait."

She watched the ule wade across, swinging its head back and forth. The water rushed around its legs, but it plowed through. Only after it reached ashore did it stop to look back for its co-travelers. Its eyes shone bright, reflecting the moonlight briefly.

"It looks shallow and safe," said Kaia, pulling the reins of the horse and directing it to take the path the ule had just taken.

The buggy swayed sideways as the water gushed through its wheels, exerting a strong force. Sidney locked her arm with Kaia's.

"What's happening?" she asked in a shaky voice.

"We're crossing a river," replied Ro, half standing to look outside the window.

"The current is pretty strong, Kaia," Brendan said.

"We are halfway there and should reach the other side—"

The buggy stopped abruptly.

Max exchanged glances with Ro and Brendan but refrained from looking outside. "I hate water," he said, clutching the handle firmly.

"Oh my God, we're going to tip over!" said Ro.

Kaia forced the back hatch open against the gushing wind and squeezed herself out. She carefully jumped into the knee-high water and waded to the front of the carriage. The horse struggled to pull the buggy.

"The wheel is stuck behind a rock," she shouted, trying to move it.

She climbed over to the driver's seat and tugged at the rein, but the horse couldn't pull the buggy. She had to do something or else the increasingly strong current would flip the buggy. "I am going to try to push that rock off, and I might need some help, Brendan," she instructed. "But for now, I want you all to stay seated."

Kaia was about to jump back into the water, but she felt something bump the buggy from the rear. The buggy rocked back and forth, but then a strong force heaved the wheel over the stone protruding underwater, freeing the buggy, which suddenly gained momentum.

Kaia lost her balance but managed to fall back on the rider's seat, yanking the reins and prompting her horse to hurry to the bank.

"How did we get unstuck?" asked Brendan, trying hard not to laugh at Kaia as she scrambled inside the buggy, wet.

"It's the ule. It came back and pushed us," said Kaia to the relieved kids.

The forest was thick, with trilight barely trickling through the dense foliage. The ule slowly led them to a large tree.

"Why is it always dark here?" asked Brendan, adjusting to the dim light.

"It is only dark for humans, not for the creatures that dwell here," said Kaia.

"Where does this oracle live?" asked Max.

"In the forest, among the monkeys, dude. Were you not listening?" Ro laughed.

"She's a tree dweller," added Kaia.

"Like Tarzan," said Brendan, also laughing.

Kaia didn't care to explain. *Too difficult to explain the oddities of the outside worlds to human children.* She jumped off the buggy onto soft ground, covered with leaves and twigs. The kids followed.

"Look, monkeys!" shouted Max. "Are they the tree dwellers?"

Two shiny creatures with silver fur, looking more like sloths than monkeys, were swinging wildly from the strands of luminescent vines that loosely hung from the forest canopy. The sight of the visitors made them restless and they started hurling twigs and large fruits at them.

"Shoo. They have come to see me, so no need to get anxious," said a voice in the rakshasi language that only Kaia understood. "Go on and show them the way inside."

That voice is familiar, thought Kaia.

One of the sloth-monkeys cautiously climbed down the tree, wrapping its long tail around the branches to balance itself. Avoiding any eye contact with the strangers and maintaining distance, it then darted toward the enormous trunk of a green tree and disappeared.

"Just follow him," said the voice.

"Who's talking?" Ro asked Max.

"Don't know and don't care. Those monkeys scared me," replied Max.

"We have just seen vampires, trolls, and big dudes on wild bulls with four horns, and you are scared of these monkeys?" asked Ro.

"And we are following a monkey into a tree," said Brendan.

Concealed by the large, bulky, and intertwining roots, a flight of crude stone steps descended somewhere beneath the tree. The sloth-monkey paused by the steps, but upon seeing the visitors, it hurried inside. Candles placed in holes cut into the damp wood gently lit the curved stairs. A narrow corridor at the end of the stairs led them into a spacious enclosure, whose walls were made of dense roots woven together. Brendan was astonished to see the peculiar chamber that opened up under the tree, tapering upward into the massive trunk. Hanging ladders and steps carved on the side of the roots provided multiple access points to the network of branches above. Although the place was cool and damp, a stone fireplace with a low flame provided warmth. Huge ape-like creatures were busy cleaning, cooking, and tending to the broken roots on the wall.

Sitting crouched by the fire, clad in a colorful skirt and matching blouse, was an old, heavyset rakshasi. Even while seated, she towered over the tall fireplace, and despite a puffy face with two slender canine teeth protruding from her mouth, she appeared calm and friendly. Her feline eyes were intense and matched the hazel color of her curly and unkempt hair. "We meet again, Kaia," the oracle said in a welcoming voice. "You've heard the legend of the widow-maker and the venom of a sergon that poisoned my queen? It's true. I was there that night. I watched the whole thing unfold," she said, speaking fast.

She paused and observed Sidney. "So, this is the child with Indra's blood?" She nodded. "She is a brave one, just like you, Kaia. I remember when you were a child. You were always brave. I admired you, but never thought you'd grow up to be a knight…Chasing my own kind."

"You know I chase only the bad ones."

"Sit here." She spoke to the perplexed kids, pointing to where a furry animal hide covered the floor. "Make yourself comfortable. My vasanas are harmless to my friends."

"Is Queen Suhela alive?" asked Kaia, quickly getting to the point.

"Barely, but this girl can still help. I had a dream not too long ago…"

"The child has already helped. Can you take us there?" Kaia raised her voice.

"I can sense you are eager to get there, but it is not that simple. Unfortunately, I cannot take you there."

She sprinkled something into the fire. "As long as this fire is green, she is alive. If she dies, the fire will become red and will die as well."

"Why is she in the Ruins? What happened to her?" asked Kaia.

"The queen knew she was dying. The only thing she wanted was to be by her sleeping king before she died, but with the help of the rishis and the keeper, I was going to cure her with my antidotes. We were on our way to the inner sphere. Somehow, the theel found us and abducted Queen Suhela. If she dies, then Kumba will blame the rishis and the immortals. I am still at a loss as to how the theel got past the keeper and infiltrated Mayastella."

"It's not the theel. There is someone evil and more powerful than the theel. A sage who has betrayed the order," said Kaia.

"That explains it. Someone with the power of the rishis but one who cannot spend time in Mayastella without being noticed. Someone who is using a soulless creature like the theel to infiltrate Mayastella."

"How do we get to the queen?" asked Kaia.

"The forest floor is covered by flesh-eating plants. The only safe way to get to the Ruins is by traveling well above ground. The banyan trees of the forests are all connected. It would be safe to travel on its thick branches."

"*Crawl* on the branches? For how long?" asked Ro.

"Don't worry; getting there is the easy part." With a soft whistle, the oracle signaled to her large apes, huddled in one corner, eating fruits. "My vasanas will take you there on their backs. I think you'll have fun as long as you hold on to them."

"What?" the boys shouted in chorus.

"Uh-uh, I am not getting on those," said Ro.

"It's that or the flesh-eating plants. You pick, bro," said Max.

"But first, we have to locate Queen Suhela. We need to read the keeper's notebook."

"We're only supposed to open it when we get to the Ruins," Brendan said.

"You are already there, young man," the oracle said.

Kaia nodded her head approvingly.

Sidney took the folded notebook from her pocket and handed it to Kaia. "I like her."

When Kaia tapped the notebook, it unfolded, as it had done many times before.

The oracle looked puzzled. "The pages are blank."

The kids huddled around the notebook.

"I think only Sidney can tell what's in the notebook," Brendan said.

"Shh…I can hear something," Sidney said.

"What you see with your eyes might just be lies. So be smart and follow the innocent heart."

"The clue is spoken and not written," said the oracle. "Follow your heart? There are many decoys, all false ones. They all look like Queen Suhela, and if you pick the wrong one, it will kill you when you exit the Palace of the Ruins. No one has survived the Ruins."

"What about the lies?" asked Brendan.

"You don't always trust what you see. Poiz are nothing but illusion… Just *lies*," said Kaia."We need to get to the Ruins before the theel arrives," she suggested.

Five large vasanas, each about the size of a fully grown silverback gorilla, lined themselves up next to each other, presenting their massive backs to the oracle. The oracle and Kaia wrapped each person with a harness made of woven vines.

The kids were at first disgusted by the odor of their rides, but the oracle disguised their smell by applying just a drop of fragrant oil to their noses.

"My vasanas are very fast. Hold on to them tight," the oracle instructed. "You'll be at the gates soon."

"How will we get back?" asked Kaia.

"If you succeed in finding the queen, she'll take care of you. But if you don't, you won't live to worry about returning," she said without feeling.

"I am sure we'll see each other again," said Kaia.

"I am confident that you'll find Queen Suhela, but if you are in doubt who the real one is, throw this fire salt on her and ask her to tell the name of her loyal subject. The answer, right or wrong from anyone other than my queen, will burn them down."

"Thank you!" said Kaia.

Before she got a response from the oracle, the vasanas jumped onto the hanging ladders and climbed for the branches with great speed. The ride was wild. Although the kids were speechless, hanging on to their harnesses tightly, they enjoyed the ride when the vasanas found their rhythm. The ape-like creatures swung from one hanging root to another and jumped from one branch to another with great dexterity. On occasion, they ran over massive branches. They did it in unison with precision and accuracy, and before long, the visitors reached the Ruins.

Chapter 14

The Palace of Ruins

Behind the dark moat stood the doomed palace.

Flames shot randomly from the Ruins; torn flags fluttered noisily in the howling wind.

"We are not going in there, are we?" Brendan's dry throat made his voice barely audible.

Kaia gripped her sword in one hand and held Sidney's hand with the other. She hustled with the children across the wooden bridge over the moat and into the corridor behind the stone wall. She continued along a dirt road flanked by dilapidated living quarters on either side. Torches crackled, but the place was empty.

"Over there," she whispered and guided the kids toward a large door to the palace.

The wooden door was heavy, but with the help of the kids, Kaia opened it just enough for them to squeeze through.

The instant Sidney set foot inside the palace, a burst of light struck her.

"Are you all right?" asked Kaia, reacting to Sidney's jerky movement.

Sidney cupped her eyes with her hands. "There is too much light here. It's hurting my eyes." She squirmed.

"It's dark here, Sidney. We can't see a thing."

Kaia adjusted Sidney's parka to cover her eyes. "Is this better?"

"No." Sidney tucked her head into Kaia's coat.

Kaia pulled a black bandanna-like cloth from her pocket, folded it a few times, and gently tied it around Sidney's face, covering her eyes. The light slowly faded away in the hallway, and Sidney began to see blurry images. There were several dark and run-down rooms, but down the hall across from where they stood, Sidney spotted a faint glow.

"I can see faint light over there," Sideny whispered.

"I can feel her presence in this building," Kaia said, switching to her night vision. "She could be in the dungeons. Pull all your hoodies up and stay together," she ordered the kids.

The crumbling rooms were dark and dusty. Thick cobwebs hung low. Shattered furniture cluttered the floor. Other than the sound of their own footsteps echoing across the hallway, the palace was unnervingly quiet.

A high-pitched scream shattered the silence. The kids froze. Kaia positioned her sword in front of her, anticipating a tantric to jump out. A second scream rang out, louder and closer. Total darkness enveloped them as a gush of wind extinguished the nearby torches. Other sounds followed—wailing, crying, mumbling, singing, and laughing.

Max shivered, tried to say something, but managed to only blurt out incoherent words.

"Is it the queen?" Sidney asked.

"I don't think so," replied Kaia. "Be still," she said as she twisted the handle of her sword.

A bluish light from the crystal on the handle of the sword provided enough light for the visitors. Kaia inched toward the wailing sound, kicked the door of the room, and directed the light inside.

In the corner of the room, a woman in royal clothes was crouched on the floor. Her head was tucked under her folded arms that rested on her knees. Her legs were shackled to the wall. She slowly raised her face and looked directly at the visitors. Her face was pale, and tears rolled down her cheeks. She was stunningly beautiful.

"Help me!" she pleaded. "Please help me."

Kaia stood there by the door, studying her.

"We found her," said Brendan.

"I don't see anyone." Sidney continued to focus on the light at the far end of the hall.

The shackled prisoner slowly picked herself up and inched toward Kaia.

"Stay where you are," ordered Kaia. "One more step, and I'll cut you into two. Where's the queen?" she demanded.

The wailing woman's expression changed. Her cry turned to laughter. "I am the queen," she said, laughing. "I am the queen. You'll never leave this place alive. I am the quee—"

The voice faded as Kaia tossed some fire salt at her and rushed the kids out of the room, slamming the door shut behind her.

"That's one of those other ones that the oracle warned us about," said Kaia.

"How did you know?" asked Brendan.

"The light from the crystal and the oracle's salt. We need to go to the basement," she said, searching for the stairs.

The dangerously narrow, winding staircase leading to the basement was jagged and shattered. Stone tiles were loose or missing, revealing bottomless holes. Kaia carefully guided the kids.

"Beware of the false queens," she cautioned to the children at her heels.

"It's like a Halloween spookhouse," said Ro.

"Except these can really bite our heads off!" said Brendan.

"Not if you stay close to me," said Kaia.

Surprisingly, the cellar was well lit by brightly burning torches mounted on every other pillar supporting the ceiling.

The first few cells were empty, but Brendan spotted a figure behind the bars of one.

"Is someone there?" he said.

"I have been waiting for you so long," the shadowy image said in a soft voice. "I am dying," she added.

"Is she the queen?" asked Max, his heart beating fast.

"I am Suhela, the queen of Kumba," the frail prisoner said, covering her face with her slender hands. "Please don't shine the light on me. It is so bright," she said.

Kaia continued shining the light, taking a closer look at the queen. "You are not the real one. Can you tell me where we can find Suhela?"

"You'll never find her," the false queen said, laughing, and quickly disappeared behind the dark walls of the cell.

"I think we are looking in the wrong place," said Sidney. "I don't see any light," she said, removing the blindfold.

"It is brighter here than in the hallway upstairs, Sidney," said Ro, holding on to her hand.

Sidney searched for the dim light that she had seen before but couldn't find it. "Where did the light go?" she asked, slowly moving away from her friends, feeling the cold wall with her hand to guide her.

Sidney drifted away from the watchful eyes of Kaia. She was thrilled to see the light again and was attracted to it like a magnet. As she approached the light, she began to see images around her—the walls, the steps, the iron bars on the cellars.

Sidney walked confidently in the direction of the light without using the wall as her guide anymore. She ignored a false queen who rushed at her from a cell.

"You are not the queen," she said without looking at her, "and I am not afraid of you."

She stopped at the entrance of a doorless room. A small candle burned at the far end. She saw the silhouette of something on the ground, directly beneath a small hexagonal opening at an unreachable height on the wall, through which faint trilight seeped. Sidney adjusted to her newfound vision and tried to focus on the heap on the floor. It was a person, curled up on the ground.

"Could it be Queen Suhela?" she thought when she noticed the long, wavy hair that almost entirely covered her pale face.

Although the woman's legs and hands were mostly covered by her loose, tattered robe, she could see the painful, long shackles that kept her in the room. Sidney was engulfed with sorrow as tears rolled down her cheeks.

"Hello...I am Sidney." Her voice was shaky. "Are you Queen Suhela?"

There was no response.

"Are you the queen?" repeated Sidney. "We are here to help you."

Still, no response.

Struck by sorrow, Sidney's tears poured like the melting wax of a dying candle. The light was steadily fading, and Sidney knew something bad might happen when the candle died. Sidney shuddered and felt a sharp pain in her stomach when she took a closer look at the frail figure. Her body was skeletal underneath the musty robe. Rusted clasps covered most of the bony ankles and wrists. Her nails were black and long. Her face was pale with a protruding thin nose, sunken cheeks, and dark, chapped lips. She did not look anything like the queen Sidney had imagined or the one she had encountered when she played Chadurang with the jala sorceress, Neeria.

This is a trap, her brain warned. *Run away from evil.* But her heart felt otherwise.

At that brief moment, she followed her heart's will and gently laid her hand on the queen's cold but soft face.

A door to a secret room was inadvertently discovered when Max accidentally grabbed onto the tongue of a stone gargoyle. The tongue moved, dislodging the creature's eyeballs, which rolled somewhere underneath into the darkness, triggering a cascade of mechanical movements. A well-lit chamber with an ornate red metal door was exposed.

No one, not even Kaia, noticed Sidney's absence. Everyone was busy trying to figure out what to do next.

A mechanical trigger? Kaia thought to herself, baffled, since the worlds of dark magic rarely intertwined with the mechanical world. She inspected the door.

"Scriptures from the ancient Earth dwellers," she said.

Ancient Earth dwellers, relatives of the rakshasas and vampires, and ancestors of the current Earth dweller, were widely known for their mastery of the mechanical world.

"Maybe they abducted Queen Suhela?" Brendan said.

"No, they don't belong here. Tantrics or poiz must be attempting to copy them. Either way, I suspect this room has something to do with the queen," Kaia admitted.

"I was the one who found it," said Max.

"I was the one who tripped you," said Ro.

"Guys! Let's focus here," Brendan snapped. "What does the door say, Kaia?"

"You'd better know how to unleash the power of what you seek to destroy or create. You'll be the first to face its wrath. The key is in the heart…Not in the eyes," read Kaia.

"I don't get it," said Brendan frowning. Max and Ro shook their heads.

"It is a warning," Kaia said. "I think there is only one queen, but she could take two forms—the good and the evil, the real and the false. What we unleash is up to us."

"How do we open the door?" asked Max.

"The world of mechanics again. Look for symbols," she told the boys.

Still, no one thought of Sidney. The thought of rescuing the queen was uppermost in their minds, pushing out all other thoughts.

Kaia uncovered two holes in the engraved scriptures. The hole in '*eye*' was shaped like an eye, and the one in '*heart*' like a heart. She pushed a blunt object into the heart-shaped hole and waited. There was a series of clicks and motorized noises and then silence.

When Brendan was about to push the door, they heard a rumble. The door opened, exposing a rectangular chamber, and from the floor emerged a large marble tomb with a statue of a queen lying on her back, facing upward. The tomb continued to rise until its base was flush with the floor.

"This IS a tomb," said Brendan. "The queen must be dead."

"Is her body inside?" asked Max nervously.

Kaia examined the tomb. The theme was obvious. There was a bright side and a dark side, like night and day or good and evil. One side of the queen appeared royal and beautiful, her face serene and joyful, her luminous eye gazing straight ahead. The other side—the shadowed realm—personified evil in a thick, tattered robe, torn in many places. Her shriveled skin revealed bony features, her bulging eye was shut, and a curved fang protruded through her puckered lips. Her sharp, black nails jutted out like talons. In one hand, she held a sword, and in the other, she held the sergon by its tail, its body coiling around her and its head resting on her chest. Three stone gargoyles guarded the queen on the day side while three sergons guarded the queen on the dark side.

Kaia thoroughly inspected the tomb and read the writing at the base of the crypt.

Something didn't make sense.

"What is it, Kaia?" asked Brendan.

"The key is in the heart…Not the eyes," read Kaia.

"Sidney, can you repeat the clue from the notebook again?" asked Brendan. "Sidney? Sidney!" His heart skipped a beat. "Where is Sidney?"

"Sidney!" Kaia shouted, disregarding her surroundings and the need to be stealthy. "When did anyone last see her?" Kaia's tone was unusually intimidating.

"She…She was there…" Brendan was trying to think.

Max began to cry.

"By the gargoyle, where we found the room. She told me that it was dark. I remember her telling me something about a light," Ro added.

"How could I have done this?" Kaia was engulfed with guilt. "A child who cannot even see, lost in a dangerous place." Kaia heightened her senses.

"Stay here," she ordered the children, concealing her panic. "I think this is a safe place," She handed Brendan her sword with the glowing handle.

"Quick! Draw a large circle around you and the others with the sword," she told Brendan.

Brendan obeyed. He blamed himself for taking his eyes off Sidney. Kaia snapped her bag open, hurriedly removed a small glass container, cracked it open, and sprinkled its contents around the circle that Brendan had etched on the floor with the sword.

"This circle of fire will protect you. The creatures cannot cross the circle. Pull up your parkas over your head and stay put, and nothing will harm you." She activated the tiny crystal that dangled around her neck to send an urgent distress signal to Aarjen and Yan, and then disappeared into the darkness, retracing the steps they had taken earlier.

The instant Sidney touched the sleeping person, she felt as though she had unloaded the heavy burden of sadness. The touch felt cold, but her heart felt warm. She closed her eyes and thought of her mother, but when she opened them, she found herself staring into the deep, penetrating hazel eyes of the shackled prisoner who seemed to be lost in the sea of gray emptiness that shrouded the room.

Tears rolled down the prisoner's cheeks, but before they left her face, drops of Sidney's tears mingled with them and struck the shackles on the queen's fragile hands like a hammer, shattering them to pieces. Somehow, the child's tears seemed to have washed away the dark poison, transforming the prisoner into a beautiful person. Sidney was now able to see things that brought happiness and color to life. Everything around her seemed vivid and real, no darkness, no blurry vision or bright, blinding light.

"You look beautiful," said Sidney.

"I am Suhela, Queen of Kumba. Thank you, my dear, for washing my pain away. You were the only one who could see me for who I am."

"I can see…I can see!" Sidney said with great enthusiasm.

"You and I are connected, my dear. Thank you for freeing me with your tears of concern. We first need to get out of here. I can sense the creatures are arriving."

"Please take me back to Kaia and my friends. They'll be worried."

The queen glided across the dusty floor like a bird freed from its cage. "I feel so rejuvenated," she said. "Let's go find your friends."

Kaia was stunned to see someone or something moving with Sidney. She reached for her disk. The deadly serrated weapon went into motion, recognizing her signature.

Queen Suhela froze when she heard the discomforting, high-pitched whir of a knight's disk. Concerned that Sidney could fall victim to the friendly fire, she snapped out of her instinctive paralysis and slipped behind a stone column.

"Stop your disk, Kaia. I am Suhela, the Queen of Kumba. The child has rescued me," the queen spoke in a steady and firm voice.

"Liar!" shouted Kaia.

"Kaia!" Sidney ran out from her cover. "I found the queen."

Kaia hesitated and held her hand back from launching her disk. She grabbed a handful of the oracle's salt from the pouch, slid across the floor, rolled over, and tossed the green crystals at Suhela.

"Una, the oracle, is my most loyal subject," shouted the queen as the salt crystals harmlessly sparked and dispersed into the darkness.

Sidney ran to Kaia. "I can see you clearly," she said, hugging her, pushing Kaia to the floor with joy.

"I finally meet you," the queen greeted Kaia.

Kaia kicked herself up from the floor and bowed to the queen. "I bring you the support of the great rishis I serve," she said.

"We need to fight the theel and the rakshasas together and get to my king before they do. But first, the children are in great danger in the tomb. If a false queen is revived, they will never leave this place alive. I can sense that the theel is already here."

Back in the tournament hall, Nora jumped with excitement when Sidney promoted her pawn and said, "Queen, please."

"She's playing as though she could see the board," Turner whispered to Nora.

Having found the gateway the hard way, fumbling through false trails with dead ends and struggling to pick up the scent of the humans and the knight, the theel and the rakshasas were more determined than ever to defeat their enemies. They had already been deceived and misled and were facing the wrath of the theel's evil master for being led astray. Since punishment for failure was often death, it was now a matter of life and death for the theel and its recruits to succeed in their mission of abducting Kumba's queen. Their minds clouded by revenge, they stormed through the forests, destroying anyone who resisted them. By threatening to wipe out the ule village, they succeeded in marching through the gates of the Ruins with the hopes of stopping the knight and her human accomplices.

"We were tricked, and someone will pay for it," said the theel, lashing out at the shapeshifting marisan. "No more failures!"

"We expected you to guide us," grunted a potbellied rakshasa. "Don't blame us for your inability to lead—"

A sharp, stinging lash from the theel stopped the potbellied rakshasa from finishing his statement. "No more mistakes. No more arguments."

"Where is she?" asked Max, worried about Sidney, but more worried about being alone by the crypt.

"I can't believe we are alone here by this tomb. I am scared, dude," said Ro in frightened misery.

"Shh…" Brendan raised the sword. "I hear something."

They tensed and huddled closer to each other with their parkas fully covering their heads as Brendan tightened the grip on the sword. They heard grunts and the heavy stomping of rakshasas.

"Kaia! Kaia!" Max panicked. "They are here!"

The theel was the first to enter the chamber of the false queen. Alerted by the smell of humans in fear, it was the only one to identify the terrified human children under their protective garments, standing next to the tomb. It let out an ear-piercing shriek.

The potbellied rakshasa, along with the beefy marisan, strolled into the chamber. The theel examined the tomb, ignoring the sword Brendan brandished. "Helpless humans, covered under their false security blankets, in that corner." It hissed at the petrified children.

"Um, what? Where?" The surprised potbellied rakshasa sniffed the air.

A bright bolt from the theel's slender tail cracked, arcing across the room and striking the ground a few inches from the protective circle. Unable to see from the effect of the temporarily blinding flash, Brendan thrust Kaia's sword in front of him. Max panicked and tugged on Brendan's parka, dislodging the hood from his head.

The potbellied rakshasa cursed angrily and rushed toward the boys, but the ring etched on the floor combusted instantly around the boys and scorched its legs. The creature backed off.

"Circle of fire! Don't kill yourself, you fool. Let me have the pleasure of hurting them," the theel said, laughing. "Where is your protector now?" the theel asked.

None of the kids spoke; they stood there, trembling.

The theel danced around the circle of fire and then quickly slithered inside like a snake. Brendan swung the sword, but the theel ducked under the moving blade and clutched Brendan's arm. Its touch was cold and scaly.

"I can smell your fear and feel your hopelessness. The so-called kings are counting on such pathetic souls to save them." It let out a villainous laugh.

"You tell me where the knight is, and I'll let you die quickly. Otherwise, this one painfully dies first." It snatched Ro by his robe.

Ro and his horrified friends screamed.

"Let him go," Brendan shouted. "I…I don't…don't know!"

"Let him go if you care to stay in one piece!" echoed a stern voice.

The theel dropped Ro and swooshed away from the circle.

Kaia stood in the doorway at the far end of the chamber. An exposed disk whirled rapidly around her index finger, ready to launch. She was acutely aware of a stealthy marisan crawling across the ceiling and positioning itself for attack.

"Where's Sidney?" Brendan whispered.

"I don't know. I think I am dead," Ro swallowed hard and could barely speak.

"Only one of us can have the queen, and it will be me," the theel snickered.

"What makes you think so?" Kaia unleashed the disk at the marisan. In haste to evade the disk, the marisan lost its grip and fell to the floor with a thud, revealing itself. Spewing sparks, the disk altered trajectory, severed the fallen marisan, and circled back to Kaia's finger, preparing itself for its next launch.

"Ahh, I know the knights fight until death…" the theel said. "But will they sacrifice the people they have sworn to protect?" The theel slipped back inside the ring of fire and charged its tail. "I can kill all of them in one hit before your disk is launched."

"Leave them alone!" Kaia knew the theel could easily kill with the slightest discharge of its tail.

"Not until you put the disk away," it demanded.

Kaia raised her finger with the spinning disk. An awkward standoff ensued between Kaia and the theel.

Mustering courage, Brendan repositioned himself, ready to strike the theel even though his arms were tired from holding the heavy sword.

There was a rumble. A crack ripped through the faded and peeling plaster of the curved ceiling. Dust spewed over the marble tomb, and the slender stone columns shook. Fissures erupted on the gargoyle statues positioned atop the columns, as though they bore the weight of the ceiling. Chunks of stone from the ceiling crashed to the ground, narrowly missing a potbellied rakshasa. An uneasy silence followed.

Kaia knew the theel would have to race against the clock. The mechanics of the false queen's chamber had already been activated, and the place would be collapsing soon. Wasting time arguing over the lives of humans would be useless for the theel. She saw the theel zip closer to the tomb.

Without reading the markings on the surface, the theel ordered a potbellied rakshasa to uncover the tomb.

Kaia, seizing the opportunity, dashed into the chamber and pulled the boys away from the theel. She knew what was about to emerge and wanted to exit the Ruins as quickly as possible.

"Run!" she yelled.

"Where is Sidney?" Brendan shouted over their noisy footsteps.

"She's safe," Kaia yelled back, speeding through the corridors of the Ruins, encountering dead false queens and rakshasas.

Only when they reached the gates of the Ruins did they stop.

"Sidney's over there!" Max tried to catch his breath. "Someone's with her."

"Meet the real Queen Suhela," said Kaia, and she quickly recounted her encounter with the queen.

"Then, what's in that chamber?" asked Brendan.

"The mother of all false queens will be storming out of that thing," warned Suhela. "My oracle will take us out of here, but we'll only be safe if we return to the outer sphere."

"Yan will show us the gateway before the false queen can reach us," said Kaia.

Inside the chamber, a potbellied rakshasa clambered over the tomb while the two surviving marisans tried to pry the tomb open by pushing the stone gargoyle. Nothing moved until the potbellied rakshasa accidentally stepped on the head of the sergon beside the statue of the queen. The head shattered. A thick blood-like fluid oozed from tiny fissures that veined through the statue of the queen and emptied into the gargoyles. The stone creatures sprang to life, fluttered their stone wings, and stretched their necks, as though awakening from a deep slumber.

Ignoring the rakshasas, they attacked and pulverized the stone sergons that sat facing them while the bewildered rakshasas watched the action. The victors perched on the sepulcher in anticipation of the emergence of their queen. From the open tomb, a queen slowly rose. One side of her body was living and healthy while the other side was dead.

The theel was the first to approach the queen, but when the protective gargoyles attempted to block the worm, it instantly vaporized the stone beasts with its powerful bolts. The queen shrieked in anger, completing her transformation into her demonic form.

"Suhela, we are here to help you," said the theel.

The queen's hysterical laughter reverberated across the chamber. "I am not Suhela, but you will help me find Kumba," she demanded.

The theel finally realized its blunder. This was no Suhela. It had succumbed to the trap set by Neeria, the jala sorceress, who had abducted the real queen in its absence and set false queens as traps. The theel had succeeded in liberating the mother of all false queens.

"You need to stop the real Suhela," the theel ordered the rakshasas, desperately hoping to still prevent Kaia and her helpers from escaping the Palace of the Ruins.

"The human souls belong to me!" shouted the false queen.

Abandoning most of its recruits, the theel shot out of the chamber with the false queen, hoping to intercept Suhela and her newfound rescuers. On her way out, the false queen evoked the remaining impostors to follow her. Their combined cackle echoed across the Ruins as they stormed toward the back gates in search of the escapees.

Suhela and Kaia hurriedly escorted the kids to the entrance of the Palace of Ruins, where the oracle was waiting with her vasanas, ready to transport them to their buggy.

"The theel and his cronies will be out soon," cautioned Suhela.

"Great. We get to ride the apes again," said Ro.

"And no oil this time to mask the odor," said Max.

"Who cares? I just want to get out of here," said Brendan.

The return ride to the buggy was quick. As the ule and horse-drawn buggy sped along the pathway, they saw the light shift a little. The portal opened, and the children saw the familiar stone building where Yan had opened the gateway to the middle sphere. The buggy came to a stop in front of the stone building, but the laughter from behind continued.

"They're following us," said Brendan.

Yan emerged from the shadows with his prisms and the faintly lit key stone. He waited for the noisy followers to reach the gateway, and when they were about to escape and enter, he slammed the gateway shut by separating the prisms, hurling them back to where they had come from.

Silence returned to the outer sphere.

###

Brendan and the kids stood at the back of the private room, listening to Turner rave to the parents about the team's splendid performance.

"Board One has been good for us today."

"It feels weird," said Brendan, leaning over to Max. "Days spent there are just hours here."

"I agree. It all seems like a dream, and I barely remember playing the game."

Ro, who was standing beside Sidney, touched her shoulder. "I was really worried for you."

"I am sorry for walking away without telling you," she said, smiling. "I could see everything in that place when I was with the queen."

"When's the next round?" asked some parent.

"Not until 2.30 p.m. We have another three hours to kill," said another parent.

Tasha handed a note to Brendan. "This is from Kaia," she said.

The note said, *Brendan, bring the team down to the stained-glass exhibit #7—The lady in the church, in the Navy Pier, as soon as possible. Kaia.*

"Now?" asked Brendan, but Tasha had already walked away.

Chapter 15

The Stone Wall

Among the exhibits at the Smith Museum, it was the largest display of stained-glass windows that had found its permanent home at Navy Pier. Colorful pieces of glass panes, large and small, were neatly assembled to form a wall-sized depiction of the inside of a medieval church, where a young woman sat on a pew, praying with her head tilted forward and arms clasped. The place was almost empty and quiet, and Brendan and his friends stood there, admiring the artwork.

"That looks like a safe place," said Kaia.

"The lady in the church by…" Brendan read the information on the wall next to the art. "Where is this church?" he asked Kaia.

"It's right here."

"That it is. But…" Brendan stopped midway through his sentence.

The light distorted. The glass pieces forming the images stretched and suddenly snapped. When Brendan opened his eyes, he found himself inside a quiet church, seated next to Kaia, several rows behind the praying young woman. The woman turned back to look at them briefly but went back to her prayers.

"Now, we can discuss our plans without being overheard," said Kaia.

Deep inside the secret Cave of Ice, the theel's master hovered as usual—cross-legged in the lotus pose, his bony frame draped in a thin black robe. He levitated silently over a massive block of ice, as if drawing strength from its bitter cold. The theel nervously waited in front of the block, motionless, suspended in air.

"I am disappointed," said the master without opening his eyes. "You were tricked by the mortals."

"Correction, master. I was tricked by the keeper and the trap by Neeria, the jala sorceress," the theel incoherently defended itself. "You never warned me about Neeria's false queen," it added.

"You failed, theel," said the master without raising his voice. A layer of water gushed as the ice melted, taking the heat from him. "Neeria is my doing in Mayastella. In your haste, you fell for her decoys. You have awakened your own soulless kind without thinking things through, and now, you must deal with the consequences. However..." the master continued without pausing for a response from the theel, "I must warn you, if she succeeds in finding me what I want, then she will replace you. I don't need two of you."

"Master, after all I have done for you..." the theel tried to protest.

"Save your meaningless whining. I have neither the time nor the patience. If you fail to get to Kumba before the humans do, then your existence will cease," the master warned. "The false queen will go with you."

"She's here?" the theel hissed, its eyes bulging. Like a kite caught in gusty wind, it swayed from one side of the ice block to the other, searching for her.

The false queen emerged from inside the cave. The theel wanted to strangle her slowly with its bony hands, but the master was in no mood to appreciate such gestures. Yet, though her lips didn't move, shivering peals of laughter echoed through his mind at the very sight of her. "*I will use her for now,*" it thought, "*but will find a way to dispose of her later.*"

"They might have found Suhela, but they'll never be able to get past the stone wall before us," said the false queen. "The water world is a dangerous place, even for your rakshasas. We can trap the humans there and hurry to the inner sphere of Mayastella."

The theel resented the false queen's arrogance.

"You'd better get to work then," said the master.

The ice block had melted to half its original size.

"Round Two," said Turner. "Austin and Sidney will go first, followed by Max and then Ro. Brendan's round will start last. The good news is, you are all playing on Board One again," he said with a grin. "And the bad news is…" Turner raised his left eyebrow as he typically did and shrugged. "*All* of you are playing tough opponents."

"Hey, man, you need to slow down a bit, man." A Caribbean accent boomed from the doorway of the large hall. "Make sure to attack the center, okay, man?" said Bob Raj to Ro. "Did you go over clearance with your coach?"

"Yes, we did," lied Ro, not in a mood to strike up a conversation with Coach Bob Raj about chess moves.

"Remember, man, you cannot poke a hole in your roof and wonder why it is raining inside the house. Don't create a hole in front of your king and wonder why you're being attacked there. Also, watch out for back-rank checkmate."

"Okay," said Ro. He had heard the same advice from Bob Raj at every tournament. Though repetitive, he knew it was good advice.

With ten minutes already on the clock, Max searched the hall, puzzled as to why his Earth dweller opponent hadn't shown. The wait was aggravating, and the sounds of kids moving the chess pieces and hitting the chess clock felt annoyingly amplified. He attempted to notify the tournament director, but the TD brushed him off. He searched for Kaia and Tasha, but neither were inside the tournament hall. Max rapidly shook his leg up and down and focused his attention on his notation pad. "Are you ready to get killed?" asked his opponent, suddenly appearing from nowhere and slumping into the chair across from Max.

He moved a white pawn and slammed the clock to stop it.

"Huh?" Max was startled by the sudden appearance of the noisy opponent.

"You heard me, wimp. Make your move."

"What's your rating again?" asked Max with a tinge of sarcasm in his voice, staring down his rival without fear. He then abruptly moved his pawn and hit the clock.

Nothing happened.

"Are you on the right board?" Max asked.

"Are you?" asked his challenger, equally bewildered.

"We'll know soon, won't we?" said Max.

"Looks like the kid playing Max is playing Stonewall. Have you prepared him for this?" asked Bob Raj, watching Max's game on the monitor.

Max kicked his legs and stretched out his arms to reach the surface. He tried to shout but gulped water and gasped. Someone pulled him by his shirt as he swung his hands wildly to grab on to something.

"Are you all right, son?" asked Yan, lifting Max out of the water.

Max coughed uncontrollably to expel the water he had swallowed. "Wh—where am I?" he asked, shivering.

"Sorry, Max. Yan's timing at steering his chariot-watercraft was a bit off, and he made you land in the water."

Max hated water, but was relieved to see Aarjen. Queen Suhela sat right across from him.

"Are we inside a boat?" he asked about his curious surroundings. Made of a shiny black metal, fitted with an oversize bow resembling a wild bronco at the front and a long, protruding rudder at the back. Despite its odd rook-shaped build, the black vehicle was slicing through the water at a very high speed. "You can call it a chariot or a watercraft, but not a boat, son," said Yan with a twinkle in his eyes.

Max took a deep breath, slumping into the futon-like seat. "Where are we going?" he asked.

"The Water World of Mayastella," said Queen Suhela. "The entrance to the inner sphere, Kumba's kingdom."

"Do we have to go on water?" asked Max. "I hate being on water," he said with a scowl.

Barely touching the surface of the water, the chariot sped down a large, winding river, flanked by rugged mountainous banks lined with tall trees. Spiky roots, like mangroves, covered the edge of the banks. The river erratically split around rocky islands as the raft followed the flow.

"Where is this kingdom?" asked Max, holding his stomach, as he fought a sensation of wooziness.

"The game you are playing will lead us to it," said Yan.

"Our journey becomes more intertwined with your game as you get deeper into Mayastella—your chess moves, your actions, and their consequences here are interconnected," Aarjen reminded him.

"Where is Brendan?" asked Max.

"Your friends should be here soon," said Aarjen. "Let's study the clues in Yan's notebook."

Yan flipped open his notebook, allowing it to illustrate the image of the river that flowed into the blue sea, but the river stopped abruptly before it reached the sea. The page was blank.

"Why does everything stop here?" asked Max, a bit puzzled.

"Looks like some information is missing or has been erased," said Yan, taking a closer look.

"Are there any clues?" asked Aarjen.

When Max carefully examined the replica of their surroundings in the notebook, the words appeared in the dark area where the images were missing.

As you near the mighty stone wall,

Lose your fear and let it fall.

"That's it? Something about not being afraid of a wall?"

"Are you afraid of a wall falling down?" asked Yan.

"Well, if I were standing close to it and if there were an earthquake or a tornado, I would be," said Max, shrugging.

"So, we first need to find this wall," said Aarjen.

"I don't think there are any walls in this place," said Yan.

"Is it a gateway of some sort?" asked the queen, shuddering at the thought of the stone walls that had kept her imprisoned.

"No, I can't recollect any gateways here. I guess we'll find out soon what the clue really means," Yan was optimistic.

Max sat back and watched the water fly by. "There!" Aarjen directed their attention to the sky. There was a flash of light, followed by a small shock wave. And just like that, Brendan and Ro stood next to Yan.

"Much better timing." Yan was pleased with himself.

"Our games just started," said Brendan. "I am playing against someone with a forked tongue."

"My Earth dweller opponent snarled at me and made her fangs grow. I was happy to get out of there," said Ro.

"By the way, you are playing against the Stonewall, Max. Good luck," said Brendan, referring to the chess tactic that Max's opponent was employing.

"That's it. It's the *stone wall*. It's my game in the tournament," Max cried out, connecting the dots.

Brendan frowned. "What about your game?"

As you near the mighty stone wall,

Lose your fear and let it fall.

"It's the clue from Yan's notebook," said Aarjen.

"I never liked the Stonewall opening," Max admitted. "Maybe if I overcome my fear against Stonewall and play well, we'll succeed here as well," he added thoughtfully.

"But you were never afraid of the Stonewall, Max," said Ro. "You are just a bad chess player." He chuckled and poked at Max.

"I think Max is right," said Queen Suhela. "It's his fear of losing. It affects his game particularly against the Stonewall opening."

"In this journey, the rook will play a big part for you, Max," Aarjen said. "Kaia has told me that you have the ability to analyze things well, and she feels you will use it to your advantage. There is more to the clue than the type of opening that you are playing at the tournament, Max."

As the chariot glazed through the water, Max and Ro explored it.

"I love the view from the front. It's like you are on a speedboat, but without the bumping," said Ro.

At a distance, spanning the horizon in front of the bow, Max spotted the outline of a structure raised above the water. At first, it looked like a wave swelling far away, but soon, Max realized it was a solid structure, whose height seemed to exponentially increase as the chariot sped closer to it at an alarming speed.

"*Stop!*" Max screamed. "Yan, *stop* the boat! You are going to hit that thing…The dam…The *wall.*"

Panic-stricken, Max darted into the cabin and grabbed Yan by his hand.

"What wall?" asked Aarjen and Yan in unison.

As Max continued to scream, Yan reacted by pushing some levers and pedals to quickly decelerate the watercraft.

"We are going to hit! We are going to hit," cried out Max, running backward.

He then jumped off the chariot but managed to hang on to the rudder. His body bobbed up and down on the surface of the water as the watercraft continued to slow down. Water splashed over his face, making it difficult for him to see or shout for help.

Controlling his balance, Yan reached over and yanked Max back into the shaky chariot. "You are going to get yourself killed, kid."

"By the wall or the water?" Max coughed water.

"What wall are you talking about?" Aarjen asked, perplexed.

"That wall." Flustered, Max gestured toward the endless, towering wall that stood just inches away from the chariot.

"I don't see any wall, Max," Brendan said, his voice conveying concern for his friend.

Yan inched the raft forward. Max ducked and covered his face with his hands in anticipation, but to his amazement, the raft slowly passed through the wall as though the barrier did not exist.

Max, who had deliberately anchored himself at the back of the chariot, relaxed when he saw everyone ghost through the wall. He closed his eyes as the wall approached him, and then he felt the impact. His stretched hand hit the wall first. He tried to grab on to its cold and rough surface but got pushed away as the chariot continued to move underneath his legs.

"*Stop!*" Max shouted again as he got pushed to the very edge of the raft, hanging from its frame. He prepared to jump out of the raft, afraid of being crushed. "*Stop, the wall is pushing me. Stop please!*" he screamed.

"*Stop, please,*" Brendan joined in the hysteria. "Something is wrong." He saw Max get pushed back, and he rushed to hold on to him.

Yan had already reacted to the situation and brought the chariot to a dead halt. Aarjen held on to Max.

"Are you all right, Max?" Aarjen asked.

"No, I am not, Aarjen," Max cried with rage, thrusting his hands out, scraped red by the wall, at Aarjen. "I am getting crushed or thrown in the water to be drowned. Do you think I am all right?" he said, his voice shaking. He adjusted his ripped hoodie, pulled his wet sleeve back, and examined his elbow. "That wall would have killed me!" His tears poured down uncontrollably.

"I...I saw everyone else go through it, but it hit me. It's real. I can see it, and I can feel it," Max stammered as he desperately tried to convince them the wall was indeed real and not imaginary. Water emptied out of his squeaking shoes as he moved away from everyone.

"I think this is an object of your imagination, son," said Yan. "Your mind is tricking you."

"Oh, yeah? Is that why I am bleeding and getting tossed into the water? This wall...This wall is *real.* I cannot even see where it begins or ends..." He looked around, and then he removed his water-soaked shoe and hurled it at the wall. Everyone watched it sail past the front of the raft and splash into the water without being stopped by Max's wall. Suhela rushed to comfort Max.

"The wall is real for Max. I get it," she said. "No more trying to pass through it," she instructed.

Yan used a long net and fished the shoe out of the flowing water that was forming a strong whirlpool ahead of them. Max watched the net briefly disappear into the wall and reappear with his shoe dangling in it.

As you near the mighty stone wall,

Lose your fear and let it fall.

"So, maybe you shouldn't be afraid of the wall, and it will fall."

Yan's theory made sense to Max. "Okay, you can try it one more time. I'll close my eyes, and maybe the wall will disappear. But go really, really slow, just in case this stupid thing doesn't disappear."

Max moved to the front of the chariot, shut his eyes tightly, and stuck his hands out as Yan allowed the current to gently push the watercraft forward.

Thump! As soon as Max hands bumped against the wall, he clambered to the rear of the raft. "It's still there. I am going to die."

Yan reversed the vehicle.

"Yan, what can you tell us about this wall?" asked Suhela.

"The wall exists," Yan looked at Max and assured him that he believed in what the boy had experienced. "It is both physical and mental. And it has to be brought down with physical and mental strength."

"Max," Aarjen gently laid his muscular arm around Max's shoulders and sat next to him. "Can you tell us how big the wall is?"

Max looked across. "It's everywhere, endless. It is from there to there." His stretched arms spanned across the entire width of the river. "It is made out of large blocks of stone, sloping, not straight up."

"How tall is it?" asked Aarjen.

"I can see the top from here." Max eyeballed the height of the wall— taller than a building several stories high.

"Why can't we just go around it?" asked Ro.

"It might not be that easy," said Queen Suhela. "Especially if we don't know where it starts or ends."

"What do you all see behind the wall?" Max asked with curiosity.

"Nothing. Just more water. This is where the river meets the sea. Whirlpools," added Yan.

"You said the chariot can fly. Why can't we fly over the wall?" asked Ro.

"I am going to show you how to control the chariot. You take it wherever you think you can get around the wall," said Yan.

"Are you really going to let him drive this?" asked Ro.

"It will be fine," Yan reassured.

The wall seemed never-ending. Max traversed from one end of the river to the other end. With the help of Yan, he guided the amphibious craft over land in either direction, but every time he thought he'd neared the end, the barrier seemed to extend into eternity. Once, Brendan and Ro even got off the chariot and walked across into the woods to show Max that there was nothing. Despite their efforts during each attempt, the wall seemed never-ending.

"I am not afraid of this wall. Yet this doesn't fall, as it says in the notebook. I bet it's my game. Perhaps you should leave me and go," Max was frustrated.

"Can't go anywhere without you, Max. You need to find the place for us," Suhela comforted Max. "You need to bring this wall down, and we are going to help you."

A distinct line separated the wall from the sky.

It's not too far, he told himself, scoping the skyline as the chariot ascended.

The chariot-watercraft hovered above the water and rose over the clouds, but to Max's frustration, the edge of the wall remained at a constant distance.

"This is useless," he said, disappointed. "How do I find a way through this wall?" He sighed.

When it descended back to the water, he slumped on the seat next to the queen, trying to hold back tears. When Suhela touched Max to comfort him, she sensed his deep-rooted turmoil. His fear was creating a wall around him.

"Something else is bothering you, Max. What is it?" asked Suhela.

"My coach says that I overanalyze everything and get stuck sometimes. And my father believes that I create my own time pressure. I am sure that I am just stuck in my game again," he said.

"Don't worry. We are going to help you break the wall," said Suhela.

"Hey, what are those?" asked Brendan curiously, drawing everyone's attention to large cylindrical green objects that intermittently bobbed in and out of the water.

"Oh, those are just monster sea turtles. They come up to breathe. They are harmless," said Yan.

A curious and daring creature surfaced close to the raft and thrust its head above the water to observe the strangers.

"He looks so friendly," said Ro.

"Most of them are," said Yan.

While Aarjen and his crew were briefly distracted by the monster sea turtles, stealthy mudalas raced toward the preoccupied visitors. The unusual smell of humans attracted them to the watercraft. They dove deep and maneuvered silently in the shadows of the gentle giant turtles, approaching the raft for the kill.

"Can we pet it?" asked Ro, pointing to the giant turtles.

"You can get close, but do not touch them," cautioned Yan.

The mudalas seized the opportunity to attack the boys from three different directions.

Aarjen jumped from his seat and dove into the water, deliberately drawing the attention of the mudalas. Aarjen's sudden move prompted Queen Suhela to follow suit. The stealthy crocodile-looking creatures rushed toward Aarjen in a frenzy, each hoping to beat the other in getting the larger portion of its voluntary meal. Aarjen, who waited with his long dagger, flipped underneath the first creature with perfect timing and slit its throat with one swift motion. He then went head-on at the second pursuer and drew blood, leaving it severely injured and at the mercy of the scavengers of the river. With similar ease, Suhela finished the last one. She was about to follow Aarjen back into the chariot, but something under the surface of the water caught her attention.

In the submerged, jagged reef below, a shiny object was swaying back and forth. Suhela plunged back into the water to take a closer look. A jala, stuck in the crevice of the reef, was desperately trying to free herself, her shiny, long silver hair swaying back and forth. Her struggle attracted a mudala that zeroed in on her with its mouth open.

Suhela timed her flip turn underwater to land a powerful kick with her brute rakshasi strength, instantly cracking its jaw. The injured mudala was swept away by the swift current.

"I am going to help you," Suhela signed to the jala and freed her from the reef that had trapped her.

As the jala expressed her gratitude, she was joined by others of her kind, who had come in search of her.

"How can we repay you?" asked a large, older jala, who was her father.

Suhela was quick to take advantage of the offer of help. "I am Kumba's queen. I am here with my friends on a quest to find my king. We need some help in finding the path to his resting place, which we hear is through your world."

"It is a dangerous quest, my Queen, but we'll honor our word and help you in any way we can." The jala handed Suhela his thin golden chain with a small, dangling conch. "Use this to send a signal when you need our help, and we'll come to your aid."

"One word of caution," he said as an afterthought. "As you get closer to the entrance, speed is most important. No one has ever outrun the ghost riders of the underworld."

"The theel has arrived with his crew. Let's take cover," Aarjen said. He was the first to sense their arrival.

"There! Max, do you see that heavily wooded island in the middle of the river at 10 o'clock? It's slightly to the left, just ahead of us."

"Yes, I can see it. The wall is only behind it."

"We'll be safe there. The smell from the tree barks of these forests should overpower human scent." Yan proceeded to steer the chariot toward the island.

"Sounds like a perfect hiding place," said Aarjen.

A brushed-nickel chariot-watercraft with an ule-shaped bow appeared to deliberately slow down in front of the island. The marisan controlling the chariot appeared to be having a heated debate with a potbellied rakshasa and kept gesturing at the island. After staring in the direction of the human hideout, the marisan steered its chariot toward the island, but abruptly halted and reversed the vehicle. The theel emerged from the shiny chariot, floated in the air, as if reconnoitering, and slid back.

"Are they picking up a scent?" Suhela asked.

"That's impossible," said Aarjen. "The aroma of the oil from the santalum trees are too strong. It could be something else they saw. Maybe they spotted our chariot."

"No," Yan assured them. "It is well concealed from the eyes of the rakshasas."

"Hey, that's the guy I am playing against! He's my opponent," Max said, nudging Brendan with his elbow while looking through a peculiar-double tubed, brass telescope, from inside their camouflaged chariot.

Brendan looked into the telescope. "Looks like the guy who's playing against me is also there."

"Let me look!" Ro squeezed himself between Brendan and Max and took over the telescope. "I don't see my opponent...Oh, wait. There she is, just stepped out."

"Shh! These creatures can pick up on your sound," Aarjen cautioned the kids.

"Someone just fell overboard," Max whispered. "Looks like they are going back for him."

Brendan took over the telescope. "I think he's dead. He's just floating in the water."

There was a long silence as both Ro and Max tried to push each other to see what was going on.

"Dead?" asked Max.

"Um, the theel is doing something to him. Looks like it's your opponent."

Max watched the theel lift the fallen Earth dweller and set him on the floor of the chariot. Something the theel did seemed to revive the Earth dweller, who waved at the creatures in the front end of the chariot and then jumped into the water again.

"He jumped into the water again," said Max.

They took turns observing the drama unfolding at a distance.

"Guys, it's the wall. The wall is pushing him down as well. He has the same stone wall," said Max, his voice booming with excitement. "I am not the only one who is stuck."

"You are correct," said Yan. "Stay low and hidden in this chariot for a while until we figure out our next move."

Max froze when he saw a pair of large green eyes staring directly at him through the opposite end of the scope. Whatever or whomever he was looking at was very close and had spotted him. Snapping out of his temporary paralysis, Max pulled himself away from the telescope, waited, and slowly peeked again, hoping that he had just imagined what he saw, but the unblinking eyes were still there.

He rotated the lenses and zoomed out to see what he was looking at. A tall, skinny lad with green eyes and red hair stood, smiling and waving at him. He appeared to say something. Max waved back out of sheer instinct.

"Who are you waving at?" asked Ro.

"Check it out. Someone with red hair is waving at me."

"Yeah, right." Ro grabbed the telescope and looked through. All he saw was commotion in the dark chariot. "Stop waving at them, Max. That theel will spot us."

Max pushed Ro and looked through the telescopic instrument again. The red-headed stranger had disappeared.

Max checked the surrounding area through the telescope, and there he was. Perched on the branch of a tall tree near Yan's chariot, the lad waved at him again and signaled Max to meet him by the thickets under the tree.

"Me?"

The friendly fellow stretched his thin long hands, as though placing them on the wall behind him.

Max handed the scope to Ro. "Here. Nature's calling."

"Be careful!" warned Ro.

But Max had already slipped out and headed to the tree.

"Hi, I am Max. Who are you?" he asked the friendly chap standing next to him.

"Max. Me Run-Nier. Friend to Max, Sidney, and Austin." The stranger spoke with an accent, stretching each word deliberately.

"How do you know my friends?"

"I am here to help Max with the wall."

Max's mind warned him against the tantrics, but there was certainly something about the big-eyed fella that put him at ease.

"Thanks. Can you see the wall too?" Max was surprised.

"I see what Max see. I help."

"The wall seems to go in all directions. I can't get around it. Is there an opening somewhere?"

"Opening?" Run-Nier thought for a while, and then he shook his head. "No. I show you the way."

"How come there is a wall only for me?" Max felt short next to Run-Nier. The thick, unruly red hair seemed to add several more inches to his already-lanky frame.

"The wall is in your mind." He leaned over and tapped Max's forehead. "In there." His slender but soft index finger was cold.

"Absolutely not," Max disagreed. "The wall is real, and I can't even see what's behind that wall."

"Max afraid. What Max fear? Max, think. The wall is your fear."

"What am I afraid of?" Max collected his thoughts. "Everything…I'll be honest with you. I am afraid of everything. Lots of crazy creatures here that want to kill us and eat us."

"Max…No. It is a fear in your mind you have carried a long time."

"Water! I am terrified of water."

"Why Max fear water?"

"Long story," Max paused, but considering the inquisitive and helpful nature of the stranger, he volunteered an explanation. "Well, okay…I was once a good swimmer."

Beads of sweat formed on his forehead. A shudder passed through him as he tugged his hair, trying to think of events in the past he had tucked away.

"One day, we, um…A bunch of kids were playing in a swimming pool, and suddenly, my friend had a seizure and began to drown," said Max, stuttering. "I tried to help him out but got sucked into the water. Luckily, we were saved by a lifeguard. I ended up drinking a lot of chlorinated water, and my friend was seriously injured." Max paused. "We almost died, and ever since, I have been afraid of water."

"Max cannot go underwater? There is no stone wall underwater."

"What?"

"There is no wall underwater," he repeated.

As you near the mighty stone wall,

Lose your fear and let it fall.

Max analyzed the situation in his mind. Even if that were true, there was no way he was going to dive inside a crazy river in some strange world where weird creatures, looking like crocs, were lurking to bite the head off any human kid—not to mention a watercraft full of rakshasas chasing them. None of this made sense. It was just not logical.

"How do you know there is no wall under the water? If it's never-ending in all directions, why not under the water?"

"Max think too much and get stuck." Run-Nier echoed the very warning that Max's coach had voiced innumerable times. "This is Max weakness. Make this your strength."

"How?"

"Okay, Run-Nier will go underwater and under wall. Max can see Run-Nier with scope." Run-Nier mimed to Max as though he were looking at the wall through the telescope. "Trust me, I help you. You go underwater alone."

"Alone? Why alone? No." Max vigorously shook his finger at Run-Nier. "I am not going underwater."

"You jump alone in water."

"Will you help me?"

"Help you with what?" asked Ro from behind. He'd come looking for Max since he had been gone for longer than he had expected.

"Ro, this is Run-Nier. He knows…"

But Run-Nier had disappeared.

Ro frowned, unable to comprehend what Max was mumbling.

"Never mind," Max said. "I need to talk to Yan. He can help me with the wall."

With great difficulty, Yan maneuvered the chariot to the other side of the island without being spotted by the rakshasas.

"Once we enter the main river, they'll spot us," cautioned Yan. "But Max will have enough time to go underwater."

"Thanks." Max's voice was shaky.

Suhela reassured him that the plan would be successful.

Yan's chariot sped silently on the river, and Max nervously awaited the wall.

"Okay, *now!*" he shouted and jumped into the water just before the chariot knifed through the wall.

At a distance, the theel's acute senses picked up the noise. "Follow them!" it screamed.

Max was disoriented. The water was bone-chilling, and the rapid current swept him downriver. Determined to stay underwater as long as he could, Max held his breath tightly and battled his fear of drowning. As he struggled, his eyes caught a glimpse of the thick red hair of Run-Nier, waving in the water at a distance. Run-Nier motioned with his hands for Max to follow him, and as Max kicked his legs hard to push himself under the wall, it seemed to dissolve as he got closer to it.

Max felt like his lungs were about to explode, yet he continued to push forward. When he had nothing left in him to give, he felt a sudden tug on his arm, pulling him forcefully as the wall crumbled. Large blocks of stone above the surface crashed into the water but safely disintegrated without a trace just a few inches above Max. Max felt a sharp pain in his head, and he couldn't hold his breath any longer. He waved at Run-Nier and let his breath slowly escape.

Max woke up gasping for breath as two heavy hands pushed against his chest. It was Yan who had pulled him out and restored his breathing.

"Welcome back!" said Yan, his voice softening with a touch of concern. "I must admit, you scared us by being underwater so long. Do you still see…"

"It's gone!" Max weakly pumped his fist in the air. "It's nowhere." He coughed more water out. "I did it, and I am not afraid of the water anymore." He tilted his head sideways and shook his ear rapidly with his finger to drain the water.

Brendan and Ro huddled next to Max on the long, comfortable seat. Brendan squeezed Max's arm and patted him on his shoulder a couple of times. Ro leaned over and put his arm around Max.

From a distance, the theel's stationary chariot fired a bolt of electricity, rocking Yan's chariot but doing no harm.

"Why are they not chasing us?" asked Max. "The wall is gone."

"It has only become worse for them," said Suhela. She gently pushed his dripping hair away from his eyes and put a towel over his head. "Not even the theel, nor their chariot, can get through the wall now, let alone the Earth dweller."

"When you broke your wall, the notebook revealed the next phase of the journey and how to get to King Kumba," Aarjen said. "Suhela can now take us to the inner sphere."

Suhela blew the mini conch attached to the golden chain, and several large jalas surrounded the water chariot.

"They'll take you to the forbidden inner sphere," said the jala who had given the conch to the queen.

Suhela returned the chain and thanked them. The chariot changed its shape into a submersible and torpedoed through the deep waters to the entrance to the inner sphere, guided by the jalas.

###

Turner couldn't believe his eyes.

"Are you sure we are watching Max's game?" he asked Bob Raj.

"It is the K-10, Board Number One, right? So, it's Max. Why do you ask?" Bob Raj was surprised.

"I have never seen Max attack like this." Turner was jubilant. "He has doubled up his rook and opened up the e-file of his opponent. Usually, when he's stuck, he's really stuck!"

"Is this the boy who often gets defensive and runs out of time?" asked Bob Raj curiously.

"Yes," said Turner.

Bob Raj patted Turner on his shoulder. "Well, your boy is about to crush the other guy—unless he stalemates."

Max's father watched his son's aggressive game with a big grin on his face.

Max quickly rolled his rook on the e-file and traded his opponent's rook. He then forced a check, pinning his opponent's queen. Within the next few moves, he checkmated his opponent, using his rook and queen, with more than 30 minutes to spare on his clock. Turner and his group jumped with joy.

"You did well," Suhela complimented Max. "You should be proud of yourself for being courageous and leading us to the entrance to the inner world."

Max expressed his earnest gratitude to Suhela, Aarjen, and Yan.

"It's time to go," said Aarjen, looking at the portal. "If the rakshasas find a way to move in, Yan will defend. It will now be your turn, Ro. Let's prepare."

The boys said goodbye to Max as they prepared themselves for the next adventure. Max felt as though he had just snapped out of a dream, suddenly finding himself in front of an angry Earth dweller, who was staring at him. His eyes were bloodshot.

"How's your stone wall, dude?" Max prodded.

"You are going to die, human." The Earth dweller's voice was deep. He sank his dark, protruding nails into the table and kicked the chair, sending chess pieces flying in all directions.

A TD rushed to the stage, where the Board Number One players sat. Many others, mid-game, were drawn to the commotion.

Max calmly stepped back from the Earth dweller.

"You are losing the games," said Max. "You cannot attack us here."

"Cheaters! We are going to get you one way or the other." He pushed the table at Max.

"Stop playing around!" shouted a TD, who had no clue as to what was going on. "You just got yourself disqualified." He rushed to intervene, but when he saw the Earth dweller's red eyes and foamy mouth, he froze.

Tasha moved quickly.

She reached for a tiny device in her vest, which looked like a pen, and pressed a button, injecting a serum into the arm of the frantic Earth dweller, who had turned into a hideous creature.

The serum took effect immediately, reverting the Earth dweller to its original human form.

"Kids were just goofing around," Tasha said to the confused TD.

Within minutes, the Earth dweller was escorted out by Tasha, and without further distraction, the kids were back, focusing on their games.

Chapter 16

The Ghost Riders of the Plasma

The chariot came to an abrupt halt. "Why did we stop?" Ro held on to his seat and strained to peek outside. He had been in the middle of telling a joke to Brendan, who was listening reluctantly and refusing to laugh.

"We are back to the surface of the water."

An ominous storm had rolled in, and sporadic flashes of lightning struck the water. It began to rain. "This is where we leave you, great Queen of Kumba," said one of the jalas from the water below. "The dangerous world you are seeking is beyond those storms. That world belongs to the vicious ghost riders, also known as the vegas. No one has ever outrun the vegas, but I hope you do."

The boys watched the jalas disappear into the water.

"We have reached the entrance to the underworld," said Yan. "This place is neither water nor land."

"Then, what is it?" asked Brendan.

"We call it suspended space," said Yan. "It is the space between the middle sphere and the inner sphere and is filled with a type of cold plasma."

"I know plasma," said Ro quickly. "It is considered to be the fourth state of matter."

"It's like quicksand. If you stay in one place or even slow down, you'll be trapped. The plasma will slowly suck you in, ultimately crushing you with its weight."

"As we cross this space, we have to find a way to race against the vegas."

"Las Vegas?" Ro said, chuckling.

"Vegas are creatures that hunt in groups. They derive pleasure from chasing their helpless victims and taunting them, eventually trapping and collecting their souls. Only then can they exit the plasma and go anywhere they want to. Without the souls, they are stuck in plasma," Yan tried to explain.

"How do these things survive in the plasma?" asked Ro.

"The bodies of the ghost riders can disassociate into tiny particles so that they can move through the layer of plasma with ease—almost like smoke dispersing in the wind, but with the ability to regroup."

"We won't be alone." Yan paused. "We will be racing against the rakshasas."

"Great! We are going to be racing ghosts and rakshasas in some plasma that could crush us," said Ro.

"We are getting close," said Yan, watching the storm intensify.

Lightning struck all around them. Yan made some mechanical adjustments to the chariot by spinning a few wheels and pushing levers.

An uneasy silence followed.

Brendan looked outside through the tiny window. "I can't see anything. It's foggy."

"I can detect plasma." Yan displayed the various features of his chariot and showed them how to measure plasma using his instruments.

Ro looked at Suhela, who had moved to the other end of the chariot. She was leaning against the window, resting her cheek on one hand and making tiny pleats on her gown with the other hand. Her eyes constantly shifted, as though she was reading something, with an occasional subtle shaking of her head.

"Queen Suhela…Are you okay?" Ro asked politely, standing close to her.

"Thanks for asking, Ro," Suhela said, shifting her attention to him with warmth evident in her gaze as she reached out and touched his arm. Her piercing yet kind and friendly expression welcomed him. "Come sit here." Her voice was soft. "Something about these vegas…I sense a strange, uneasy feeling."

She looked outside the window and drifted away a little.

Ro leaned inward with his hands clasped. While he wasn't quite prepared to discuss inner turmoil with an adult, he managed to continue his conversation with the queen. "Have you felt this before?" he asked.

"I have rakshasi blood, which means I have a sinister side deep inside of me," she paused. "Emptiness or sadness could evoke this emotion. It seems the evil vegas have done just that…"

"Don't worry. We are here to make sure the creatures don't get to you," he said as he tried to comfort her.

"I am lucky to have you by me." Her soft, warm touch suddenly felt cold and made him shudder.

Suhela rubbed her wrists. "I have the same feeling I had when I was in shackles." Her breath fogged the window glass. Her body shivered.

Ro held on to Suhela's trembling hand. He wanted to help her. He grabbed the heavy robe that was hanging on a rack behind them and wrapped it over her shoulders, covering her body.

"They are here," she whispered. "I can hear them say, *Your soul is mine.*"

"I see them." Ro looked through the windows.

The smoke-like ghost riders appeared in front of the partially frosted window, their bodies elongated, like elastic bands. "*Your soul is mine,*" she repeated after them.

"Queen Suhela, they are getting to you. Please don't look at them." Ro's voice was stern and loud enough for others to hear. He shook Suhela lightly by her shoulders.

"Don't look at what?" asked Brendan.

Ro raised his voice. "We saw them, the vegas."

"The vegas?" Yan moved closer to the window. He peered outside into the vast expanse of haze.

"Everyone, stay away from the windows." Yan removed his folded notebook.

Ro paced between Brendan and Suhela. "Isn't it my turn?" He wished this were not his journey.

"I think so. Let us see if you can read the clue," replied Yan.

Fog drifted out of the blank pages, and they gathered over the edge of the propped-up notebook.

"I think the plasma is trying to form words," he said, squinting and adjusting his glasses. "I can't make them out. They are like disintegrated sky writing," Ro said.

Yan attached the notebook to a small, flat wheel by the instruments he'd used for measuring the plasma and fastened its corners. He then covered the notebook with a pane of glass.

"This should hold it in place." He made room for Ro. "Step in here and see if you can read the words while I spin."

As Yan spun the wheel, foggy plasma gushed out of the page, like the dancing fumes of incense sticks clustering together. It filled up the enclosed glass casing and overflowed into the chamber of the chariot, as though someone had dropped a smoke bomb.

"I feel heavy. The air is pushing me down," said Brendan.

"I can feel it too," agreed Yan, holding on to his seat.

"I actually feel light, as though I were floating through space." Ro stretched his arms out and flapped his hands in the air.

Words began to form, and Ro read them aloud clearly.

For in your haste, the time you waste,

Trying to outlast the Vegas, so fast.

You might never win to get in.

Greed is their creed, you shall use not to lose.

"It is about speed, outrunning the vegas without wasting time," said Yan.

"When you play a long game, you waste a lot of time by walking around, dude," said Brendan.

"Huh?" Ro skewed his upper lip sideways.

"I am not sure I understand," admitted Yan.

"Ro gets bored with long games. He doesn't use his clock much and wanders around the tournament, watching other games while his opponent is thinking about the next move," Brendan swiped at Ro's shoulder with the back of his hand.

"I am a fast thinker." Ro shrugged his shoulders.

"When he loses, he loses fast, too."

"Hey, it's my style. I win fast, lose fast. I don't get stuck, like Max," argued Ro.

"That's it," said Brendan, as though a light bulb had gone on. "This clue is about playing fast games."

"Blitz!" Ro said with a sparkle in his eye. "It is blitz, and I rule in blitz. Just five minutes on the clock. No time to waste," Ro was unable to conceal his excitement over blitz.

"And he *has* finished top five in the nation." Brendan nodded.

"Is blitz part of the tournament?" asked Yan.

"It is a separate event…The second night of the tournament," Brendan said. "Tonight."

"The faster I play, the faster I'll travel through that plasma, right?" Ro asked. "I think that's the secret."

"Looks like you solved the puzzle," Suhela said. "Let's regroup with Aarjen and Kaia. We have the advantage now, so let's do it together."

"The pairings will be up and posted on the main hall and by the registration desk, but please don't crowd the tournament halls," the tall tournament director announced loudly to the crowd of tired parents and children sprawled across the waiting room.

Kids representing various schools across the country crowded around chessboards, yelling chess moves and noisily hitting chess clocks. Coaches were going over won and lost games with their students, younger kids were running around, and food and snacks were consumed in large quantities.

"Will this be posted on the tournament app?" a parent asked.

"Nope. We are having some technical issues," he shouted back.

"You should have held the blitz tournament yesterday," yelled a man from the back of the crowd.

"Are you going to have Round Six?" asked a parent in a rude voice.

"Probably not, if you all are not patient," the TD snapped back and walked away.

"Hey, Ro!" Kaia called out, intercepting him as he was darting to the coaching room, where his parents and friends were waiting.

"Kaia, I have won all my games so far."

"How many more rounds to go?"

"Not sure. We were supposed to go for six rounds, but since it is already late, they might not hold the last round," said Ro. His casual response and tone of voice betrayed his disappointment.

"You will have the final round," said Kaia.

"Are you sure?" Ro asked breathlessly.

"This is your round, Ro. Prepare yourself to face the ghost riders."

Ro's heart raced. He had won 10 out of 10 games and had a real shot at the title. He enjoyed playing blitz, but the thought of facing creatures who hunted for souls in a faraway world made him squirm. Suddenly, he wanted it all to be just a dream and go away.

"Will I be playing them *now*?"

"Yes, but don't worry, both Aarjen and I will be going with you," Kaia reassured Ro. "Let's talk after you come back from the coaching room. Your parents are waiting for you."

Ro disappeared into the crowd. Kaia waited for a while. When he returned, she watched him hug his mother with joy. He had won five rounds of blitz and just one more to go. He was on fire. "What are you looking at?" Aarjen tapped Kaia on her shoulder and pulled up a chair next to her.

Kaia was focused on Ro, who was explaining how he had won his game against the top player in the tournament. It was an upset. "He has a good head on his shoulders," Kaia remarked warmly. "I feel a strong connection with them," she added, her eyes reflecting genuine understanding and affection.

Aarjen changed the subject swiftly. "With the proliferation of the nijaz, the vegas have been able to collect so many souls and have become stronger—more than ever."

"Yes. These poor nijaz have not yet learned about the perils of Mayastella and are attracted to the plasma like moths are attracted to light," said Kaia. She slid her chair closer to Aarjen to remove a few specks of shiny red and blue foil confetti that had settled on his rugged brown hair from a nearby chess team's victory celebration, but then decided to just hold his hand.

"I am worried for Ro and the queen," said Kaia.

"The queen?" Aarjen asked, raising a quizzical eyebrow.

"Yes, the ghost riders kindle her dark side," said Kaia. "Their presence could tilt the balance between good and bad within the queen. I am afraid we will not like the consequence."

"I will go with Ro. You should stay back here," said Aarjen. "Yan and Suhela can travel with you after we have found the entrance to the underworld."

Kaia thought about the plan. She shook her head thoughtfully. "I think I should be in the plasma instead of you."

"And why would that be better?"

"If we want to be fast in plasma, Ashvat will be able to help me. Once we find the entrance, we can switch places. The inner sphere is the place for you. You and Brendan will be better paired in the endgame."

"The plasma is too dangerous for—"

Kaia placed her finger on Aarjen's lips and interrupted her companion before he could fully object.

"You forget that I am a knight too, Aarjen. Speed is my nickname," she said, patting Aarjen's stubbly, chiseled face. "I feel that I need to be with the queen when she's challenged by the vegas."

Aarjen grabbed her finger playfully and nodded. "Brendan certainly will need me in the underworld, I agree. We'll wait for you in the chariot."

"Only one game left?" asked a young player, standing on a chair and scratching his head. "But each round of blitz is always out of two games."

"You can't change the rules at the last minute," shouted an angry father with a thick accent.

"Yes, we can, sir, *especially* if it is blitz. Technically, we don't want to start one minute later than 9 p.m., and if you all keep arguing, I'll cancel the last round." The TD slammed his notepad on the desk, sending notation sheets and pencils flying.

"Let 'em play the last round. At least this will serve as a tiebreaker," shouted another TD. "That's eleven games all together, just one short of the planned twelve games."

"Why can't they play all of them? You don't need to post another pairing, and they can simply switch colors," shouted one of the school coaches.

"One game or nothing!" yelled the TD. He pulled a crumpled wad of napkins from his loosely fitted coat pocket and wiped tiny beads of sweat from his forehead. His face turned red. He then pushed a chair away before walking back into the tournament hall, mumbling to himself.

Kaia pulled Ro aside. "Our plan to keep this to just one game has worked. Play as fast as you can."

"I will," said Ro.

"I'll see you on the other side." Kaia winked.

"See you soon." Ro waved at Kaia, not wanting to think about the longest five minutes he'd ever have in his life.

"Where are we?" Ro's breath condensed, like it would on a cold winter day in Chicago. Shivering, he squinted and tried to focus on the dim surroundings.

Kaia greeted Ro inside the fully enclosed chariot-watercraft by gently wrapping him with a warm, thick robe. Narrow beams of golden light from tiny lamps on the roof of the chariot appeared to lose the battle against the dense fog, creating an illusion of light dispersing into a bottomless tank. Ro was relieved to feel the floor's hard surface. He noticed Yan's shadowy figure at the front of the chariot, fiddling with the instruments and gadgets.

The stationary chariot's door slowly unfurled upward, like the falcon winged door of a Tesla Model X. Ro's eyes adjusted to the surrounding darkness, but there was nothing but gray thick haze. He followed Kaia, Yan, and Suhela and stepped outside cautiously.

"I am standing on a hard surface," said Ro.

"We are still on land, but we are about to be challenged by the vegas to play their game," said Yan.

"What kind of game?" asked Ro.

"A cold-blooded one they call a soul trap—a cat-and-mouse game of chasing and trapping souls," said Yan.

A group of looming vegas awaited their arrival.

"Welcome to the world of plasma. Get ready to lose your soul," announced a sinister, hollow-sounding creature. "I have not started the clock yet, so you can have a head start."

Ro found himself standing next to Kaia, staring at a vega, whose skin was loosely hanging on a cartilaginous body. Its sunken eyes were barely visible, buried inside the socket of the bony skull face. Its wide, lipless mouth exposed its rotten teeth from cheek to cheek, creating the expression of a wicked smile. The tattered dark leather outfit, exposing bones and flesh, was loosely wrapped around its body. It carried a long, luminescent whip, coiled and tucked behind in the wide belt that kept his saggy outfit from falling.

"I see you have company," the vega bellowed.

It disappeared from where it stood and appeared in front of the marisan, who had just arrived with the theel and the false queen.

"We are here to help you get a human soul," hissed the theel.

"A proposition from the worm?" replied the cynical vega.

"My master will reward you with your own world of plasma and an endless supply of lost souls for your kind to keep," advised the theel.

"An empty promise from another soulless creature. You need to give us more than the human souls." The vega went close to the marisan. "We'll take a few of these," it said, sniffing the marisan's head.

Two other vegas whisked by the marisan and laughed.

"You can have as many of them as you want, but I must warn you, these shapeshifters are as fast as the vegas."

"The faster, the better!" declared the vega as it zipped through the plasma to demonstrate its speed.

"Listen up. You'll not only play each other, but you'll race the other ghost riders," the leader yelled. "The clock is about to start on a soul hunt, and here are the rules," the vega said.

"Rule number one." The vega stuck out its pale spike-like finger and zoomed from Kaia at one side to the theel at the opposite side so fast that it appeared to be on both sides at the same time. "We have two primary players: this human"—it appeared close to Ro and touched him with its sharp but lithe nail, just short of tearing the skin; Ro gasped. "And you."— the vega swooshed to the Earth dweller standing next to the theel and squeezed the Earth dweller's head.

A protective marisan attempted to push the creature away from the Earth dweller, but the vega had already moved away in one fluid motion.

"You race against each other."

"A human soul is worth more than this filthy one here," the vega ridiculed the Earth dweller. "I like that," it added, quickly shifting to Ro, but Kaia shielded him. "The two primary players are the kings of this game. We are after your souls."

"Rule number two! You can bring your own force—your queen, your knights, your bishops, or your rook—but we'll provide you with the soldiers. Dead soldiers, like us." The vega held hands with another ghost rider and danced. "They'll obey your orders and do as you command. However, if anyone is captured, their souls will remain trapped." It paused and closed its eyes, its wrinkled eyelids only partially covering the large eyeballs. It inhaled fog and smirked. "I love souls," it said before returning to its rules.

"We'll be happy to trade the captured souls back to you if it means so much to you, but only in exchange for another soul with the same or higher value. Do you understand what I am saying? A queen for a queen, a knight for a knight, and so on. While we don't like this, it gives your friends one more chance." For a fleeting moment, the vega sounded almost sincere.

"Until we chase them down again and collect their souls," the sidekick ghost rider chuckled.

"Rule number three! If your time runs out first, you lose. We'll find you and take your soul." The vega gloated at the prospect of collecting more souls.

"Rule number four. The game is over." said the vega, just inches away from Ro's face, "when the soul of the primary player is captured and your king is dead."

It put its bony hand on Ro's chest and gestured as if tugging at his heart. Ro gasped again, but the vegas burst out laughing like a pack of hungry hyenas preparing for a kill. "Your soul will be mine," the vega said, its sunken eyes fixed on Ro.

"Do you have any questions?" asked another vega.

"Does the winner get to open the door to the inner sphere?" asked Yan.

"Ahh…The winner, of course, has a chance to find the door." The vega winked at its sidekick. "But there will be no winners," it whispered to Ro. "Now, who is on your side?"

"I am!" said Kaia.

"I'll play as well," said Suhela.

"Lovely. The souls of Kumba's queen and the rishi's knight are priceless," the vega said. "Who is on *your* side?" asked the vega as it dissolved and reappeared next to the Earth dweller.

"I have picked his squad. It will be me, the marisan, and the false queen," said the theel.

The vega abruptly stopped close to the theel, unafraid of its lethal sting. "The ghost riders will be on your side if you help us take the soul of Kumba's queen and the human child," it whispered to the theel.

"I'll give you more than that," promised the theel, who was pleased with its ability to strike an alliance with equally heartless creatures.

"Let the clock tick," the vega cried out.

The ground began to liquefy for Ro, and fog descended. He found himself alone, moving through the cloudy surroundings with great speed.

"*Where's everybody?*" Ro wondered. He felt a sudden sense of urgency, as though someone were chasing him. He spotted a ghost rider flying toward him, but it disappeared.

"Kaia! Where are you?" Ro cried out. "Can you hear me?"

Ro moved up, down, and sideways, but the disorienting gray medium filled the space, and he lost all sense of direction. He kept hearing the cackle of the ghost riders, and he did his best in outrunning them to nowhere.

"You safe behind me," he heard a voice say with a strange accent.

"What?" Ro tried to find the source of the voice. "Who is it?"

"I am foot soldier. Your Pawn. You safe here." It sounded like the leprechaun from the game he had in his computer.

"I can't see anything," replied Ro. "Who are you?"

"You play blitz, Ro. Close your eyes and feel the game," the voice with the accent continued.

Ro stopped briefly, closed his eyes, and tried to focus. He could feel he was moving the chess pieces and rapidly hitting his clock in another world. When he opened his eyes, he saw a file of soldiers marching in front of him.

"Look!" shouted Ro to one of the soldiers. "You are being attacked by a ghost rider."

The soldier waved to Ro, ran toward his fierce attacker, and fought him. The ghost rider struck him with his weapon, and his body dispersed into tiny particles into the surrounding plasma.

"I can take the ghost rider," said one of Ro's soldiers. "Gimme your command," he requested.

Driven by his instincts and finally relating the live events in the plasma to the chess game played in his own world, Ro ordered the foot soldier to attack the ghost rider. The soldier stormed through the space, displacing the plasma like a heavy truck. He struck the ghost rider with his sword and scattered it into smithereens.

"You did good, my friend," said one of the soldiers standing in front of Ro. Not only was his voice and his accent familiar, but he also looked different from the rest of the soldiers. He was tall and skinny, and his thick red hair awkwardly sprang from his helmet. His large green eyes brought Ro some comfort.

"Who are you?" asked Ro.

"I am your friend, Run-Nier," replied the soldier.

"You are Run-Nier, the one who helped my friends?" asked Ro.

"Yes. I am here to help you, too," said Run-Nier. His words were reassuring. "You need to be careful and pay attention, Ro. This is more dangerous than the other places you've journeyed. Stay behind me and keep moving."

"What should I do to get to the door?" asked Ro.

"Move faster," said Run-Nier. "First, give up your knight and your queen," he recommended.

"What? Give up Kaia and Queen Suhela?" Ro was perplexed by Run-Nier's suggestion.

"For equal ones, of course," added Run-Nier.

Ro thought for a minute. "You mean, like exchanging the pieces?" he asked.

"Yes, yes," Run-Nier agreed. "Let them fight their equals. Tell them to attack the theel and the false queen."

"Why?" The plan sounded suicidal to Ro.

"No time. Ro, you need to save their souls. Easy to trade now when the powers are equal and your enemy is not expecting an exchange."

"How do I do this?" asked Ro.

"Just play like you play chess. Close your eyes and feel the game. You'll see your enemies and your friends just as you see the positions of the pieces on your chessboard. You will also see the time remaining on your clock." Run-Nier spoke slowly to ensure

Ro understood him. "If your position is good, then exchange without wasting your time."

Ro was not convinced that it was the right time to trade his most valuable pieces. He closed his eyes and took a deep breath. He could see the chessboard with the pieces. One by one, they were all positioned, and his game was rapidly developing. His knight was in the middle, controlling the center. But when he opened his eyes, he saw Kaia on Ashvat at the heart of the battlefield. Obviously, she was his knight at the center.

Ro closed his eyes again and studied the position of his queen. She was already out, attacking on the king's side of the opponent in accordance with Suhela's attack in the plasma.

"Do it, Ro!" said Run-Nier, his voice assertive. "They will not be harmed this way. They'll safely get out of the game. Otherwise, the plasma will affect their ability to fight." he explained.

Although Ro was hesitant, he somehow trusted Run-Nier's instinct.

"Kaia…Queen Suhela, go for the attack," Ro instructed.

"Are you sure? Their knight might be protected, and if we are traded, you know we will not be able to help you," Kaia said, surprised by Ro's call to attack this early in the chase.

"Uh, yes, I am sure," Ro said, but his voice conveyed hesitation.

"I think we should wait," suggested the queen. "Take them by surprise."

"Let's do it. I can see where everyone is now. It might be too late, and I don't have too much time," Ro said.

Kaia followed Ro's instruction. She ambushed the enemy knight, a shapeshifter recruited by the theel to be their knight, but a swift counterattack followed.

"I guess I have been trapped and eliminated from the game, Ro," she shouted. "I see ghost riders all around me. But I cannot get out of here."

"I can hear you, Kaia. Don't worry, you have been traded equally," Ro confirmed. "Can you tell me how many soldiers you eliminated?"

"Two," Kaia replied immediately.

"Where are you now?" asked Ro, unable to see her.

"I am trapped in a place, surrounded by tall stone columns—like Stonehenge," said Kaia, surveying her new surroundings. "I cannot get out of here," she added.

"Hey, release me or else..." she ordered a ghost rider that was looming around.

"Just as I expected, the humans don't have it in them," the ghost rider said and scoffed. "The boy's chances of crossing the plasma were never good, but now, with you gone, his fate—and along with it, yours—is sealed."

Out in the open plasma, Ro saw Queen Suhela hesitate, but the hesitation cost her. The false queen jumped from behind and struck Suhela first with force.

"Your soul will belong to the vegas, and I'll take your place." Her crazy laughter echoed around the plasma.

"Queen Suhela, did you capture any soldiers?" asked Ro and waited for an answer.

He never got a response.

"Run-Nier, what's happened to Queen Suhela?" asked Ro.

"She has been captured, not traded. You need to quickly set a trap for the false queen with in-between moves. You have to ambush her, Ro."

"Ah, I see it now," Ro said, vividly seeing the in-between move, the move to gain another piece in chess between two forced moves. He quickly retaliated and captured the unsuspecting false queen.

"Get them back, theel," the trapped false queen screamed. "Don't let him get away!"

Like Kaia, both of the queens were stuck in a circular, floating patch of land, surrounded by pi-shaped stone columns.

"Thank you for your quick thinking, Ro. You have liberated me with an equal trade. But be careful, there are hidden enemy soldiers," Suhela cautioned.

Ro continued to advance through the plasma, staying closely behind Run-Nier. Run-Nier had asked him to keep a tally of all the enemy soldiers that were removed, but he had already lost count. Things were beginning to get blurry.

"I cannot see clearly." Ro, rubbed his eyes and tried to stay focused.

The game was exhausting.

"Only soldiers and the primary players remain in the game. Now, do you remember the enemy soldier count?" Run-Nier asked again.

"We have captured six or seven soldiers? I have lost count," said Ro, shaking his head. He knew the importance of the pawn count to his endgame.

Ro closed his eyes and tried to concentrate on the game. He could see the Earth dweller pushing the pawns around his king, but the other end of the board was blurry. Ro strained his eyes to see through the plasma. "I can spot two soldiers with the Earth dweller. Same as us. But what if she has more?" Ro was concerned.

He knew foot soldiers had the ability to reach the patch and release the imprisoned players from the Stonehenge prison, thereby making the attacking team more powerful—like promoting the pawn in chess.

"Don't slow down, Ro," Run-Nier advised. "Just keep moving as fast as you can, and you'll be fine," he said reassuringly.

For the first time as he moved through the plasma, he saw floating landmarks all around him—circular, mossy green areas, unevenly distributed across the foggy plasma. Intermittent gray lines marked the edges of the patches.

"Look, Run-Nier! We must be close to land," Ro shouted with relief. "Have we reached the end of the plasma?"

"These are the Stonehenge patches, Ro. Gates to the inner sphere for those who find the right one," Run-Nier explained.

Ro briefly slowed down to observe the massive circular patch with enormous stone columns.

"These must be the soul traps that Kaia and the queen described," he guessed.

"The gate will not open without the right soul. And that's why the vegas use them to trap the souls inside the patch, hoping it will open into the inner sphere," said Run-Nier.

"So, any soul in any patch won't open the door?" asked Ro.

"No! Only the right soul in the right patch will open the door. Hopefully, when we finish this, we will have found the right patch."

"How do I release the queen and Kaia?"

"When *our* foot soldiers enter the patch where a soul is trapped, they can liberate the trapped soul with renewed powers," Run-Nier explained. "But if enemy soldiers enter the patch, then these souls will join them to fight against us."

"Like promoting the pawn in chess to a queen or knight or rook?"

"Yes, and the game is over when the vegas trap you—a checkmate," Run-Nier warned.

"What happens if *I* enter a patch that already has a trapped soul?" Ro asked.

"It would be a no-win situation. You are the king. You don't want to trap yourself. You cannot go anywhere from there," Run-Nier said.

It was only when Ro neared the patch that he felt the enormity of the dark pi-shaped stone columns that lined the edges like a giant floating Stonehenge.

Run-Nier spotted a soldier running toward a distant patch where the false queen was trapped. "We need to stop him. Your soldier over there can take him."

Under Ro's command, his soldier threw himself on the speeding enemy just before he entered the patch. The impact instantly dissipated their loosely held body particles into the plasma, but within seconds, the particles coalesced back into their original forms.

As the enemy struggled to reach the patch, the soldier commissioned by Ro yanked him back with his glowing whip, snapping the ghost rider, and rushed toward the patch. But another attacker emerged from the shadows of the stone column and ambushed Ro's unsuspecting soldier. With no one to stop him, the lone enemy foot soldier entered the patch. A tall stone column shifted, allowing the soldier to reach the center.

"Oh no, he just released the—" Run-Nier's voice was drowned in the hysterical laughter of the false queen.

"Perish in the plasma!" She circled around the Stonehenge screaming. Invigorated with renewed power, she smashed a few columns before charging at Ro.

"Ro, they might have more power now, but just keep moving," Run-Nier advised. "I am sure we can find a way to reach an empty patch before they do."

"Run-Nier, I think this game's over," Ro said. "We have no way of knowing how many more enemy soldiers they have in hiding. They can all become as powerful as the queen. How are we going to outrun the rakshasas?"

"Don't give up, Ro. We can still figure this out," said Run-Nier.

"They are trying to get our queen or our knight to join them." Ro was frustrated and tired. He stopped for a brief second to catch his breath. He could see a stealthy enemy soldier emerge from the plasma.

"Can you tell me the words to the clue from the keeper's notebook?" asked Run-Nier, briefly appearing beside Ro.

For in your haste, the time you waste,

Trying to outlast, the Vegas, so fast.

You might never win to get in.

Greed is their creed. You shall use not to lose.

"So, it is not about winning, Ro. No one can outrun the vegas, the ghost riders." Run-Nier moved toward a nearby patch but abruptly stopped at the entrance of the patch where Queen Suhela was trapped. A soldier who attempted to ambush Run-Nier missed and crashed into the patch instead, releasing the queen. The false queen then ordered the last enemy foot soldier to enter the patch where Kaia was imprisoned and forced the knight to join the vegas.

Ro watched the transition. "They just took control of our queen and knight and are going to make them fight against us," he cried out.

"Ro, now, you know how it's going to end," Run-Nier said.

Ro closed his eyes and studied his position. He saw the pieces on the board. He was the lone king with no support. The single pawn that protected him was about to be captured. His enemies had surrounded him. He had no place to go.

"I know what to do. Their *greed is their creed*, and we are not going to lose."

"Now, destroy the last soldier protecting him," the false queen ordered Queen Suhela with sadistic pleasure.

Summoned to fight against those who had saved her, Suhela transformed into her true bloodline rakshasi form and swept out of her patch.

Taking advantage of the vacant patch that Queen Suhela had just created, Ro snuck past the stone column and entered the patch, unnoticed by his enemies.

He waited at the center and watched the queen attack Run-Nier.

Without resisting, Run-Nier sank himself into the queen's trembling, knife-wielding, extended arm. She held on to him as he slumped.

"No, no, no. Queen Suhela, he's our friend," Ro cried out at the sight of the bloody knife in her hand as plasma began to surround the fallen Run-Nier.

It was too late.

Kaia stood by Suhela, also unable to protect the dying foot soldier.

"Please take me inside the patch," Run-Nier begged the queen. "I would like to die by my friend Ro."

The queen instinctively recognized the sacrifice made by an unknown soldier.

"Who is this soldier?" she asked Kaia as they managed to enter the patch with Run-Nier before the columns closed behind them.

Overloaded with souls, the columns sealed the patch, rendering it inaccessible to the vegas or the other chasers.

"Kill the human! Kill him!" ordered the false queen from an adjacent patch.

Vegas surrounded the patch that Ro had entered.

Ro knelt next to the dying Run-Nier, holding his hand.

"It's a stalemate," whispered Run-Nier. "We didn't lose, and they cannot win."

"That's right, Run-Nier. you did it. There's no place to go for us, and they cannot chase us anymore. Look at all the vegas; they are stuck outside this patch. They cannot take our souls anymore. It's a no-win situation."

"The game is over," Kaia declared to the false queen, who desperately circled the patch, trying to somehow break her way through the Stonehenge column.

"No! No! This can't happen," the false queen screamed.

"Oh, yeah, it just did," shouted back Ro. "It's a stalemate."

A stream of tears ran down his cheeks. "Run-Nier! Run-Nier!" he called out, but the thin, long body of Run-Nier lay still. "He told me he had no soul, but he has a soul greater than anyone I know," Ro said.

The blurry images of the surroundings sharpened, allowing Ro to see clearly the rough surface of the gray stone columns, and the soft, mossy grass that covered the ground where the still, cold body of Run-Nier lay. As the plasma began to disperse around Ro, he began to feel the weight of his body and his heavy heart pulling him down.

The ground trembled, and the Stonehenge shook. The thin layer of plasma surrounding the patch began to churn, forming a funnel cloud as the Stonehenge patch spun. One by one, the adjacent patches with the vegas, the rakshasas, the wicked false queen, and finally, the theel disappeared into the vortex.

All that remained was one circular, mossy green patch of land floating in space. At its center stood the queen who had returned from the dark side, the knight who had almost lost her soul to the vegas, and a human child, crouched over the lean limp body of a newfound friend.

Yan's chariot quietly descended into the patch without much obstruction and landed on the green turf.

"It was not about winning against them; it was about not letting them win," said Yan. "A clever draw allowed you to uncover the entrance and, along with it, a good friend," he told Ro.

"Who is this foot soldier?" asked Kaia, puzzled.

"I believe his name is Run-Nier," said Yan, taking a closer look at him and referring to his notebook. "He had followed the kids at all the levels. He was somehow helping them uncover the answers to my clues, but he's been quite evasive."

"He is a mystery to me," Kaia admitted. "It is quite strange that someone had the power to freely travel throughout Mayastella, unnoticed."

"So…What do we do now?" asked Yan, kneeling next to Ro. "Should we take him with us?"

"No!" said Ro. "He told me this is where he wanted to be. He also told me, someday, he hoped to get a soul."

"I heard him, too, and sadly, I agree that we should leave him here. Perhaps we can get the help of the rishis when we return," she proposed.

It was time to leave. They had uncovered the entrance to the underworld. Although they were winning against the rakshasas, Kaia knew that the theel and its evil master would change things around and try to take control.

The crowd's roar jolted Ro to his senses.

"No way!" screamed one of the kids standing behind Ro.

"I can't believe this," said another one.

The room was filled with moans, groans, and cynical laughter.

"Stalemate?" shouted one TD to another.

"Crazy!" replied the other.

Ro's opponent, in the final seconds of the game, had promoted another pawn, only to place the queen on the board in a hurry and hit the clock to stop his time. Ro's lone standing king was cornered and had no place to go. It was a silly stalemate.

Run-Nier had helped Ro become a national champion in blitz, and Ro knew that many would talk about this game for years to come. Not about how he had defied the hunting vegas, but instead how a player on Board Number One had blundered by hastily promoting too many pawns and stalemating his opponent.

Ro's opponent slumped into his chair, confused, unable to comprehend what had possessed him to get the second queen.

Brendan ran to Ro and shook his hand. "Dude, I don't believe this. You got lucky. So, what happened out there? Were you able to find the door to the inner sphere?"

"Would I be here if I didn't?" Ro smirked. "Run-Nier helped, but—"

"Who?" replied Brendan, puzzled.

"Don't you remember Max and Sidney throwing out that name? Run-Nier!" Ro reminded him.

"Um, yeah, I kind of remember them mentioning something." Brendan couldn't remember exactly and the noisy crowd was distracting.

"He is real and helped me too…But he died…Sacked himself." His voice was subdued with sadness.

"What happened?" Brendan asked. "Let's talk about it later," Brendan suggested upon scanning the crowded room. "We need to find Kaia," he said.

"She's with Aarjen," Ro said.

Brendan felt a sudden chill. It was his turn.

The theel felt the force of the plasma squeeze its wormy body, its eyes bulging under the external pressure. It was also having to deal with the defeated and infuriated vegas, swarming around it in circles to scavenge the souls of the defeated creatures. Selfishly, the theel focused all its efforts on formulating a quick escape from its looming entrapment inside the plasma for eternity. Although it blamed its master for allowing the senseless false queen to partake in executing its plan, the theel quickly sought its master's assistance in fleeing from the plasma hell.

"I see you have not succeeded in finding the door to the inner sphere," the master said.

Although his voice reverberated across the plasma, only the theel could hear his master.

"Master, the vegas were on my side, and I was very close to being successful, but the stupid false queen ruined my plans with her greed," the theel desperately whined. It then sought its master's empathy. "If you feel I have let you down, then I deserve to rot in this plasma with these hopeless creatures. But I can still serve my master. Show us the entrance, and I'll build you a force in the underworld like no other to finish the job for you." The theel clearly knew that it had to quickly demonstrate the value of its existence to its master. "The false queen, my master, is a distraction to your grand plan. Her loyalty and skills pale in comparison to mine. Please allow..." the theel pleaded, as the opportunistic vegas dangerously closed in.

The force of the plasma was steadily draining the theel's strength, and it struggled to communicate with its master. "Please allow me to continue to serve you...My master," it pleaded one last time.

"You are pathetic but loyal," its master spoke finally after a seemingly deliberate silence, as though deriving pleasure in watching the theel suffer.

"The false queen is of no use to me anymore. I'll order the vegas to keep her and release you in exchange," the master said, releasing the theel from the plasma. The freed theel burst through the plasma, fleeing away from the soul seekers. "Cannibals!" it shouted and hurried to sneak through the gate the humans had opened before it closed.

It then resentfully thanked its master.

When it neared the gate, the theel paused to hear the voice of the false queen, which, much to its delight, had changed from the annoying laughter to a painful moan and then to a gut-wrenching scream.

"Enjoy your eternity in the plasma with the filthy vegas. If you are lucky, you'll find a way to die soon," it mumbled with joy.

Someting at the entrance of the inner sphere caught the theel's attention and it momentarily stopped. It was Run-Nier.

"*This is the foot soldier who sacrificed himself to cause the stalemate,*" thought the theel, irritated that the body was blocking the entrance to the underworld.

As the theel zapped the body of Run-Nier to move it out of the way, it felt something strange—a connection.

"*A soulless creature, like me,*" it thought as its electric bolt passed through the lifeless body of Run-Nier.

Soulless, but not purposeless, like the vegas, it reminded itself.

The theel then quickly descended through the gates. Long after the theel's departure, its charge lingered on the body of Run-Nier, disseminating a bluish haze around the patch and across the plasma.

"I see him," Ro's father said to his mother, peering through the door that partially opened and quickly closed every time a player walked out. Board One was located at the far end of the hall. "Where? I don't," replied Ro's mother, anxiously trying to get a glimpse of her son on the top table.

"Is he done? Can you tell if he won?" she asked nervously. "Why can't they put the blitz games on the screen or the app, like all the other games?"

"He's just standing around, talking to Brendan. How many times have we told him to come out after his game?" Ro's father complained.

"It's okay. Let him have his time, hon. We forget he's only fourteen." She usually restored the calm in their family. Finally, Ro's father threw his arms up, waving and trying to catch his son's attention, but any attention-garnering gestures were lost in the sea of chaos.

"So, did Ro win the game?" asked Bob Raj, the third person to sneak into the room, adding fuel to the fire.

"We are trying to find that out, Raj," said the father, exasperated. "Why is he always talking after the game?"

"Kids!" said Bob Raj. "They just want to be cool."

The crowd around Ro and Brendan got animated, and there was a brief argument with Ro's opponent and a TD. Turner rushed to the table.

"What's going on?" Turner asked the TD.

"We just had a stalemate, but suddenly, there's an argument. The team over there seems to have a problem."

"Did Ro just stalemate his opponent? Is there a dispute in the results?" he asked the TD.

"No, no, that kid drew, and the opponent agreed, but now, their crazy coach is adamant about one more game," complained the TD, throwing his arms up in frustration.

"We are not going to have another one. We are done for the day!" another TD shouted.

Brendan and Ro noticed that the Earth dwellers were getting increasingly unpleasant and impatient. They were worried that the creatures were about to retaliate against the humans. The chaos subsided when more TDs and coaches congregated by the Earth dwellers and ruled in favor of Ro by declaring that the blitz tournament had concluded. The Earth dwellers were warned and escorted out of the hall.

Ro was delighted that he was declared the tournament blitz champion as his friends erupted with joy.

Ro finally waved to his parents, gave a thumbs up and a reassuring smile, then slowly walked toward them with his clock in one hand.

"I was watching it," said Brendan to his father, shaking his head. "That guy lost it. He promoted a pawn on the A file and got a queen, then promoted another one on the C file, got another queen without thinking, and ended up stalemating him."

"Today, it looks like Ro really used his weakness of playing too fast to his advantage." Turner put his hands on Brendan's shoulders. "It is going to be a long day tomorrow for you kids."

Chapter 17

Final Preparation

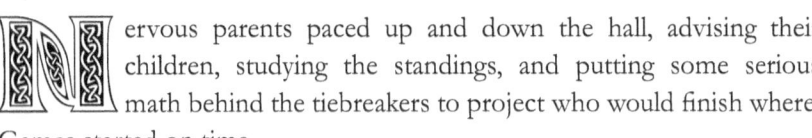

ervous parents paced up and down the hall, advising their children, studying the standings, and putting some serious math behind the tiebreakers to project who would finish where. Games started on time.

There were no major upsets to talk about, and the festivities at Navy Pier continued to entertain the families of the contestants during the long gaps between rounds. Navy Pier turned out to be the perfect location for the families to participate in a chess tournament.

"Coach Turner?" said a deep voice.

"Yes, who's this?" the distracted coach asked, not bothering to look at the caller ID of his old Samsung phone.

"This is Tom." There was a brief pause. The speaker playfully waited to be recognized but soon gave up. "Tom Moxley, from New—"

The *York* portion was lost in the coach's sudden verbal explosion. "*Mox?* Where in the world are you? I came looking for you in the New York skittles room, but just couldn't find you," Turner shouted into his phone.

"Hey, Turner, is this a good time to talk?" Mox sounded unusually serious.

"It is always a good time to talk to you, Mox. What's up?"

"I heard there was some trouble at the tournament with an unruly team?"

"Yes, a group from your state. Behaving strangely."

"That's why I am calling," Mox said.

"You know these kids?"

"No, no, they are actually not even from New York," said Mox quickly.

"Yeah, I heard…Apparently sponsored by the New York student exchange program. Go figure."

"It's a fake entry, Greg." Mox was abrupt.

"How do you mean?"

"Coach, listen to me," Mox said in his deep voice. "I need to talk to you in person."

"Where are you? Are you coming to town sometime?" Turner asked, surprised.

"I just landed in Chicago, and I am ubering to Navy Pier. Just don't mention that to anyone yet and keep your eyes on your kids."

"How long will—"

"I'll text you when I get there," he said and hung up without waiting for Turner to respond. It had been a while since Turner had last seen Mox, and he'd almost forgotten how big he was. Mox squeezed himself out of the Toyota Prius Uber ride and threw his heavy hand on Turner's shoulder, almost dislocating it. Turner winced as Mox greeted him.

"How are you, old man?" Mox beamed.

"I was all right until you knocked my arm out of the socket, big guy."

"Didn't I tell you not to take your eyes off the kids? I don't see them here!" Mox scanned through the sea of people on the move around the pier.

Reggae beats from a live show thumped from the speakers as spectators cheered the performers. The place was festive and colorful. "They're fine." Turner shrugged. "What's going on?" he asked nonchalantly, more intent on catching the lively music while soaking up some sun.

"You know what I do for a living, right?" Mox slipped on a pair of dark Ray-Ban aviators.

"Yeah…You are a lousy chess coach, but I hear you are a fine NYPD cop," Turner snickered. "By the way, I like your new look, fully shaven head and dark shades."

"A special unit detective," Mox said, rubbing his shiny, bald head.

"What special unit? Are you making up stuff again, Mox?" Turner laughed.

"The kind of special unit that you will not find if you google." Mox wagged his finger at Turner. "I have been investigating some shady activity that has recently surfaced in your neck of the woods."

"Chess-related? A gang of knights who checkmate their unsuspecting victims," Turner joked, but his humor was not reciprocated by Mox.

"Let's sit down." Mox headed to the far end of the pier, where a couple had just cleared a bench. "But first, some cinnamon almonds." He stopped by a lemon-yellow kiosk and handed a ten-dollar bill to the girl behind the elevated counter that was surrounded by neatly hanging snack packages and bags of lemons. "Two, please," Mox ordered despite his friend's protest. "Almonds are good for you. They make you think." He tapped Turner's forehead.

"I love Chicago in the summer," he continued, savoring the addictive pleasure of mixing toasted almonds, sunshine, and the beat of live music. He slumped onto the bench.

"Is your investigation chess-related?" Turner dug into the newspaper cone containing warm, sticky almonds.

"It is now, since your kids got involved," Mox responded enigmatically.

Anxiety shot through Turner. "What?"

"It is connected to the fancy board that Scrappy took from you."

"How do you know about that?" asked Turner.

"It's my job to know these things, Coach. Where did you get that board from anyway?" he calmly inquired.

"We think it was a delivery mix-up. There was no return address, and Scrappy claimed it was his, but I didn't believe him. You know we are using these boards at the tournament." Turner gave a hurried account of the events.

"There is more than one?"

"Some detective you are." Turner restlessly got back onto his feet. He explained to Mox how he had heard about the company setting up multiple boards in exchange for commercial exposure. "These boards are high-tech; games are easily streamed live." Turner crumpled the newspaper cone and tossed it into the nearby recycle bin. "What does this have to do with my kids?"

Mox thought for a minute. "Have you ever heard of Earth dwellers?"

"Us, the people? Humans?" Turner asked, sarcasm creeping into his questions.

"Yeah, I had the same reaction when I first heard of them." Mox said, nodding his head and briefly watching the people in front of them enjoying a nice summer day in Chicago. "It's like in those TV shows where they have aliens and creatures who live among us, looking like us, but only a few know about them. Do you get it?" he asked abruptly.

"No!" Turner had a baffled look.

"Then, just hear me out. They are the scum of the earth, living among us, causing trouble—"

"What kind of trouble?"

"One can say they are the source of many evil things in the history of mankind," said Mox.

"That's pretty broad, Mox!" Turner threw his arms up in the air.

"Look, all I know is, they are some kind of underworld creatures who live among us, posing as humans. I know it all sounds weird, but it's true. We humans have been aware of these dwellers for centuries. We are just getting to know more about them, like who they are, where they are from, who influences them, et cetera."

"I think the heat's getting to you." said Turner. "Stop messing with me."

"Let me get to what's more relevant to you now," said Mox, ignoring his friend's comment.

"Ok, go on." Turner and Mox walked by the edge of the Pier, crowded with noisy seagulls looking for scraps.

"These creatures are emerging from their cover—"

"No Mox, these seagulls have been here even before us." Turner shooed a couple of the birds away from him, but Mox remained serious.

"And at the heart of all these activities seems to be the game board they are using in this tournament. There is reason to believe the Earth dwellers are posing as players from New York and want to use this board for some other reason."

"These kids from New York—these Earth dwellers—are here for something besides winning the championship?"

"I told you to go with this, Coach." Mox was stern. "You have to trust me. I have told you what I know of the Earth dwellers. Now, let's talk to your kids."

"My kids have nothing to do with the board. Do you want me to alert the chairman?" Turner was concerned.

"We cannot alert anyone now. It is not a job for the association or the chairman or even the local authorities. We need to find help from external sources."

"Like who? *The Men in Black* or *Ghostbusters*?" Turner's cynicism surfaced again.

"I believe they call themselves the knights of the rishis," replied Mox calmly. "They are said to keep things under control."

"This is all a joke, right?" asked Turner.

Mox shook his head regretfully and squeezed Turner's shoulder again. "There are real special forces that track these creatures and terminate them when they get out of control." He then offered to share some of his knowledge of the knights and rishis with Coach Turner. Perplexed, Turner thought for a moment. Mox was not the kind of person who would come up with such nonsensical fantasy. "I need the kids to be safe," he said finally. "I also need to let the other parents know immediately."

"Not yet. That's why I am here, Greg—to make sure the kids are safe." Mox offered his strong hand to Turner.

Turner gripped Mox's hand firmly. "Mox, the safety of my kids is my number one priority…Even if that means I should pull them out of the tournament," he said, his voice steady and emphatic.

Turner's appreciation of the festive surroundings suddenly waned with Mox's revelation of gangs and goons. They quietly walked to their assigned skittles room to meet the chess kids.

"Let's talk to Brendan," said Turner. "Maybe he has noticed something."

"Guys, you remember Coach Mox from New York?" Turner announced to Brendan and his friends in a private room marked *Chicago Chess—Pass Pawn*.

The boys were busy playing bughouse. Brendan stopped the clock and stood up to greet Coach Tom Moxley. The others waved quickly and got back to their game.

Turner pulled up a chair next to Brendan and asked in a calm voice, "Do you know anything about Board One and why those kids from New York were acting up?"

Brendan exchanged glances with Ro and Max. He hesitated while making his otherwise snappy move of capturing his opponent's piece. "Just upset over losing," he responded smoothly.

"They just don't like the new boards and complained about delays." Max chimed in.

"Should I tell him?" whispered Brendan, when Turner and Mox were loudly interrupted by Bob Raj, who was also a friend of Mox.

"Maybe he can help?" Max mumbled back.

"How?"

Max shrugged. "Then, go find Kaia while I tell him the story," Brendan suggested to Max. "It's about time he knows what's really happening, and Kaia can help."

"What are you guys mumbling about?" Turner asked as soon as Bob Raj left.

"Dad, I want to tell you something."

Ro kept his eyes glued to the game while Brendan recounted his encounters with the other world with calm sincerity.

"What are you talking about?" Turner burst out.

Mox pressed Turner's arm, trying to calm him.

"Dad, it is all true," Brendan was hardly surprised by his father's reaction. "When we play the game, it takes us to another world."

"It is real, and we are in it. The board that Scrappy took from us is magical. It takes you to places far from this world—like you see in movies."

"Like *Jumanji*," Ro said.

"So, let me get this straight. You were in something called plasma and raced ghosts who caused that kid to stalemate you?" Turner asked Ro. "But none of you left the room while playing the game. What am I missing?"

"Dad, it is hard to see logic in all of this! Unless you experience this on your own, it is very hard to describe. When we move a piece on that board, we open up some kind of a portal to another parallel world, which allows us to be here and play the game while we are in the middle of a mission somewhere else. Again, it's not easy to explain." Brendan was frustrated.

There was a long silence. Turner looked into Brendan's eyes briefly.

"I can try to clarify," said a woman's voice from behind.

"Perfect timing, Kaia!" Brendan was never so happy to see her.

"Coach Turner, we met briefly once at your chess club. We were interested in the antique chessboard you had." Without waiting for the puzzled coach to make the connection, she sat next to him. On cue, the kids left them alone.

"You must be Mr. Moxley from New York, special unit." Her demeanor was pleasant, and her handshake was firm.

"Please call me Mox. How did you—"

"I am supposed to know the people on our side." She paused and qualified her statement. "A knight is supposed to know—even information that one cannot find by googling." She winked at Mox.

"So, it is all true?" asked Mox.

"As true as it can get," Kaia affirmed.

"Why now?" asked Turner. "Why have you decided to tell me about this now?"

"Timing is important. Your son and his friends from the chess club were chosen for something big, and it's approaching a tipping point. Things are going to get ugly, and we need to work together."

"How? Sorry, but this sounds bizarre to me!" Turner waved in exasperation.

"Two ways. First, Mox can help with his special unit to contain any uprising from the Earth dwellers here. Second, it is important for Brendan to know that you believe in him every step of the way." Kaia looked directly into the coach's eyes.

"Of course I do! He's my son!" Turner responded without hesitation.

"I know you do as a father." She spoke clearly but fast. "As a coach, you must make Brendan confident of your faith in his potential. Last year, Brendan had some challenges and was accused of not trying hard enough. The most important thing for him now is to feel that you believe in his ability to win. That's the confidence that will let him be who he really is without the anxiety of letting you down."

Turner knew he was different from most fathers and coaches. He encouraged his kids and students with positive reinforcement. He had witnessed many ugly scenes in the tournaments where parents who claimed that chess was "only a game" often came down hard on their kids for not delivering a winning outcome. He had seen children accused of not "stepping up" when they lost to higher-rated players and made to feel worse when they lost to lower-rated players. The tournament last year was different, and he might have questioned Brendan's appetite to win on a few awkward occasions. These occasions, however few and far between they might have been, had eroded ever so slightly Turner's confidence, as a coach, in Brendan's ability to be a champion. A shade of doubt was all it took to shatter the foundation of confidence carefully built over many years.

"There is not a moment in my life when I am not proud of my children," he said. "But I don't understand what that has to do with all of this. I am not going to let Brendan participate in your game even if it means we'll have to pull out of this tournament." Turner abruptly pushed his chair back to stand up, but Mox intervened by subtly holding him down.

"Coach Turner, it's too late to walk away now. The war game has begun and kids are bound by the rules of the game whether we like it or not.

The creatures are in attack mode, and stopping now will only divert more attention to the kids."

"What will happen if we walk away?"

"The creatures will hurt the kids and make them play without our help. You will be putting them in harm's way. We will not be able to protect them since we might not know when or where they'll strike."

Turner shook his head disapprovingly. "I don't think—"

"We need Brendan's help to break this curse. Brendan and his friends have what it takes to outsmart the creatures, and they have already demonstrated that. We will protect them with our lives!" Kaia assured him and sought Mox's assistance before Turner walked away. "You'll meet Aarjen, my partner, tonight. He'll provide you with more information on how to deal with the Earth dwellers."

"Greg, let's join forces. If you believe in Brendan's ability to play chess, if you believe you have taught him well, then let him play this game," Moxley pleaded.

Finally, the coach reluctantly agreed that the kids could continue playing. "If any of those things act up, I'll personally go in there and smash that board. No one's going to mess with my kids," Turner warned, even if he did not fully understand the role of Chadurang or the curse.

"Kick some butt tomorrow, son. I know you are awesome at chess and a great kid. Just be yourself," Turner said, placing both his hands on Brendan's shoulders and looking into his eyes.

"Sure, Dad, I will," Brendan said with a fist pump.

Mox's team of eight, including some FBI agents, had set up shop in a special room assigned to them by the city of Chicago. "You are on Board One, Brendan," said Austin, who had dashed into their room, just to wake up Brendan. He was carrying his bright yellow backpack.

"Who's my opponent?"

"Someone from New York. A 2,000 rating," said Austin, puckering his lips, his Rs pronounced as Ws.

"That's a monster of a rating!" said Brendan.

Coach Turner, who was making coffee, heard him. "I am sure you can get him," Turner said and poured himself some coffee.

"You can do it, Brendan," said Austin. He reached into his backpack and handed Brendan his stuffed elephant. "Here, keep Mr. Trunks. He'll help you."

"I know he will, and I want *you* to keep him. He's going to help you become the K-1 champion."

"Thank you, Brendan." Austin heard Sidney calling out for him and he dashed out.

"Have you thought about your opening?" Turner offered his son a cup of coffee.

"I am going for something simple…Modified English attack maybe. I have a feeling that my knight will be very active."

The phone rang. It was Kaia. She asked Brendan to join her right away.

The inside walkway at Navy Pier that usually bustled with tourists and shoppers was oddly quiet in the early hours of the morning. Brendan clutched the handles of his nylon chess case tightly as he rushed through the empty hallway. A tall, thin man in blue coveralls was mopping the already-clean floor of the Häagen-Dazs ice cream parlor. Light poured through the large glass windows. Brendan quickly strode across the wet floor, and the man, without looking at Brendan, acknowledged him by nodding.

"Watch your step, brother!" he cautioned.

"Sure." Brendan adjusted his stride to step only on the dry surface of the floor. He exited the first building through large sliding doors, crossed the driveway between the two long buildings that formed Navy Pier, and continued through the winding walkway inside the next building.

"*Welcome to the maze! Kids under five are free,*" the muffled motion activated sign blared, startling Brendan when he walked by the entrance of the Chicago Maze—a quirky indoor maze created with mirrors and optical illusions.

The brick red walls of the maze entrance made the walkway dark. Brendan glanced at his reflection in both the funhouse mirrors by the sign—one showing a skinny, tall, and considerably bent-in-the-middle reflection and the other showing him looking short, fat, and awkwardly disproportionate.

He chuckled, but his amusement abruptly changed to fear when he saw the reflection of a creature standing behind him—something he had only seen in the other world.

Out of sheer reflex, he wildly swung his chess bag behind to strike, but as he swirled, he lost his balance and fell to the floor. His muted cry echoed through the empty hallway.

Under the frame of the mirror, a sparkly object attracted his attention. When he rolled over to get a closer look, he recognized the safety wristband with the crystal that Aarjen had asked him to wear. The thin leather strap had snagged on an exposed hook on the wall, snapped, and slid under the mirror.

The broken strap was tucked under the frame at an awkward angle. Brendan pushed his fingers underneath the side of the frame, pressing his head and shoulders against the wall. A thud shook the rough red plaster wall he leaned on. A short squeal erupted at a distance, followed by what sounded like sticks clashing. The noise moved all around him. Brendan closed his eyes and focused on retrieving the wristband.

Finally, his fingers touched the strap, fuzzy with a ball of dust. He patiently guided it to the outer edge of the frame before pushing it free. The crystal lit up like an LED light. Brendan sat, leaning against the wall, with his eyes closed and ears covered with his hands until the uneasy emptiness of the hallway returned. When he opened his eyes, he found himself staring at the face of a tall man in a blue coverall with a mop in his hand.

"You okay, dude?" the Häagen-Dazs man with the deep, friendly voice asked.

"Yes. I slipped," Brendan lied.

"Slipped, huh?" The man extended his arm, his face expressionless. "Must have been that patch of water."

"Uh, I guess." Brendan locked his hands. "Thanks," he said. "I was in a hurry. I have—"

"I know. You are the chess kid on Board Number One. It's a big day today. Be careful, brother," the man cautioned.

"I will." Brendan was surprised the stranger knew about him.

The man watched Brendan turn the corner and enter the stained-glass museum. Without waiting, the man with the mop dove into the small puddle with a tiny splash and disappeared into the world of the jalas. His mop turned into a bloodstained sword, and his legs transformed into a fluke. He had just prevented a kateri vampire from assaulting a very important human kid.

Brendan quickly ran up the stationary escalator to the game room. Only when he reached the top of the escalator did he look down at the lifeless hallway to see if anyone had followed him and was puzzled to see the same man in the blue coverall with a mop in his hand.

The man waved. "You're doing fine, my friend. You go get 'em!"

Brendan waved back. A sudden comfort settled on him when he realized that this chance acquaintance was somehow looking out for him. Kaia and Aarjen were talking to each other inside the tournament room. Finally feeling secure, he allowed his mind to focus on chess.

"There you are!" Kaia cheerfully greeted Brendan.

Brendan stopped and plopped down in a chair to catch his breath.

"Were you running through the hallway? Something startle you?" asked Aarjen.

"No, just an empty hallway with no lights," he said trying to regain his cool.

Mox and his team had arrived to hear Aarjen's game plan. "Seriously?" asked one of the FBI agents, pushing his coat behind his holster as a display of confidence. "You are a self-proclaimed *knight* who goes after creatures from another world?"

"That would be me," said Aarjen. "Not self-proclaimed though."

"And this kid here is going to save the—"

"We have gone over this, Frank," interrupted Mox. "Sorry. He's the skeptic I told you about," Mox told Aarjen.

"No apology needed, Mox," said Aarjen.

A lady in a security uniform called out to Kaia. "Ma'am, the video file has been transferred to your tablet."

Kaia handed the tablet to Aarjen.

Aarjen watched the hallway surveillance video from the maze and the stained-glass museum with Mox.

"What do you think?" he asked Mox.

"I wouldn't show this to Frank yet," suggested Mox. "If he wants proof, let him get it the hard way!"

"I agree," said Kaia. "In person."

Brendan's opponent was half his height with an abnormally big belly. A close cousin of the potbellied rakshasa, he didn't look anything like a high school kid. A large gray hood loosely covered most of his expressionless face, but his cat-like greenish-yellow eyes remained fixated on the chess pieces, ignoring the other players who meandered to the isolated Board Number One for a quick chitchat with Brendan.

An uneasy feeling fluttered through his stomach as Brendan thought of the unknown dangers that awaited him in the other world. But seeing Alex alleviated his anxiety.

"Ready?" she asked, with a quick, one-handed hug.

"I will be, but what was he saying to you?" asked Brendan, motioning his head at Scrappy Junior, who was walking away from Alex.

"He just came to say hello and, believe it or not, to wish you luck."

"He probably wanted to jinx my clock so I don't end up playing the next round," Brendan said sarcastically, much to Alex's surprise.

"Brendan, he's cool. I don't think he cares for these fake New Yorkers. I think these guys are messing with your mind," she said in a kind voice.

"Whose side are you on?" Brendan was annoyed that his best friend was supporting his nemesis.

"Your side, but trust me on this one, Brendan," she assured him.

Brendan managed to snap out of his irritable mood. She was right. The creatures were getting into his mind. He exchanged glances with Scrappy Junior, who offered a casual wave and quickly settled on Board Number two. Scrappy Junior was the only other person who had won all his games and was under the constant surveillance of his stepfather.

Brendan was happy to see his father at the entrance of the hallway, waving before the doors closed.

"Gentlemen, start your clocks," yelled the TD.

Chapter 18

The Knight's Game

The portal transported Brendan directly to the floating Stonehenge patch on the plasma—the gate to the underworld that Ro had managed to open. Aarjen was already waiting for him. "This time, we are not the ones being chased," said Aarjen, seated on the flat portion of Stonehenge rubble that littered the grassy patch. His sword and his leather bag lay by his side. His looks, style, and gear were drastically different from his appearance at the tournament. His outfit made him blend into the dull background.

"We are the followers. You can tell your opponent has gotten here with the theel." Aarjen referred to the destruction caused by the rakshasas. "They are trying to slow us down," he added.

"Is it working for them?" asked Brendan, his eyes sweeping over the large mass of broken stones.

"Not really. Random destruction serves no purpose. But the theel will leave no stone unturned," said Aarjen, his lips twisted in scorn.

"I can see that." Brendan chuckled. "But Kaia said the theel was stuck inside the plasma."

"It has connections," Aarjen said.

"Is this where Ro finished his blitz?" Brendan asked.

"Yes. The stalemate was brilliant thinking by him."

"What now?"

"When the shadow of the stones—at least from the ones still standing—from the three moons converges at the center, the gateway to the inner sphere will appear. We wait."

Brendan noticed the faint light from the three large bluish celestial objects casting shadows of each remaining pi-shaped column that had survived the rakshasa's destructive rampage.

It was strangely fascinating to see streaks of lines, differing in length and the shade of grayness, crisscrossing the surface of the patch.

"Ro said he got help from someone called Run...Run-Nier...who died here."

"He remains a mystery to me. Someone who appears to have helped all your friends. We left his body here, but it looks like it, too, was scavenged," Aarjen said with disgust.

"Would they really eat him?" Brendan felt nauseated.

"Oh, yes. Many of these creatures are flesh-eaters." Aarjen spoke matter-of-factly. "The theel's servants are not kind even to the dead."

There was a brief silence. Brendan wasn't sure what to say, but his inquisitiveness caught up with him.

"How did Kumba get inside?" Brendan asked.

"Maya took help from the jalas."

"Jalas? They could cross the plasma without water?"

"Jalas can enter any world using tiny portals made of water tunnels with just a tiny splash of water. You wouldn't even notice it. Especially when you are nervously walking in the early hours of the morning across a dark corridor filled with stained-glass exhibits."

"Aha. I knew it! The guy with the mop in Navy Pier. He appeared out of nowhere," Brendan said.

"He splashed in and out of your world quickly to snatch your shapeshifting attackers away from you."

"So, do they live on Earth?" Brendan wondered aloud.

"Of course. The jalas love Earth and humans. After all, more than two-thirds of the Earth's surface is covered by water. But the plasma is nothing like water. Not easy to get through, even for the jalas."

"So, how do they go through the plasma?"

"Maya created specific doorways called the patches," explained Aarjen. "Certain patches let you in, and only a few know which ones. We believe someone evil, but with the skills of a rishi, introduced the tantrics into the plasma. Someone with the goal of nurturing evil and abolishing the good works of the rishis."

"Why was this place not just destroyed?" asked Brendan.

"Destruction was one of the options, but rishi Vyas thought it would be a good hideout for Kumba—to keep him protected until the time was right, to unify the rakshasas, and to bring peace to the underworlds. The inception of life in the form of nijaz had already begun in Mayastella and the rishis did not want to destroy a world with real lifeforms. It was too late for total destruction. The theel's master saw this as an opportunity to somehow infiltrate Mayastella and take advantage of the curse. "Oh, the columns are moving," shouted Brendan.

"No, it is not the columns that are moving. The entire patch is turning around, like a giant disk." Aarjen guided Brendan to the center of the patch.

The surrounding plasma dispersed, like thick smoke swirling around a fan, as the patch churned the plasma. "What's happening?" he asked nervously.

"As the plasma becomes thin, the patch will descend to the core below— the inner space of the Mayastella. This is the only way to get to the inner sphere," said Aarjen.

"You would feel much safer at the center…" Aarjen's words faded.

Brendan felt the ground beneath his feet loosening. Within seconds, it completely disintegrated into sand-like particles. A gush of air rushed onto his face as his stomach churned. He found himself falling into the emptiness below.

"Aar-Aarjen!" he tried screaming, but his voice failed.

The fall was short as he gently landed on a soft, sandy surface. He remained disoriented, since nothing was visible. When he tried to move, his head spun. He wobbled and fell flat.

Brendan heard Aarjen's muffled voice, and as his eyes adjusted to the surroundings, he could see the silhouette of the knight. A greenish hue highlighted the horizon behind him.

"Are we in the inner sphere?" asked Brendan. He was dizzy and light-headed.

"Apparently, we are. My first visit—and hopefully, my last." Aarjen switched to his night vision mode.

"I thought you had been here before. How did you know what to do at the patch?"

"Knights don't belong in the world of illusion. And as far as knowing what to do, I am just following Yan's instructions—without which I'd be as lost as any other poor soul." Aarjen laughed.

"The sky looks weird."

"The glow is not from the sky; it's from the water," he said, squinting at the horizon. "We are on the shores of a sea."

Brendan examined the ground. His feet sank into the fine black sand of the beach. Shadowy rocks of all shapes and sizes littered the place. He could hear the sound of water gently washing ashore. He briefly sensed the beauty of the calm inner world.

Aarjen jumped up onto a tall boulder and surveyed the landscape. Brendan followed him. They could see miles and miles of rocky shoreline touching the vast endless span of green sea, spiked with tall columns of jagged ridges.

Aarjen perched on a flat boulder and tapped on Yan's notebook. They studied the unfolded page together to pinpoint their location. The 3D images on the map rearranged, changing shapes until a tiny island surfaced from the middle of the sea. "That is the island we need to go to." Aarjen followed the map with his index finger. "If we can get to this point on land, we'll be at the shortest distance across the sea to this island."

"The Sea of Poison," Aarjen read the words that came out of the map. "This sure explains the glow in the water."

"Do you have one of those chariots to take us there?"

"No. We have to find a way to get there somehow." Aarjen turned the pages. "We should see some daylight soon."

Brendan rubbed his forehead and temples. He stumbled, but Aarjen kept him from falling.

"I am dizzy." He hurriedly stepped away from Aarjen to empty his stomach.

"Our bodies are weak from traveling through the gateway. We have a long journey ahead. Yan has advised us to find Indra's Camp first and get acclimated to this place." Aarjen handed him a tiny slice of dry ingee. "Chew on this. It's like ginger and mint."

"Where is this camp?"

"Just follow me, and you'll be fine," instructed Aarjen.

"Of course. What else can I do?" Brendan mumbled.

After a tiring walk across a beach riddled with treacherous rocks and eroded stones, Brendan was disappointed when Aarjen called a pile of rubble "Indra's Camp."

"Not much of a camp." He strained his eyes to see the details of the shady structures. "Why are all these places broken-down ruins?" His mouth was dry, and his head hurt.

"Wait here for me while I confirm this is the camp. I'll be back before you know it," Aarjen suggested, tossing his leather bag at Brendan, who caught it out of sheer reflex. "You'll find some fruits, water pouches, and my knife in there. I'll keep Yan's notebook." Aarjen waved the notebook at him.

"Sure," Brendan muttered, finding a flat surface—a right-sized boulder to lean on. He was too exhausted to take another step. He shoved the soft bag under his head and watched Aarjen disappear into the night, unaware that he was being watched.

"What? What?" Brendan muttered incoherently when he heard a voice talking to him.

He was in a daze, unable to wake up from his nap. Leaning against the boulder, he wasn't sure if it was a dream or if Aarjen was talking to him.

"What is a human doing in this place? It is dangerous here," said a hollow voice from behind Brendan. It sounded as though someone was talking through a metal pipe.

"I am with Aarjen." Brendan checked around himself. He didn't see anyone.

"You cannot trust a knight. They hunt, and they kill. It is just a matter of time before you become a victim, too," the voice warned.

Brendan froze when he finally saw the creature.

An awkward stone structure, assembled with chunks of large gray rocks, moved around him with surprising agility up on the boulder that was at his shoulder height. When it neared him, Brendan noticed it looked like a lion, but its large face had a trunk and small tusks, like an elephant. With disjointed moves, the stone lion moved close to Brendan, who was wedged against the boulder, startled.

"I can get you what you want, kid, and if you listen to me, I can make you the master of your games." The creature was close enough to whisper in his ear. "Don't be afraid. If I had to kill you, I would have by now."

"Who are you?" asked Brendan, his courage returning. "*Another strange creature with elephant-like features,*" he thought.

"I am a yaali, the guardian of the stone mountains. They call me Kal. I am your last chance to live," it warned.

The crystal dangling from Brendan's wristband did not glow.

"*At least this thing is not a rakshasa,*" Brendan thought, comforting himself.

"*Aarjen!*" Brendan shouted. "Aarjen! Where are you?" he yelled. "Something is talking to me."

"You can call me Kal," the stone lion repeated. "The knight can't hear you, son. He is busy planning to terminate you."

"He is a knight," Brendan said, wondering what a yaali was. "Why does he have to kill me?"

"Sacrifice," whispered the stone lion deliberately. "He becomes the Seventh Knight if he sacrifices a human."

Brendan felt a sudden chill crawl down his spine. Aarjen had alluded to sacrifices on a few occasions, but the context had always been vague.

"Aarjen is the knight of the Dark Forest, the most powerful knight. Even Kaia told me he's the most powerful of all the knights." Brendan raised his voice and moved away from the stone lion.

"Knight of the Dark Forest, yes! And he desperately wants to be the Seventh Knight. And of course, she is with him. I guess they work in pairs," Kal instigated.

"What's the Seventh Knight?" Brendan was suddenly curious.

"*The most powerful of all the knights!* The knight who rises above the devas, asuras, and jalas. The only knight who will be able to challenge a rishi— good or bad—my friend." The stone creature was emphatic.

"That doesn't make any sense," argued Brendan. "Aarjen and the knights serve the rishis. Why would he want to challenge them?"

Once again, the large creature inched closer to Brendan's face, exposing the weathering on the ancient stone the creature was made of.

"It's about power, kid. The power to be the master," said Kal loudly, deliberately scraping Brendan with its cold and heavy trunk.

Brendan shuddered. "But what about the curse? The rakshasas are out to destroy the worlds."

"They are all just stories." It lowered its voice, causing the change in resonance to increase the hollowness of the sound. "The rakshasas have uncovered the truth about Aarjen and Kaia, and they are just trying to protect their own world. It's a long story of rivalry, but do you really want to get tangled up in this and throw your life away?" Its tone was friendly. "I am giving you a chance to get out of this mess."

"What's in it for you?"

"I am the guardian of the truth. My job is to protect souls."

The stone lion leaped to lower ground with a muffled thud of hollow rocks colliding. The creature was as tall as Brendan. Its mane was comprised of an intricate and careful network of artistically woven stonework while its trunk seemed to have been constructed hurriedly with a collection of cylindrical stones.

It let out a short grunt through its trunk. Its cold breath rolled toward him before dispersing into the thick air. "Yaalis are natural friends of humans. I am here to help you and your friends." The stone lion continued to try to convince Brendan to betray Aarjen. Brendan moved around, jumping from rock to rock, buying time to think, and the massive creature made of rocks followed him at a close distance. When he saw a narrow opening between two tall boulders, he quickly slipped into the gap.

"Are you paying attention to what I am saying?" the irritated lion grunted.

Brendan could hear the stone lion moving around, searching for him as he wandered deeper into the shadows of the crevice. It had clearly lost track of him. He stopped to catch his breath. He crouched at the base of the boulder and searched for Aarjen's knife inside his bag.

"Are you looking for this?" a voice with a strange accent whispered from behind Brendan, startling him again.

Brendan fell back and swung the bag wildly at the voice, like he had done at the entrance of Navy Pier mirror maze, but a cold, slender hand stopped him and cupped Brendan's mouth lightly.

"Shh. The stone lion can hear you, Brendan," the stranger with piercing green eyes and fluttering red hair said.

Brendan sat still with his eyes rapidly scanning the stranger who was staring at him. The stranger had Aarjen's knife in his hand. But his friendly face had a calming effect on Brendan.

"I am Run-Nier, friend of Ro, Max, Sidney, and Austin," the lad said, pulling his hand back slowly. "The stone lion is behind that rock, looking for you. Listen to me carefully."

"Aarjen said you were killed in the plasma," Brendan wiped the sweat from his forehead with his sleeve. He could barely speak.

"Run-Nier is alive because of the theel." Run-Nier quickly explained how he had suddenly woken up in pain, as though lightning had struck him, and had seen a furious theel cursing and descending down the gate.

"The theel had found Run-Nier on patch and become angry," said Run-Nier in his funny accent. "It sent 'shock' to burn Run-Nier body, but its shock saved Run-Nier," he said, knocking his chest lightly with his closed fist.

"Like a defibrillator," said Brendan.

"Run-Nier glad to be alive to help Brendan. But first, we get rid of the stone lion."

"Why?"

"The stone lion is not a real yaali. I know this fake yaali was sent by theel to make Brendan go against knight. The stone lion lying to you."

"How can you tell?" Brendan felt he could trust the stranger more than he could trust the stone lion.

"Ask stone lion who killed Run-Nier. If it blames knight, then it is lying," said Run-Nier in a low voice.

There was a loud grunt, followed by the unpleasant sound of big rocks colliding, from the far end of the fissure that Brendan had slipped through. The boulder shook, dislodging loose rocks several feet away.

"Hey, kid, where are you?" the stone lion called out in a resonating autotuned voice. "If you are not careful, you'll get crushed by falling rocks."

"Let's get rid of this fake yaali before it hurts you," Run-Nier said.

"Make it follow you to the edge of the cliff," he suggested, motioning at a massive rock formation on the other end. "Fake yaali don't like height and very unstable. Easy to push it off by kicking in the back."

Run-Nier lay on his back on a flat surface and showed Brendan where and how to kick the fake yaali. "You should go now," he said.

"I am coming out from the other end," shouted Brendan so the stone lion could hear him.

He climbed over the rocks noisily and let it follow him. He could hear its pounding footsteps approaching him rapidly.

Brendan called out to the stone lion, "So, why did the rakshasas steal the soul of Run-Nier? He was our friend, too."

"Um… uh…" The stone lion appeared to be at a loss for words.

Brendan could tell his question had taken it off its guard.

"Why couldn't you save Run-Nier if you are such a good friend?" He continued his line of questioning.

"Run—who?" The lion stumbled for words while trying to locate Brendan. "I am telling you, son, it's the knight's doing."

"I see." Brendan pulled himself up another steep rock with great effort.

When he reached the summit, he looked over the edge carefully. Just as he'd imagined, he was at the rim of a deep canyon that dropped precipitously into the green hue of the sea below. His knees trembled when he realized how high he had climbed. The yaali continued to tail him over the jagged terrain, pouncing like a little kitten despite its mass. When it reached the top, it slowed and moved away from the sharp drop.

"You have to be careful, kid. It's a dangerous place. I am here to help you live."

"Do you know how Run-Nier died?" asked Brendan.

"Killed by the *knight!*" The lion raised its voice, displaying its impatience. "Let us talk about you instead," it said, quickly regaining its composure and changing the subject.

"Wrong answer, Kal!" shouted Brendan and jumped from one tall rock to another.

He lay low on his back and waited for the stone lion to leap. Its front legs safely landed on the rock over Brendan's body, but before its heavy hind legs could secure its footing, Brendan landed a powerful kick on the stone lion's back with all his strength. He felt as though he'd jammed his legs against a heavy boulder that wouldn't move, but the timing and the angle were just perfect to throw the leaping stone lion off-balance. The hill was too steep and slippery for it to regain its shifting center of gravity. Brendan heard the stone lion smash into the side of the rocky cliff and shatter into pieces.

"Good kick," said a voice from behind.

"Thanks for showing me what to do with that pile of stone."

"It was tantric, sent by theel. An impostor. Aarjen will be here soon. When you find real yaali, seek his help. I see you later." Run-Nier gently placed his hand on Brendan's shoulder.

"Where are you going?"

"Knight is in danger, and you help him," he said, jumping and climbing down the rocky hill.

"Wait, please don't go." Brendan was uncomfortable with the thought of being alone. "If Aarjen is in danger, why don't you stick around and help him?"

"The return of Seventh Knight!" shouted Run-Nier.

"*Why is everyone suddenly talking about the Seventh Knight?*" wondered Brendan. "Who's the Seventh Knight?"

"There you are. Why did you get up here?" The familiar, stern voice of Aarjen from behind surprised Brendan. "I told you to stay close."

"Run-Nier! Where did he go?" Brendan asked incoherently.

"The foot soldier is dead. The journey is messing with your mind," Aarjen said. "You have to rest up, and you are going to get plenty of it at Indra's Camp," he added enticingly.

Brendan was too exhausted to argue or recount his encounter with Run-Nier.

The beauty and ostentation of the interior belied the stone-ruins facade of Indra's quarters. Brendan inhaled sharply in surprise.

"Look at this place." He gestured at the marble walls and the pillars, adorned with colorful stones.

He was inside an opulent palace, unsure where to look or what to admire. When he entered a room with a massive cot, he slumped into its softness.

"This is Indra's inner sphere base camp, created for him by Maya. Rest up well. We'll be battling…" Aarjen's words faded away as Brendan drifted into deep sleep.

"Alekhine?" asked Turner, surprised.

Bob Raj, who stood by the tall coach, raised his eyebrows, not comprehending.

"Look, Brendan is playing the Alekhine opening." Turner turned his laptop toward Bob Raj so he could see the live streaming of the game.

"I am sure your boy has a reason to move his knights out first. It *is* a strange choice, though."

"I am confident you know what you are doing, Brendan," Turner mumbled at the screen.

This time, he knew his son had traveled to another world.

Although a bit confused, Brendan woke up refreshed. The room was magnificent and bright with soothing crystal lights. It was decorated with life-sized marble statues, large gold-framed oil paintings of royalty and knights, rich crown moldings, colorful curtains, and furniture.

"Your meal is on the stand next to your bed. We will leave soon."

"Who is the Seventh Knight?"

Aarjen set the instrument he'd been working with on a stone pedestal next to him and looked directly at Brendan without speaking. Brendan couldn't tell from his frown if he was surprised or annoyed.

"Sorry," said Brendan, "I didn't mean to pry. The stone lion told me that you are not the Seventh Knight. Just wanted to know if I can be of help…"

"A stone lion?"

"It called itself Kal—a Yaa…Ya something." He had already forgotten the word.

"A yaali! A lion with a trunk," Aarjen finished. "Where did you meet this creature? What did it tell you?"

Brendan sensed Aarjen's discomfort. "It asked me not to trust you or the other knights. But it turned out to be a fake one. A tantric."

He explained how the stone lion had accosted him when Aarjen was away and tried to convince him to betray the knight. "Run-Nier taught me how to push it down the cliff."

"Are you sure it was Run-Nier?" Aarjen scratched the stubble on his cheek. "Kaia and the queen told me that they had left his body in the patch and I thought the body was scavenged."

"He's alive!" Brendan said. "Why is he always helping us?"

"It is all a mystery to me as well…"

"He mentioned the Seventh Knight too. He said that you were in danger, Arjen, but he disappeared, and then you showed up," said Brendan.

"Follow me," Aarjen said, leading Brendan into an adjacent chamber.

Inside the nearly empty chamber, lit with silver lamps, the walls were covered with many strange symbols. Brendan quietly stood by Aarjen. Silence consumed the room, occasionally broken by the crackle of the flames from the silver lamps.

Finally, Aarjen spoke. "The knights are the order of the seven rishis, commissioned to protect the worlds and the lords of the elements. Each of us serves one of the seven rishis." Aarjen's voice echoed across the empty chamber.

"So, there are seven knights?" Brendan quickly made the connection.

"Six!" Aarjen corrected.

"Why only six?"

"The Order is led by the Seventh Knight, the one who can combine the power of all the knights."

"Isn't that you?" Brendan asked.

"I am not destined to be the Seventh Knight." Aarjen was sincere and the tone of his voice was humble. "The time has come for the true knight with all the power bestowed by the rishis to rise from a world of darkness and join forces with us to defeat the theel and his master."

"Is that what Run-Nier was trying to tell me?"

"I am not sure exactly who this Run-Nier is and what he's trying to say. But whoever he is, he must have heard something about the Seventh Knight either from Maya or from the theel's master," Aarjen guessed.

"Why did he say you are in trouble?"

"He could be delivering a message, but from whom, I don't know." Aarjen left the room. "Let's look at Yan's notebook. "

"Aarjen, I'll make sure that I don't let you down," he said politely, suspecting that Aarjen might be in some sort of danger.

"Thanks. I am counting on you." Aarjen reached for the encased sword in front of him. "Here, you should have my sword." He turned it sideways and offered it to Brendan with both hands. "This sword was created by the rishis and will protect you."

Brendan searched for words, looking at the long sword that Aarjen held in front of him. Without saying much, he accepted the sword. He felt the weight of the sword bearing down on him as he tried to slip it through his belt.

"The sword now belongs to you, Brendan." Aarjen unfolded Yan's notebook. "What do you see?"

Brendan focused on the blank pages of the notebook. "All I see is a hazy green hue—the glowing sea?" asked Brendan.

Aarjen brought a lit crystal closer to the notebook and flipped the page.

"Ahh...I see something," said Brendan.

> *If you cross the poisoned sea,*
>
> *Kaling will have no mercy.*
>
> *By night's fall, you'll recall*
>
> *All along that they were wrong*
>
> *About the weak and the strong.*
>
> *When you fight with the knight,*
>
> *You need wings as she stings*
>
> *And a flying dart*
>
> *To strike the heart.*

"This is long," Brendan repeated the verses from Yan's notebook.

"We are up against a deadly foe. Kaling is the mighty kin of the theel, an enormous five-headed sea serpent. Many devas and asuras have attempted to fight Kaling and have been petrified by its poison."

"Can we just avoid the sea altogether and just go on land? Is there a way around?"

"Unfortunately, no." Aarjen read the map in the notebook. "This is the island where Kumba is resting." He followed the rugged landscape projected on the page. "The only way to reach the island is by getting to this point where the strip of rocky land extends into small fragments leading to the island. I anticipate this will be the most heavily guarded location in the inner sphere."

Brendan tried to follow the map.

"The green glow of sea is caused by the venom that has been seeping into the water over the years. The water is acidic and corrosive. The chain of rocks is the only place where we can try to cross with the least contact with the water." Aarjen carefully mapped bits of tiny fragments of land on the notebook, like connecting the dots of a picture. "Unless, of course, we find a way to—"

"Fly?" Brendan asked.

"Well, I was going to suggest a chariot, but, yes, flying would be even better," agreed Aarjen.

"*You need wings as she stings.* Don't you have one of the flying chariots, here at the camp?"

"No." Aarjen seemed to quickly dismiss the thought and focus on the clue. "It's time for us to leave this camp."

###

At daybreak, Aarjen and Brendan embarked on their long and difficult trek across the seemingly endless expanse of black, interlocking volcanic rocks. The columnar formations, perfectly hexagonal in places, rose and fell like a vast, rocky staircase connecting the islands. Brendan couldn't help but think of the Giant's Causeway in Ireland, a landscape so otherworldly it felt as though it had been crafted by giants. "How long do we have to climb through these rocks?" Brendan complained.

"The journey has just begun, young man!"

"There has got to be a better way." Brendan took a break, looking around to see if he could find a solution.

Aarjen finally stopped several paces ahead of Brendan. "I agree," said Aarjen. "The sooner we reach the end of the strip, the more time we'll have to plan for a defense against Kaling. There has to be a better way to get there," he admitted. "If only the poiz were here—"

"Wait!" Brendan burst out. "Run-Nier told me that this island is full of petrified poiz, who can help, but they need energy."

"I think Run-Nier is on to something. Theoretically, poiz that have become petrified will be very useful if you supply them with energy."

Aarjen removed a baseball-sized crystal from a leather bag and showed it to Brendan. "Crystal energy is like sunlight."

"I thought you said you had some fruits and a knife in that bag," Brendan frowned.

"And one crystal the size of a fruit." Aarjen held the crystal next to an orange-sized fruit from the bag, comparing the two. "The fruits nourish us." He lobbed the fruit to Brendan. "The crystal nourishes the soulless creatures. Now, I just need to find a poiz who can take us across this difficult terrain," said Aarjen.

Aarjen led Brendan into a small burrow between two large boulders. "Stay here and don't drift away, talking to strangers." With the large shiny crystal in his hand, Aarjen disappeared behind the rocks.

Chapter 19

The Rise of the Seventh Knight

hen Aarjen returned, Brendan couldn't take his eyes off the creature he had brought with him—it looked exactly like the stone lion he had encountered the night before. Although the creature's large face and its long trunk appeared less threatening in daylight, Brendan was terrified of being anywhere near another one.

"Relax, *this* is a yaali, but he's the real one," Aarjen assured Brendan. "Meet Komo, a kind yaali who has offered to help. Komo is a poiz in the form of a yaali, but has been petrified into a stone lion."

"I am privileged to serve the great knight," said Komo.

"Why does it have to be another stone lion?" asked Brendan.

"What did you expect, a stone bird that could fly?" asked Aarjen.

Both Aarjen and the yaali chuckled. Aarjen converted the leather straps from his bag and sheath into a makeshift harness. He stuffed washed-up dry kelp under the harness and crafted a cushioned seat. He fluffed the filling and tested its sturdiness as Brendan watched.

Brendan burst out laughing when the yaali turned with its bulky seaweed saddle, almost knocking Aarjen to the ground. "You look funny, trying to tie that on something that looks like a big statue from the Field Museum," Brendan said, laughing. "Are you sure this is going to be faster than walking?"

"Watch what you say, kid. One tip, and you'll find yourself dipped in acid," said Komo.

It was Aarjen's turn to laugh. "Thanks, Komo," he said, patting Komo on its stone mane as he effortlessly hurled himself onto the seaweed cushion. "Hop on, kid. You don't want to miss the bus." He motioned to Brendan, who was keeping a safe distance away from the big thing made of stone.

With great hesitation and difficulty, Brendan pulled himself onto the surprisingly soft saddle.

The motion on the high-riding stone lion was a stomach-churning combination of swaying sideways and rocking back and forth. But once Brendan became accustomed to the rhythm of the motion under the warm daylight, he was impressed with the agility and speed of the creature.

For a while, Brendan tried to listen to a conversation in an unknown language between Komo and Aarjen, but soon his mind drifted. He had so many questions. He patiently waited for the opportunity to talk to Aarjen.

"If yaalis are poiz and just illusion, how come they are solid matter?" asked Brendan abruptly during an opportunistic moment of silence. "You said something about them being gaseous forms with loosely connected molecules."

"Poiz are weak and transient in the outer sphere," Aarjen agreed. "In the inner sphere, they have evolved into nijaz, true life forms. But here, like Komo, they have become petrified and low in energy. My crystal will sustain Komo for a while, but by nighttime, his energy will be dissipated. We need to get to the edge of the land by nightfall and prepare to cross the sea."

There was a brief silence as Komo pounded on the rock. *Clickety-clack. Clickety-clack.* "*Need wings as she stings,*" thought Brendan to the rhythm of the yaali's movements.

"Can any of the poiz fly?" asked Brendan.

"No. Rocks can't fly, even in this world," replied Aarjen.

A short break seemed to have helped Komo. The stone lion was agile as it found the path of least resistance and pushed itself along the flat rocks.

They traveled for hours, yet the landscape remained unchanged—an endless terrain of flat and protruding six-sided rocks, flanked by rough greenish sea. Aarjen signaled to Komo to stop, transferred more energy from the crystal to Komo, and had a brief conversation with the stone lion. "We are almost there," he told Brendan, who offered help in tightening the harness that held the remnants of the flattened seaweed pile.

"All along they were wrong…About the weak and the strong. The curse is about the weak becoming strong, but the words from the notebook seem to contradict this idea," Brendan said. "Maybe it is about me and my weakness—my inability to use your sword or finish what I came to finish."

"I think you have demonstrated enough courage, Brendan. Just focus on the task ahead and trust your instincts."

"Need wings as she stings. A flying dart to strike the heart." Brendan recited the words of the notebook again. "We need to find a bird or something that can attack from the air with a dart—an *arrow*?" Brendan said, raising his voice. "Make a bow and arrow."

"I told you that there are no flying creatures here," Aarjen stressed. "While I like your idea of using a bow and arrow, it's not practical against the enormous Kaling."

The journey continued as Komo transported the visitors to the tip of the rocky cape before the day ended.

"This is the land's end, the farthest I can take you. I…I…" Komo paused and continued. "I should just leave now," he said, bowing to Aarjen.

"Do you have something on your mind, Komo?" Aarjen asked politely, sensing Komo's hesitation to speak.

"May I speak frankly, oh great knight of the Dark Forest?" Komo's voice resonated from deep within the hollow, hardened cavities, like that of the first yaali Brendan had encountered. "I have something to share, if the knight would care to hear from a poiz."

"Of course. Please speak your mind freely, my friend. You have been of great help to us, and I am indebted to you."

"Thank you, great knight of the upper worlds. I couldn't help but overhear your conversation with your human companion about Kaling." Komo lowered his massive head and approached the knight.

"There is no way to avoid the wrath of Kaling when we cross the Sea of Poison," Aarjen acknowledged.

Komo nodded slowly. "No creature with a soul has ever succeeded in crossing the poisoned sea since the keeper disappeared. If the poison doesn't kill you, Kaling will. We fear Kaling despite our hardened form."

Komo directed their attention to the remains of the petrified creatures strewn on the rocky shore.

It then moved closer to Aarjen and lowered its voice. "But last night, one of our kind heard a conversation between Kaling and her evil sting-tailed kin. I thought it might be of interest to you," Komo said in an offer to disclose the information it had gathered from its eavesdropping source.

"I have known about the theel's connection to Kaling even though they don't trust each other. Nevertheless, I am curious to learn about what they spoke about," Aarjen said.

"I heard the conceited Kaling was singing its own praise of immortality, but the sting tail warned her of her vulnerability." Komo paused.

"Vulnerability?" Aarjen asked keenly.

"Yes! The sting tail was heard telling Kaling that a napoptaksha's immortality was vulnerable at the time of secreting hot venom. It warned Kaling that a clever enemy could locate her heart and slay her if she was not careful, but Kaling simply dismissed and disparaged her cousin."

"Interesting fact, Komo." Aarjen appreciated the value of the information. "Didn't know that Kaling is a napoptaksha," he admitted.

"What does that mean?" asked Brendan, trying to follow the conversation.

"Napoptakshas are a type of rakshasa that have found a way to stay alive when their blood spills…Like the cancer cells in humans that avoid cell death," Aarjen explained to Brendan.

"Kaling's wounds will heal instantly," said Komo.

"So, how do you kill a napo…na-pop-tak-sha?" asked Brendan.

"Death has to come from within and not from outside," stated Aarjen.

Komo nodded his assent and began walking away from Aarjen, but when he passed Brendan, he slowly turned and looked straight at him. "If you try hard, you should be able to find something that will take her out—from the inside—and always ask for help."

"How? From who?" asked Brendan, searching for answers.

"I have a feeling you'll figure it out, kid, when the time is right." Komo paused, feeling the effect of the attenuation of energy, and spoke to Aarjen. "I know I don't have much time, but I want to let you know that it has been my greatest honor to serve you. I wish you success in your quest."

"Thanks, Komo. When we are successful, I'll make sure that Indra provides you and your kind with the gift of crystal energy so that the yaalis can be free to roam anywhere in Mayastella."

The stone lion didn't reply. He had already solidified.

"He'll regain limited movement at daybreak," Aarjen said, as if to comfort Brendan.

The view was magnificent from where Brendan and Aarjen stood. They could clearly see the outline of the enormous, mountainous island rising abruptly from the calm green sea not too far from the thin strip of land where they stood. It had been a long journey to the edge of the cape, and the sunless daylight was already waning, allowing darkness to slowly descend.

"That is the island of Kumba," Aarjen said.

"Is this the end of land?" Brendan's eyes widened in wonder.

"The end of continuous land. If you look closely, all these tiny, fragmented islands lead to the main island."

Brendan followed the clusters formed by the columnar, interlocking rocks, and small hills. They curved like a tail of an animal toward the main island.

"That's a long way to go," he said.

"This is where I would expect to encounter Kaling," Aarjen cautioned. "Something tells me that she'll invite us to the dance when she's ready."

The shore was short, jagged, and littered with heavily eroded boulders of various shapes and sizes, battered by the rough sea. Lodged among the boulders were the fossilized remains of poiz and nijaz who had attempted to cross the sea.

Aarjen inspected his weapons, one by one. They were neatly concealed in different parts of his attire. Komo had provided them with crucial information. The battle could be won if he pierced her heart when her venom was hot and about to be expelled from her sacs.

Aarjen shared with Brendan his secrets for quickly mastering the sword. Of all the weapons Aarjen had displayed, the chakra captivated Brendan's attention most. The mechanical sound it made when activated and the speed with which it spun around Aarjen's finger before being unleashed enthralled him.

"You can cut off the serpent's head with that thing," Brendan said, carefully feeling the serrated edges of the chakra with his finger.

"It will only grow another one. We need to find the venom sac and puncture it while you get to her heart with the sword," Aarjen reasoned.

"Where is the venom sac located?"

"I don't know, but since the venom is hot, I should follow the heat map," Aarjen guessed.

"What's a heat—"

Before Brendan could ask his question, Aarjen's hand moved over his mouth and covered it to prevent him from speaking. Brendan froze, but Aarjen pulled him behind a rock.

"Listen," he whispered, motioning toward the sea.

Brendan's eyes moved rapidly as he strained to listen. He could hear a splashing sound in regular intervals from the calm water.

"Kaling?" He moved his mouth silently.

Aarjen nodded. He held a shiny object in his palm with a reflective surface. He tilted the object to show Brendan multiple pairs of flaming red eyes bobbing up and down on the surface of the water, slowly advancing.

The slithering monster let out an ear-piercing shrill.

"This is no chess game," Brendan whispered as he slumped by the rock next to Aarjen, pulling his parka up.

But the noise subsided, and the splashing stopped altogether.

"It's gone!"

"Probably waiting for us to make a move," Aarjen cautioned. He kept his eyes focused on the reflective surface. "We need to split ways here, Brendan. Do you see that tall rock across the water?" It was a sheer, towering formation with a flat top, rising sharply above the water. "I am going to climb to the top, but right across that cliff, on the base of where this land ends, there's a cave," Aarjen paused to make sure Brendan spotted the well-concealed cave. "Get inside the cave and wait. You can easily get up there by going over this strip of land across the shore. When I reach the top, I'll draw her toward me. I'll sever her poison sac with the disk as soon as I pick up the heat signature when the venom gets hot. Kaling will have to squeeze through the narrow stretch of water. When I give the signal, you'll surprise her from behind with your sword."

"What will your signal be?" asked Brendan. "It all seems too complicated for the timing to be perfect."

"When you see the light from my crystal, plunge the sword deep into the back of Kaling's center head. The tip of the V-shaped marking on the center head marks the spot for the heart inside. Striking her heart and exposing it to her own poison will finish her."

Brendan nodded. "Will I be able to get to Kaling from there? What are the chances that she'll be exposing her back to me close enough for me to strike her?"

"I will be able to force Kaling through this channel with my chakras." It was a narrow strip of turbulent water between the sea cliffs. "I'll hold her in position. You'll have to do the rest. It's not going to be perfect, but I'll give you the best position to execute your attack. You can do it, Brendan," said Aarjen with confidence.

"I wish you were with me, but I get it," he said, locking hands with the knight.

Aarjen gripped Brendan's hand firmly, said goodbye, and disappeared into the darkness.

"You remember the knight's game?" were the last words Brendan heard after Aarjen left him.

Startled by the sudden but familiar voice from behind, he lost his footing on the slippery rock and went tumbling down the bumpy slope. His head hit a flat rock, and the world went black.

Coach Turner hastily dug for his phone in his jeans pocket, attempting to pick it up before the first few vibrations turned into a ringtone. He had stepped into the tournament hall to watch the game and did not want to be thrown out by an overzealous TD for not keeping his phone on silent mode. He raced to the door.

"Hello?" he whispered into the phone after stepping out.

"Dad?" It was his daughter Tara on the other end.

"Hey, Tara. How are you?" Turner continued to speak softly into his phone despite having exited the tournament hall.

She was calling him from Edwards Air Force Base in California.

"Dad, has he started his game?"

"He is plum in the middle, hon." Turner had his eyes glued on Brendan and bumped into another parent.

"How is his position?"

"Um…It's tight…But, um…He's playing a strange game." Turner analyzed the game quickly with Tara, who was very skilled at the game.

"It is a little odd. I don't understand why he traded his active knight for two pawns, especially since they were holding his bishops. He must have a reason for taking such a risk."

"I am sure he does."

"I wish I had talked to him before the game," she sighed. "Um, Dad, I have some exciting news."

"Are you getting married?" The coach chuckled loudly, startling the lady who stood next to him, staring at the players inside the hall.

"Nooo. Stop it!" said Tara, laughing.

"What, then?" Turner quickly moved away from the annoyed lady.

"I am about to fly a new aircraft. No one has flown this beauty before. Just wanted to tell you before I took off." Tara's voice conveyed her exuberance.

"That's really awesome. I am sooo proud of you! What is it? A new type of Stealth or something?"

"You know I can't say much, Dad. I'll call you after I come back to check on Brendan's game. Oh, by the way," she quickly added, "I am taking the family pic with me, so you are all going to fly with me. Love you, Dad!"

"Good luck, kiddo. You are the best!" Turner tried to hold back his emotion. "Make sure to look over your shoulder when you change lanes."

"Okay, Dad. And I'll also stick to the speed limit." They both laughed before hanging up.

Turner slipped his phone into his pocket, and gazed out of the window at the choppy blue water of Lake Michigan until Bob Raj interrupted his thoughts.

"He gave up his knight for a pawn, man! I watched it closely, you know, and it was not a forced exchange. Not sure what he has in his mind," Bob Raj said, shrugging his shoulders.

When Brendan regained consciousness, his eyelids fluttered in an effort to adjust to the lightless surroundings. He blinked at the rough edges of a dull ceiling. His cold body trembled. His head throbbed with pain. He saw a faint light at a distance but could not pinpoint its source or location; it was blurry. He found himself leaning against a hard surface that felt like ice, his legs stretched on the floor.

Only when he felt his loose parka did he recall his journey to the inner sphere with Aarjen. He remembered seeing Run-Nier just before he hit his head. He strained his eyes to see where he was and finally realized that he was inside a cave.

Where was he and how long had he been there? Aarjen had assigned him a specific task. Had he already signaled? His stomach sank with the crushing realization that he might have let Aarjen down. Shaky and disoriented, he was unsure of what to do next.

"Aarjen might still need help. I cannot give up," he told himself.

Then, from the corner of his eye, he caught a glimpse of something rapidly moving across the cave. Brendan pulled himself up hurriedly and took cover behind the dark jagged formation of the cave's wall.

"You okay?" It was the voice of Run-Nier again.

"Run-Nier?" Brendan was relieved to have the company of someone who always seemed to be there during crises. "How…How…" Brendan searched for words, his head throbbing. "How did I get here?"

"Run-Nier carry Brendan…You fell on rock and hurt your head. Run-Nier bring you up to the cave the knight wanted you to be in."

"But how? How could you carry me this far?" Brendan was puzzled.

"I have to leave you here and go." Run-Nier, waved something at him.

It took a few seconds for Brendan to realize Run-Nier was holding Aarjen's sword.

"Hey, wait, I need that sword!"

Run-Nier was already heading for the entrance.

"Stop, Run-Nier!" Brendan followed Run-Nier. "Aarjen gave me the sword. Please give it back to me!" Brendan was puzzled by Run-Nier's behavior.

Run-Nier paused at the cave's entrance. "Run-Nier keep knight's sword." His tone was unusually harsh. "The sword belongs to Run-Nier."

Brendan was taken aback. Was this the helpful Run-Nier, or was it an impostor, posing as a friend to cart off the valued weapon?

Aarjen had entrusted the sword to him, and Brendan was determined to reclaim it. He lunged at Run-Nier and tugged the sword by its hilt. But Run-Nier's reaction was equally swift. He jerked back and yanked the sword away from Brendan. Brendan's grip on the sword handle slipped, but he managed to pull loose the spherical object attached at the end of the hilt. Unable to balance himself, Brendan stumbled and crashed into Run-Nier, ejecting him from the cave.

Run-Nier let out an awkward cry, shouting, "Nights fall…The weak and strong," as he plummeted into the poisoned sea below.

Brendan stared after him. *Was that an impostor of an already-dead Run-Nier, or did Run-Nier betray Aarjen?*

Run-Nier's words continued to echo in Brendan's ears, and then it dawned on him that the words night's fall he'd read in Yan's notebook probably meant *fall of a knight*.

Is it the fall of Aarjen? he wondered.

Brendan tried to remember the words.

By night's fall, you'll recall

All along that they were wrong

About the weak and the strong.

When you fight with the knight …

"Then, who was the weak?" Kaling? Theel? Run-Nier? Or himself? Nothing made sense to Brendan.

From where he sat, Brendan got a glimpse of the spherical crystal piece he had dislocated from the hilt. He had seen Aarjen use the object to communicate to Kaia.

Brendan retrieved the object, placed it in the center of his palm and repeatedly rolled it like a snowball, but nothing happened. He let out a deep sigh, and realizing his efforts were futile, he slumped back against the raised rock formation, but something in his pants poked him. It was his phone, and surprisingly, it had a full charge. It lit up with a picture that he had recently saved as his wallpaper. It was of Tara with her thumbs-up from the cockpit of an F-16 Fighting Falcon aircraft.

"I could use your help, sis."

But as he was about to put the phone away, he noticed a faint glow from the crystal he held in the other hand. The closer he brought the crystal to his phone, the brighter it got.

"*Interesting,*" he thought, placing the object on his phone.

A loud static noise erupted from his phone. There was distant chatter. Brendan moved around, hoping to pick up a better signal.

"Hello? Hello? Can anyone hear me?" His voice echoed across the cave.

He listened carefully to the chatter, but the noise died abruptly.

The silence didn't last long. The ground shook violently. Brendan slid the crystal into his pocket, pulled his hoodie over his head, and slipped back into the concealed enclosure from where he could observe the open sea below. A chill ran down his spine when he saw the monstrous serpent slithering across the water, a few hundred feet away. The very sight of the vicious and cruel creature shocked his senses momentarily. Its collection of five different heads, clustered together, with large fiery red eyes, towered over reefs that rose from the water. Its forked red tongues flicked in discord underneath the puffs of moisture that swirled from large nostrils. The center head of the serpent, with a V-shaped mark, was the largest and the only one with two curved fangs several feet in length. Brendan prayed Aarjen was still alive and ready for the attack, as he had planned.

Aarjen waited patiently in the shadows. He could finally see Kaling rolling toward the boulder, searching for its victim. He planned to lure Kaling toward him at the opportune moment, and in that instant before she spewed her hot venom, he would strike her venom sack with the chakra and signal to Brendan to plunge his sword into the back of her head.

Aarjen prepared for the attack, but his instinct warned him of the presence of intruders. He would deal with the intruders later. Without delaying, he let out a cry to draw the attention of Kaling.

Unseen by Aarjen, Run-Nier climbed up the rock, carrying Aarjen's heavy sword. His destiny hinged on perfect timing. As Run-Nier neared the summit, he could feel the electric charge in the air. His body tingled, and his hair rose with static. He sensed the presence of the theel.

When Run-Nier reached the apex, he was just in time to see Aarjen emerge from the shadows and let out a cry to draw Kaling's attention.

The theel gloated over its vantage, observing from where it prepared to ambush its archenemy. At last, it felt it had outsmarted the knight of the Dark Forest. It had masterminded the alliance with Kaling and the poiz of the underworld to lead Aarjen to a fatal trap. This was the turning point it had been waiting for—a revenge for all the humiliation it had faced. It was about to eliminate an unsuspecting knight. With great satisfaction, it charged its tail. Within seconds, it would incapacitate Aarjen, allowing Kaling to deliver the fatal blow.

Kaling spotted the knight atop the flat surface of the boulder, deliberately signaling to her to duel him. She knew a direct duel with Aarjen would prove to be a fatal mistake, but she was certain that death would be delivered to the knight with assistance from her clever and deceitful kin. With her venom sac overflowing with hot venom, she raced toward Aarjen.

Brendan felt helpless. The crystal was all he had. He knew that, somehow, he needed to stay involved. He focused his thoughts on finding a way to import the most lethal flying hardware that his sister had access to.

Turner and Bob Raj analyzed Brendan's position on the monitor carefully. Brendan's knight had just gotten pinned to his king by his opponent's bishop.

"He might have to trade his knight for a bishop," said Turner.

"Yeah, I can't see any other way out," Bob Raj acknowledged.

Although it was an even trade, Turner did not want Brendan to trade an active knight, but he realized Brendan might not have a choice.

After considerable deliberation, Brendan traded this knight for a pawn instead, completely surprising Turner and Bob Raj.

"What?" Turner blurted out, unable to conceal his surprise. "He just gave up his knight!"

"I don't, um…Unless…" Bob Raj mumbled as he tried to interpret the move.

Tara had ascended to 35,000 feet when her test jet lost power and began a premature and uncontrolled dive. Her reflex and training took over. She made rapid adjustments to take control of her test fighter jet without panicking, but her aircraft spiraled and plunged to the earth, like a peregrine attacking its prey. A dark cloud engulfed the plane, and a shock wave rippled with a loud boom. Tara felt the surge of G-force just before she passed out.

It was the crackle from the radio that helped Tara regain her consciousness. She had a sharp headache. She was still strapped into the cockpit of her test aircraft, which was still in one piece. Darkness surrounded her, except for a bright green glow permeating from the outside. She radioed in, but there was no response, and then the familiar voice of her brother cracked through her earpiece.

"Tara, I can hear you!"

"Brendan, what the heck's going on? Where are you, and how am I talking to you?"

"Tara, listen to me. I need your help. You have been pulled into this new world—"

"What are you talking about, Brendan?" Tara was not sure whether she was hallucinating. In a few brief strokes, Brendan gave Tara a picture of the events that had propelled him and his friends into a bizarre world and a strange mission. "You are my weapon, Tara, and my only hope," Brendan sighed.

Tara was silent. The white noise and the strange aberrations in her instruments suggested entry into a different world from where her brother had reached out to her.

"Where are you, and where do I find this monster?" Tara asked.

Brendan gave her a description with landmarks and topography but finally gave up. "I am not sure how to guide you. It is so huge that you won't miss it if you fly low. Don't you have devices to look for these things, heat sensors, laser thingies?"

Before she could respond, Tara saw the thing in her radar first and then a visual with infrared. "Oh my God! This thing is enormous, Brendan, and I see two hot spots on it—one on the top and the other below the first one. The heat's really building up."

"You need to hit it as soon as I tell you to."

"Brendan, I am only carrying dummies. But it has the guiding system and the sensors, and it should certainly put a hole through the beast," she said.

Tara locked on to her target and waited for the signal.

Through his night vision, Aarjen saw the two hot spots of the venom sac under Kaling's hood. He aimed his disk at the sac, but a fraction of a second before he released his disk, bright flashes lit up the darkness, and powerful bolts of lightning struck him from behind. His knees buckled, and the impact knocked him forward. He had lost control of his weapon. Just then he realized he had been ambushed by the theel and was about to be struck by the hot venom of the raging Kaling. With great difficulty, he tried to regain his strength, but the intensity of the current was too strong. Before he fainted, he saw a figure rushing toward him. It was not the theel.

From a distance, Brendan saw the drama unfold. Flashes of light illuminated the scene as Aarjen was struck by bolts from behind. The disk he awkwardly launched initially soared past Kaling but veered back, severing her fifth head from the large, arching trunk of her body. He watched in horror as a stream of blood spewed from the serpent's sliced torso, and to his amazement, as the blood thickened and oozed out of the stem of Kaling's neck, she rapidly reconstructed a new head. The head began to function normally almost immediately, hissing and emitting a loud shrill at Aarjen.

Brendan watched the knight struggle to regain his strength amid the flashes. And then it happened. A thin, shadowy figure with a sword in its hand raced across the rock and crashed into Aarjen, hurling him from the edge of the cliff and disappearing into the darkness just as a stream of poison sprayed from Kaling's fangs at the spot where Aarjen had stood, melting the rock. "Oh no...No." Brendan was unable to comprehend what had just happened to Aarjen.

"Tara, fire your missiles now."

Turner finally saw the move. "He's going for the pawn," he said.

"Looks like your son found a magic pawn, Coach," said Bob Raj. "How did we not see this? He's brilliant. No wonder he let his knight go. Now, he can get a queen by promoting the pawn."

"Or a knight?" said Turner, watching Brendan reach out and choose a knight instead of a queen and place it on the board. "Check," he said.

"I guess he wants to check his opponent," added Bob Raj. "He should try to checkmate his opponent. A knight is only going to let him check, but not checkmate," he joked.

"Didn't you just call him brilliant?" mused Turner, raising his eyebrows. "I am sure he's got a reason."

Brendan watched the fighter jet rip through the dark sky, discharging blue flame from its rear. Two fiery flashes were followed by smoky trails that separated from each other as the missiles roared toward Kaling in curvilinear paths. Brendan watched the missile attack with eager anticipation of a serious impact, but his attention was diverted by an intruder entering his cave. A mysterious figure crept toward him.

"He's not dead! Thanks to you, Aarjen will live," said the deep voice. "We still have some unfinished business."

Brendan slipped into the veil of darkness and responded with silence.

"I know you are there, Brendan. Aarjen needs you," the voice advised.

"Who are you?" asked Brendan, nervously stepping out from behind his rocky cover.

When he saw the tall, muscular figure slowly lay Aarjen on the floor, Brendan cautiously approached Aarjen and the towering person leaning over Aarjen's pale, limp body.

"I am your friend Run-Nier," replied the voice. "Don't you recognize me?" he asked, gently placing the sword by Aarjen. "Sorry I had to forcefully take the weapon from you," he added.

Only when Brendan noticed the piercing green eyes and the shiny red hair under the faint glow of the crystal, was he convinced that the person who stood in front of him was Run-Nier. Somehow, the skinny lad had transformed into a muscular warrior. The deafening noise and the commotion that followed distracted Brendan. Just outside the cave, the serpent violently rocked back and forth. Two small fireballs had erupted from its head and dissipated into plumes of smoke behind its head.

"You chose the right weapon, Brendan," said Run-Nier. His strange accent had all but disappeared. He sounded more like Aarjen. "We don't have much time. Do you still have the crystal?"

"Yes, I do."

"I'll finish the beast," said Run-Nier, taking the crystal from Brendan.

"Brendan, it's hit. Did you see it? But it is still alive!" He heard his sister's voice coming through his phone.

"Tara, I saw the strike. Thank you."

"We are grateful for your help," said Run-Nier. "You have saved our lives. You may safely return to your world."

"Great. Be safe. I'll see you back at…"

Things went quiet.

"You stay here with Aarjen. I'll be back soon." Run-Nier plunged into the poisoned water. This time, Brendan didn't fight for the sword. The injured serpent thrashed until the corrosive water frothed. One of the missiles had lodged into the center head of Kaling, ripping the poison sac. Even though a portion of Kaling's head was shattered, it had already begun the reconstruction process. Sizzling violet poison oozed from the gaping hole where the sac had once existed. The second missile had slid right through the hole and slammed against a tall column of rock behind the serpent, where the theel had ambushed Aarjen, causing heavy slabs of rocks to fall and crush Kaling's body.

Badly injured and dazed, Kaling set out to destroy everything in her path, knocking massive rocks into the sea. Undaunted by her violent response, Run-Nier swam toward her. He could finally feel the effect of the poison seeping into his skin, making him stronger and stronger with every stroke he took through the acidic water. He felt his skin stretch, his muscles bulge, and his bones expand, but he remained focused on his enemy.

"He's growing like the Hulk," mumbled Brendan, sitting next to the stiff body of Aarjen and watching Run-Nier morph into a giant.

"It is the effect of the poison," said Aarjen, his voice shaky and barely audible.

Brendan jumped at hearing Aarjen's voice. He had helplessly witnessed the theel assault Aarjen, its retribution evident by the bruises and burns on Aarjen's body.

"Are you all right?"

"I'll be fine, Brendan," said Aarjen, his voice weak. "How are you holding up?"

"Good. Run-Nier saved you."

"Yes, but you, my friend, have just helped me discover the Seventh Knight."

"Run-Nier is the Seventh Knight?" asked Brendan.

"Of course. I should have known. He's the soulless wanderer who not only sacrificed himself to save a mortal being, but also threw himself in the line of a deadly attack to protect me from sure death."

"Look!" Brendan interrupted.

Run-Nier had turned into a muscular giant, swimming across the sea, causing enormous waves that crashed into the rocks. He lunged out of the water and grabbed Kaling by her neck.

"Like Kaling, the Seventh Knight has the rare blood of napoptaksha. He can use the poison as a stimulant that will grow his body," Aarjen mustered up energy to explain.

"So, the notebook was describing Run-Nier?" asked Brendan. "*All along that they were wrong about the weak and the strong.*"

"Yes," said Aarjen, adjusting his body to lessen the pain.

Run-Nier squeezed Kaling's neck, and the monster writhed in pain as she let out an ear-piercing cry. He then pulled her defenseless body out of the water and plunged Aarjen's sword, which looked more like a knife in his giant fist, into the exposed underside of Kaling's body. With her venom sac emptied and heart pierced, she coiled around Run-Nier to crush his body. But Run-Nier refused to compromise. He continued squeezing her neck until her own venom slowly drained into her punctured heart, killing her. Kaling's body slid out of Run-Nier's hand like a loose cord and disintegrated in the corrosive water.

His mission completed, Run-Nier swam back to the cave. By the time he reached the cave, he had reverted to his original but stronger self. With poison dripping from his body, he climbed into the cave to be greeted by the two admiring spectators.

"I apologize for allowing the theel to hurt you, oh great knight." Run-Nier spoke to Aarjen. "I had no choice but to time my encounter with you on the rock during the theel's attack." Run-Nier knelt beside Aarjen, who was resting against the wall in pain.

"The theel had saved its best for me. Without you, I would have been petrified by Kaling's poison," Aarjen said.

"Why didn't you just explain your plans to me?" asked a puzzled Brendan. "I would have just given you the sword."

"My mind was drawn to the sword, as though I had a connection with it, and it was the sword that helped me defend Aarjen from the theel's electric bolts. The bolt struck the weapon and the charge went through my body. It was exactly how I'd felt at the patch when I was struck by the theel. This time, its effect on me was many times stronger."

Run-Nier rubbed his hands together and generated a soothing aura in his palms, which he gently spread across Aarjen's body to begin the healing process. "This should heal you soon," he said.

There was momentary silence.

"Run-Nier, *you* are the Seventh Knight," said Aarjen. "The rishis have chosen you to lead us in the battle against the theel's evil master."

Aarjen studied the perplexed reaction on Run-Nier's face. His penetrating green eyes somehow seemed to accelerate the soothing effect of the healing aura.

Run-Nier shook his head in disbelief. "I don't understand…"

"Of course. You do not have any memories of your past since you found your way to Mayastella. Let me give you a quick account of who you are," Aarjen offered to explain.

Brendan leaned over with interest to listen to the story. He looked at Run-Nier with great admiration and could still see the same innocence that he had seen in his eyes before.

"You are the son of the rakshasa warrior, Zuri, who helped the rishis raise and protect Queen Suhela. Pleased with your father's bravery, dedication, and loyalty, the rishis granted him a wish." Aarjen paused to regain his strength.

Run-Nier tried hard to remember his father. Fleeting memories flashed but disappeared.

"Zuri's only wish was for his son—you—to have a chance to become a knight, to be accepted into the knight's ashram, where young prospects trained. And the rishis created the opportunity despite the fact that you are mostly a rakshasa," Aarjen continued.

"Are rakshasas not allowed into the ashram?" asked Brendan.

"Rakshasas in general are not trustworthy and are the enemies of the rishis who have sworn to protect other life forms from these creatures. But there are exceptions…Queen Suhela, Zuri, and Kumba are examples of such exceptions," Aarjen clarified. "Your father was loyal to the rishis."

"Acceptance of Zuri's son into the program worried the devas and the asuras, but you were given a fair chance and taken under the wings of the rishis until…" Aarjen paused to collect his own thoughts and shorten the sequence of events. "Things changed when the battle with Kumba was about to begin. Your father left the rishis to be with Suhela, to protect her. He promised he would return, but he never did. Some feared he had been killed in the battle. Soon afterward, the rishis decided to close the ashram until the war ended."

"What then happened to me?" asked Run-Nier.

"The exact account is not known," Aarjen confessed. "During the war, many of the students went back to their families and assumed different roles, except for one lost disciple, who continued to practice his skills, waiting for the right opportunity to prove his courage. But the opportunity never arrived, and the grief-stricken young disciple slowly drifted away, forgotten over time. At least by most."

"I remember my father a little," said Run-Nier. "I missed him so much. Do you know what really happened to him? It seems so long ago."

"Your father tried his best, Run-Nier," Aarjen said reassuringly. "But he was deceived by his own. Eventually, he was captured and killed by the theel's creatures. His only wish was to see you become a knight, and if he were here today, he would be very proud of you."

"Mayastella is the only place I remember," Run-Nier said. "This is my world. I saw the devas and the asuras come and go during their quests and journeys. No one ever noticed me or interacted with me, and those who saw me thought I was poiz. I found Yan's notebook inside the Blackstone Cave after he disappeared, and I familiarized myself with all the information he had stored in his notebook. I knew they were clues to hidden secrets of this world."

"Run-Nier, your willingness and ability to save a knight of the rishis from mortal danger, even if it required sacrificing your own life, was the ultimate act of loyalty and courage that impressed the rishis."

"Brendan is about to win his game," Run-Nier said. "The rakshasas are not going to be pleased with this outcome, and the Earth needs protection against their uprising."

"Kaia and I will protect Earth, but I have one last thing to do for you, Run-Nier," said Aarjen. Mostly healed, he asked Brendan for the crystal that had been separated from the hilt of Aarjen's sword.

When Aarjen reattached the crystal to the hilt, magic happened. The cave was illuminated, and the images of the seven rishis appeared from seven corners of the cave. They walked toward the center, where Run-Nier stood. One by one, they initiated him into knighthood. When the ceremony was completed, rishi Vyas spoke. "Run-Nier, you are the true Seventh Knight. You have saved Aarjen and helped the children. You are now the protector of our immortal and mortal worlds. Do you accept the Seventh Knight's responsibilities?"

"Yes, until I die, oh great one," swore Run-Nier.

"Your weapon will be your sword, and its powers will protect you from any harm. We'll see you at the ashram once the Curse of Bhrigu is erased for eternity."

"My father," said Run-Nier. "I would like for people to remember him."

"Your father was a great soul. You have made his wish come true. Your memories of him will return, and you'll see his greatness in your own."

The rishis showed images of Zuri, and Run-Nier watched, his lips quivering, tears welling up in his eyes. He gripped his sword tightly.

"You bear the soul of your father. He will live on through your greatness," Vyas promised.

"It's time to go, Run-Nier. We have our work cut out for us." Then, Aarjen spoke to Brendan. "And you, my friend, your choice of weapon was splendid. You should thank your sister for me."

"You are welcome, Aarjen. Um…I…I…" Brendan hesitated. "Can I ask you for something?"

"Yes, whatever you want," replied Aarjen.

"The crystal—how much power is left in it? You know, the one you used for Komo?"

"Not much. We drained most of its energy. But that one—" Aarjen pointed to the sword that he had given Run-Nier. "—on the sword has plenty of energy."

"What's plenty?" probed Brendan.

"Depends on what you need it for." Aarjen frowned and shrugged at Brendan. "For a poiz, that could last an eternity. Why do—"

"Can I have it?"

Aarjen exchanged a glance with Run-Nier. Without saying a word, Run-Nier removed the spherical object and tossed it to Brendan.

"It's yours," he said as Brendan eagerly caught the crystal and shoved it in his pocket.

"The portal will be opening soon," said Aarjen, guiding them back to the rocky shoreline, where the yaali had left them.

On the sandy shore of the poisoned sea, when Aarjen and Run-Nier were engaged in what appeared to be a busy conversation, Brendan quietly slipped down to the beach where the petrified yaali rested. Brendan greeted the yaali, who could barely move. "I see you are still alive, kid," Komo said slowly. "The word is out that Kaling is dead. I knew you would help the knight accomplish his task," the yaali said, moving his large stone head with great difficulty.

"I had a lot of help. Thank you!" Brendan said politely.

"No need to thank me, kid. I was just trying to do the right thing this time."

"This time?" Brendan frowned at the yaali, not quite understanding what he meant.

"Never mind. We all learn our lessons." The yaali's voice resonated from the depths of its hollow stone trunk. "Now, most importantly, remember to be yourself and follow your heart, and you'll do well, kiddo," he said, mustering his last ounce of energy.

"I have something for you," said Brendan, digging into his parka pocket.

"You have already given us what we want." The yaali's hollow tone was sincere. "Freedom to live without the fear of Kaling."

Brendan placed the active crystal into Komo's trunk, instantly powering up Komo. Brendan narrated the battle between Run-Nier and Kaling and how Aarjen had been saved from the theel.

"You deserve freedom, Komo. The crystal should provide you and other poiz the strength you need until the rishis find a permanent solution."

"You are kind and thoughtful, kid," the stone lion said, shaking his enormous body and leaping from one boulder to another with his newfound vigor. "On behalf of my kind, I take a pledge of allegiance with the human race," he promised. He then moved close to Brendan and whispered, "Now, I have one other secret to share with you."

Chapter 20

Metal Birds

rendan was back from Mayastella, and only he knew that his game was over, even before he promoted the pawn to a knight, which his opponent didn't see coming. The knight's attack on the Earth dweller's king was devastating, and eventually, the opponent realized that the game was all but over. The crowd of kids who stood around Board One, including Nicolas, began to cheer Brendan, infuriating the Earth dweller.

This time, the game's outcome elicited a severe reaction from the Earth dwellers. Finally, the creatures had received the much-anticipated signal from the theel to break all rules and engage in the attack of the humans—a retaliation that Kaia and Moxley had anticipated and were prepared to counter.

The defeated Earth dweller's yellow eyes turned red, and his talons began to protrude. Before the game officially ended, he swung his hairy arm across the chessboard, propelling the few remaining pieces on the board at the handful of kids watching the game. He awkwardly stood, pushing his chair away. Players from the nearby boards curiously rushed to the scene. The Earth dweller pounced on the table, but unable to bear its weight, the laminated surface split and crashed to the floor.

The fallen Earth dweller began hurling broken objects at the helter-skelter crowd.

Tournament directors rushed to the upheaval, only to back off in fear and confusion when they encountered the teenager turned into a ghoulish creature. A confused crowd converged from all sides of the tournament hall and blocked access to Board One, preventing Kaia from reaching Brendan. Other Earth dwellers, scattered within the halls, unveiled themselves, fueling the confusion.

Brendan swung a partially folded chair and smashed it on his creature-turned-opponent, who was clutching his leg and pulling him down. Before the creature could recover, Brendan managed to kick the attacker and get back on his feet. Moxley moved in with his crew and discreetly controlled the attackers with crystal-laden flashlights that subdued the creatures.

Relishing the thought of eating humans, mudalas crept into the world of humans through the waters of Lake Michigan at Navy Pier. Their masters had yielded to their reasoning, and their patience had been compensated. They announced their arrival by creating huge waves that slammed into the concrete walls of the pier, smashing boats against each other.

"How do we stop the mudalas without their blood spilling?" asked Aarjen. "The human weapons will only create bloodshed, triggering uncontrolled spawning of these creatures."

"We will summon the ispat pakshis, the birds of steel," said Kaia.

"That's impossible. The birds of steel have to rise from Earth to be effective. Their inception will take years, not hours or days," reminded Aarjen.

"Earth has already been seeded for this, Aarjen," replied Kaia.

"Where?" Aarjen asked with a frown.

"The stainless-steel bean you saw at Millennium Park is actually an egg of the ispat birds."

"That bean?" asked Aarjen, vigorously gesturing to the south side of the building. "When did this happen?"

"Two rishis will pour water from seven mighty rivers of Earth onto the steel bean to hatch the steel birds. We need to get there now," she said, pulling Aarjen's hand and rushing out of the tournament hall.

CHADURANG: THE CURSED WAR GAME

The random civilian faces on the two giant electronic screens of the contemporary water fountains at Millennium Park on Michigan Avenue transformed into two aged, gray-bearded men with long hair knotted over their heads. Water flowed from the mouths of the sages, as it had from the thousands of faces displayed on the screens every day at the park. Gentle streams meandered over the concrete steps and across the park toward the giant steel bean. As the swirling water splashed against the massive stainless-steel structure and the surprised tourists, thin cracks zigzagged across the shiny bean, randomly intersecting with a metallic scratching noise.

"Everyone, listen up! Please move away from the bean," ordered Moxley as the crowd around and underneath the bean noticed the hairline fissures snake through the structure.

"The bean is cracking," someone yelled.

"It's the water! The water is breaking the bean!" shouted a kid.

Moxley and his crew herded the crowd to a safe distance and secured the perimeter with makeshift barricades.

"What is that noise?" asked another tourist as the frequency and intensity of the tapping increased from within the bean. "Is this a show?"

"Kind of," replied Kaia, who had joined Moxley. "Just watch what comes out."

"What comes out?" asked Mox.

The bean imploded into tiny pieces, prompting the nervous crowd to duck and draw farther from the barricade. Six gleaming stainless-steel spheres—several feet in diameter, five of the same size and the sixth twice the size—rolled through the puddle of water where the bean had once stood.

"The egg was carefully assembled by our friend Anish Kapoor with these seeds. The water will do the rest," Kaia reasoned.

Moxley and the stunned onlookers watched the spheres unfold into large birds. "No kidding. Can steel birds fly?" asked Mox.

The birds ambled across the floor, staring at their excited audience. Occasionally, they stopped to groom themselves, just like real birds, and ate bits of the shattered steel. The smaller birds gathered around the giant mother bird.

"Pakshis!" Kaia called out to the large bird. "The creatures have begun their attack, and we need your help in removing them from this world without bloodshed."

"I am honored to serve a knight," replied the mother bird, her voice metallic. "I'll eliminate their leader while my children battle the mudalas before they emerge from the water."

The birds unfurled their wings, each spanning between ten and twenty feet, as the bewildered crowd cheered at the strange sight of talking metallic birds. Within minutes, the birds soared across the blue sky.

"Mox, call your people. Phase two is a bit more challenging, and we'll need extra help. I'll explain when we get back to Navy Pier," she said, getting into Mox's fortified car. "How fast can this thing get there? I really want to watch the birds dive into the water."

People by Navy Pier watched the metal birds circle the lake, sounding as though metal sheets were being tossed around in a gale. Alerted by the sudden and unexpected arrival of their enemies, the mudalas submerged into the depths of Lake Michigan in an attempt to be stealthy. The birds abruptly folded their wings midair and plunged into the lake, hurling themselves at the mudalas.

The jalas, who were waiting on the other side of the portal, timed the opening for the precise moment of impact, allowing the steel ispat birds to blast the mudalas through the portal with a bang. But the birds knew that they wouldn't survive the entry through the portal. They were born on Earth, and so they would die on Earth. They would rise like the phoenix, but in another world, when the great rishis required their services. Kaia quickly paid homage to them. She knew that the jalas would retrieve the seeds of the birds. "The kateris will be next," said Kaia. "Aarjen and I will prevent them from entering this world."

"Just the two of you? How will you know where they are and when they'll enter Earth?" asked Mox.

"The kateris are waiting for their alpha to arrive and lead them in an attack against the humans. If we eliminate the alpha, the others will not be able to enter our world."

"What about the people? The news?" he asked, wondering how the public would react to the day's events.

"It will all be forgotten tomorrow. The rishis will take care of that," assured Kaia. "The kids have one last game to play, so we should meet with them soon before the final round starts," she said.

"Do you really want me to trust the words of a tantric?" Kaia asked Aarjen after reading the message he had delivered from Yan. "Tantrics know no loyalty. They hunt for souls. What's the catch?"

"Yan didn't think much of it either when the tantric offered to help. But after all, he did spare its life inside the cave of Mount Ely. Perhaps it wants to show its gratitude," said Aarjen, grinning, not attempting to conceal his sarcasm.

"Really?" Kaia scoffed.

"It wants to live in the outer sphere of Mayastella. The reward of life is quite a carrot." Aarjen was sincere this time.

"And Yan gave in?"

"The stakes are high, Kaia. These creatures have nothing to lose, but a lot to gain. But I do hate the tantrics," he admitted.

Kaia quietly slipped into her long, dark trench coat, tied her thick brown hair back, and armed herself with a long silver poniard with a crystal handle. "I'll need this," she said, feeling the sharp tip of its shimmering blade. She embraced Aarjen gently.

"Be careful out there," said Aarjen, squeezing her hand gently. "Never trust a tantric," he warned, "just trust your instincts."

Kaia took a couple of steps and ran through the wall, which distorted slightly, sending ripples across the room like disturbed water. When she disappeared, Aarjen heard a muffled scream echo across the ceiling. He ignored the sound and walked away, leaving behind the orange glow of dusk, which silently bathed the open room at the end of the Navy Pier building.

The other end of the portal was quite a contrast to the one from which she'd entered. It was gray and damp, and a strong stench of decay filled the air. Although Kaia was no stranger to this world, she loathed everything about the home of the kateri vampires. The kateris—winged, vampire rakshasas—were ruthless. Driven by anarchy, they lived in nomadic groups, feeding on dead and weak creatures. On occasion, opportunistic drifters ventured in and out of the human world, causing problems. Under the knight's strict vigilance, they mostly remained as curious observers.

Kaia moved cautiously, not because she was afraid of the kateris, but because she wanted to remain stealthy until her rendezvous with Ashvat.

The day was winding down. The dull, filtered sunlight that struggled to penetrate the thick, frigid mist was being replaced by hazy white light from the moon. Shadows began to stir silently across the dense forest, but the undaunted knight of the Earth stayed focused on establishing contact with her ride. She whistled twice at a frequency only Ashvat could hear and waited for a response.

Out of the shadows galloped the majestic Ashvat ran toward Kaia, like wind gushing down the great plains. His breath condensed into puffs of clouds. Without missing a stride, Ashvat continued past Kaia, who elegantly vaulted onto his back.

At a distance, a tantric in the form of a hideous kateri quietly followed them.

The village of the kateris wasn't much of anything. Kaia felt Ashvat tense his muscles as he entered its vicinity. "Trust me, Ashvat," whispered Kaia while stroking his neck. "I am here to protect you. Besides, their speed is no match for yours."

Kaia scanned the broken shacks and dead trees with sharp, dangerously hanging icicles. Barren gray hills with patches of snow surrounded them, peppered with large, pockmarked boulders. Kateris hung in clusters like bats on the branches of the dead trees. Kaia was less concerned with these smaller scavenger vampires that fed on their dead. Some of them opened their bright red eyes, only to gaze at the unannounced visitors before resuming their winter slumber.

Kaia knew the one she was pursuing, the largest and most powerful, was well protected and tucked deep inside the network of sheltered caves that littered the hills.

"You have to choose carefully," said a hoarse voice from above.

"I knew you would find me soon." Kaia did not look up. "I have one hand on my poniard, and you are just a few photons away from instant vaporization."

"That won't be necessary," the tantric replied as it maintained a safe flying distance from the galloping horse at Kaia's eye level. "My word to Yan holds."

"Words of tantrics are lies of the theel. I trust my silver blade and not your promise," Kaia prodded the tantric without exchanging looks.

"A knight should know when a tantric is hostile." The tantric treaded carefully. "Yan's kindness in the cave of Mount Ely has given me life. My allegiance is with him, my liberator." It continued on a path of reassurance. Its scaly, flapping wings displaced large volumes of damp, fetid air.

"I am not sure if I need you," she argued despite the tantric's consistency in its reasoning.

"How are you going to find the alpha you are looking for without my help? If you are not careful and choosy, you might end up disturbing a bunch of nests unnecessarily, and you and I both know that would be messy," it cautioned. It then hurriedly flew past the speeding Ashvat, and perched on a large, uprooted tree.

Kaia let Ashvat ease a bit past the tree and then signaled him to stop. She finally turned around to look directly at the tantric for the first time. It was less unappealing than she had anticipated. Unlike the other kateris, it sat upright with its thin, scaly legs bent underneath its folded wings and its curved black talons partially embedded into the dead wood. Its penetrating red eyes gazed at Kaia. Out of sheer instinct, it sneered, exposing large vampire fangs, but then quickly converted it into an ugly expression.

"There! The fourth hole from the far right in the middle of the hill." The tantric pointed its long, slender forefinger without extending its winged arm. "It will take you to the drifter of the two worlds. She'll awaken from her sleep to assist the theel, and if she lays her eggs on the other side, even the rishis—"

"That's enough, tantric," snapped Kaia. "You've done your job of disclosing its location to me. I'll take care of the rest."

Kaia whispered something into Ashvat's ear, and as though helping her to avoid thanking the tantric, he sped toward the rocky hill.

The fourth hole, she thought, looking up the hill and simultaneously setting her chakra in motion and charging her crystal.

"It's a bit steep, Ashvat," she cautioned her horse, but unfettered Ashvat maintained its stride up the hill despite the tortuous path.

Ashvat was the first to encounter the ambush. To protect Kaia, he lunged at the first attacker—the smaller kateri with a wingspan twice the size of its body. The kateri was quick to tear a piece of Ashvat's hide with its sharp claw but was not quick enough to avoid the powerful legs of the mighty horse that had once belonged to the greatest asura king. The force was too much for the kateri to regain balance or initiate flight as it awkwardly toppled. Its bones crushed, it tumbled down the hill until a spiked-branch of a dead tree abruptly ended its descent and life.

The more opportunistic second attacker lodged itself on Ashvat's back and attempted to throw its weight on Kaia, its talons ripping through Ashvat's thighs. To prevent further injury to Ashvat, Kaia threw herself off her horse and rolled down the hill, dragging the kateri along with her. With one hand, she squeezed the neck of the rabid kateri, which relentlessly attempted to sink its fangs into her neck. With the other, she plunged her crystal poniard into its heart, instantly vaporizing the beast. When she regained her balance, her first task was to tend to Ashvat's injury.

"Filthy creatures have laid a trap, Ashvat." Kaia was fuming mad as she inspected his wound. "The cut is deep, but this should heal you fast."

She cauterized the wounds by shining the light from the crystal and then spread a thin piece of medicinal cloth-like patch across the cuts. Ashvat winced but seemed far more worried about his master's safety than his own injury. He gently nudged her face with his and let out a soft whinny.

"There are a lot more of them waiting for you," said the familiar, hoarse voice from behind, startling Ashvat.

"You again?" Kaia casually displayed her bloodstained poniard to the tantric that had continued to follow her. "You sound disappointed."

"You fled before I could warn you."

"Ha. Warn me of your own traps?" she said, raising her voice. "Did you see their fate?"

"The two of them? Yes, that was quick," said the tantric, kicking the remains of the mostly vaporized kateri. "Just these two. But what about those?"

Four big kateris lay dead in a dark corner beside a large boulder.

"I am sure you didn't see them," the tantric said, perched on the boulder.

Ashvat tensed at the creature's close presence.

Kaia was surprised to see the dead ones with the distinct marks of a tantric attack.

"The kateris might never succeed in killing a great knight like yourself, but they will kill your horse and drain the last bit of your energy until help arrives, giving the alpha drifter enough time to get to your world." The tantric paused and then continued, "Your cause will be defeated if you spend all your time fighting these scavengers who will die to protect the drifter."

"What do you suggest I do?" asked Kaia, tending to Ashvat and allowing herself to listen to a tantric.

"Thought you would never ask." The tantric relaxed its scaly shoulders and receded its talons. "Allow me to do the job for you. Your crystal." The tantric's eyes shifted to the poniard. "Give me the crystal, and I'll get rid of the drifter kateri for you."

No tantric had ever survived long enough to ask a knight anything, let alone for a deadly weapon like the light crystal. Could she trust a tantric with her crystal?

"You know the light from this could kill you too," she stated.

"A risk I am willing to take," the tantric acknowledged.

Kaia was puzzled by the tantric's response. "For what? I thought tantrics wanted to live in flesh with a stolen soul?"

"I am willing to give up mine in exchange for another."

"Whose life would that be?" Kaia sounded skeptical but was truly surprised.

"My mate! She's a tantric kateri inside Mount Ely. She'll be willing to cross over but has not done enough to earn her life. Yan will help her live in the outer sphere if I do the job for you," the tantric explained.

Kaia sensed the tantric was telling the truth. She was touched but continued to be cold to the creature. It was the first that she had ever heard of a tantric willing to die for another. Yan's good deed inside Mount Ely seemed to have paid off.

"Makes no sense to me," said Kaia, deliberately attempting to push the tantric. "You want your mate to live, but you are willing to kill yourself? I don't see a purpose."

"Yes, you do!" the tantric snapped, fluttering its wings in remonstration. "I know you would do this for your soulmate—the strong knight of the Dark Forest," said the tantric, much to Kaia's amazement. "There's something else," the tantric hesitated.

"What is it?" asked Kaia, strangely impressed by the tantric's intuition.

"The keeper will spare not one, but two lives since my mate is about to lay our egg inside Mount Ely," confided the tantric. "Perhaps the next generation of tantrics, loyal to the keeper," it said with an awkward pause.

Kaia tossed the poniard with the crystal to the tantric.

"This will do the job for you." She then removed her large trench coat and handed it to the tantric. "When the crystal fires, cover yourself with this. You don't have to die. I think you'll be a good father," she said, endorsing a tantric's existence for the first time in her life.

The tantric looked at her thoughtfully. "We have a lot to learn from your kind. Your trust is overwhelming."

Kaia broke into a smile for the first time and jumped on Ashvat's back. "Keep the crystal and the blade. It will protect your child from your enemies. But I want my coat back!"

The tantric sneered—this time, it was a genuine attempt at reciprocating her gesture. It then spread its massive, skinny wings and lifted itself into the air toward the fourth hole up above the hill.

Ashvat raced downhill with Kaia on his back.

"The portal should open any minute now," she told Ashvat.

A flash of bright light lit up the slopes of the hill, and the screams of kateris briefly echoed through the barren terrain. When a shadowy creature flew past Kaia, a tattered, burned coat fell on her.

"See you and your family at another place, another time," shouted Kaia.

Ashvat leaped into the portal.

"What happened to your coat?" asked a surprised Aarjen.

Kaia was known to be protective of her favorite knight's coat, even in serious combat.

"Loaned it to a friend."

"A friend?" Aarjen raised his eyebrows. "A cool kateri with red eyes?" he asked with sarcasm.

"No. A smoking tantric," Kaia replied.

Her soulmate would hear the full story sometime later.

Chapter 21

The Bughouse

hings had quickly returned to normal. Local TV channels and newspapers reported on the "Hooligans of Chess," describing the unsportsmanlike conduct by a team from an undisclosed country behaving badly after losing to the American kids. An article described how the unruly team, which had struggled against the local team, vandalized the tournament hall and disrupted the games wearing masks and costumes. The Chicago kids were praised for staying cool and continuing their winning streak despite their opponents' actions.

"For the first time, two local kids, both from the northern suburbs of Chicago, face off in the final round," Ro read the news article aloud.

"It's showtime tomorrow!" cheered Bob Raj, who was playing chess simultaneously against six different kids. "Your time to avenge your defeat, huh?" Bob Raj asked.

Brendan remained quiet. While he had nothing to prove, there was still a task to be completed. The curse was still active. Coach Turner was also dismissive of the hoopla surrounding the final round between Brendan and Scrappy Junior. He was acutely mindful of the greater events influencing the tournament outcome, putting his kids in peril.

"What about them robot birds, man?" asked Bob Raj in his usual accent. "What a waste of money." He laughed, showing the pictures on his phone of the metal birds crashing into the water with a caption in large font—*Millennium, Metal, and Malfunction.*

"It came out of the bean and all but perfectly flew right into the water. They tried to do too much, you see. It is like being up by a queen and suddenly losing on back-rank, you know," he said, reading the article on the failed robot show at Millennium Park again while the kids exchanged glances and rolled their eyes.

"Something happened, oh great one!" the theel muttered to his master, who was unusually calm, considering the enormity of the theel's fiasco. "Kaling is dead! Someone saved the knight from my bolts."

"You failed because of your inability to harness the power of Kaling and combine it with yours. I am beginning to question your capacity to serve me," the evil master said with uneasy calmness.

"Master, it was a good plan," the theel defended furiously. It had planned and rehearsed the sequence of events repeatedly in its mind. "The ambush was timely, and the attack on Aarjen was carried out simultaneously. But someone intercepted the attack and absorbed the electric bolts intended for the knight."

"A plan is only as good as its execution. I blame myself for allowing you to continue."

"I reckon a bigger force has risen, oh great one, and I suspect—" The theel suddenly held its words.

On its way up to its master's secret abode, it had noticed for the first time a sudden influx of tantrics. It appeared that his master was preparing for a mission without informing the theel. It had already lost its master's trust.

"Fool, there are no bigger forces than ours. You have become weak," his master concluded.

The theel refrained from revealing the rise of the Seventh Knight.

"Your attempts to disrupt Earth have failed as well. You should have sought my approval to get the kateris and mudalas into the human world."

"Forgive me, my lord. I wasn't aware of the ispat birds. The rishis placed an egg in the human world."

"Precisely my point. I would have warned you had you consulted with me. Instead…"

"But your tantric betrayed you," the theel said, carefully deflecting the blame. His master's own creation—a tantric—had betrayed him by helping the knight and slaying the kateris.

"Betrayed *you*, theel, not me! Never underestimate your enemies."

"But, master…" the theel protested.

"Do not come back until you have completed your mission in Mayastella." He continued to speak with his eyes closed. "Your existence depends on it." The sage of the dark side raised his hand and struck the theel with a lightning flash. "Here's a taste of your own medicine," said the evil master and laughed at the theel for the first time.

The theel was hurt, both mentally and physically. He knew the support from his master had ceased. He felt abandoned and alone. "I will find a way to awaken Kumba, but when he does, the end will come to the devas, asuras, the humans, and…" The theel let out a scheming grin, despite reeling in pain, as a devious thought played in its mind "…*then I'll kill the master.*"

Aarjen spoke of the courage and valor of the human children at length to the kings and lords of the immortal worlds, along with their council, who listened without interrupting. Indra, who normally sat on the throne that was placed on the highest pedestal, sat beside the radiant Surya, his most revered member of the council. Baga, the lord of the asuras, and Samudra, the queen of the jalas, sat beside each other on a dual throne as a symbol of unity.

The exuberant Maya gracefully floated across the courtroom, distorting the light from Surya and creating a spectacular aura.

Indra addressed the knights. "We are indebted to you and the human children. You have saved the worlds from the demons. We…"

"Lord Indra," Aarjen interrupted politely. "We still have to complete our mission to savor victory and ensure that the curse is broken forever. But before I reveal my plan, I would like to introduce to council one who is chosen by the seven rishis, the long-awaited Seventh Knight, the knight of Mayastella who saved me and the worlds from the throes of destruction."

A noisy chatter disrupted the silence. Most suspected Aarjen to be the Seventh Knight, but the announcement of Run-Nier caused some excitement. Run-Nier walked into Indra's courtroom for the first time as the kings cheered and welcomed him.

"This is Run-Nier, the knight of Mayastella who has the power to defeat the real enemy of the rishis," Aarjen spoke loud and clear.

"Welcome, great knight of the knights!" said Indra, walking up to Run-Nier with extended arms.

"He has the blood of asuras," added Baga. "And he is the son of the great Zuri."

"A magnificent warrior," said Samudra. "We are lucky to have him on our side."

"The theel will try to finish what it has set out to do until the curse is truly broken. It can still find a way to make Kumba serve his master," said Aarjen.

"We should not let this happen," said Samudra, and the council agreed in a chorus.

"The children have been successful at every stage of the quest, yet you feel the theel could make true the curse? It makes no sense, Aarjen," commented Baga.

"The humiliated theel has a real chance to reach the conch of life before us. It still has a network of tantrics and commands the fear of its underworld allies. They could help with its quest for Kumba."

"What is the theel's plan now?" asked Agni, the lord of fire.

Run-Nier spoke this time. "We think the theel might use another human child, skilled at this game, to play against Brendan."

"Would the curse be effective?" asked Surya.

"Yes. This child is a mixed blood. An Earth dweller with human blood, the only known descendant of Leela, the vagabond queen of the people with no land."

"The nadodis, who settled in the human world?" asked Varuna.

"But I thought Leela died—killed by rakshasas—before the child was born," said Chandra.

Maya displayed images from the past to the council. "It's a well-kept secret," she said. "Leela's child was secretly raised by humans who have sworn to protect the queen's lineage, hoping that, one day, a prince will be born to rule the Earth dwellers and defeat the enemies of the nadodi vagabonds."

"The boy's name is Nicolas; he is part-human but has all the powers of an Earth dweller. He has no idea who he actually is. He's about the same age as Brendan. After his grandfather—his true guardian—passed away, the kid has been raised by a crooked dealer who is disloyal to his own kind."

"This is the one who smuggled the board and aided the Earth dwellers with the tournament arrangements?" asked Agni.

"Yes. They call him Scrappy. He is the kid's stepfather. A traitor who abets the Earth dwellers in committing many crimes," said Aarjen.

"The portal will open when this boy plays against Brendan. No one can stop the theel, and the kid has a chance to get to the shunk first. But he, too, will be quickly eliminated by the theel after the task is completed," said Run-Nier.

"If the task is completed," added Indra.

"How good is he at this game?" asked Varuna, the lord of the rain.

"There is already some rivalry between Nicolas and Brendan, fueled by Scrappy. I think the more relevant question is, how helpful will Nicolas be for the theel in the inner sphere?" explained Aarjen.

"He is not quite as good as Brendan, but he does have additional powers that are beginning to show," added Kaia.

"How can we stop him from playing or accessing the inner sphere?" asked Varuna.

"I don't think we should stop him," replied Kaia. "We'll use this game to get to the theel. Let the kids play," she said.

###

The young chess players from Chicago were thrilled to hear from their coach that they could play bughouse. As a diversion from all the distraction that preceded the final round, the tournament officials decided to move forward with the bughouse event—the modified version of chess where players played as partners in pairs against their opponents. They hoped this quick and fun version of chess would excite the participants and rekindle the sportsmanship or spirit of the game before the final championship round of the tournament.

"Sidney, your partner is Ro. Max, with Austin. And, Brendan…"

"I was thinking of Alex," said Brendan before his dad suggested a partner for him.

"Alex?" asked the surprised coach.

"Yes! She's good at it. Dad…Remember, this is bughouse, where kibitzing is allowed, so it would be fun to tag team with her." Brendan referred to the aspect of the game where the partners could discuss with each other and strategize while playing. One strong player could take the lead and shape the outcome of the game.

"Don't you want to win, Brendan?" asked Alex, equally surprised by her friend's choice of partner.

"This *is* my winning move. You are stuck with me." Brendan nudged Alex. He leaned over to her and mumbled, "If you don't want to play with me, then I'll have to partner up with Scrappy Junior over there."

"I heard his father wouldn't let him play bughouse. He's preparing him for the final game against you—*no distractions!*" said Alex with an irksome smirk.

Brendan glanced over his shoulder and looked at Nicolas, who was talking to someone several tables away. Their eyes briefly met. Nicolas nodded, as if to say good luck to Brendan, and Brendan awkwardly responded back.

"That was a first," said Alex. "I see I do have a positive influence on you."

"Oh, shut up."

Out in the dilapidated, abandoned sawmill, the theel convened its dejected troops. The creature sensed mutiny and retaliation brewing within the ranks. The only other thing the rakshasas could smell quicker than blood was fear, and the theel knew that it had to ruthlessly instill fear in its subordinates before they sensed its own. It was on the offensive and was prepared to kill any creature that opposed it.

"I have found a cunning way to play the final game with the humans. This is our last chance," it hissed to the disgruntled leaders of the rakshasas and Earth dwellers.

The theel knew that its troops were not privy to his master's recent negative sentiments toward it. They still believed the theel exerted full command over those who served it.

"What happened out there?" asked an irate marisan. "Many of my brothers and sisters sacrificed their lives, helping you and Kaling, but you failed. We were very close to crossing the Sea of Poison, but the portal closed and sent us back here. You abandoned us." The creature grunted accusingly.

Infuriated, the theel charged its tail. "It was all part of my strategy, you fool!" it lied. "Are you questioning my plan?"

"No. You were the one who said we cannot fail while playing the game here or at our quest …"

"Yes!" yelled out an Earth dweller that sat next to the marisan. "You even gave us orders to reveal ourselves to the humans. We lost because of you."

"Useless Earth dweller!" the theel muttered angrily. "You are all losers."

"You are blaming us?" Before the Earth dweller could take cover, he was vaporized by the theel's fury. The electric bolt then ricocheted and struck the marisan, who fell to its knees, clutching its neck. Its sharp horn lodged into a decaying stump as it leaned forward.

The theel held its charge back. It wasn't about to waste its crucial resources—not yet at least.

"Any other suggestions or comments?" sneered the theel, backing away from the creatures. As a demonstration of its strength, it ascended in the air several feet above ground and enlarged its body to twice its original size.

A shapeshifter marisan uncloaked in front of the puffed-up theel and spoke hurriedly. "Hold your fire, theel. I have an idea."

"Speak only of your idea and nothing else," the theel warned, its tail fully charged for several kills.

The marisan said cautiously, "I hear from the Earth dwellers that there is another form of this game that allows them to play in pairs. I am told the humans will be engaged in this game and will not for a million years expect us to play against them—just like we didn't expect them to play the speed form, which helped them defeat the vegas." The marisan paused, allowing time for the theel to calm down. "We can play many quick games, and when the portal opens, no one will be there to help the human kids. We can kill them before the knights arrive."

"I had plans of using the nadodi kid to surprise the knights, but your idea would put an end to this war sooner," acknowledged the theel, exposing its ugly, spiky teeth.

"Will the curse work with this game?" asked a marisan.

The theel thought for a moment. "It will as long as we use the Chadurang and our pieces."

"Do you all know how to play this version?" asked a potbellied rakshasa, looking at a group of scared Earth dwellers crouched on a dead tree trunk.

"Yes, we do. It's in our blood. This game was created by the asura king, Baga. 'Baga asura' is what these humans call 'bughouse'. It was designed to bring multiple forces together, and it is our chance to get all the rakshasas united without the knights' knowledge."

"We can get this done, master," shouted the largest Earth dweller. "We can change back into our human form and enter the tournament again."

"But we were kicked out of the tournament," shouted another Earth dweller, a short one, as it kicked an old, dirty, broken plastic crate.

"I can handle that. We have connections," countered the largest Earth dweller, spitting at the short one.

"And surprise the life out of the humans," echoed another.

The Earth dweller quickly described the game to its leader, and the others attempted to show off their knowledge to appease the theel. The theel snaked around the suddenly motivated crowd, discharging its excitement as intermittent flashes of electric charge. "I like this game. It is quick, and the player gets to place the captured pieces given to him by his partner anywhere on the board against his opponent." The theel abruptly stopped talking and opened its mouth wide, exposing most of its two ugly fangs as it thought through the scenarios in its mind. "I need to recruit some support," it mumbled.

"What are you thinking, theel?" asked the marisan.

"I am thinking of the little chataans of the underworld. Like the jalas, they can appear and disappear at will."

"The pesky little creatures that devour their enemies and *friends*?" asked the marisan with a scowl.

"Precisely. I can smuggle them into Mayastella and manipulate them."

"Brilliant thinking, theel," said a newly recruited and ambitious marisan, who appeared ever so eager to praise the theel. "This is a great idea. Let the pests attack the enemies while we get to the conch and blow it to wake up Kumba."

"Don't be a fool," barked the theel. "This is not any ordinary conch. This is the *shunk* and you *don't* touch the shunk that is not given to you. The master has warned of the dire consequences. It will burn or petrify any unauthorized holder."

"It has to be given to you, not taken, you idiot," echoed the marisan who had suggested playing bughouse to the theel.

"But how do we use it then, sting tail?" asked the new recruit.

"A guardian poiz in the form of a yaali is the only one who can use the shunk."

"Poiz cannot be guardians. They are weak and worthless, and they are not real," argued the shapeshifter.

"The shunk cannot be guarded by any life form. It is too dangerous. The poiz exist without really existing," the theel said.

"So, why can't the master use the yaali to get the conch for us? Wouldn't that be easier?"

"The master has tried this, but forcing or tricking a poiz to meddle with the shunk only petrifies them."

"Didn't we encounter some of these petrified and useless yaalis on the shores of the poisoned sea of the Kaling?" asked the furious marisan.

"They are useless indeed," agreed the theel, painfully recollecting its failed attempt to recruit a real yaali and finally having to depend on a tantric to pretend to be a yaali. The one that slipped and fell to its death from the edge of the precipice.

"If we succeed with our mission, the yaali will have no choice but to hand me the shunk."

Within moments of the order cascading from the theel, Scrappy secretly entered the computer room and carefully altered the bughouse pairings.

Scrappy hated variations in chess. He considered them instruments of chaos, and although he didn't understand why the Earth dwellers were wasting time on bughouse, he assumed it involved some form of gambling somewhere.

"Each pair has five minutes on the clock," Turner explained to Nora's sister Vicki, who was new to chess.

"You said Sidney and Ro are partners, right?" asked Nora, trying to make sense of how bughouse was played.

"Yes. The partners sit next to each other on two different boards and play against two different opponents across from them. If Sidney plays black against her opponent, then Ro will play white against his. So, when Ro captures his opponent's black piece, he will give it to Sidney, and she can place this black piece from Ro anywhere on the board as her own. Do you get it?" asked the coach.

"And I guess Sidney can give the white piece she captures from her opponent to Ro, who could then place it anywhere on his board, right?" asked Vicki, making the shrewd connection.

"Often, the player will watch his or her partner's game, especially the stronger of the two partners, and suggest that the partner make certain moves or capture certain pieces that would be of help to his game."

"Ro can stall too, mom," said Sidney to help her mother explain the complex game to her aunt.

"But wouldn't you lose if you let your time run out?" Vicki asked with curiosity.

"Only if you let all of your time run out. Let me explain to you," Brendan said and removed his Chronos digital clock from his bag. He turned it on by hitting the center red button. The clock lit up. "Everyone has five minutes on the clock," he explained. "See this digital timer? This clock is more like a stopwatch. There are two timers in each clock for the two players who play against each other. After you make a move, you hit the clock, and your opponent's time starts to wind down from the five minutes that was originally allocated."

"That's just the time for bughouse and blitz," interrupted Sidney. "The other games vary from 30 minutes to two hours per person."

"Phew, two hours each? You guys can play chess for four hours?" asked Vicki.

"In any of these games, the more time you take to make your move, the less time you have on your clock, and, yes, if you lose all your time, you lose the game," reminded Brendan.

"But if *stalling* is running out of your own time, then why would you do it?" asked Nora.

"In bughouse, if your partner is winning or about to win, then you stop your opponent from playing against you by simply running down your clock and not making a move. Of course, you don't run out all your time—just enough to let your partner win or get closer to victory. The game is over when one of the partners checkmates his or her opponent," said Brendan.

"Or the first team runs out of time," added Ro.

"Also, in bughouse, you can change your mind after moving your piece and make a different move any time before you hit the clock. It is not like the other versions, where, when you touch a piece, you have to move that piece, and you cannot take back your moves," Brendan went on.

"Your opponent cannot make a move until you hit the clock," said Ro.

"Ahhh," said Vicki, dramatically pulling her hair. "How do you guys remember all these rules? You are all nuts." Then, she leaned over to Nora and asked softly, "Will Sidney be able to play this game?"

"She'll use the special board, and Ro is her partner. They have good chemistry, and they play this all the time at the club," she said, smiling at Ro.

Amid the renewed chaos of kids, coaches, and parents running around, looking up pairings and the noise that engulfed the tournament hall, Brendan and the Chicago chess kids were immersed in bughouse-related stories from the past. It was only when Brendan leaned over to shake his opponent's hand that he noticed the board and the pieces.

"Hey, where did *these* boards come from?" he asked Alex with a perplexed look.

Alex shrugged her shoulders and searched for the other team members who were seated in their respective grade level sections, spread across the hall. Both Alex and Brendan spotted the special boards placed in front of Max, Austin, Sidney, and Ro. Realizing what could be happening, Brendan immediately studied the eyes of his opponent, but they appeared human.

"This cannot happen now!" Brendan thought, but before he could formulate what was going on, his opponent hit the clock.

"Let the game resume, human. No knights to save you now."

"Wh—where are we?" asked Ro.

Sidney stood beside him, holding his hand.

"No one said anything about going through the portal."

"I smell a big belly rakshasa," said Sidney, pinching her nose and reaching for Ro's hand.

A grunt and deep laughter were followed by twisted words of English. "We trapped the human kids. Ha-ha-ha!"

When Sidney entered the alien place, her vision slowly returned. A fat, hairy, potbellied, bluish-skinned rakshasa stood in front of her, its red tongue sticking out and dripping with saliva. Its blood-red eyes glowed under a flat, wrinkled forehead with two tiny, protruding horns.

Ro stood there, terrified, tightly holding on to Sidney.

"Funny but cute," she said.

"What? It's ug-ugly. R-r-run," he stammered.

"I am talking about you, Ro." Sidney giggled, ignoring the rakshasa that was thumping its chest and making guttural noises.

"You can see me?" His voice squeaked with surprise.

"Yes, I can see that thing, too."

"Okay," Ro tried to find his voice. "It's not a friendly one." He quickly turned around and pulled Sidney with him.

She held on to his hand and ran alongside him.

"We need a knight between us and the beast," said Ro, panting, alluding to the bughouse game, where a chess piece could be placed anywhere on the board.

The potbellied rakshasa was gaining momentum and was only a few paces behind them.

"How about a queen? I got you a queen." Sidney waved at Queen Suhela. "Where would you like her to be?"

"Between us and that thing, of course." Ro was delighted to see Queen Suhela. "Thank goodness," he said, slowing down.

"I heard you." The queen jumped in front of the rakshasa.

The clumsy rakshasa adjusted its step awkwardly to face the new obstacle that had suddenly landed in front of it. It pulled its bone dagger and lunged at the queen, but she was too agile. She side-stepped the attacker and swept her leg across the leaping potbellied rakshasa, knocking it off-balance. Before the creature hit the ground, she slid on to her back, planted both feet on the creature's dough-like belly, and leveraged its momentum. Gravity did the rest. The potbelly flipped over her in the air and crashed with a thud.

Ro and Sidney finally stopped running.

"He won't bother us anymore," assured the queen, ruffling the kids' hair. She then crouched to Sidney's height to look directly into her eyes while touching her cheeks gently. "How are you, little princess? It is good to see you again." Her soft voice instantly lifted Sidney's spirit.

"I can see you." Sidney threw her arms around Suhela with joy, who responded by embracing Sidney tightly.

"It was supposed to be only Brendan against Scrappy Junior in the final round. What happened? Why are we here?" asked Ro, confused with the turn of events.

"The theel tricked us this time by switching the board so they can get a head start," Suhela said. "We need to find out where your friends are."

The familiar, encumbering darkness of the underworld was replaced by a bright and colorful world in contrast to all the ruins Brendan had witnessed at the various stages of his journey.

"Where are we?" asked Alex, who had not had the experience of being transported through a portal before.

The place was unfamiliar to Brendan. "I think we are in the inner sphere, where Kumba sleeps. But this doesn't look anything like what I imagined. We are not supposed to be here now, Alex."

"This sure is a dark, cold, and run-down place, just as you described, Brendan," Alex mocked.

"Ah, shut up. You have no idea how different this is from all those places I have been to."

"The theel would have followed us, and the only way we can contact Aarjen and Kaia is with a crystal."

"Don't you have one?" asked Alex.

"I gave mine to a friend, not far from here. We both have our wristband crystals." He examined the large pockets on his baggy jeans. He felt something else in his pocket.

"I do have Yan's notebook." Brendan sounded relieved.

"Brendan, look!" Alex alerted Brendan to something across the lush meadow.

Brendan, who was focused on Yan's notebook, didn't pay attention.

"Hey, look!" Alex shouted. "Something is coming at us. Several of them."

"I don't see anything," he said with a half-hearted glance, unfolding the notebook and studying the page.

"It was over there. I swear there were at least three hairy creatures with large eyes and big dog ears—"

"I didn't see…"

"*Yak, Yak, Yak, Yak*—"

Before Brendan could finish his sentence, three creatures not more than three feet tall suddenly landed in front of them. Making a weird laughter-like noise, the creatures inched awkwardly toward Brendan and Alex, as if they were unable to walk.

"What the heck are these?" whispered Alex, unable to take her eyes off the short creatures with large facial features, enormous teeth, sharp noses, and pointed ears.

Each creature pushed and pulled the other just to move forward.

"They look like the troll dolls without the colored hair," said Alex. "I can tell that they love trouble."

"Let's get the heck out of here." Brendan started running away from the creatures, while simultaneously searching the pages of the notebook for any information on the creatures.

Alex hesitated for a moment, but her instincts prompted her to follow her friend, and being a faster runner, she quickly outpaced him, but only to encounter the creatures again. She slid and hit the ground hard, and in the process, she knocked into one of the creatures, sending it tumbling down the slope. "These things jump from one place to another...But they can't seem to walk."

"I don't care how they move." Alex scrambled to get up. "I just want to get out of here before they get us."

"I am calling for help." Brendan read lines from the pages of the notebook aloud.

Before the creatures could jump again, something appeared in front of them and sent the remaining two creatures flying through the air.

"Someone called me?" said the leather-clad, hatchet-wielding person in front of them.

"What the—"

"This is Yan, Alex," said a jubilant Brendan. "He is the guardian and the keeper of this world, in his rider form. Yan, this is my friend Alex."

"Hello, young lady," said Yan, offering his stubby hand. "I have heard a lot about you. You are the ballplayer," he said.

Alex felt the ground shake as Yan walked toward them. The towering figure with an elephant face and hatchet rendered Alex speechless despite the friendly tone of his voice.

"I do this to people," joked Yan.

"How come you became Mr. Trunks again?" asked Brendan, surprised to see Yan revert to his original rider form. "I thought—"

"You forget, Mayastella is a world of illusion. My little friend Austin must be looking for me. I like this look. Don't you?" Yan said, laughing.

"You bet!" Brendan laughed at his bughouse partner, who remained dumbfounded.

"Those creatures are called chataans. A mischievous lot that mostly live in the narrow dry lands of Jalastella, but I kid you not, they can be manipulated to bring harm to others. They are easy to handle as long as they are not in large numbers."

"Why are they only jumping?" asked Brendan.

"Uhhh…" Yan looked around, as if studying the surroundings. "I would advise you both to just slow down a bit; otherwise, you'll end up like those chataans."

Alex raised her eyebrows, not able to understand any of what she was hearing.

"I—" When she was about to ask a question, she noticed another airborne creature—red in color—flying toward them. "Watch out! Here comes another one," she said, ducking quickly from the live projectile that struck Brendan and knocked him down.

"Pull that thing away from Brendan," Alex hollered to Yan, who stood next to Brendan, laughing.

The jumping creature that had landed on Brendan was none other than Max.

"I tried to warn you guys," said Max, sprawled on the ground, unable to move. "Ahhh, that hurts."

Yan continued laughing.

Max rubbed his head and examined his arms and legs for bruises. "I think Austin is right behind me."

"Oh—nooo—shoot!"

Thump!

Max couldn't avoid the impact as he flung backward in what felt like slow motion and hit the ground on soft grass, entangled with Austin. The strong arms of Yan heaved them upright.

"Mr. Trunks!" Austin cried out joyfully. His glowing bishop talisman hung loosely around his neck.

"The gravity gets weaker and weaker as you get toward the palace of Kumba," explained Yan to the kids. "At the center of a pyramid-shaped palace lies the sleeping giant, gently floating above his bed. The lack of gravity prevents his bones from being crushed under his own weight over the many years he has been sleeping.

"If you move too fast toward the palace, you end up airborne, like jumping on the moon, but if you change direction, the gravity gradient will make you fall faster. You will be able to use the change in gravity as a means to travel, but if you're sloppy, like the chataans, you will get stuck. Let me show you how to work it," said Yan.

To demonstrate, he took a couple of steps and began to ascend tens of feet in the air, maneuvering himself in circles and then skillfully landing. It was an odd sight to see a large elephant person move so gracefully through the air.

"Yan looks like a big Macy's float." Max laughed, but when he attempted to jump, he spun out of control and landed at a distance. Yan picked Max up and dropped him back where he started.

"I would be careful who you make fun of." Alex said, poking Max.

"The palace is invisible," said Suhela to Ro. "But I know it is over there," she said, looking in the direction where the invisible place would exist. "Sometimes, you can see the light bend, as though there were a layer of… some kind of, um…bubble…" she said. "The palace is visible only when you enter the bubble."

Ro strained his eyes.

"I see it! I see it!" hollered Sidney. "I can see an outline of a triangle," she said, unable to contain the excitement in her voice. With every jump, she went higher and higher until Suhela held her down.

Only when Ro began jumping, too, was he able to see the light shift a little at a distance, creating an outline. "It looks like a giant glass bubble," Ro said with equal excitement. "But I cannot see anything inside. How can we go inside if we can't even see the pyramid?" he asked.

"I'll find a way." Suhela's heart began racing with excitement and joy. She was finally going to see her king.

"We should get there before the rakshasas arrive. Let's keep moving. When you get tired, we can take breaks." She guided the kids through the open meadow, deliberately staying away from the thickets of the woods, where danger often lurked.

At a safe distance, two marisans patiently watched Suhela and the kids.

"The orders are only to follow her," said the larger of the two cloaked marisans. "Keep your cloaking and resist the temptation to attack the children," it warned its accomplice. "The queen is a strong warrior of rakshasa descent, and you'll only end up like that ignorant potbellied one. She will lead us to Kumba. Once we get close to the palace, we can warn the others."

"There they are," shouted Austin, excited to see the queen arrive with Sidney and Ro. "How did you spot them, Mr. Trunks?" he asked the keeper.

"I saw Queen Suhela out at a distance when showing you how to move around," said Yan.

After greeting each other, the kids readily shared their adventures.

"You should see these little creature things jumping around," said Max.

"I fell on Max." Austin uncontrollably laughed while trying to demonstrate how he jumped around.

"Brendan, I can see again." Sidney looked closely at Brendan. "You're much taller than I imagined."

While the kids were busy talking, the queen had a private conversation with Yan. "A large army is gathering," she warned. "There are many armed creatures from the underworlds, and many more are arriving through the portal."

Yan nodded, affirming Suhela's observation. "The battle of the worlds is about to begin here unless the curse is broken."

"They know they'll succeed in getting close to Kumba without the knights' protection. You and I can stall them while the kids go inside the palace," she suggested.

"I doubt the pyramid is a friendly place for the children." Yan looked into Suhela's beautiful eyes; he could see her joy as she was about to unite with her husband after an eternity. He felt happy for her. "Why don't I stay outside and try to contact the knights while you guide the children?"

"Promise me that you will not try to fight them alone. These creatures are formidable in numbers."

"The question is, how do we—" Yan abruptly stopped speaking and stood still for a moment. He then pushed Suhela away from him and dove beside her.

An arrow pierced the ground where Suhela had stood, almost a third of its length burrowed into the ground. The exposed shaft vibrated, absorbing the impact.

"The children!" Suhela scrambled to protect them.

Yan, who resembled a large, fallen varsity mascot, arched his heavy back and flipped himself into an upright position. He twirled his hatchet in the air, destroying several arrows plunging toward him in succession. He waited until Suhela ushered the children away from the shower of arrows and into the thickets.

The attack had begun. The infuriated Yan leaped into the air, and after a series of arrow-dodging maneuvers, he crashed into a group of diminutive archers, hurriedly taking aim. When he returned, he pummeled an entire delegation, albeit small in size and numbers, of bow-wielding chataans who had begun their premature attack.

"We'll be safe here," Yan assured the kids.

He had quickly created a makeshift but secure bunker by felling small trees and arranging them on the face of a rocky hill with a naturally carved-out shelter. He sat next to Brendan, slowly flipping through the unfolded pages of his notebook and studying the 3D images of hills, meadows, and forests. At its center, a large, dark pyramid, as though made out of polished granite, stood above all.

"That's the palace?" asked one of the kids.

"Yes, the pyramid of Kumba," replied Yan. "Look for clues."

"I see some words." Brendan strained his eyes.

As it had in the past, words that only one person could read began to appear across the pages of the notebook. Brendan read the lines.

At the center sleeps the king,

Protected by the burning ring.

"This path goes down like a shaft to the center," he said, running his index finger along the passage inside the pyramid. "I bet this is where the king is sleeping. But I don't see anything burning. Is it fire?" asked Brendan.

"I see something shiny," said Austin, who was looking at the book upside-down.

"Where?" asked Brendan, turning the notebook around.

"There!" Austin grabbed the notebook from Brendan. "Right next to those words."

"I don't see any words," said Ro. "What does it say?" he asked.

Austin tried to enunciate the words. *"A floating…Sh-un-k could be found. And used to make the a-w-a-k-e-n-i-n-g sound."*

Austin spelled out the hard words, and Brendan and Alex stitched the words that Austin read into sentences.

The floating Shunk could be found

and used to make the awakening sound.

"It is the sound from the shunk that will awaken the king," said Suhela to Yan.

"The shunk is a conch," Yan reminded the kids.

"I remember from your notebook. It's shiny and about the size of a football," Brendan acknowledged.

"But where is the fire?" asked Max.

"Maybe we'll see it only when we go inside," said Yan, turning the page. "Perhaps there's more."

"This page is blank," said Max.

"I see the words on this page," said Sidney.

You should see without your sight

While you play without the knight.

Sidney barely finished reading when the dark, glossy pyramid rose from the blank page and words began moving across the faces of the pyramid like an electronic marquee. Brendan and Alex finished reading the words in succession.

Trust your friends to win the fight.

The poisoned lips will make it right.

The words swirled briefly before being sucked through the apex. The pages turned blank again.

"What? What happened?" asked Brendan, helping Yan flip the pages. "Your entire notebook went blank."

"It is your endgame, Brendan. The notebook has gone silent in case it falls into the wrong hands," Yan cautioned. "I must have programmed it to shut down as a precaution. You and your friends should remember these words." Yan repeated them.

At the center sleeps the king,

Protected by the burning ring.

The floating Shunk could be found

and used to make the awakening sound.

You should see without your sight

While you play without the knight.

Trust your friends to win the fight.

The poisoned lips will make it right.

"I am not sure if we understand what this all means," said Alex, shrugging her shoulders.

"As you did with all your previous challenges, I am sure you'll figure out what these words mean when you enter the pyramid," said Suhela. "Let's not waste any more time trying to decipher them."

The chataans that had survived Yan's retaliation were severely punished by the commanding marisan under the order of the theel. The marisan itself was admonished for its inability to control the clumsy chataans.

"Never underestimate your enemies," reprimanded the marisan, repeating everything the theel had told him. "They are still strong, and we need to wait to outnumber them."

The marisan hated the chataans. They were worse than the selfish potbellied rakshasas—no real sense of strategy, courage, or discipline—but they existed in large numbers and were willing to fight for the theel, who had promised them a large chunk of Jalastella upon successful completion of this mission.

The army continued to swell as swarms of small, armed chataans, potbellied rakshasas, and mudalas arrived. The excitement of battle reeked in the air as the creatures let out war chants in unison. The theel and a select few watched the build-up patiently.

"I'll command this army," said the theel. "A small group will enter the pyramid to obtain the shunk. When the shunk is sounded, Kumba will awaken, and the battle will begin."

"And our master will join us to defeat the devas, asuras, and jalas. All the worlds will be ours," roared the marisan.

The theel sneered at the shapeshifter. Despite the sweet scent of victory in the air, the theel hated the fact that a lowly marisan thought an unknown, dark sage was its master. It blamed itself for constantly highlighting the eminence of its master.

"But all that will change," thought the theel. *"When Kumba is awakened, my master will be betrayed."*

###

The pyramid attracted Suhela like a beacon. Her dark side began to possess her. Even though she savored the feeling, she knew she had to resist her instincts for the sake of the children.

Sidney was the only one who noticed the queen's transformation. "Queen Suhela, what is happening to you?" she asked, concerned.

The queen remained silent, attempting to suppress her feelings.

"I think she's getting sick," whispered Sidney to Brendan. "I can feel her pain."

Suhela's condition rapidly and visibly deteriorated. She felt dizzy, and her steps faltered. Her appearance changed as her skin shriveled and loosely hung on to her frail skeleton. Her beauty had all but disappeared as her eyes bulged and her cheekbones protruded. Her hair twisted into unkempt dreadlocks, and her nails and lips blackened with poison. She began to choke and gag.

Suhela clutched her neck and dropped to her knees.

Everyone, except Sidney, was terrified and stepped away from Suhela, not knowing what to do. Sidney, teary-eyed, gently held on to the queen and comforted her.

"The poison!" Suhela showered saliva on Sidney. She understood that Sidney's presence kept her from slipping totally into the other side. "The bubble...Open...Now." She scrambled words together and motioned toward the pyramid. "Enter...Pyramid...Get help...Poison!"

"I am going to find some help." Sidney ran toward the pyramid without warning anyone.

"Stop! Stop, Sid..." Suhela struggled to get her words out, barely mustering enough energy.

When she finally managed to get back on her feet, a marisan ambushed her, knocked her back to the ground, and began to strangle her. The unsuspecting queen screamed, startling the boys. They stood, petrified by the sight of a hideous creature strangling the equally hideous figure Suhela had been reduced to.

Before they could contemplate their next fight-or-flight move, they found themselves entrapped in a heavy, rawhide net, cast by a clumsy potbellied rakshasa, who seemed to have appeared out of nowhere. The rakshasa hurriedly bundled its terrified victims like chickens and tethered the net to the branch of a nearby tree. It peered into the net, poked Brendan with its dirty nail, and chuckled. Austin screamed. Brendan tried to kick, but the net was too restraining. The rakshasa laughed until a large marisan charged toward it and slapped its head, yelling something in its language.

"Alex, do you see Sidney anywhere?" Brendan muttered.

"No, she took off into that clearing before I could go after her. What do we do now?"

"Don't know, but these things are trying to kill the queen," said Brendan, unable to bear the sound of Suhela wailing in pain.

"I have a pocketknife. I think I can cut through this net." Max tried to reach into his pocket.

Enticed by the reward that awaited anyone who captured the queen, a larger marisan intervened to take control. The rivalry between the two marisans yielded some wiggle room for Suhela to retaliate. Seizing the opportunity, she sank her protruding fangs deep into the thick hide of her strangler's arm.

Infuriated, the marisan drew its weapon to strike the queen, but suddenly clutched its own neck, gasped, and dropped dead. The lethal effect of venom from the queen was nearly instant. Greenish-red blood oozed from its skin where Suhela had bitten.

"I think it's dead," said Brendan.

Quickly taking advantage of the pinned queen, the larger marisan carefully stuffed her mouth with thick ule chamois to prevent her from biting. It maintained a safe distance from the restrained but dangerous captive, and watched Suhela slowly pass out.

The marisan and its gawky cohorts celebrated while the entangled kids watched in horror. Within minutes, an argument broke out over what appeared to be who would deliver the prisoners to the theel.

"Things are about to get nasty," thought Brendan.

Unaware of the attack on her beloved queen, Sidney ran into the forest in search of help. She reached a long tunnel-like clearing carved into the dense thicket. The ground was soft and packed with dry, powdery sand, as though someone had laid a trail. A black wall abruptly ended her path. It was the outer wall of the pyramid. Sidney stopped running. "Help! Help! Someone, please help Queen Suhela," she shouted, hoping to find help. "Someone, please help Queen Suhela. She's dying!"

Without warning, the ground shook; the fine sand particles formed geometric patterns that danced loosely to the frequency of the vibrations.

A distant roar echoed through the forest. Sidney backed herself against the smooth, glossy wall. She stood, paralyzed, as an enormous dragon-like creature snaked furiously toward her.

Ro peered through the net, at their captors. "They are going to fight each other."

"Maybe they'll kill each other," said Max.

"Maybe not," said Alex. "That thing with the knife is coming at us."

"Come on. Let's all try together to see if we can force ourselves out of this net," suggested Brendan.

Alex and the boys struggled to stand up from under the net, but the net was too restrictive. They tumbled like bowling pins, knocking each other down. Brendan rolled over to protect the others from the attacking marisan.

The ground shook suddenly. The marisan paused, as though to examine the cause of the tremor. A loud hiss ensued from behind, and and the marisan who was about to hurt Brendan let out a scream before being tossed over the net and into the trees like a rock.

"What the…" Brendan was perplexed.

"What is *that?*" asked Ro.

"Looks like a dragon," said Alex.

"How do you know? You have never seen a real dragon before," said Ro.

Austin began to cry.

"Whatever it is, it's going after the rakshasas. And where's that pocketknife?" Brendan asked Max.

"Hey, guys, look up!" It was Sidney. "This is Azi."

"Oh, look, Sidney is on top of that thing," shouted Ro.

She was carefully tucked between two large vertebrae on the back of the creature. This must be the sergon that Queen Suhela had forced to bite her." She's huge," exclaimed Brendan.

A startled potbellied rakshasa's attack ended abruptly when Azi picked it up and tossed it away like a rag doll. A third marisan cloaked itself and fled, probably to alert the theel of the unexpected sergon ambush.

Azi pushed the dead marisan away from Suhela's frail body and closely examined her. "I've been waiting for the queen all these years. I can keep the queen alive, but she needs to get to King Kumba soon. I'll take you all to my den, where you'll be safe."

Sidney's mystified friends climbed up onto Azi.

Yan had found a way to use the portal, just like the theel had, to build a formidable force. Within hours, he had built an army of his own, comprised of the elephants of Mount Ely, ules, ule warriors, and petrified poiz— revived by the generosity of Brendan, who had given them the power of the crystal at the shores of the Sea of Poison. Yan had even recruited two powerful tantrics from the cave of Mount Ely.

"We are at your service, great keeper of Mayastella," said Marra, the chief of the ule warriors, to Yan. "The knight and the children saved us from Neeria, the jala sorceress."

"The chataans are a menace, especially when in large numbers and the theel has amassed a powerful army."

"The chataans are no match for our might, oh great keeper," affirmed Marra. "Should we surprise them now while they are waiting?"

"No…We are here only to defend and not to attack," Yan informed him. "We'll wait for the knights to arrive."

Azi's den was an ensemble of large, crisscrossing tunnels, burrowed into the base of the pyramid. The tunnels merged at a central chamber with a domelike roof, where Azi resided.

The kids were pleasantly surprised when they entered the chamber. It was festooned with rich furniture, a large cot, walls lined with books, marble statues, wood trims, and even a stone fountain, from which a gentle stream flowed silently around the room.

"Wow, this place is like a palace," said Brendan.

"For people and not a dragon," mumbled Ro.

"Yes," said Azi, transforming herself into a beautiful woman. "Sergons are changelings." She gently placed the queen on her bed.

"You…How…How did you change into a person?" asked Max.

"We will transform only in the presence of those we trust. Make yourself comfortable here." She tended to Suhela.

"Azi, you are here," whispered Suhela. "I thought…" She was too weak to finish her sentence.

"It is a long story, my queen, which I'll tell one of these days. My poison is affecting you again."

"Find the shunk, and it will guide you to what you are looking for," Azi told the kids. "It's the only way to save the queen. The shunk is the conch of life."

"You don't know where it is?" asked Brendan.

"Where it resides inside the pyramid depends on who the seeker is. It is different for the queen, for you, Brendan, for you, Alex, and for you, Sidney," Azi explained, addressing each of them individually.

"Aarjen told me that there are only a few shunks," said Brendan.

"This is one of them," Azi said. "The keeper of this conch will become ruler of Mayastella, and an alliance with this mighty king will depend on who receives the conch first. And if the theel receives the conch first…"

"How do we stop the theel from finding the conch first?" asked Brendan.

"You don't find the conch. It finds you," she corrected him.

"Could you please take us inside the pyramid?" Brendan requested Azi politely.

"I need to be with my queen now, but I will show you the way. The pyramid empties into the vast openness of the endless universe, a strange place for the mind. Each one of you will experience a different path," she explained.

Azi then led them through the smallest of the tunnels that took them into a small, circular, stone-walled room. The ceiling was a partial dome that telescoped endlessly above the room.

"Don't look up until I tell you to." She was polite but firm. "Go to the center of the platform and select a ring to stand on," she instructed, referring to the colored rings embedded at the center.

"Are you ready?"

"Ready for what?" Brendan looked at Alex.

"I take that as a 'yes'." Azi transformed back into the sergon and spun the platform like an amusement park ride.

Brendan felt his head spin. The walls began to deform and eventually became blurry. "Now, look up," Azi instructed. "Look directly into the middle of the dome."

Brendan found himself floating through a space littered with stars. His feet were still securely planted within the ring, which served as a floating disk. Alex and the others were nowhere to be seen. Then, as though someone had turned on a spotlight, a beam of light appeared in front of him. He could see people.

The crowd was intensely watching something. When Brendan navigated through the people, he was surprised to see himself seated in the middle, leaning over the table and staring at a chessboard. The setup was familiar. He had seen it a million times.

When he saw Nicolas, he knew he was seeing a replay of when he'd lost time on his clock. His attention was automatically drawn toward the clock to see how much time he had, but the numbers were fuzzy.

"You have questions. We have answers," said an old man who stood at the back of the crowd, slowly stroking his white beard.

"What?" Brendan was unsure if the man had spoken to him.

"Answers. Haven't you always wanted to know what happened? And what would have happened?"

Brendan thought for a minute and then spoke clearly. "Is that going to change anything?"

"Don't you have a burning desire to know?"

Brendan walked through the crowd, reached in, and hit the timer on the clock. "It already happened." Without looking back, he walked away from the table.

The applauding crowd behind him dispersed, except the old man. His expressionless face remained fixated on Brendan as he slowly drifted away into the darkness.

The light got brighter and brighter as Alex floated toward it. She was beginning to see images at a distance.

"*It looks like I am moving toward some sort of city,*" Alex thought to herself, but it soon occurred to her that the lights were shining on a football field.

"*This is odd,*" Alex told herself when she recognized the stadium. She felt the cool autumn breeze blow on her face. The scene felt so familiar.

"*I am watching my own game,*" she realized, looking at herself in her Mustangs jersey. It was the game against the rival Hawks.

"*I should have adjusted for the wind and kicked the ball more to the right to score the field goal,*" thought Alex. "*I am about to miss the field goal.*"

Before the ball was snapped, Alex was of two minds—to kick the ball a little to the right, into the wind, or straight toward the center of the goalpost. The autumn wind was picking up speed, so Alex wanted to kick slightly to her right. But when she saw the ball snap and positioned on the ground, she stepped toward the ball and kicked it straight. The ball seemed to head in the right direction; however, to the crowd's despair, it curved away from the center, hit the post, and ricocheted away from the upright.

"Do you want to know what would have happened to you if you had kicked it into the wind?" asked a white-bearded old man.

Alex thought for a moment. "No, not really. I knew I should have adjusted to the wind," she replied.

"Don't you have the desire to find out more about yourself?"

"No, thanks." Alex was emphatic. "This doesn't change anything."

The lights turned off, and Alex drifted away from the stadium.

"You don't seem curious about what I have to offer," remarked the shaky voice from behind Brendan.

It was the bearded old man again.

"Sorry, sir. I am certainly curious, but I just don't see the point of looking back at the past. I was never good at it."

"These are *your* memories." The old man paused, then continued without waiting for Brendan to respond, "Events that you wish had had a different outcome surface in this pyramid. Yet, you shun the alternative and seem to want to move on."

"Correct," agreed Brendan, vigorously nodding his head. "As much as I can. Everyone talks about the past—the should-haves and could-haves." Brendan closed his eyes and took a deep breath. "My mother never did." When he opened his eyes, he could see her smiling at him. Her face was pale. Her eyes displayed the intense pain that she never revealed to her children.

"She found purpose, even in the dreadful cancer that took her life. 'There is always a cause, Brendan, just learn from it and make it better the next time,' she said. 'Never look back.'"

"Do you want her back?" the old man probed.

"What do you mean?"

"I can make sure that she's always with you," he proposed.

"Thanks. But she *is* always with me," Brendan responded.

"What do you desire then?" the old man asked bluntly. "I can rid you of your fear, make you strong at the game you play, and give you powers beyond your wildest dreams. You'll always be a winner."

Brendan was surprised by the offer. "I appreciate the offer, sir." He paused. "I have seen a lot the past few days. Things I never imagined. Things with more power than any human can ever have. But they all suffer. Big and small, good and bad."

"So, are you declining my offer?" the old man questioned without changing the tone of his voice.

"Only because I am certain now that true happiness does not come from what you offer." Brendan's answer was sincere.

"Pretty deep for a human kid," remarked the old man, a touch of astonishment coloring his voice.

"I mean it, though."

"I know you do."

The wise old man was silent. His pale, wrinkled face was partially exposed behind the silver hair. Stars twinkled in the distant background. The light on and around him intensified.

"You are here for something. What is it that you are looking for?" the wise man finally asked.

Brendan carefully worded his thought. "Just want to do my duties, you know. The ability to do the right thing."

"There is no right and wrong here," the wise man cautioned.

"Then, I guess I am not looking for anything," Brendan concluded.

The wise man unfolded his hands and began stroking his beard. "I met your friend as well. The girl."

"Alex?"

"She thinks like you. Doesn't care about the past."

"Of course," Brendan agreed proudly.

"Didn't want any powers either."

"Not surprised."

"But she did have a purpose. She was looking for something."

Brendan hoped Alex hadn't mentioned the shunk

"She did," said the old man, reading Brendan's thought. "She wanted to know where one can find the shunk."

"Not for herself," Brendan said in defense of his friend.

"The shunk is elusive for those who seek it."

Brendan was not going to argue. He knew Alex had meant well.

"Doesn't the shunk belong to Kumba?" he asked.

"It belongs to no one. The holder of the shunk holds the key to life in Mayastella. And Kumba will be the keeper of this life. With this comes immortality."

"*Aha, and that's why the rakshasas are after the conch. If they can take the shunk, they can become immortal,*" Brendan thought to himself.

"No one can take the shunk. It is given and not taken. The theel might desire immortality and seek the conch, but it will never receive it. Not the theel, not the rakshasas, not the devas, the asuras, the jalas, and not even the theel's master—the betrayer of the rishis."

"What if someone took it from the one it was given to? Wouldn't it be wrong?"

"As I said, there is no right or wrong. What's wrong for someone is right for someone else. Let's just say that one will have to face heavy consequences," the wise man spoke, his voice trembling with wisdom yet carrying a deep sense of satisfaction. "Now, young man," he continued, "like the game you play, even here time is relevant. The mouth of the shunk will stay open only for a while. If no wind passes through it, no sound will be made, and the shunk will disappear for ages."

"Isn't it true that only a poiz will be able to make sound with the shunk?"

"You ask a lot of questions. Now is your time to choose wisely," said the old man.

"Choose what?" asked Brendan, perplexed.

"I have a gift for you." The bearded man stepped back.

In front of him appeared a pinkish-white conch as large as a football. It was a simple yet spectacular shell, spiraling anticlockwise, gradually tapering like a cone. A plain silver ring adorned the mouth of the conch, which was sealed. The exposed inner side of the conch was shiny, like a pearl, dispersing light into different colors.

As the wise man slowly faded away, Brendan began to see more of the surroundings. The conch was gently resting over a purple lotus, floating on a pedestal at the center of a circular fountain with crystal-clear water.

"This must be the shunk," he thought.

Brendan found himself on the top step of the fountain at the end of a long, nave-like hallway with tall marble columns fanning into pointed ceilings. The fountain had a charred circular border. At the far end of the hallway was a large altar, covered in silky sheers.

Brendan heard the voice of the wise man who had all but disappeared into the background.

"You are at the heart of the pyramid, where Kumba sleeps. In front of you is the shunk that will allow you to break the curse. But it comes with a choice—a choice which will involve doing what's right or wrong for you. As you can see, your friends are here with you, and your enemies will be here soon."

Brendan slowly walked past the fountain toward the altar. He felt light, easily able to move toward the center. Statues lined the walls of the nave, statues of kings, rishis, and even rakshasas—some he had encountered before and others he had never seen or imagined. As Brendan approached the decorated altar, he could hear someone crying. It was eerie. It felt as though he were at a wake.

He slowly stepped up to the bed and moved the sheers to see who was behind it.

The armored body of the sleeping giant levitated a few inches above the bed. A large shield lay on one side and a long sword on the other. His body was covered up to the waist with a golden sheet. Brendan could see Kumba's serene face, most of which was hidden by a mustache and thick eyebrows. The king's long, curly locks of hair spread to his shoulders. Except for the curved canine pair of teeth that jutted out from the corners of his mouth, any overwhelming resemblance to the rakshasas was absent. He rather looked like a Viking.

The muffled cry came again from the side of the bed not quite visible from where Brendan stood. When he walked around the bed, he noticed Queen Suhela was crouched by the bed, softly crying. She didn't look at Brendan.

"What do I do? Where is the poiz?" he asked himself, looking around. He knew the queen was dying.

"I can save the queen," said a voice from the opposite end of the hallway, startling Brendan.

This time, it was not the wise man. Brendan recognized the floating theel from the distance. It was hovering around the shunk at the other end of the hallway, its long tail glowing with a charge.

"The shunk!" Brendan suddenly remembered, quickly getting off the altar.

"Don't worry. I can't take it even if I want to. It's yours," the theel said calmly.

"Step away from it," ordered Brendan.

The theel snorted. "You are not listening to me." It moved impatiently in the air, snapping its tail. "You'll give it to me—for the sake of your friends."

Brendan stopped. He noticed that three marisans had already joined the theel. They spread themselves across the hall. Two other marisans uncloaked just a few feet away from him. Brendan looked around. He saw Azi in human form, moving toward the altar with his friends.

Alex was nowhere to be seen.

"This is your final stop, kid. Unfortunately, you are stuck on the other side. Just say I can have the shunk, and all will end well," said the theel.

"No. The shunk belongs to no one—certainly not you."

"Good things will come out of it, if you just say I can have the shunk," the theel advised him calmly.

"Nothing good will come from you."

"Really? How much do you like the queen?"

"Where is this conversation heading?" Brendan asked himself. *"Is this the choice the wise man was talking about?"*

"The only way she's going to live is if you let me have the conch," the theel insisted.

"You are lying!" Brendan snapped.

"Am I? The shunk will create and protect only your kind of life, if you accept it. But all the rakshasas who have left their world to get here will die," the theel warned.

"You should have stayed where you belong."

"It's not about me. Don't you know Suhela is a rakshasi? If you blow the shunk, the conch of life and activate it, then she dies."

"No human will blow the shunk. It will be the poiz that will blow the shunk."

"Um…Look around you. You are on the wrong end of the hallway, *and* you are surrounded by rakshasas. The shunk will open in moments, and you'll never be allowed to get close to it. And your loyal poiz is bound and helplessly standing by your queen, awaiting its fate."

Brendan turned back toward the altar to find a potbellied rakshasa holding a large net. Trapped inside was Komo, the yaali who had helped Aarjen and Brendan get to the sea of Kaling. His eyes met Komo's.

"Komo! Hey, let him go," Brendan shouted at the potbellied rakshasa.

"Sorry to let you down, kid. It is my job to make sure that the conch is given to and activated for the rightful person, but I let the theel trap me." Komo, a poiz in the form of a yaali, apologized.

"Shut up!" The potbellied rakshasa grunted and yanked the net, pulling the heavy stone lion toward it.

Komo's legs tangled in the net as it crashed to the marble floor with a loud thud.

"Queen Suhela is dying," said a tearful Azi. "She won't live too long, Brendan, but there is a bigger cause. She is willing to sacrifice her life for her husband. Do not offer the conch to that creature. You can do the right thing."

"There is no right or wrong," Brendan reminded himself.

"You have to save the queen, Brendan," Sidney cried. "She saved us, remember?"

Prrrummmm, prrrummmm!

Two short blasts of horn, originating from the fountain, echoed across the hall. Tiny waterspouts emerged from the fountain. At the center, where the shunk rested, steamy water percolated like a hot spring.

"You don't have much time, kid," said a dejected Komo, struggling to free himself from the tangled net. "I will not be able to get to the conch in time."

The theel let out a villainous laugh. "Ahh, how ironic," it sighed. "Ever wonder why your knights are still not here?"

The theel glided toward the shunk, its eyes bulging and its tail wildly fluttering in the air. It then swished back up and laughed.

"It's your stupid game of bughouse," the theel continued, laughing. "We are holding on to all the knights so that they'll never get into the game. We beat you at your own game. You lose!"

"You don't win either," argued Brendan. "I would rather see the shunk disappear than give it to you. Even if I gave it to you, you couldn't use it."

"Yes, I can. I am a soulless creature, like the poiz. Your weak mind will allow me to take the conch."

The theel flicked its long tail. A bolt of energy landed on Brendan and knocked him to the ground. A marisan appeared before his fallen body and forced him up. Brendan was dazed, but in all the confusion, he noticed something from where he stood. At the far end of the hall, from behind a tall marble column, Alex was signaling to him. Only he had seen her.

The silver ring on the shunk began to move as the spiral outer rings rearranged themselves. Slowly, like the shutters of a camera, the opening in the front dilated, allowing water to flow into the shell. A luminous blue liquid oozed out of the conch, and Brendan, although severely hurt, could feel the magic in the air.

Brendan noticed Alex watching him writhe in pain, her heart reaching out for him. He could tell she badly wanted to run into the theel, who was just a few feet away from her, and take it down, but he knew she had to wait for the right opportunity. He saw her signal to him, but he was unable to respond to let her know that he had understood her hand signal.

The second bolt of shock jolted Brendan. His knees buckled under him, but his trembling body hung loose in the strong hands of the marisan.

"Stop! Stop! Don't kill him, let me talk to him. I can convince the kid. I don't think he understands your power, like I do," Komo pleaded.

The theel hesitated.

"Trust me, master," said Komo. "The shunk will have to be activated soon; otherwise, my purpose will be lost… Forever! I can—"

"Poiz are worthless. You serve no one other than yourself," the theel responded angrily.

"I am sure you can appreciate that, master. Our survival instincts brought us this far. It is this instinct that will help us finish this journey. I might not have succeeded at the sea of Kaling but this is even better."

"It was you at the poisoned sea, where Kaling was killed?"

"Yes, it was. But I couldn't help you there for the right reasons. I needed to get to the shunk," it confessed.

"I don't need you," sneered the theel. It seemed to be further infuriated upon hearing the yaali reveal its identity. "I can activate the conch without your help."

"I know…I know that you are soulless, like the poiz, the vegas, and the tantrics, and can find ways to activate the shunk. But the kid still needs to *give* you the shunk of his own free will. The human mind could become tricky if you are only using force. So, let me help you, theel. I can get into their minds, like I did before. Don't kill the kid now. You'll get plenty of chances later," Komo reasoned.

"Let it loose," the theel commanded the potbellied rakshasa. "Hurry, you sloth. Make your pitch before I kill you too."

"I will, master theel." Komo lowered its head in respect. "You will not regret this."

"*Hurry!*"

"The circle of fire is less than halfway completed, Master, but we still have time," Komo shouted to the theel with a heavy rakshasa accent as it walked slowly toward Brendan.

"Traitor!" Suhela shouted desperately at Komo so that Brendan could hear her. Across the hall, the theel hissed while Komo walked slowly toward Brendan, ignoring the queen and the other impatient rakshasas. "Leave the boy alone," Suhela pleaded, staggering toward Komo, but Komo just turned around and grunted at Queen Suhela. She slumped by the bed, barely holding on to a pedestal by the bedside.

"Komo, you cannot switch sides," barked Brendan. He tried moving away from the slowly approaching Komo, but the marisan shoved Brendan toward the yaali.

Komo leaned over to Brendan with great difficulty and whispered, "Signal your friend to throw the shunk to me and not to you. Trust me, Brendan, I'll never betray my true friend, but now, pretend as though you don't like hearing what I just told you. Azi knows of my plan to trick the theel and she will back me if something goes wrong."

Brendan shook his head violently while Komo continued his one-sided discussion for what must have seemed an eternity to the theel.

"When your friend makes her move, make them believe that she's going to throw the conch to you," Komo said. "Do you have Yan's notebook?"

Brendan gently made a subtle nod of his head and confirmed to Komo that he still had the notebook.

"After I catch the shunk, read what the notebook says loudly, kid. Everything will be okay," the yaali whispered.

"That's enough," the theel snapped, signaling to the Marisan to interrupt the conversation.

The ring of fire rapidly spread around the shunk, and Brendan knew that all access to it would end soon, and all their efforts would end in vain. He signaled to Alex.

Alex, who had managed to remain unnoticed by blending in with the statue next to the column, swiftly made her move. She raced toward the pedestal.

The theel appeared stunned to see another human darting out of nowhere. It reacted by firing several bolts at Alex, but they were random and erratic. A potbellied rakshasa hastily jumped into Alex's path, but she spun around, and the awkward creature ended up hurling itself uncontrollably across the floor.

Alex found a narrow, nonburning opening and jumped into the water that surrounded the pedestal. She stumbled and gasped, as though not anticipating the shallow-looking puddle to be waist deep and frigid.

Soaked and shivering, she managed to pull herself onto the base of the platform and removed the shunk.

The theel zipped toward the unexpected trespasser; its random discharge of electric bolts continued to streak through the pool.

Alex grabbed the shunk with ease in one hand. "Brendan, over there!" Alex yelled, pump faking a couple of times toward the corner of the hall.

Brendan shook himself free from the marisan and ran to where Alex had directed him. He threw his arms up in the air, signaling Alex to throw the shunk.

"Stop that boy now," the theel ordered the nearest marisan. "They are going to ruin my shunk."

Alex dodged two potbellied rakshasas rushing at her. One plopped into the water, and the other slid straight into the ring of fire. The fire intensified, and Alex's hand trembled. She suddenly struggled to move, as though gravity was weighing her down. The force seemed to steadily move up her body from her feet, legs, hips, and arms.

Brendan knew she was beginning to pay the price for touching a forbidden object.

Alex was giving it her all. As the fire closed in, she made one last pump fake and heaved the football-shaped object. As the conch spiraled out of Alex's cold hand, she froze like crystallized ice, even before her action was completed.

The creatures pushed themselves in front of Brendan, hoping to intercept the conch safely, but the conch was moving away from them, heading in the direction where Komo stood.

Tackled by creatures much heavier than him, Brendan hit the floor but managed to keep his eyes on the conch. He knew his best friend would have understood his signal to throw the conch to Komo and not to him. As the shunk traversed across the hallway, the forward thrust and the spiraling motion forced the air through the silver opening.

Voooooooom. The sound from the conch blared across the hallway.

A potbellied rakshasa that stood in the trajectory of the moving object slowly reacted by clasping its hands together in an attempt to catch it or prevent it from hitting its face. But the shunk never made contact with it.

From under a pile of rakshasas, Brendan watched Komo's rigid trunk unfold and snatch the shunk safely before the potbellied rakshasa could intercept it. Like a snake coiling around its prey, Komo's trunk curled around the shunk. Brendan quickly reached into his parka pocket, pulled out, and unfolded Yan's note book to its last page.

"Say it now, Brendan," said Komo.

Brendan immediately shouted out the ancient rakshasa words that formed using English letters even though he didn't recognize the words, "I hereby relinquish the shunk that was offered to me as a gift by the wise man of this pyramid to Queen Suhela, the queen of Kumba, with Komo, the yaali, as my witness."

"Thank you, my friend," said Komo.

It then placed the shunk on the pedestal that was by the bedside inside the altar and asked the queen to repeat the words it was about to say.

Queen Suhela, who appeared to be shocked by the turn of events, quickly followed the instruction and carefully repeated the magical words

Komo chanted. The statues of the seven rishis that surrounded the chamber moved closer, and water poured from the tiny copper spouts they held in their hands, mixing with the pedestal pool. The ring of fire on the other side of the hall abruptly extinguished as steam gushed across the hallway and through the shunk. A powerful sound blasted through it, like pressure releasing from a steam engine.

The floating king stirred. His body settled on the bed. He rubbed his eyes and reached for his sword. Without faltering, he stood up next to the bed and raised his sword. He studied the chamber.

Komo and Azi dropped to their knees instantly.

Komo was the first to speak as the others watched the towering king descend the platform. "Long live King Kumba. Long live the savior and the protector of all life of Mayastella."

"I see my queen is dying," said the king, who was at least twice the size of Brendan in both height and build. "I'll save her, but my first order of duty is to serve the one who awakened me. The one selected by the rishis to receive the shunk."

"A kind human has made your queen the rightful bearer of the shunk. Your queen's enemies are your enemy, oh great king," said Komo.

"A human?" asked King Kumba in a quizzical voice. "Humans are weak and cannot cross worlds. How can they enter the forbidden land and possess the shunk?"

"Yes, oh great king, the humans are weak." The theel quickly piled on to the king's sentiments.

"I know you," Kumba said thoughtfully, keenly observing the theel. "My loyal council warned me of your deceitful schemes to turn the rakshasas against me. They told me you are manipulative and repeatedly tried to infiltrate my kingdom to instigate. My generals pleaded to get rid of you, to lock you away. Some even wanted you dead. But I refused to take action because I believe you are innocent until proven guilty. We might be rakshasas, but we don't have to live without laws."

"I am innocent, oh great sleeping rakshasa king of Mayastella," the theel said, shrinking in size, bowing to King Kumba. "I have come to offer my alliance. The combined power of my master and your might will be matched by no rishi, no deva, asura, jala, or any gods of the world. You'll rule all the worlds if you join us. The rakshasas will rise above the immortals," the theel proposed. "The humans, they are with your enemies. They are in it for the power…To control life and immortality. You should punish those who did this to you and your queen."

"I beg to…" Komo tried to intervene.

"My lord, the theel is—" Queen Suhela couldn't finish what she was about to say. She tried to warn Kumba, but she fell to the floor in mid-sentence.

Sidney dropped down next to the queen and held her hand. "I cannot see anymore, Queen Suhela, and if you don't wake up, I'll never be able to see you again," she sobbed.

"The residual poison is about to kill your queen, oh great king of all rakshasas," said a teary-eyed Azi. "She saved your life, only to suffer under the shackles of your traitors who prevented her from joining you at your resting place. Now, you must save her."

"My master will rid her of the poison your disloyal Azi injected your queen with. It was the rishis who convinced your queen to poison you. They took everything. Do not let them get to you again, oh mighty one," pleaded the theel.

"My lord, only you can save queen Suhela," Komo spoke. "Do not trust the soulless creature. The humans might be weak in strength, but they demonstrated unmatched courage and loyalty."

The king was silent but acknowledged Komo with an affirmative nod. He knelt beside Sidney, who looked like a speck by his side.

"Help her," she pleaded to the king.

Kumba held his wife's frail hands and lifted her toward him.

To Sidney's delight, the queen opened her eyes. A last bit of energy still remained in her. She uttered something in the rakshasa tongue, and Kumba leaned over to hear her. He brushed his mustache with his fingers and shook his head.

"Do you think I should kiss my lovely wife?"

Sidney nodded, and before the queen could say anything, her husband gently kissed her hand. Kumba's lips blackened as the residual poison immediately transferred from his queen to him; the poison spread through his body while Suhela's spectacular beauty returned.

"Oh…No!" cried Sidney, instantly reaching out to the king's hand and holding on to it tightly. She attempted to stop the king. "That's enough. The poison is going to hurt you."

"Thanks for the concern, young lady," said Kumba, who had already extracted the poison from his beloved wife and would soon be feeling its effects.

"She is the one who saved me, dear," said the recovered queen and spoke briefly to the king in the rakshasa tongue.

"In the name of the seven rishis, I designate Queen Suhela as the ruler and the protector of Mayastella and all beings of this world until the time is right for me to rise again. I am…I am…" Kumba's head wavered, and his speech slurred slightly, but Suhela's presence appeared to soothe him.

"I am grateful to those who have remained loyal to me," he said, regaining his strength. "I am grateful to those who have saved my queen. To this extent, I promise to protect all those who have been loyal to my queen or me," he said, looking at Komo.

The theel, desperate, moved closer to Kumba to avail one last chance to make good of the situation. Kumba was once again under the influence of the deadly poison of Azi. His tail fully charged, he could still orchestrate a surprise attack that could bring down the sick and the unsuspecting king. It prepared to strike Kumba with a swift bolt.

"*Watch out!*" Brendan cried out.

But Kumba had already anticipated the attack. Wielding his sword in one hand, he grabbed the long, lashing tail with his other hand, allowing the theel's charge to harmlessly seep through his thick skin. He wound the tail around his arm and yanked it toward him. The theel rolled helplessly in the air, like a floating balloon caught in a wild gush of air. Kumba then swiftly swiped his sharp pewter sword across the tail, rendering the theel powerless.

"You are not much without your sting, are you, theel?" asked Kumba. "I'll spare your life, but I can't promise what will happen to you outside of my home," he warned. "Let's put all this energy to good use, Komo. Can you step into the fountain of life?" Kumba directed them to where water gently flowed from the statues through the conch.

The stone lion obeyed the king.

"Could you please help my friend too, Your Highness?" requested Brendan.

Kumba dropped the dazzling whip-like tail that had once belonged to the theel into the shunk-activated liquid.

The current zipped through the luminescent water, sending steam into the air. The blue hue deepened and spread across the hall into the fountain, where Alex's crystallized body stood like a statue of a football player in action.

Magic happened.

Both Komo and Alex appeared to thaw. The crystals melted like icicles on a warm spring day, and Komo's rocky body came to life. Komo pounced out of the water like a lion and awkwardly bowed to his king. He then shook his beautiful, long golden mane dry, much to the amusement of the kids.

"You have given me eternal energy, oh great one, for which I will serve and protect you for all my life," Komo said with gratitude.

Alex jumped from the fountain as though a burst of energy rushed her and completed her football throwing action. She looked to see if Komo had caught the conch. But to her surprise, Komo stood next to her in a non-petrified, full-of-life form. "That was a fine throw, young lady," Komo praised Alex. "The curse is broken. You saved the day."

Brendan ran over and hugged Alex, who was still soaked.

The theel scrambled to the entrance, attempting to flee, but Azi was quick to trap it.

"Let it go," commanded the queen. "We'll not harm anyone here. The creature will have to face its own fate outside this kingdom."

"You can follow your leader if you choose to," Kumba informed the other rakshasas. "You are all free to leave."

The potbellied rakshasas grunted and ran to the exit, and one of the marisans followed, but the other chose to stay back. It desired to lead its kind to serve the queen of the Mayastella.

"Yan is building an army to defend against our enemies. He needs help," reminded Suhela.

"With the theel gone, will they even think of a war against us?" asked Azi.

"Unlikely, but I'll make sure that we send our forces to Yan and stop the war before it begins," promised Kumba. "Bhrigu's curse is broken, and I can rest peacefully."

"Do you have to go back to sleep again?" asked Sidney, reaching for King Kumba's hand, her vision all but faded away.

"The king has seven Earth weeks before the residual poison will begin to shut down his senses," said Azi. "We should leave the queen and the king alone."

"Don't worry, Sidney. I'll always be with him," Suhela assured. "Azi has worked on new medicine for this poison. I am sure this time, it is only for a short while."

Kumba leaned over to Sidney and rubbed her temples with his two fingers, which were disproportionally large compared to her tiny face. "Close your eyes, little princess," he said, "and think of your favorite thing."

Sidney thought of her mother, her sweet, soothing voice and her gentle touch.

"Don't worry, you'll get to see her soon," Suhela whispered to Sidney.

"Thank you," said Sidney, unable to hold back her tears of joy.

Back at Yan's camp, the kids were excited to see Kaia and Aarjen, who had heard everything from Maya before the kids' arrival. King Kumba's reinforcement had joined the thousands of Yan's nijaz.

The chataans were no match to Kumba's army, and they quickly scattered in the absence of the theel, who was nowhere to be seen.

"Is this the end of the journey?" asked Brendan.

"Yes, the curse is broken," said Kaia.

"Then, how come we are still here?" asked Ro.

"Wouldn't the bughouse game be over by now?" inquired Max, wanting to go home.

"Almost, but we have made arrangements for things to continue a little bit longer."

"We are having a special event," replied Aarjen. "A celebration."

When the kids entered the pyramid with Kaia and Aarjen, they barely recognized the place. They walked across an enormous courtyard, flanked with tall stone pillars. The palace hall was decorated with white flags with silver borders and banners in the shape of a conch with seven bright stars in the middle. The marble walkway was accented with plants with colorful and exotic blooms. Hundreds of small and large elephants, embellished with fancy ornaments, stood in orderly rows, along with the warriors of Kumba, clad in shiny battle gear. The crowd erupted in delight upon seeing the visitors. Little gajaz thrust their trunks in the air and waved.

"Look at those trunks! They look like the long thingies that people wave at basketball games," said Ro, laughing.

"Who are they waving at?" asked Max.

"At us," said Alex.

"Look! Yan is riding Ely." Austin was jubilant to see Yan and Ely.

Yan, who was seated on top of the largest elephant, waved at the guests.

The majestic Ashvat proudly trotted alongside Kaia. She made the crowd roar by galloping around at full speed.

A long and wide red carpet spanned the courtyard and into the hallway. Inside the grandiose hall, several people were seated on tall chairs—some with long, flowing beards, wearing simple robes, and others dressed like royals. At the center sat Kumba and Suhela, both wearing their crowns. Run-Nier sat next to Kumba. Komo, Azi, and Una, the loyal sorceress, along with other prominent rakshasa generals, stood behind him.

"Wow," said Alex. "Everyone is looking at us."

"Who are all these people?" asked Brendan. "They all look royal."

"Except those over there," said Ro. "They look like the rishis Aarjen talks about."

"The ones with the long beards?" asked Max.

"Yes. There's one…two, three…"

"Seven," Aarjen completed the count. "The seven rishis."

"Queen Suhela looks lovely." Sidney was enthralled to see the beauty that surrounded her as she rode with Kaia on Ashvat.

A sudden blurt of horns sounded, and the crowd chanted. Aarjen led the kids over to the steps after Sidney joined them. The devas, the asuras, the jalas, the nijaz, and the poiz all stood up and greeted them. The rishis remained seated.

"O great rishis and the kings of the world, I present to you the brave human children who helped us defeat evil. The curse is broken, and we have found our Seventh Knight, Run-Nier," said Aarjen in a thundering voice.

The crowd applauded for Run-Nier and the kids.

Rishi Vyas stood up, his robe flowing to the floor. He briefly chanted in an unearthly language and then spoke in English, "Let there be peace in the mortal and immortal worlds, and above all, let life prosper in Mayastella. Let the ceremony for Kumba begin in the presence of the rishis, the kings of all worlds, and our honorable guests from the mortal world."

The ceremony began with Maya creating images of the kids. Many—including Run-Nier, Yan, and Komo—spoke about the bravery and the achievement of the children.

"The festivities will last for several days, until Kumba returns to his rest," said Aarjen, who sat next to Brendan at the dinner table.

"I am glad Queen Suhela is with him," said Brendan, genuinely happy for her.

"She spoke very highly of you, Brendan. Very few are capable of what you did inside that pyramid," Aarjen complimented Brendan. "You can achieve great things. I am sure you'll choose your path wisely."

"Thanks. I have learned a lot already, and I have a lot to learn, starting with the final round at the competition."

"That's right, you have one last round. But this time, you won't have any trouble from disruptive creatures. Do you still have the crystal?"

"No, I gave it to Komo at the sea of Kaling," informed Brendan.

Aarjen shook his head and rolled his eyes. He pulled out his knife and cut his wristband with a dangling crystal and handed it to Brendan.

"Here, keep this. You'll know where to find me when you are in need."

"Thanks. What about Kaia? Will she go back with us?"

"She doesn't have to be on Earth anymore. We are planning to settle down," Aarjen said with evident happiness.

"Don't you need a knight on Earth?"

"*You* are there now." Aarjen jokingly nudged Brendan.

"Me?" Brendan laughed.

"Actually, there is a vagabond earthling who, when the time comes, will bear the coat of arms of Kumba and will be the leader of the Earth dwellers. He'll also be the knight of the Earth dwellers, but he'll need a lot of help from you, Brendan." Aarjen leaned over the squeezed Brendan's shoulder.

"How will I meet this person?" Brendan was curious.

"You'll know when you see his coat of arms. You'll recognize it immediately."

"Hmmm…" Brendan was unsure how to respond. "When are we going home?" He switched gears suddenly. "I want to see my father."

"Actually, I don't mind staying here for a while," confessed Alex.

Everyone laughed. There was entertainment, stuff that the kids had never even dreamed of. They got to meet the lords of the elements and ride on flying horses, elephants, and ules.

It was then time to say goodbye.

Chapter 22

The Final Round— The Championship

he confusion ended when the bughouse tournament finished. Sidney slowly walked out of the tournament hall alongside Ro. She held his hand for emotional support. She couldn't wait to *see* her mother. The other kids followed her. Sidney was overwhelmed by the lights, the colors, the facial expressions of people whose voices she could only hear before. Her eyes wandered around in search of her mother, who she knew how to recognize only by touch and her soothing voice.

"Don't tell me who she is," she had told the boys. "I want to guess on my own. I can't wait to see my mother's expression when she finds out I can see."

Turner waited with the parents of the Pass Pawn chess kids outside the hall amid the sea of people.

"There's my dad, in the maroon polo, waving at us," Brendan clued Sidney in. "And there—" Brendan was about to reveal Nora, who was behind Coach, but stopped himself.

When Nora called out, Sidney focused all her attention on the voice to spot her mother. And there she was, as beautiful as Sidney had imagined. Sidney hurriedly walked to embrace her mother.

"Be careful!" Nora shouted to Sidney when she saw Sidney navigating through a crowd of people, crisscrossing the hallway, before landing in her arms.

"You need to be careful, pretty princess."

"I can see, Mom. I can see now. I can see how beautiful you are in that green dress."

"What! How?" Nora looked down at her lime-green outfit. "How did you…" She looked into Sidney's blue eyes and began to cry.

Kids and parents surrounded the heavily stapled notice one last time to check the final round pairing. It was the long-awaited last round of the tournament. The phones were buzzing.

"It's official. Brendan is playing Scrappy Junior for the championship!" Ro announced.

"As expected," said Turner. "It's just a game, son. You have battled bigger things the last few days. I am proud that you are back on Board One, fighting for the championship the old-fashioned way."

For the first time in the tournament, Brendan and his friends felt at ease about playing chess, without worrying about traveling to another world, filled with strange creatures. It brought an unusual sense of relief.

"Good luck, Brendan. I know you can get him," said Alex as they headed to the top table of the tournament.

The high school open was the highest level and most popular section of the tournament, and its winner would be crowned the tournament champion.

"Do you wish you were playing someone else?" asked Ro.

"No, I am fine. I am ready for him."

"Make sure you take your own clock," advised Max. "Are you playing black or white? You know black calls the clock."

"I'll play white, like last time, so it will be his clock, but it doesn't matter."

When Brendan arrived at Board One, Nicolas was already seated, his eyes closed, and he was listening to music through the massive over-the-head headphones, a hoodie pulled over his head. It took him a few minutes to realize Brendan had sat across the table.

"*Something's different with Scrappy Junior,*" thought Brendan.

"You can use your clock," Scrappy Junior offered, sliding one of the speakers away from his ear underneath his hoodie. His face was expressionless.

"Black calls clock," Brendan replied sternly.

"I didn't bring one—to not complicate things. We can borrow one or maybe even play without a clock?" he suggested, pushing his headphone to his neck.

"*Not a bad idea,*" thought Brendan. He looked around and didn't see Scrappy.

"My stepdad won't be bothering us today," said Nicolas, as though reading Brendan's mind.

"Um…Okay," Brendan said uneasily.

"No one has seen him since this morning. I got a call from a cop who found his truck in a ditch. He had left in a hurry."

"I am sorry."

"Don't be."

Brendan suddenly felt sorry for him.

"Nicolas," he said, deliberately not calling him 'Scrappy Junior', "let's just ditch the clock and shock everyone."

Nicolas finally nodded thoughtfully. His focused gaze swept over the board as he carefully adjusted each chess piece to sit precisely in the center of its square, ensuring perfection before the game commenced. When he pulled his sleeve of his loose hoodie back, Brendan was shocked to notice his tattoo—a yaali crouched on its powerful hind legs, its two forearms clasping a long sword, pointing down. Behind the sword, the yaali's long trunk curled at the end, touching the ground.

"*Symbol of Kumba's kingdom,*" thought Brendan. "*How did Nicolas suddenly get a tattoo that represents Kumba?*"

He had never seen this tattoo on Nicolas before. Was there a connection, or was it all just mixed-up memories that were confusing him?

"When did you get it?" Brendan asked.

"The hoodie?"

"No, the tattoo," Brendan almost reached out and touched the exposed tattoo, but stopped short.

"Uh…Recently," Nicolas muttered, hurriedly pulling down his sleeve to cover it up.

"Today?"

Nicolas didn't answer.

"What is it?" Brendan continued his questioning.

"Um…" Nicolas hesitated and searched for words. "It is…It is…I believe…Or I was told that it is my ancestor's coat of arms. I *just* found out."

"Your ancestors?"

"Yeah…Long story. Don't ask." He shrugged and tugged his sleeve down again to ensure that no part of the tattoo was visible.

The conversation ended.

Brendan remembered what Aarjen had told him. "*There is a vagabond earthling who, when the time comes, will bear the coat of arms of Kumba and will rule the Earth dwellers.*"

Aarjen had told him that he would recognize the coat of arms.

"Who is this person?" Brendan had asked Aarjen at the celebration dinner.

"You'll know him when you see him," Aarjen had told him. "Your respect he'll earn, your friendship he'll desire, his protection you'll receive, as you look beyond the past and join hands with him for a secure future."

Brendan remembered Aarjen's words.

"*Ahh…This cannot be that person, could he?*" Brendan wondered.

A gong sounded, permeating its vibration across the room. The chairman briefly addressed the crowd before dispersing the spectators out of the tournament hall.

"All right, let's go at it one last time," he announced to the players. "You may begin the championship round."

"No clock it is." Brendan stuck out his hand to kick off his final game against his nemesis in chess.

They shook hands.

Brendan leaned over to make his first move and touched the e4 pawn, but instead of moving it, he hesitated, lifted the piece off the board, and set it at the side of the board.

"What are you doing?" asked Nicolas, frowning at Brendan.

One by one, Brendan removed pieces from the chessboard. Pawns, knight, bishop. He then rearranged the remaining black pieces on the board in different positions as Nicolas watched him in bewilderment.

"Ahh, I see where you're going with this," said Nicolas, nodding his head and pinching his lower lip. He, too, removed and rearranged his pieces before anyone could inspect them.

"I hope no one sees us doing this," said Nicolas as a couple of kids began wandering toward them to watch their game.

"It's too early for kids to check out other games."

"It's never too early. Here they come," said Nicolas, just finishing the familiar setup on the board—the beginning of the endgame from the controversial past.

One middle school gawker frowned at the chessboard; the other one shrugged his shoulders.

Someone else whispered, "How can they be this far along? Like blitz."

"Board Number One must have started earlier," the one from behind rationalized discreetly, fearful of getting caught for talking to a fellow player while the games were on.

They studied the game briefly and hurried back to their seats.

"Let's finish the game we started last year, Nick," Brendan suggested.

"No clocks, no external influence, and all the time in the world. And I like being called Nick." Nicolas reached across the table and shook hands with Brendan one more time.

Then, it happened again! Brendan felt the light distort, and for a second, things went dark.

He found himself in a circular chamber, leaning over the large marble game board that had been the source of the Curse and their extraterrestrial journeys. Ornate pieces remained arranged as they had set them up on the board before transporting.

The person across from him was in a long, silky red robe. A hood covered his head like a boxer ready to enter the ring. The large golden symbol of the yaali holding a sword was neatly embroidered on the robe.

This time, Brendan noticed the sergon behind the yaali as well. Nicolas appeared as puzzled as Brendan.

"Nick, what the heck is this?" asked Brendan.

"You tell me!" snapped Nicolas. "Apparently, you have had more experience with this than I do."

Brendan looked around. He was surrounded by royal spectators. Indra, his council, Maya, Aarjen, and Kaia were all seated together.

Kumba and his queen were seated behind Nick. Accompanying the royal couple were Azi, Komo, Una, and the ule warriors—Marra and Karro. Banners of Kumba lined the circular auditorium behind Nick. Clearly, the chamber was divided into two. Brendan's side appeared to belong to the devas, the asuras, and the jalas while the other side across him belonged to Kumba's kingdom from Mayastella. It was obvious—Nicolas represented Kumba.

Brendan paused, trying to grapple with the unexpected change of venue. He searched among the kings who were seated behind him. Aarjen was smiling and nodded at him.

"I thought this was over. What are we playing for now?" Brendan asked, shrugging his shoulders.

"Ahh. Let me explain, son," said Indra, waving his hand, as though he'd expected Brendan's question. "Before putting away Chadurang for good, we had one small discussion among us about humans and your quest to win. We wanted to see who has the most desire to win—the Earth dweller or the humans." Indra exchanged glances with Kumba.

"We had a small disagreement," said Kumba from the other side.

"So we wanted to find out."

"Earth dweller? Nick?" asked Brendan, pointing to him and trying to put two and two together.

"Vir is the son of the nadodi queen. The rightful leader of the Earth dwellers."

"Did you know?" Brendan asked Nicolas.

"You kidding me? The tattoo appeared this morning when I woke up. I thought my stepfather had drugged me and tattooed something on my hand because he's crazy. But that lady sitting behind you tried to explain some of this just before the game started. I thought she was messing with me at first…But then she showed me some cool stuff about my family that made me wonder."

"Kaia?"

"Yep."

Kaia waved to Brendan.

"And since you both have the same burning desire to finish your unfinished business from the past, we thought we could watch how this will end," explained Indra.

"So, you represent the Earth dwellers?" Brendan asked Nicolas.

"I guess so." He shrugged, just like Brendan had. "Somehow, I always represent someone else," he mumbled.

Suddenly, Brendan hated the idea of being tested and challenged.

"Is this about me stepping up or having a winning attitude or whatever?" he asked Indra, his voice expressing irritation for the first time.

Indra's thunderbolt weapon reacted to his emotions by charging up, but Maya took the heat away by intertwining her glassy form between Indra and the players. "Brendan," Maya said kindly, "Kumba's kingdom has created a place for the poiz, nijaz, and other non-humans. The Earth dwellers will be relocated to Mayastella slowly. This game allows us to compare the thinking and mental endurance of the Earth dwellers with that of humans, how close or different you are in pursuing a desired outcome."

"By means of a simple game? Even humans are not alike. Sorry, but this makes no sense to me," said Brendan. "My sister didn't even want to play this game, and she is better at this than I am."

"This is a special game, as you already know." Maya moved across the hall and got the nod from Indra, who had calmed down, to continue to explain to Brendan. "You both are the perfect match. You have competed against each other in this game since childhood, and you both think alike."

"Only in how we play this game," said Brendan. "Otherwise, I think we are very different."

Nicolas nodded in agreement with Brendan.

"Exactly. That is why we are using this common link to understand the similarities or differences in behavior."

There was an uneasy silence.

"I would like to say a few words," Aarjen finally spoke.

Indra and Kumba nodded.

"Brendan, you don't have to play if you don't want to. This is not a life-or-death situation," he acknowledged.

"Um...I..."

"No need to explain. I meant everything I told you at the dinner event a few days ago."

"I have to prove—"

"No! You don't have to prove anything to anyone." Aarjen stood up. "Do you trust me?" His question instantly comforted Brendan.

"Of course, Aarjen, I do."

"I have already told everyone here what the outcome of this game is likely to be."

"And what is that?"

"Play the game and prove me correct, Brendan. Only if you play the game, you'll know that I have earned your trust."

"But—" Brendan held his words and thought for a moment. He trusted Aarjen. He bit his lip, ran his fingers through his hair a few times, and studied the board. He counted the moves. He could possibly win.

"We have analyzed the game," Maya spoke, approaching the players. "And each of you has one winning combination. The first one who makes a mistake will lose. Now, do you want to play?" She was direct but polite. The players nodded thoughtfully, both staring at the board, trying to figure out their winning moves. Brendan looked at Nicolas, who gave an affirmative shrug.

"Okay," they both said simultaneously and shook hands one more time.

Brendan made the first move.

"*It's all about the pass pawn,*" he told himself looking at one of the two pawns to his left.

He slowly pushed his pawn toward the other end of the board, but so did Nicolas from his side. It was a race of the pawns across the board. The first one to promote to the queen would win; the first to blunder would lose. They both made intense calculations for what seemed to take hours, carefully executing each move.

Brendan finally made a move that suddenly presented Nicolas with two distinct options—to move a pawn or move the king. The obvious and safe move was to continue to push the pawn forward, but moving the king presented an opportunity—albeit a risky one. Nicolas realized that moving the king could bait Brendan into making a wrong move. After considerable deliberation, Nicolas thoughtfully approached the pawn, looked into the eyes of Brendan for a few seconds, changed his mind, and moved the king.

Brendan responded by smiling. At last, he saw mate in 5 for him, and he wondered if Nicolas realized it.

He pushed his pawn again and gestured to Nicolas with a curled hook-like finger inside his cheek, pulling as though it was Nicolas who had gotten baited.

That was not the move Nick had anticipated. He realized Brendan had deliberately baited him with two options, and the riskier move hadn't paid off.

"*Clever,*" he thought.

Although it signaled the end of the game, Nicolas hoped he could still force Brendan to make a mistake.

Indra grinned triumphantly at Aarjen, a subtle pride discernible in his expression. Kumba, on the other hand, raised his eyebrows in thoughtful anticipation, his gaze flickering between the unfolding moves, aware of the potential for Nicolas to lose. Kaia, gently patted Aarjen's arm, silently acknowledging his foresight and supporting him.

"It's not over," whispered Aarjen to Indra, but Brendan could still hear him in the near-silent theater.

"I think it is," concluded Indra.

Brendan recalled the events that had unfolded over the past few days. He had traveled to worlds that he hadn't known existed, interacted with kings, knights, and creatures, and helped save the worlds from near destruction. He had been told that it was a matter of life and death. He then remembered the old man in the pyramid who had offered to show the outcome of the game if the clock hadn't unexpectedly run down—the outcome of the game that Brendan never cared to know.

"This is just a game," he told himself. *"After going through all that trouble of breaking a curse and restoring peace, how significant could the outcome of this particular game be?"*

He shook his head, squinted his eyes, stretched his arms. He stood up and walked around, ignoring the gazing eyes of the powerful kings of the different worlds. His mind clear, he returned to his chair.

"It's just a game," he whispered to himself but loud enough for Nicolas to hear.

Silence followed.

"What are you thinking?" asked Brendan.

"I can see it. But you can take it if you really want it."

"Can you defend it?" asked Brendan.

"Maybe."

"You know, there is a third outcome." Brendan lowered his voice.

Stroking his cheek, he wondered why Nicolas, a very conservative player, had chosen to make a risky move at a crucial time in the game. He should have seen it.

"Was it a deliberate move?" he questioned.

The royal spectators watched—some amused, some concerned, still others confused that the players were engaging in a conversation.

"What are they saying?" Agni asked Varuna.

Maya deliberately had screened the kids from being heard by the audience.

"Um…" Nick sighed. "Continue playing? Maybe you can close this one."

Brendan glanced at Kumba's coat of arms, tattooed on Nick's arm. The shy boy he knew as Scrappy Junior, a rival he had come to dislike, was now an ally he'd learned to respect.

"How about a draw, my friend?" Brendan extended his hand to shake Nicolas', totally catching him off guard.

"A draw? A draw, Brendan? That would mean that I could win the national championship on a tiebreaker. Would you really want that?"

Brendan just shrugged. "You are a winner, Nick," he said sincerely. "It looks like you have already won," he said, pointing to the tattoo.

"You would have won this game—forced mate in five—but I accept your offer. Good game." Nicolas shook Brendan's hand to conclude the game.

"Friends?"

"Friends," he said.

Aarjen nodded at Indra and walked to the players. He put his hands over the shoulders of the players. "This what I predicted. This is *just* a game."

All the kings and their cohorts stood in respect for Brendan and Nicolas and cheered the outcome.

There was loud applause.

And the boys found themselves back in Chicago.

They were surrounded by kids and TDs. They all seemed surprised but pleased with Brendan's decision to offer a draw.

Brendan turned and looked at the exit at the end of the hall, where his father patiently waited, unable to see the game. He raised a hand in acknowledgment but knew his father really wouldn't worry about the outcome of the game

They collected the pieces and tossed them into the Ziploc bags, rolled the vinyl board, and walked right through the sea of kids, who stood, watching in amazement.

"I'll see you around, Nick."

"I owe you one, Brendan—just ask when in need." He exposed his tattoo. "I see your dad's waiting for you. I'll turn in the result slip to the TD so you don't have to justify to these mortals why you offered a draw," he said sarcastically. Brendan readily agreed to Nicolas turning in the results of their game to the TD. It was just a formality in their case since many of the officials had lurked around Board One and watched most of their endgame.

While only the experts would have seen a victory for Brendan at that stage, he sensed they would have been confused by the sudden offer of a draw. "Let me know if they still want confirmation from me. I'll wait here at the door and signal back to you," suggested Brendan.

"I offered a draw," Brendan announced to his dad at the entrance to the tournament hall. "It was a good game, Dad," he added while checking on Nicolas, who seemed to be having a surprisingly long conversation with the officials who collected the game slips and noted the results of each game.

After several minutes of talking and gesturing, Nicolas turned around and signaled to Brendan. When the officials looked at Brendan, Brendan nodded and waved at them, as if to authenticate and agree to the outcome noted in the slip.

The TD shrugged his shoulders and gestured a thumbs-up at Brendan.

"Thanks, Nick," shouted Brendan. He then looked at his dad and said, "Looks like the officials were questioning the outcome of the game. They are just curious and confused."

"It's the right outcome, my son. You played well."

"I thought you said you offered a draw?" Bob Raj yelled out to Brendan, startling several kids and parents in the vicinity. He had his cell phone to his ear and was wildly wagging his finger at Brendan.

"I did." Brendan shrugged nonchalantly.

"I just talked to the tournament director." Bob Raj beamed, thrusting his cell phone. "The results of the tournament are up. I know you saw mate in 5, man," Bob Raj continued to holler with excitement, drawing a crowd.

"Brendan did the right thing, Bob Raj," Turner jumped in. "Nick could have still pulled something. Since it wasn't a forced mate, it is premature to come to any conclusions. I support Brendan's decision to offer a draw."

Bob Raj frowned at the coach, confused. "Are you messing with me? The TD just told me the opposite of what you guys are saying, Nicolas resigned when he saw the mate in 5. It's official. That's what Nicolas told the TD when he turned in the slip."

"Congrats, man. You're the champ," Bob Raj cheered.

Brendan shook his head in disbelief when he realized what Nicolas had done. Nicolas had offered to turn in the result slip on his own so that he could convince the officials that he had resigned and Brendan had won. When Brendan was about to protest to Bob Raj and his cheering posse, a text message alert from his phone distracted him.

It was a text from an unknown number, and it simply read: *"It's just a game, my FRIEND! See you soon—Nick."*

###

The stadium was packed, and the crowd was on its feet, wildly cheering the home team on a chilly, windy autumn evening. Among the fans was Brendan, who sat with Tara, Maddie, Max, Ro, Sidney, and Austin. Coach Turner sat next to Nora. The Pass Pawn kids and their families seemed to have occupied several rows at the bleachers to watch their favorite kicker play for Millburn High School.

For the first time in its history, the school was playing for the state championship, and Alex had been instrumental throughout the season in scoring winning field goals. There was excitement and anxiety in the air as the Millburn Mustangs trailed by two points and only a few seconds remained in the game. Once again, Alex was faced with the pressure of scoring a field goal to win the game, but she knew that this one was clearly out of her range.

The home crowd erupted with excitement as the team lined up on the line of scrimmage to snap the ball. Alex planted one leg in front of herself and waited for the ball to be snapped by the long snapper to the holder, who would then hold the ball upright on the ground for Alex to kick the field goal. At that instant, her mind wandered into the courtyard inside the pyramid, racing to the pedestal upon which lay the shiny shunk. She remembered water splashing all over her as she had jumped into the pool of water and reached for the conch. She had successfully tricked the rakshasas with a pump fake and ended up throwing the shunk to Komo.

Amid the roar of the crowd, Alex took her well-paced strides to kick the ball, but the ball was snapped poorly and it deflected off the fingertips of the holder, bouncing erratically near Alex as a wall of adrenaline-rushed players stormed at her. Without slowing down, Alex snatched the ball on a low bounce, spun around a defender who had dived to take her down, jumped over a pile of linemen, and headed straight for the end zone. Alex felt the slushy snow splash under her heavy cleats.

Slosh, slosh, slosh.

She picked up a rhythm and felt as though the crisp autumn wind had lifted her. She tucked the ball under her arms and breezed to the end zone, more than 30 yards away. One by one, the rest of the defenders fell under her feet. The crowd erupted, and the noise drowned the stadium. The touchdown Alex had scored won the championship for the Millburn Mustangs.

Brendan scanned the sea of the crowd that had flooded the field.

"Are you looking for Alex?" asked Max.

"Um, no. I see Alex." Brendan continued to survey the stands.

He finally spotted the person he was looking for at a distance, seated alone in an isolated corner of the bleachers, wearing a hooded raincoat with a large golden image of the stone lion. He stood up, waved at Brendan, and signaled a thumbs-up. Brendan responded by gently pounding his chest with his fist a couple of times and waving back.

Inside the Cave of Ice, the evil master, Dur-shi, sat alone with his eyes closed, deep in thought, holding the crystal that had once been given to Brendan but was stolen by the theel. The kids might have broken the Curse of Bhrigu that he had cleverly activated, but the dark sage sought revenge against the seven rishis for refusing him when he had been a mere apprentice. He was scheming to unleash the wrath of Kaling and bring death from within.

Shiva's Coaching Tips

Shiva Maharaj is an accomplished international FIDE chess trainer based in the Chicago area. He has inspired and trained numerous students, many of whom have gone on to become chess masters. Known for weaving humor and life philosophies into his coaching, Shiva brings warmth and wisdom to every lesson. Many of his friends fondly refer to him as the "Yoda of Chess".

- ABC—Always Be Careful! DEFGH – Don't Ever Forget Good Habits!

- Between two good moves, find the in-between move that makes both even better!

- Think you've got a good move? Stop, take a breath, and find an even better one!

- Control the center like a boss—because the player who owns the middle calls the shots!

- Watch out for the back-rank checkmate—don't let your opponent score a touchdown while you're still tying your shoelaces!

- Always ask why. Try to get into your opponent decision cycle!

- When your opponent is ahead, don't just sit back—throw them off with unpredictable, unorthodox moves!

- When you poke a hole in your roof, don't be surprised when it starts raining inside—always protect your king!

- Leaving your king open is like playing without a goalie—you're asking for trouble!

- A knight on the rim is dim—keep your pieces active, or they'll be as useful as a benched player!

- If you're ahead in material, don't just sit on the lead—close it out before your opponent mounts a comeback!

- Your pawns may look small, but when they stick together, they're stronger than a brick wall—use them wisely!

Acknowledgements

Writing *Chadurang: The Cursed War Game* has been a journey much like a game of chess—full of strategy, unexpected moves, and moments of reflection. The inspiration for this story came from the many years my wife, Deepa, and I spent as 'chess parents' to our two sons, Roshan and Rohit. Watching them, their close chess friends, and countless other young players navigate the emotional highs and lows of scholastic chess tournaments inspired the heart of this tale. Your passion, resilience, and unwavering spirit have been a constant source of inspiration.

This story is also a tribute to the rich tapestry of Indian mythology, which forms the very framework of Chadurang. Weaving these ancient tales into the vibrant and diverse setting of Chicago—a city my family and I have called home for over two decades—has been a deeply rewarding experience. Chicago's unique blend of cultures and beautiful landscapes provided the perfect backdrop for a story that bridges worlds, both real and extraordinary.

First and foremost, I want to thank my family—Deepa, Roshan, Rohit, Jaya (my dear mother), and Uma (my sister)—for being my greatest supporters. Your patience, encouragement, and unwavering belief in me have been the foundation upon which this book was built. You are the queens and rooks in my life: strong, reliable, and ever-present.

To my extended family, friends, the amazing chess coaches—Shiva Maharaj, Alice Holt, Yuri Shulman and Frank Swindell—who relentlessly dedicated their time and efforts to bringing out the best in their students, and to my beta readers—Awonder Liang, Vicki Hodder, Rachel Strick, John Larson, Lauren Kern, Tara Sharan, and Vidyut Skanda—thank you for your honest feedback.

A heartfelt and sincere appreciation to the very first editor of this manuscript, Mrs. Kalpana Arun, an amazing English teacher who has mentored and inspired many students around the world. Without your generous and selfless help, this manuscript would never have left my laptop! I wish to express my gratitude to the many professional editors who contributed to this book at various stages: Leah Clifford, Elizabeth Ridley, Jovanna Shirley, Yamini Vasudevan and Vicki Hodder.

My deep appreciation also goes to Yamini Vasudevan and Prem Kumar for their support in helping me transform this manuscript into a finished book.

Finally, to all the readers who will embark on this journey with me, thank you for opening these pages. I hope *Chadurang: The Cursed War Game* captivates your imagination and transports you to a world where every move matters, and the stakes are nothing less than the fate of the universe.

Shankar Subramanian

About the Author

Shankar Subramanian's early years were steeped in the rich culture and heritage of South India. Encouraged by family, teachers and friends, he developed a deep love for storytelling and a vivid imagination. In his early twenties, Shankar moved to the U.S. to pursue a PhD in chemistry, where his advisor and fellow graduate students helped cultivate his passion for science, storytelling, and good humor.

Shankar and his wife, Deepa, raised two sons in the greater Chicago area, along with their beloved Wheaten Terrier, Newton, who passed away recently. Both sons developed an early interest in chess, which became an integral part of the family's life. Years of taking their sons to various chess tournaments provided the inspiration for the beginnings of this book. The family now enjoys the company of their new puppy, Myla, also a Wheaten Terrier.

In addition to writing, Shankar enjoys G-scale model railroading, cooking, watching 'Jeopardy!' with his family, crafting dad jokes, and creating wood art.